SLOW BLEED

Tim Adler

URBANE
Publications

urbanepublications.com

First published in Great Britain in 2016 by Urbane Publications Ltd

Suite 3, Brown Europe House, 33/34 Gleamingwood Drive, Chatham, Kent ME5 8RZ

Copyright © Tim Adler, 2016

A CIP catalogue record for this book is available from the British Library.

ISBN 978-1-911331-27-8

Design and Typeset by Julie Martin

Cover by Susanna Hickling & Julie Martin

Cover image courtesy of Brett Walker.

Printed and bound by CPI Group (UK) Ltd, Croydon, CR0 4YY

urbanepublications.com

FOR BASIL PHILLIPS

CONTENTS

CHAPTER ONE	13
CHAPTER TWO	19
CHAPTER THREE	29
CHAPTER FOUR	39
CHAPTER FIVE	46
CHAPTER SIX	56
CHAPTER SEVEN	64
CHAPTER EIGHT	72
CHAPTER NINE	80
CHAPTER TEN	87
CHAPTER ELEVEN	94
CHAPTER TWELVE	100
CHAPTER THIRTEEN	109
CHAPTER FOURTEEN	118
CHAPTER FIFTEEN	125
CHAPTER SIXTEEN	135
CHAPTER SEVENTEEN	140
CHAPTER EIGHTEEN	157
CHAPTER NINETEEN	173
CHAPTER TWENTY	184
CHAPTER TWENTY-ONE	194

CHAPTER TWENTY-TWO   200

CHAPTER TWENTY-THREE   210

CHAPTER TWENTY-FOUR   224

CHAPTER TWENTY-FIVE   229

CHAPTER TWENTY-SIX   239

CHAPTER TWENTY-SEVEN   244

CHAPTER TWENTY-EIGHT   248

CHAPTER TWENTY-NINE   255

CHAPTER THIRTY   263

CHAPTER THIRTY-ONE   268

CHAPTER THIRTY-TWO   276

CHAPTER THIRTY-THREE   280

CHAPTER THIRTY-FOUR   287

CHAPTER THIRTY-FIVE   292

CHAPTER THIRTY-SIX   296

CHAPTER THIRTY-SEVEN   300

CHAPTER THIRTY-EIGHT   310

CHAPTER THIRTY-NINE   322

CHAPTER FORTY   330

CHAPTER FORTY-ONE   335

CHAPTER FORTY-TWO   340

CHAPTER FORTY-THREE   347

CHAPTER FORTY-FOUR   358

CHAPTER FORTY-FIVE   363

CHAPTER FORTY-SIX   369

CHAPTER FORTY-SEVEN   374

CHAPTER FORTY-EIGHT   384

CHAPTER FORTY-NINE   395

CHAPTER FIFTY   399

CHAPTER FIFTY-ONE   411

CHAPTER FIFTY-TWO   423

CHAPTER FIFTY-THREE   430

ACKNOWLEDGEMENTS   438

EXCERPT FROM SURROGATE   441

ABOUT THE AUTHOR   455

BOOKS BY THE AUTHOR   457

'Anyone who hasn't experienced the ecstasy of betrayal knows nothing of ecstasy at all.'

JEAN GENET, *Prisoner of Love*

CHAPTER ONE

HER FIRST THOUGHT WHEN SHE saw the flash was that it was the whitest white she had ever seen. Her next thought was about her son, whom she would never see. And that she was going to die.

Toppy Mrazek first sensed something was wrong when she saw both cars coming up fast in her rear-view mirror. They were racing each other, accelerating towards her in the fast lane. Instinctively, she took her foot off the accelerator and shifted in her seat in an attempt to get comfortable. The drum of her stomach was tight against the steering wheel, and she could feel her baby moving around inside her, as if somebody was pressing a thumb against her from the inside. She had cried when she first saw him turning on the ultrasound. Now, five months later, there was barely enough room for her in the sports car she had once cared so much for. The silver Mercedes suited her image as a young female executive. Her body was changing now that her baby was on the way; climbing the corporate ladder, which had once seemed so important, now appeared meaningless.

Two lads passed by in souped-up street cars. Fat exhaust

pipes. She glimpsed one of them guffawing with laughter as he overtook her. She registered that the cars were far too close together and, again, it made her want to hang back.

Her heart welled at how her life was about to change, at the budding life inside her. Single life – which for Toppy consisted of working long hours as an office manager in the City and then coming home to a microwave dinner in an empty flat – had palled. She had longed for a baby, something that would give her life meaning, for years now. Her heart had dropped every time she opened a "We're pregnant!" email at work. It physically hurt her. Right where a baby would grow. Soon there would be two of them – it amused her to think that, eight hours away in Hong Kong, her son's father was blithely unaware of the changes going on inside her. Not that he would ever know. She had decided it was going to be just the two of them: her and her baby. She was tired of waiting for the right man to come along and marry her; she pictured her and her child living in a remote cottage somewhere in a wood. No one else. Rain pattering on the leaves as she watched him playing with his wooden blocks on the floor.

Toppy's thoughts were interrupted by the sight of both cars dropping into her lane, right in front of her. She slammed on the brakes, stopping just short of the Honda. It swung out again, trying to get ahead of the Renault. It was such a dangerous manoeuvre that she wondered whether the boy behind the wheel was drunk. His car howled ahead. Even with the motorway noise, you could hear the boom of his exhaust.

Something was wrong. The Honda started weaving, and, to Toppy's horror, it slewed and bumped the weed-choked central reservation, touching the crash barrier at more than one hundred miles an hour. Bits of plastic and metal spewed out of its back and tumbled towards her. The Honda touched the railing again, and this time it hurdled the fast lane, spinning round and around directly in front of her.

Everything went into slow motion; it was as if time had elongated. She pulled the steering wheel down, trying to swerve, and must have clipped the Honda, because the next thing she knew, her world windmilled upside down, and she was thrown onto the motorway. She knew what was about to happen. The road was coming up fast. She closed her eyes and braced herself for impact. There was a juddering crunch as the world collapsed around her. Flipped upside-down, she felt her car scraping along the road.

Toppy opened her eyes only when it had come to a stop. She was still gripping the steering wheel. The smell of petrol and burnt rubber was in the air, and the hot metal of the car ticked softly. She let go. Toppy was hanging from the driver's seat with her head jammed against the roof. Through the windscreen, she was facing the car she had just swerved to avoid. Ugly skid marks slalomed across the fast lane. Smoke was rising from the Honda's engine, and curious people were already getting out of the cars queuing behind it.

Her first thought was for the tiny baby inside her. Was he all right? She couldn't feel him moving.

Petrol was raining onto the windscreen, but all she could do was hang there, wedged in, suspended, unable to move. Her neck really hurt. Fighting rising panic, she groped for the safety belt but couldn't quite reach it. She felt too stunned to cry. She was still alive, and that was all that mattered.

"Can you hear me?"

A man appeared at the left passenger window. She nodded. He tried the door, but it wouldn't budge – the partially collapsed roof had jammed it.

"Are you hurt? Can you move? I am going to get you out of there, luv, all right?"

"I can't breathe."

"That's okay. I'm going to get you out. There's fuel everywhere. We need to get you out straight away."

The man crawled in and started trying to free her, reaching across and unbuckling her safety belt. It wouldn't open. He began tugging at the belt, as if his strength was any match for twisted steel. She started to cry once she realised what was happening. She was sitting in a petrol bomb. The car could go up at any second.

The first contraction hit. It was so painful she felt as if she was being split in two.

"Ohmygod, ohmygod, ohmygod."

"Look at me. Everything is going to be all right. I'm going to get you out of here."

Her guts twisted inside as another contraction hit. He didn't understand. She was going into labour. She was going to have her baby in this car.

"I'm going to have a baby. Right now."

This time she screamed until she thought her throat would bleed.

The contraction ebbed away. Her vision cleared, and she found herself looking into a calm, kindly face. Behind him, flames belched downward out of the wrecked Honda's bonnet. She noticed, in a detached sort of way, that petrol was pooling towards them, snaking along the oil-stained tarmac. The man turned, realised what was happening, and started pulling frantically at her belt. The bed of fuel ignited. A wall of flame shot up, engulfing the bonnet. At that moment, the safety belt released, and Toppy fell forward out of her seat. Her saviour dragged her out of the passenger window on her belly, scraping her along the tarmac and broken glass. Please be careful of my baby, she thought. A siren rang out in the distance.

Her rescuer pulled her to her feet, just as the petrol tank exploded. Her world turned silent. The blast threw her against the man, rattling her teeth as the tarmac shook beneath their feet. The sound came back with the dull crump of the explosion. A wave of heat like a blast-furnace door being opened fell across them, and she could feel the hairs on the back of her neck singeing.

Other arms were around her now, pulling her away from the burning wreck. Another contraction twisted her guts as somebody threw a blanket over her shoulders. She couldn't believe something could hurt this much, and she started to howl with everything she had. The contractions were getting stronger now. "Jesus Christ, she's going into labour," a woman said. Toppy sobbed hysterically against her rescuer's chest as firm hands steered her away. Smoke was everywhere. Toppy whimpered as they led her hobbling towards an ambulance. "It's okay, it's okay," the ambulance woman kept saying. But it wasn't okay. In fact, nothing would ever be okay again.

CHAPTER TWO

IT FELT LIKE THE LAST good day of summer, so lovely that it caught the back of your throat. Yet it was with a pang, because she knew there wouldn't be another day of such unsurpassed loveliness for another year. As she lay there gazing up at the leaves of the plane tree, Jemma reached for her husband's hand. The leaves broke up the sunlight, and she realised this was an epiphany, a moment of pure happiness. It was Saturday. They had gone to the park and taken a picnic rug and a rucksack of their five-year-old son's toys. It was such a fine afternoon that they both just lay there while the boy was off somewhere in the children's playground. Jemma watched the tree's leaves stirring in infinite perspective. Around them you could hear children shouting and the thud of a football being kicked around. Parents calling their kids. A typical London weekend afternoon.

"He has got to be joking," said her husband shaking his newspaper.

"Who's that?" Jemma said, rolling over.

"That smug, self-satisfied public-school idiot. The health secretary. He's always got this wide-eyed, how-could-this-

possibly-be-happening-to-me-I-went-to-public-school
look on his face. You know I met him once. At an NHS
conference. You could tell he was pretty dim, that he didn't
really understand what was going on. He just kept banging
on about how hospitals have to be market facing."

"What's he done now to get you so riled up?"

"He's now saying that the NHS has a lot to learn from the
American health care system. Yeah, right. I remember
the manager of a big Chicago hospital telling me that
the moment one of the big US contractors got involved
in the day-to-day running of his hospital was the death
knell. Death by a thousand cuts. First, they could use only
generic drugs. There was this constant pressure to upsell
every operation. So you went in for a hernia and walked
out with a nose job. Eventually, he said, they'd cut out every
part of the hospital for themselves apart from A&E – and
even that was sponsored by a liquor company. Which was
ironic, since most people were in there because of booze.
By the end they had hacked out every profit-making bit of
the hospital and there was nothing left. The patient was
dead on the table."

"Tony," she said. "Remember what we said? No shoptalk at
weekends."

She and Tony, her husband, both worked for the same big
London NHS hospital. That was where they had met. Tony
had been brought in as a management consultant, while
she was a house officer, the bottom rung of the surgical

ladder. Like a lot of couples, they had met at a party. Two years later they had married, and their son, Matthew, was born a couple of years after that.

"I mean, he's got brown fingers. Everything he touches turns to shit. Yet he keeps being promoted. I just don't get it."

Jemma cupped her head and thought how tired her husband looked. This was the first Saturday they had spent together in weeks. The NHS budget was being squeezed, and their hospital was feeling the pain along with everybody else. You noticed small things first. Blown light bulbs not being replaced. Equipment looking out of date. A creeping sense of slovenliness. Last week Jemma had seen a cockroach scuttling along an A&E corridor. She knew Tony felt as badly about it as she did. He was trying to keep the entire hospital together on less and less money. She reached up and touched his hair. The words of an old song, Together Alone, came back to her: that's how she thought of them sometimes, the two of them lying here clinging together, while the farther away they moved from this spot, the more hostile the world became.

"Mummy. Push me," Matthew called out from the swings.

"I'll go and get him. You stay here," Jemma said, getting up.

"What are we going to do about lunch?"

"There are some bits in the fridge that need eating up."

Jemma walked over to where Matthew was sitting on the swing. Other fathers were pushing their children with one hand, some of them furtively checking their mobile phones. She felt a twinge of resentment at how the division of childcare had worked out. It always seemed to be her who looked after Matthew. She remembered one bitterly cold afternoon when it had just been the two of them in the park; Tony was always working. He rarely got home before nine o'clock.

She started pushing Matthew, and he laughed as he kicked his legs out. "Higher, Mummy, higher," he called.

Jemma felt her mobile vibrating with a sinking feeling. She fished it out of her pocket, hoping it was her mother calling. Instead, it was a text message:

"Urgent. M25 car crash. Woman in labour. Ambulance on way."

It meant going into hospital. She was on call that weekend, so her family time was over. She wasn't even supposed to be working; she had volunteered to cover for a colleague whose sister was getting married. Jemma slowed the swing down to a stop and Matthew jumped down, running off towards the roundabout. Keeping one eye on him, she called the number she had just been texted from. Jemma spoke to Guaram Chandra, her obstetric registrar. Guaram was on secondment from a big Mumbai hospital that handled just obstetrics. Soon these new super-hospitals that specialised in heart surgery or cancer treatment would be coming here too. Guaram had a slightly pompous way of talking, as if he was her superior rather than the other way round. Or perhaps he just didn't like women.

"Hi, Guaram, what's up?"

"We've got a 33-year-old woman who's been in a motorway accident. She's going into labour. Paramedics say she's just in her third trimester. Her blood pressure is dropping and her heart rate's high."

"How far apart are the contractions?"

"Every few minutes." She heard him say something on the other line. "She's also got a fractured hip."

"Okay, I'll be straight in. Oh, you'd better call the ortho registrar. Get Frank in to deal with the hip fracture."

"Do you want Doctor McCracken as well?"

Duncan McCracken was the consultant anaesthetist she sometimes worked with. Usually a registrar, one down from a consultant, would be fine for a woman giving birth, but this case sounded fraught with complications.

"Yes. I'll meet you in A&E. I'll be in as fast as I can."

Jemma rang off and couldn't help cursing her luck. Her one day off.

Putting her phone back in her jeans pocket, she fluttered with panic when she couldn't see Matthew. Then she spotted him. There was a wooden train he liked to hide in. Soon he would realise that when Mummy's phone went, that meant playtime was over.

"Matthew. Come on. We're going," she called. He deliberately ignored her. She pushed her hair away from her eyes, feeling anxiety building in her stomach. This was going to make her late. But how do you explain what a surgeon does to a five-year-old boy? She walked over to the train and found her son hiding in one of the dark windowless carriages. He was laughing. She caught his wrist a little more firmly than she intended and he yelped. Then he started to wail. Jemma felt another mother looking at her disapprovingly. "Come on, Matthew, I haven't got time for this," she said loudly, partly for the other mother's benefit. "Mummy's got to go to the hospital."

Dragging her straining, protesting son back to where Tony was still lying down, she said: "The hospital called. I've got to go in. There's been a car crash, and a woman's going into labour."

Tony put down his paper and said, "Oh God, I am sorry, love. Don't worry about us, we'll be fine. We can go and get something to eat at the café. Would you like that, Matthew?"

"Ice cream," said Matthew solemnly.

"No ice cream," said Jemma, packing up her things from the picnic rug.

"What time will you be back? Remember, we've got Emily

and Adam coming round for drinks tonight."

Jemma raised her eyes. "Oh, I forgot. I'll pop in on my way home and tell them that I'm going to be late. I'll pick up something to shove in the oven. You can get started without me."

Her voice had an edge in it she hadn't quite intended. Tony raised his hands as if to say there was no problem. She leant down and kissed him, her mind already going through what she had to do next: if there was internal bleeding, the quickest thing would be to perform an emergency caesarean. The road crash victim wouldn't be able to push with a fractured hip. If the mother's vital signs were dropping, she would have to get the baby out quickly.

Jemma was still running through her options by the time she arrived at the house next door. Their neighbours were an insurance broker and his wife. The two couples had become friendly over the summer, occasionally sharing meals in their back gardens. Emily and Adam had a three-year-old and a newborn. Emily would spend those summer evenings looking anxiously at the baby monitor strapped to her waist. Adam was nice if a bit dull, and Jemma sensed that Tony was always a little patronising towards him.

Unlike the Sands, they were renting. Very few people who worked at the hospital could afford to live locally. Jemma knocked and Emily opened her front door, grinning broadly. She always seemed so pleased to see her. There was something inside her that was genuinely good and that Jemma responded to. How much more interesting were the subtle varieties of good compared with the banality of evil.

"Emily, I'm really sorry, but I've got to go in to the hospital. I won't be back until later."

"Oh, that's absolutely fine. Don't worry. Why don't we do it another time?"

"I'm not saying that. Tony's in the park with Matthew. Why don't you come round at six, and I'll try and make it back when I can."

Inside, Jemma glimpsed the happy chaos of family life. Emily's naked three-year-old daughter ran up and hugged her mother's leg, gazing shyly up at the visitor. Her next-door neighbour had a relaxed attitude towards parenting that Jemma admired but could not quite share. Emily once told her that coming to their house felt like walking into an operating theatre, with toothbrushes and toothpaste lined up in the bathroom like surgical instruments. Never a toy left out or anything out of place.

"Only if you're absolutely sure," continued Emily. "We'll stay for one drink and then it'll be bath time."

"Yes, please do," said Jemma quickly. She glanced at her watch. It was 1:26pm and she was late. She pictured the ambulance with its blues and twos on, hammering up the Fulham Road.

Jemma let herself in through her front door and dumped her rucksack on the kitchen counter, grabbing her car keys and shoulder bag. She would have to hurry. It was now 1:40pm.

Their car was parked in the doctors' reserved bay in front of their house. Jemma tried ringing Guaram again, but the call went straight through to voicemail. Tossing the mobile onto the passenger seat, she started the engine, which bobbled reassuringly. She knew their green Subaru was slightly vulgar, but she liked the punch of the acceleration. Their London terraced street quickly became a blur as she put her foot down.

Traffic was nearly at a standstill along the Fulham Road, though. Cars were crawling along. She imagined the swing doors banging open as the car-crash victim was pushed into theatre, her saline drip jangling as Guaram got her prepped. Up ahead, four policemen swayed on horseback wearing hi-vis jackets. The horses had fluorescent quarter sheets on. Of course, Saturday afternoon. There was a football match. Chelsea were playing at home. 1:44pm. Jemma hadn't counted on this. Fat men wearing clinging soccer shirts walked three abreast along the pavement, and she felt her impatience rising as she glanced at the digital clock. 1:46pm. Traffic was being diverted. She contemplated abandoning the car, getting out and running, when the car in front edged forward. The farther they got from the stadium, the more traffic eased up.

Eventually Jemma turned right and pulled into the hospital's underground car park. The back bumper dipped as the car dropped down the ramp. There was a screech of tyres as she searched for a reserved parking space. The car park had a hot rubbery smell, and she glanced down at her BlackBerry, blinking like an angry red mosquito. There was another text message from Guaram: "Urgent. Patient crashing."

CHAPTER THREE

JEMMA NODDED TO THE NURSE on duty behind the Plexiglas window as she hurried into A&E. The public benches resembled a war zone. Drunks sat watching television with cans of Special Brew pushed discreetly behind their chair legs. She keyed in the numeric door code. The A&E receptionist told her that the car-crash victim was in the third cubicle on the left, and she hurried past a man clutching his bandaged head.

Jemma pulled the curtain back and saw Guaram and the consultant anaesthetist standing over the woman who had been brought in. She was hooked up to the ECG and a blood pressure monitor. Pop… Pop… Pop… Her heart rate was slowing. Blue digital numerals showed her blood pressure was dropping too. "My baby, my baby," she moaned, before screaming as if her guts were being wrenched. Jemma could see she was going into hemodynamic shock.

"How many weeks pregnant?" Jemma asked.

"I am guessing around thirty weeks," Guaram said.

"We need to get her into theatre as soon as possible," said

McCracken. "Her blood pressure is ninety over forty and dropping."

"What's her heart rate?"

"It's dropped to fifty. Everything's collapsing."

She glanced quickly at the woman's notes: Toppy Mrazek, age 33. Road traffic accident. Asthma.

Jemma said briskly, "My name is Doctor Sands. Your baby wants to come out now, do you understand? I am going to deliver your baby. Is it all right if I touch you? My fingers might feel cold."

The woman groaned and nodded. Jemma pulled up the car-crash victim's dress. The moment her fingers touched the patient's abdomen, she had a strange premonition that she was going to come into great conflict with this woman. Stop being so ridiculous, she thought, what an absurd thing to think. She had work to do. The woman's trunk was growing in size before her eyes and it was tense to the touch – a sure sign of serious intra-abdominal bleeding. She guessed the patient was exactly thirty-two weeks pregnant. She knew she had to save the mother and the baby. Both of them were her patients, although the mother took priority. This was not going to be easy, but she would do it; she had spent seven years of her life training for emergencies like this.

She squirted some ultrasound gel onto her palm and rubbed it on the woman's belly. Using the foetal Doppler, she listened for the baby's heart rate. The heartbeat was erratic and faint. The baby was in distress, and she had to get it out as fast as possible. Only then could she try to save the woman's life.

Together the three of them pushed the woman down the corridor towards the theatre. Toppy Mrazek howled as another contraction hit. Her baby was moving into position. They had to get it out now. Banging the doors open with the trolley, the scrub nurses raced to get her prepped while Jemma changed.

The women's changing room was empty. Jemma grabbed a set of blue pyjamas and undressed as quickly as she could. The starchy top and bottoms brushed against her skin and underwear. Pulling a dirty-looking pair of white clogs from the rack, she slipped the sky-blue disposable cap over her head. From here it was only a short jog to the sterile theatre changing room. She clacked down the corridor where they would be waiting for her. It was 2:29pm.

Inside the scrub room, she slapped the disposable gown pack onto the counter. Opening it up, she breathed in the oddly industrial smell. Turning on a pair of long-armed taps, she wet her hands, pressing the Betadine dispenser with her elbow. In her head, she pictured what she was about to do. She tried telling herself there was nothing to worry about, that it was an operation she had done many times before, but for some reason her heart was racing.

Raising her hands in the air, she felt rivulets of sweat running uncomfortably down her arms.

Somebody came in behind her. "She's just gone under," said Rose, a theatre nurse. "Could you give me a hand?" Jemma asked. She tied both ribbons of the mask behind her head, squidging the strip over her nose until the mask fit snugly on her face. Rose fastened the ties down her back. Hurry, hurry, they had to hurry.

She backed into theatre with her arms crossed over her chest like a high priestess with the scrubs nurses as her acolytes. Usually operating theatres were calm places; Jemma found them almost restful. The last thing you wanted in theatre was drama. That was partly why she became a surgeon; it appealed to her sense of order. However chaotic the world outside might be, nothing unexpected could happen here. Today, however, felt different. The air seemed stiff with tension.

The patient's chest was exposed under the harsh overhead light. Even like this, unconscious with a ventilator tube in her trachea, the woman was still beautiful. She was just the type that Tony would go for, Jemma thought. She knew that she was the exception when it came to the sort of woman Tony preferred. She was blonde for a start. Straightforward. Athletic. Tony had joked that all his previous girlfriends had been neurotic brunettes with a death wish. A few strands of hot brown hair peeked out from beneath the car-crash victim's surgical cap, and something made Jemma want to tidy them up and tuck the hair back under.

"Whenever you're ready, Doctor," said Guaram.

The radio was playing a jaunty pop song, and Jemma asked for it to be turned off. Now she could hear the pop, pop, popping from the heart-rate monitor. It wasn't loud, but it dominated the room like a metronome. The blips were getting farther apart. She imagined the baby struggling for life.

"The baby's heart rate is crashing," said McCracken. "It's going into shock."

"Doctor Sands, you'll lose the baby if you try and do a C-section now," Guaram said. "Better wait until she's stabilised."

"That will be too late," Jemma said. "She'll die if we don't get the baby out."

"But the baby isn't viable. We need to get its vital signs back up."

She saw panic in his soft brown eyes. Guaram didn't know what he was talking about, she decided.

Calmly, she swabbed the woman's stomach with iodine. Her scalpel rested just below the woman's belly button. There was a moment of resistance before the flesh gave way and she swept the scalpel down in a vertical uterine incision, working quickly through the first layers of fat and tissue. Guaram cauterised. There was a smidge of smoke and a burnt-flesh smell every time his wand touched the woman. Jemma began separating her abdominal muscles by hand, revealing the uterus. One more layer to go. There. They were through. She started pulling the baby out, cradling his precious head and scrawny, hunched-over purple-red body. Where was the noise, where was the indignant yelling? This baby was not even trembling with shock.

Flatline. She was too late.

The baby was dead.

Rose began suctioning his nose and mouth, but Jemma knew it was useless. This baby was stillborn.

She could not believe what had just happened.

The baby should have been fine, even if his vital signs were dropping. She had done everything by the book. This had never happened to her before. She cut the tough umbilical cord while a neonatal nurse waited to take the baby from her. Although Jemma knew it was hopeless, the neonatal nurse would still try and revive him.

It was only now that Jemma realised the trouble she was in. The woman's uterus was filling up with blood as quickly as a basin fills with water. Blood was rising up over the sides of the incision, pooling around Jemma's hands, with some of it spilling onto the floor. For a moment she felt overwhelmed. Everything was awash with blood. The car crash must have ruptured the woman's placenta, ripping it away from the uterus. Instinctively, Guaram plunged in, plugging vessels with his fingers. As he did so, Jemma began packing the patient's uterus with as many swabs as possible. Anything to buy more time. She felt like a sailor uselessly bailing out water. Everything began playing out in slow motion. She hesitated for a moment, wanting to turn to somebody and hand the problem over – only then did she remember that she was the one in charge. The feeling was as brief as déjà vu.

"Rose, could you see if there's another consultant on duty? I need another pair of hands," Jemma said.

Her mouth felt dry; her pulse was knocking against her ears.

Rose nodded and quickly left the room.

"I can't control the bleeding," Jemma said. "She's got a placenta previa. We need to perform an emergency hysterectomy."

The most important thing was to get the bleeding under control. Jemma could work on that until help arrived. She started clamping off big vessels, shutting down the blood supply. The other scrub nurse correctly anticipated the tools she would need and handed them to her. Jemma began cutting and tying off. Her back felt cold under the scratchy pyjamas, and her mask was suffocating. The theatre lights were also starting to make her head ache. Push and probe. Cauterise. Suction. Where was the other consultant? Surely there must be somebody else on duty; they couldn't all be in theatre.

Slowly she felt her panic subsiding now that she knew what she was doing. Everything was getting back under control. She heard Rose returning to the theatre. "All the consultants are busy operating," she said. Jemma nodded. So she was entirely on her own. More blood. She started cutting the uterus out, working in silence except for the beeps and sighs of theatre equipment. Pop, pop ... pop, pop. "We're nearly there," said Jemma. "Suction."

It was bloody, unpleasant work, but soon she felt the womb give. She lifted the bloody mess out and placed it reverently on the metal dish beside her. She glanced at Guaram, who nodded. They were done.

By now they had been working for around an hour. The suction pump hissed. "Tell Frank he can come in and get started on the hip fracture," Jemma said, touching her damp forehead with her forearm. Now all she had to do was sew her up. She felt drained as the adrenaline that had been keeping her going for the past hour wore off. One of the nurses started counting bloody swabs. You didn't want one to be left inside the patient.

Frank, the orthopaedic surgeon, came into the theatre. He, too, had his arms crossed to preserve sterility. Frank would work on the woman's hip fracture for another hour. Jemma sat on a corner stool watching numbly as Frank got busy. Once he had finished, the patient would be transferred to a bed and wheeled to the Intensive Care Unit, where she would be woken up in two or three hours.

Jemma wanted to be there when she woke. The last thing the woman would remember would be the car crash. She wouldn't know why she was in hospital or that she had lost her baby. Jemma would have a lot of explaining to do.

Snapping off her latex gloves, she dropped them in the bin. Jemma felt utterly drained as she disposed of her gown. She walked out of theatre, still wearing her cap. Down the hall was a small room they used for writing up notes. She found the correct form and started recording her operational account, making little drawings of what she had done. She began to reflect on the awfulness of life gone wrong. Another tragic waste of a life. Sometimes it seemed to her that everybody came into hospital just to lose something: a limb, a loved one, a baby. She thought of Matthew and inwardly shuddered. This was not what she had signed up for.

Her thoughts were interrupted by a welcome knock at the door. Guaram's face appeared at the porthole. He, too, was wearing just his scrubs.

"Hey, how are you doing?" Jemma said, glad of the distraction.

"Doctor Sands, I think you were a little hasty back there." His face was grim.

"What are you saying?" Jemma said, a little taken aback. It was unheard of for a registrar to question his consultant like this.

"I am saying that if you had waited a little longer you could have saved the mother and the baby."

"I didn't have any other option. The baby was in distress. You heard its heartbeat. I had to get it out."

"I don't want to cause trouble between us, Doctor Sands. All I am saying is that in my opinion things could have been done differently."

"That's all very well for you to say. I was the one who had to make the decision. One day you'll be faced with a similar situation. I wonder what you'll do then." She was astonished by his effrontery.

Guaram dipped his head, acknowledging her point.

"Anyway, the mother is out of danger now," he said. "And you did save her life. Doctor Foley is just finishing up."

She watched Guaram shut the door behind him, still angry at his impertinence. She wondered if he was going to make a complaint. She had noticed the way he tried to ingratiate himself with his superiors, complaining about things those beneath him had done wrong.

Jemma felt uncomfortable walking back to the women's changing room. Her underwear was sticking to her. It was only when she was pulling off her dark-stained bottoms that she realised why. Absentmindedly, she touched her knickers. Her fingertip was bloody. Looking down, she realised her underwear was wet with the patient's blood.

CHAPTER FOUR

THE SCHOOLGIRL HAD BEEN BROUGHT into A&E by her teacher, complaining of stomach pain. She hadn't even realised she was pregnant. The thirteen-year-old Pakistani had been very frightened when she had been admitted, and Jemma had watched her miscarry yesterday afternoon. Seeing the bloody bundle taken away to be incinerated had been like an annunciation in reverse: the mother who became a virgin. Sitting up in bed this morning with her hair brushed and a hospital gown on, the schoolgirl looked even younger. The tiny chocolate-brown letters spelled out the name of the hospital on a custard-yellow background again and again. Jemma had wanted to keep the girl in over the weekend. Assuming no further complications, the teenager would be discharged tomorrow. Her boyfriend, a frightened-looking youth absurdly dressed as an urban gangsta, was sitting at the bedside. Dressed in baggy tracksuit bottoms and a baseball cap, he was holding her hand. He looked scared stiff.

"How are you feeling today? Still sore?" Jemma asked, whisking the curtain shut.

"Better, s'pose," the girl said with a shrug.

Now the panic was over, she was back to her usual non-communicative self.

"Do you mind if I feel your tummy?"

The girl lifted up her hospital gown without a word and flinched as Jemma touched her stomach.

"I'm going to give you a prescription for some more ibuprofen. It'll take the soreness away. I want to keep you in another night and then you're free to go home."

She had said the wrong thing. The girl stared at the blanket at the foot of her bed while her boyfriend gripped her hand tighter. A tear rolled down her cheek. Jemma had seen it so often before. Regret for the baby she would never hold. The girl was so young. Jemma wanted to tell her that none of us knows what the future holds, that every one of us drives through life with dipped headlights. Nobody can see ahead. Whatever was upsetting the girl, Jemma wanted to put her arms around her and tell her everything was going to be all right.

"Your parents, they do know you're here, don't they?"

"My dad would kill me if he found out. That and going out with a white boy. They think I'm having a sleepover at Shazney's house."

"I told ya. You can move in with me and me mum. Swear down," her boyfriend said.

He looked up beseechingly, and Jemma noticed he was trying to grow a beard.

"You won't grass us up, will ya? Her dad's been in pen. No joke."

Now she realised. Not only was the teenager underage, but she was Muslim. This was the sort of thing you heard about prompting an honour killing. Dog walkers discovering the body early one morning, and police digging through undergrowth on the evening news. Jemma shuddered inside. She had once met a German woman doctor at a conference who sewed up the vaginas of young Turkish girls to make them seem like virgins again.

"It's up to you whether you want to tell your parents or not. You can tell them the ibuprofen is for period pain. What I would say is, you don't want this to happen again. You've got an appointment with the family planning counsellor. There are some leaflets on your bedside table. You're still growing. Don't wish your childhood away."

Jemma spent the next hour doing her rounds on the labour wards. Midwives handed her the patients' notes, and she would chat to the mother while she checked each baby's heart rate. She glanced at her watch. It was 6:31pm. Her next-door neighbour Emily and Emily's nice if rather dull husband would have arrived by now. She had promised Tony that she would try and be there on time, and yet she was going to be here for another hour at least. And she still had to stop at the shop to get them something to eat, and Matthew needed putting to bed. Finally, the moment she had been dreading was here. It was time to wake up her hysterectomy.

Duncan McCracken, the consultant anaesthetist, was waiting for her in ICU. The patient's bed was screened off by a nubby brown curtain.

"Is she ready to come round?" Jemma asked.

"She should be waking up just about now," he said.

They stood to one side to let porters wheeling a hospital bed go past. An alarm rang persistently in the background. A young black boy was lying on the bed, just waking up from an operation, while a nurse stroked his head.

Jemma swished the curtain back.

Toppy Mrazek was lying fast asleep with the ventilator tube still in her trachea. The ventilator stood next to the ECG monitor showing her heart rate and blood pressure. McCracken would ease her into taking over her own breathing simply by weaning her off the drugs. It would take about ten minutes for her to wake up. Jemma stood watching him while he got to work.

Once he had left, she pulled up a plastic chair and sat down. Through the window a plane was coming in to land at Heathrow. The sunset was turning everything a blood-red tawny gold, and Jemma hoped this was not going to take long.

It was a beautiful evening. She kept thinking about how late she was going to be getting home. But she knew her duty was to tell the patient what had gone wrong and how none of it could have been avoided. Right from the moment Toppy Mrazek's gurney had crashed through the swing doors of A&E, it had been like an equation you couldn't solve. All the factors had conspired against her to end in the same dreadful conclusion, and she pictured the chalk snapping as she reached the end of the blackboard.

The patient shifted in bed and opened her eyes.

"Where's my baby?" she said drowsily. "Wanna see my baby."

"Miss Mrazek, it's me, Doctor Sands. You were in a car accident. Do you remember?"

The woman spoke slowly, licking her lips. She shook her head. "Dunno... I remember the motorway. Two cars. After that, no."

"Your car hit another vehicle and landed upside down in the fast lane. You're lucky to be alive. They had to pull you out from the wreckage. Don't worry, your memory will come back. It's perfectly normal. Your hip was broken and we had to mend it." Jemma hated the way that her voice sounded so cheerful, it was all so false.

"I can't feel my baby. What have you done with him? I need to see my baby."

"You were trapped upside down in the car. They had a hell of a time getting you out. You had a terrific shock. The crash hurt your baby."

Toppy tried sitting up, but the effort was too great. Her face was swollen with cuts and bruises.

"This is going to be difficult for you to take in right now. You were dying. I had to make a decision. Either I could save you or your baby. I had to save you."

She licked her lips again, trying to focus. "Don't understand. What have you done with him?"

Tears were coming as the anaesthetic wore off, as if she already knew the answer. Jemma could not meet her eyes and stared down at the floor. Often patients didn't remember the first conversation they had coming to, and Jemma hoped to God that was true in this case.

"I didn't have any option. It was either you or your baby. If you'd just let me..."

The woman just sat there, absorbing what Jemma had just told her. "You had no right," she said finally. "You didn't ask me. How dare you. You killed my baby."

Jemma said nothing, remembering what the hospital lawyer had said about how to handle these situations. Best say nothing that might affect the hospital's legal position, he told them.

Seeing the lack of reaction, the patient tried again. "Who the hell do you think you are playing God like that? You had no right."

"We have a bereavement counselling service if you want." Jemma realised how lame this sounded.

Toppy moved her arm beneath the bedclothes.

"What have you done to me?"

"I can give you a morphine pump for the pain. There were complications. We had to perform a hysterectomy. I'm sorry."

"A hyster– I don't understand."

"We had to remove your uterus. It's standard. It was either that or–"

The patient gulped. Tears were really coming now. The golden early evening light made her look as young as the Muslim girl Jemma had seen upstairs.

"If you'd just let me explain–"

"Explain what? That you killed my baby? That I'll never be able to have another one?"

"You were dying. If there was any way to save both you and the baby I would have done so, believe me."

"Get out," she said coldly. "Get Out. GET OUT."

Jemma stood up, only too glad to be getting out of there.

Whisking the curtain behind her, she met the shocked stare of a passing A&E nurse. The nurse must have overheard Toppy's shouting. That was when Toppy began to scream. Her scream was so piercing that it penetrated the brickwork.

CHAPTER FIVE

EMILY WAS RIGHT. THEIR SITTING room was as immaculate as an operating theatre. Jemma dumped her keys on the radiator cover and glanced at the photographs on the sitting room table. Matthew laughing on a swing against a blue sky as unclouded as his future. Jemma at her graduation, looking pimply and awkward in a mortar board and gown. Tony and Jemma gazing into each other's eyes on their wedding day. Jemma clinging to a climbing wall during a rock-climbing weekend in Wales. A snapshot taken on their honeymoon when they learned to scuba dive.

"Tony, I'm home," she called. Tony's voice came from upstairs. He was probably in Matthew's bedroom reading him a story. Rather than go straight up, Jemma carried her shopping bag through to the kitchen.

Medicine, like music, often runs in families. But nobody in her family had ever been a doctor, let alone a surgeon. Jemma had known she wanted to be a surgeon since she was a little girl. She had come across a book about doctors in her school library and had pored over it all night, huddled in her plaid dressing gown, her hair in bunches. Aged nineteen she went to medical school in Scotland, where she froze in a succession of rackety cottages.

Jemma partly spent her first year as a medical student dissecting the nut-brown, desiccated body of an old woman in the anatomy class. Her flaccid breasts fell either side of her chest. It surprised Jemma how tough cutting up bodies was – like trying to saw through old shoes. Soon, any embarrassment in the class gave way to chatter about which party you were going to that night and who was going out with whom. You could see people's shoes as they walked over the dirty glass roof-window above. She wondered what pedestrians would make of what was going on beneath them – medical students scooping up massed intestines and dropping them into a plastic bucket. Most of all, what she remembered was the overpowering stench of formaldehyde.

Tony and Jemma had been together for ten years. Matthew had been born four years after they married. Jemma's thoughts flicked back to that Gower Street basement flat where they had first met. The room had been a crush of nurses and doctors. Tony caught her looking at him and mouthed a question. Jemma, intrigued, had moved forward and they had entered into conversation, she couldn't remember what about. Despite all the people clustered around them, Jemma felt they had been speaking a secret language known only to them, that they were the only two people in the room. The encounter made her feel hot and light-headed.

She knew who he was. She was still a house officer then, while he was a consultant advising the hospital. She'd heard nurses talking about him in the changing room. He was a big man with thinning hair and, judging from the smudges under his eyes and his heavy jowls, she suspected he might be diabetic. What immediately attracted her to him was his voice. It was deep and delicious, like honey poured over iron filings. That and his utter self-confidence. He never had any doubt about anything. Now she understood why the nurses had been talking about him. They went back to her basement flat that first night and she remembered kissing him hungrily in her kitchen. "Do you have this effect on every man you meet?" he asked with a big grin on his face.

She felt guilty the next morning as they came up the steps of her shared basement flat together. Feeling cross with herself, she fumbled to put on her sunglasses in an effort to look cool – unfortunately the nose-clips were missing, and they slithered down her nose. That was the moment when Tony said he fell in love with her.

She remembered those first few years as being completely happy. Memories arrested her. Tony standing naked in her kitchen, opening the window and letting in the cold winter air. Tangled together in bed, watching the reflections of orange headlights swoop across the bedroom wall. The truly awful hotel they stayed in during their first weekend away together. And standing on a bridge in the French countryside overlooking lily pads as she said, "This is exactly the tacky sort of place where somebody would propose" before noticing the tiny velvet box that Tony was holding as he got down on one knee and asked the inevitable question.

Next to the picture of them scuba diving was another photo of Matthew asleep as a baby. She thought about the girl with the dead baby this afternoon. Would her husband be sitting by her side holding her hand? Would Toppy Mrazek rest her head on his chest as they mourned their loss? They wouldn't be able to try again. Jemma had seen to that, oh yes. But she hadn't had any other choice. Of course you did, said another voice.

Putting the groceries away in the fridge, she saw a bottle of white wine and thought longingly of a drink. It had been a truly awful day. Rather than go straight upstairs, she selfishly decided to have a moment to herself. She reached into the back of a kitchen cupboard for the packet of ten cigarettes she kept secret from her husband, opened the back door and stepped out into their approximation of a garden. It was really just a square of greenish uneven paving stones. As she sucked greedily on her cigarette, Jemma wondered whether the car-crash victim would make a formal complaint. If she did, the hospital would back Jemma up, she was sure of that. She had done everything by the book. Would Toppy Mrazek understand that she hadn't had any option today? Or would she hate her forever? She shook herself again. The tobacco was making her morbid.

Flicking the butt into a corner, she went back inside.

Tony was sitting at Matthew's bedside reading him a story. Jemma groaned inwardly when she saw it was the same story he wanted every night. Matthew was clutching his teddy Ray, all the more beloved for his mysteriously singed paw.

"Sorry I'm late," she said. "I couldn't get away. The incoming was more complicated than I thought. Supper's downstairs in the fridge if you want to get on with it." Standing up, Tony grimaced as if to say, what time do you call this? "Emily and Adam were sorry to have missed you," he said, handing her the book. He was annoyed with her for being so late. Well fuck you, she thought, leaning down and hugging her son. His hot, stout body, still fresh from the bath, smelt delicious. Her throat tightened with love. "I'll go downstairs and get supper on," Tony said, sidling past her.

Jemma settled in the rocking chair in which she had nursed Matthew, and he looked at her with damp, tired eyes. Ugly acid-orange streetlight spilled through the curtains. Somewhere a telephone rang, and a plane roared into Heathrow.

"Did you have a nice time with Daddy in the park?" she said, opening the book.

He nodded. "We had ice cream and Auntie Emily came over with Matilda and we played Moshi Monsters."

"What did you have for supper?"

"Sausages." Chips and sausages and ice cream were Matthew's favourites.

She picked up the story where Tony had left off – she almost knew it by heart. She did not want to think about what had happened this afternoon, but it kept seeping into her brain like a ruptured blood vessel. Part of her mind went through the sequence of events, stopping at the point when things got out of control. She kept telling herself that her call for help had been ignored. She could not get past that moment. Stop being so dramatic, she thought. You did the right thing; you had no other choice. Jemma paused for a moment to check if Matthew was asleep yet. She wondered whether Matthew would ever know how much she loved him. Really, love between parent and child was the perfect love, an unconditional love compared to that of husband and wife. That was different. The girl this afternoon would never be able to do this, a voice remonstrated... But you saved her life, the other voice reasoned. Round and round they went, both voices, competing with each other. Eventually Matthew yawned and his eyes flickered closed. Jemma switched off the lamp and crept downstairs.

Tony was in the kitchen slicing chicken breasts when she put her arms around him. She felt him stiffen, as if he did not want her touching him.

"I'm sorry I couldn't get away. How were they both?"

"Oh, fine," said Tony, dropping breast chunks into a bowl. "I fed the kids while Adam told me about this big deal he's working on. Do you know, I don't think he's ever asked me a question about what I do."

"You're a good man, Tony Sands," she said, coming forward to kiss him.

He turned his head away.

"You should have told me about this afternoon," he said, moving towards the fridge. He wouldn't look at her. "Your registrar has made a complaint. He says you were too hasty getting the baby out. He says you should have waited."

Jemma was appalled. She took a moment to collect herself. "That's ridiculous. The baby's heart rate was dropping. The foetus was going into shock."

The bastard, she thought. Guaram had no right to go behind her back like that.

"I called for help but was told none of the other obstetric surgeons were available."

"This woman's lawyer has already been in touch. I suspect Chandra's told her about the complaints procedure. You always said he was a two-faced weasel. It doesn't even matter who's right and who's wrong. The point is that the legal meter has already started ticking." His voice was hard and cold. "If she does sue, I'll have the insurers on my back telling me to settle. It could cost the hospital hundreds of thousands of pounds. I know you've done nothing wrong, but I'm still going to have to convene a meeting of the ethics committee. I just wish you'd told me first. I had no idea what Chandra was talking about when he came to see me."

Guaram came to see him?

"It's all very well for Guaram to complain after the event. I was the one who had to make the decision. The patient was crashing. She would have died otherwise."

"Chandra says you panicked."

She felt a mixture of shame and anger.

"Look, I want to get this settled as quickly as possible," Tony said, softening his voice. "I'm going to convene the meeting for Monday."

What she needed was for him not to be so angry with her. She reached forward and touched his arm.

"Everybody knows that you're my wife, for goodness' sake," Tony continued. "They'll all be saying that I pulled some strings if the committee's too soft on you. If anything, they've got to lean the other way." He stroked her blonde hair. "Hey, listen, I'm sorry. I'm on your side, remember? There's no need for us to fight."

"But I didn't do anything wrong." She felt righteous anger welling up inside her.

"I know that. But I've got to be like Caesar's wife. Above reproach. Of course, I'll excuse myself from the hearing."

"Tony, I have done nothing to be ashamed of."

"Of course you haven't. It's just your registrar making trouble."

Jemma followed Tony to the kitchen table where he busied himself setting their places. He still wouldn't look at her.

"Who will take your place on the committee if you're not going to be there?"

"I thought of asking George Malvern."

Her heart leapt a little at the mention of George's name. George was head of the hospital's psychiatric department. He and Jemma had known each other since they were both junior doctors and had become close friends. They had met at the same party where she and Tony had met. Sometimes she found herself wondering what would have happened had she gone home with George that night and not her husband. But only secretly, to herself.

Tony looked up from arranging a knife and fork. "Listen, it's the weekend now. Try not to think about it. Let's have a nice day with Matthew tomorrow."

"How can I not think about it? You're telling me I've got a disciplinary hearing on Monday. How on earth do you expect me to enjoy the weekend?" Calming down, she added, "What's the worst thing they could do?"

Now it was his turn to be placatory. "The worst that could happen is that they'll launch a full enquiry. You know how difficult malpractice is to prove. Patients are always complaining that you doctors stick together. The likelihood is that they'll drop it," he said, taking both her hands.

Relieved, she felt the pain and anxiety ebbing away as Tony put his arms around her. She allowed herself to sink into him.

"So, what do you fancy doing tomorrow?" he said. "We've got the whole day to ourselves."

"Dunno. Take Matthew to the park. Go and feed the ducks."

He tightened his arms around her. "Whatever happens, I will protect you. That's my job."

"Oh, Tony," she said, her eyes pricking with tears. "Today was so fucking awful. I felt so isolated. I didn't know who to turn to."

He shushed her, stroking her blonde hair. She lifted her face up to his and they kissed gently.

"Everything is going to be all right," he said. "Just you see."

He was wrong. Later, Jemma would remember that night as their last moment of unalloyed happiness, but neither of them could have known that then.

CHAPTER SIX

JEMMA SAT WAITING IN THE hospital corridor outside the ethics committee meeting room. There wasn't much to look at apart from a coffee vending machine, and the sofa she was sitting on had seen better days. People glanced at her as they walked past, but they never stopped. When news had spread of her disciplinary action, colleagues reacted as if it would have scalded them to touch her. In short, she was being quarantined.

The meeting-room venetian blinds were closed, so she couldn't see inside. As she sat there, her feelings alternated between numb dread as to what she was about to face and self-justification. Her call for help had been ignored, and she had been in over her head. For a moment, deep down, she knew that she had panicked. Not that she was going to say as much to the ethics committee. She was in the middle of rehearsing her argument when the door opened. George Malvern stood in the doorway.

George was a bit older than Jemma, in his late thirties. Although Jemma had always thought of herself as a high flier, George had left her far behind. He was a member of the Royal College of Psychiatrists by his late twenties, and a consultant by thirty-one. Four years later he was appointed head of unit at St Luke's. Jemma knew that some of the older psychiatrists resented being told what to do by a younger man. For her part, she was pleased when Tony told her George would be taking his place on the ethics committee. It meant she would have somebody she could trust fighting her corner.

George was a good-looking man with a kindly, rather old-fashioned face. In Victorian times he might have been a curate. On first meeting him, Jemma's mother – always outspoken – had declared that he was the man she should have chosen. This had struck Jemma as a peculiar thing to say, considering she was already engaged to Tony. And yes, if she was honest, there was always something unspoken between them, an unarticulated regret... Jemma took her seat, ready to be interrogated.

There were two others on the panel. Christine Matlock sat on the far left. She was a tough old bird who was Tony's second-in-command running the hospital. Her grey hair was cut mannishly short, and the only time Jemma had ever seen her smile was announcing budget cuts. St John David, the committee chairman, sat between Matlock and George. David was the clinical director in charge of obstetrics. He was an arrogant man who was strongly disliked by everybody who worked under him, including Jemma. He behaved as if he alone was the recipient of some vastly amusing private joke. George gave her an encouraging smile.

"We've convened this meeting to discuss what happened on Saturday afternoon," David said, holding a piece of A4 paper. "Perhaps you could tell us in your own words, Doctor Sands." Jemma could tell he was enjoying this.

"You've read my operational notes," she began. "I was faced with a dilemma. Either I save the mother or the baby. My duty was to save the mother. I learned that the first day of medical school."

"Please could you take us through the course of events? I want to hear exactly what happened."

"At approximately one o'clock on Saturday afternoon, I received a text message from my obstetric registrar telling me that a car-crash victim was being brought into A&E. She was going into labour following a pile-up on the M25. I reached the hospital around forty-five minutes later. The patient's blood pressure was ninety over forty and dropping, while her heart rate was already under fifty. She was going into hemodynamic shock. It was clear to me that the baby was in distress. We had to get it out as quickly as possible."

"Go on," said David, leaning forward.

"I performed an emergency caesarean, only we were too late. The baby was already stillborn. Not only that, but the patient's placenta had come away from her uterus. My first priority was to get the bleeding under control."

"Your registrar says you didn't know what you were doing,"

interrupted Matlock.

Jemma shifted in her seat. "That's not true. There was a moment when I felt overwhelmed, yes," she said carefully. "There was so much blood. I asked for assistance. I felt I was losing control of the situation. To be honest, I didn't have enough hands. Every other obstetric consultant was in theatre. By the time I was told nobody was available, I'd staunched the bleeding. Everything was back under control."

"So you admit that you panicked."

"I admit there was a moment when I felt the operation getting away from me, yes."

There was a short pause, then David said: "I still don't understand how this relatively straightforward procedure could have gone out of control. Foetuses are viable these days at twenty weeks. Surely you knew that. I am puzzled that somebody of your experience couldn't have performed an emergency caesarean and still saved the mother."

Jemma sat forward in her chair. "I was trying to do that. The baby was going into shock. Things were moving so quickly. My priority was to save this woman's life. I couldn't do two things at once. If I'd had another pair of hands perhaps–"

"In other words, you did panic," said Matlock coldly.

"Not only that," David interjected. "But in your hurry to get the baby out you performed an emergency hysterectomy.

An operation that, in my opinion, was not strictly necessary. And you've left the hospital open to a lawsuit that could cost this NHS trust hundreds of thousands of pounds."

"That's not what happened at all. I couldn't deliver the baby until I'd got the woman stabilised. If you read my notes–"

"Now hang on a minute," George said. "Doctor Sands was only following protocol. She did save this woman's life. And she wasn't arrogant enough not to ask for help. Help, I might add, that was not available."

Matlock cocked her head to one side considering his point. As David turned to her, Jemma felt painful apprehension in her stomach. This was not how she had anticipated the meeting going at all.

"Has the woman issued a formal complaint?" David asked.

"Not yet. No. But we've already had an email from her solicitor, a big City firm. Turns out she knows people. Tony has agreed to meet this woman's solicitor to try and head off any legal action. Hopefully he can get them to drop any lawsuit."

"Nevertheless," David said, "it is now clear to me that a full enquiry is called for. There is clearly a case to answer. Until then I'm suspending you from theatre. You will, of course, still be allowed to do ward rounds and continue to make plans for patient care."

He began squaring the papers in front of him.

Jemma felt shock creep up on her. She had not expected this.

"How long am I to be suspended for?" she asked.

"That depends on the length of the enquiry. I would say one or two months. That will be all, Doctor Sands. If you will excuse us, we still have some other business to discuss."

Jemma did not remember how she got from the meeting room to the hospital atrium. She sat down heavily, unaware of the scraping of chairs and clatter of cutlery going on around her. She could not take in what had just happened; she wanted to cry and vomit at the same time.

"I wanted to see how you were doing," said George behind her. "I'm sorry St John David was so rough on you. I guess that's why they call him 'the bastard'."

He was holding two cups of coffee, and she was so pleased to see him. She longed for a soft word, somebody to tell her everything was going to be okay. She thought about how she had told the Muslim schoolgirl that very same thing only two days ago.

"Two months. I feel so humiliated. I always thought I was a good surgeon."

"You are a good surgeon," said George, sitting down. "He didn't have any option. Imagine the stink if it got out that this girl sues the hospital and you haven't even been suspended."

"But I saved that woman's life. It was either her or her baby. And now I'm being punished for it?"

"Look, I know that," said George, reaching across and touching her wrist. "But look at it from their position. They had to be seen to be doing something. The investigation will be over in a couple of months. You will be exonerated. Tony's real problem will be if she tries to sue the hospital."

"She would have died if I hadn't operated."

"You could go and see her, you know. She might be ready to listen. Tell her that you couldn't save her baby. If she'd lost any more blood she would have died."

"St John David would come down on me like a ton of bricks if he knew what I was doing. He's only just suspended me."

"How would he ever know? It's a five-minute conversation. You know what they say, to understand is to forgive. She might just change her mind if she heard what you had to say. And don't you owe her an explanation? She must be feeling incredibly angry and upset."

George was right. She had been so wrapped up in her own feelings she hadn't really given her patient a thought.

"Are you going to be all right?" George asked.

"I'll be fine." Beat. "I didn't do anything wrong."

They said goodbye, and Jemma left her half-drunk cup of coffee. The pain she felt was replaced by the sense of wanting to do the right thing. She would explain to Toppy Mrazek that she had saved her life, that she'd had no alternative, yes, that was what she would do. Jemma's heels clicked along the hospital corridor with purpose. How good it felt to be doing the right thing.

Puffed up with rectitude, Jemma let herself into intensive care. The duty nurse looked up as Jemma explained that she had come to see Saturday's car crash. The nurse nodded and pointed farther down the ward. A drunken Jamaican woman was standing in the corridor shouting at a nurse. An electric bell was ringing. Jemma walked up to the car-crash victim's cubicle, and for a moment she stood there wondering whether she had the nerve to go through with this. She reached up and touched the curtain.

CHAPTER SEVEN

STANDING IN THE SPACE-AGE RECEPTION of Nicolson & Chaney Solicitors, Tony wondered how much they charged by the hour. The all-white reception area reminded him of a sixties' science-fiction film. The receptionist smiled meaninglessly at him and the hospital's solicitor as they arrived. She directed them to sit on one of the white modernist sofas that looked like a Henry Moore sculpture.

"I dread to think how much this all costs. It's probably why she's coming after us for so much money," Tony said, glancing at Sky News on one wall.

"They're just doing what they have to do," the solicitor replied. Neil Watling was astonishingly ugly, with thick black glasses and a bad haircut. "Her solicitor knows the hospital did everything to try and save this woman's baby. The ethics committee has launched a full investigation. They can't ask for anything more."

"Well, you've read the correspondence. They say there's a clear case to answer."

It had been a month since the car crash and Jemma's suspension. Toppy Mrazek had been transferred to a private hospital on Cromwell Road within a few days of being admitted to A&E.

Toppy Mrazek. The moment Chandra mentioned her name when he came to see him, Tony wondered if it was the same person. Even though he tried to forget her, there were moments when he saw somebody in the street: a look, a glance, the kind of clothes she used to wear. It had taken years for him to stop thinking about her and for his heart to finally heal, and now here she was, back in his life again. The irony was that this had all come about because of his wife – the one person whom he had kept Toppy Mrazek's existence a secret from and, more important, what she had meant to him.

And it was his wife's malpractice that had brought them together again.

Private health insurance had covered her hospital expenses. The next solicitor's letter arrived shortly after that: not only was the hospital being sued for malpractice, but Toppy and her solicitor were coming after Jemma personally. The legal correspondence started flowing thick and fast. Tony remembered what Watling said when he showed him that first letter: "There's something personal here. There's none of the usual legalese. It's as if the woman herself was dictating the letter to…" he scanned for the signature, "Amy Krige. Usually we write these things in temperate language. This one's absolutely scalding. It's as if she was standing over the lawyer's shoulder telling her what to write."

If he was correct, then they were just about to meet whoever had really dictated that letter. Each letter was costing the hospital a hundred pounds to reply to. Of course, it was a war of attrition, and Toppy's lawyer was trying to wear St Luke's down to get them to this meeting. Tony also knew that he ought to say he and Toppy had met once before, that he was not entirely disinterested, but somehow he could not bring himself to do it. He needed to see her again.

Tony looked up at the sound of approaching high heels. Amy Krige was a tall blonde whose slightly bug eyes reminded him of a grasshopper. She had a cool, crisp manner as she evaluated the two of them when they rose to greet her. The three of them shook hands. Tony and his solicitor followed her into one of the smoked-glass meeting rooms leading off from reception.

Toppy was already waiting, standing beside the floor-length window overlooking the magisterial grey buildings of the City. She was on crutches. Tony took in her thick, slightly wild hair and small, sharp features. It had been fifteen years since he had last seen her, and she had not changed much at all. But then people don't really change, do they?

"Mr Sands, Mr Watling, this is my client, Ms Mrazek," said Krige.

"Hello, Toppy," said Tony.

The last time he had seen her she was sprawled

lubriciously in his bed, and he remembered the line of her neck and shoulder against the pillow. Lovelier than any work of art. He remembered the neon spill from the streetlamp outside his window. That had been when he was finishing his MBA, and she had disappeared that night without a word. Not even a note.

"Hello, Tony."

"You didn't tell me you knew each other," said Krige, surprised. "You should have told me."

"We don't really know each other," Toppy said. "We met in Cambridge once, years ago, didn't we, Mr Sands? That has nothing to do with this." She hobbled over to one of the chairs and sat down.

"How long will you be on crutches?" Tony asked, wanting to be sympathetic. They were all sizing each other up before they got down to what they were really there for.

"My doctor says another month or so. I have to go back into hospital to have my stitches out."

"We're here to see whether we can come to a financial settlement without having to go to court," Krige said.

"Hang on," Watling said. "St Luke's hasn't admitted any wrongdoing. You know we have launched a full investigation, and we're waiting for our ethics committee to report back before we discuss the possibility of any compensation. Not that we're admitting any liability."

"Do you have any idea of the trauma your hospital has put

my client through?" Krige said. "Not only did your surgeon unnecessarily abort my client's baby, but she will never be able to have children."

"Doctor Sands said in her sworn statement that she was faced with a dilemma. Either she saved the baby or your client's life."

"We have two other obstetric surgeons prepared to say otherwise. They will testify in court that there was no need to perform an emergency hysterectomy. Doctor Sands acted unilaterally and without regard for the physical and emotional wellbeing of my client."

"That's simply not true," Watling said. "She was following procedure."

"Mr Watling, let me tell you what will happen if this goes in front of a jury. They will see a young woman whose life has been blighted by a surgeon who didn't know what she was doing. I will paint a picture of a Madonna and child for them, a painting that your hospital has ripped up."

While the two lawyers were fencing, Tony glanced furtively at Toppy. She returned his gaze frankly. He was still powerfully attracted to this woman and he had no idea why. A one-night stand fifteen years ago and he had never been able to forget her.

They had met one night in a pub, and she told him she was studying at a local secretarial college. They had gone back to his hotel room that night. There was a faint whiff of death about her – and it was intoxicating.

"Toppy, please can you tell these gentlemen what you've been going through since the accident?"

"I can't sleep. I haven't been able to get in a car since what happened. All I keep seeing is the car swerving in front of me and the taste of metal in my mouth..."

"This kind of traumatic stress is perfectly normal after a car accident," Watling said. "I fail to see what this has to do with the hospital."

Toppy continued: "It's deeper than that. I lie in bed at night thinking about the son who was snatched out of me. You don't know what it feels like to know you're never going to have a child. I listen to the sound of children laughing, and it cuts like a knife. Do you have any children of your own, Mr Sands?"

"Yes, I do," Tony faltered. "His name's Matthew. He's five years old."

"Lucky you. The happy gurgle of a child's laughter is a pleasure I will never know."

"Look, Miss Mrazek," Tony said, "my consultant obstetrician–"

"Isn't there a conflict of interest here? You're not only the hospital's chief executive, you're married to the woman who scooped my insides out. You're bound to defend her, even though the truth is staring you in the face."

"That's unfair. There is a Chinese wall between myself and my wife in this matter. She has been suspended from duty pending the report of the ethics committee, which, by the way, I have excused myself from."

"We don't understand why you are suing Doctor Sands personally," Watling said. "If I may say, it smacks of being unnecessarily vindictive–"

"To make sure she doesn't do this to anybody else," Toppy interrupted. "You have no idea how it feels knowing you are never going to be a full woman."

Tony found himself digging into his suit pocket and retrieving a business card. He told himself that all he was doing was being the good Samaritan, yet in his heart he knew he really wanted was to see this woman again. Alone.

"I am truly sorry for your loss, I really am," he said. "But sometimes bad things just happen. We all look for people to blame. Everything always has to be somebody's fault, doesn't it? The cards fall wrong sometimes. My consultant obstetrician, her staff in A&E, nobody's wearing the black hat here. The tragedy of it is that everybody was trying to do the right thing."

Even as he was sliding his business card across the boardroom table to her, something was telling him no, no, no. Toppy reached for the card and, as their fingertips touched, it was if a blue electric spark jumped between them.

He had to have her. It was as simple as that.

"Yes," she said. "Wouldn't it be nice to think so?"

CHAPTER EIGHT

THE ARCHITECTURAL VISTA OF THE City of London was like a science-fiction skyline. Gazing out over Waterloo Bridge, Tony wondered what it would look like in twenty years' time.

He glanced at his watch. Nibley was late. Tony worried for a moment that he might have got the wrong bridge until he saw the custard-beige Mercedes approaching. It reminded him of those cars African dictators used to drive. The car pulled over, and the American drugs company executive got out. His driver, the copper-coloured mixed-race man who went everywhere with him, regarded Tony flatly. With his crew-cut ginger-ish hair, he looked like the result of an unlikely coupling between Mike Tyson and Jessica Rabbit. The one time he had met him before, Tony had found the driver's lack of emotion unnerving. Nibley had referred to him as "the ultimate in attitude realignment", whatever that meant. The drugs company boss said something to his driver, and the car moved off.

Nibley was dressed in a spivvy-looking camel overcoat. They started walking over the bridge against the raw autumn wind. Tony realised that he had never seen Nibley without a tan, and he wondered whether the American was vain enough to use a sunbed.

"Will he do it?" Nibley said.

"There won't be any trouble there. He was salivating when I showed him the data you emailed me. The results are off the chart. You are going to make a lot of people very happy. You could even save lives. Perhaps I should buy stock myself. Your share price is going to rocket."

"So when can the guy start?"

"As soon as you can supply him with what he needs. I explained about the others and how he wouldn't be on his own."

"What about the other thing we talked about?"

"There won't be any trouble there either. I've approached the other directors individually. They understood. After all, they have lifestyles to support. In the end, everybody has a price," Tony said ruefully.

"Yeah, well, uh, how much money to swing things?"

"A million pounds is what we agreed."

"That's a lot of grease."

"Think how much the contract is worth. You will be making millions every year."

"My chairman said I could go up to seven fifty only."

Tony felt a sudden panic. He realised that he was powerless in this transaction, that he was merely the supplicant:

whatever Nibley offered, he would have to suck it up. Money, he thought, was the one subject it was impossible to joke about.

"Have you got the next payment with you?" Tony said. His thoughts flicked to the woman he was meeting for lunch. He felt faint with desire at the thought of her. The two men stopped and looked out over the Thames towards Big Ben and the Houses of Parliament. Nibley passed over an envelope. And that was that. The transaction was complete.

Sitting on the Tube, Tony kept worrying that he might lose the envelope or that he might be pickpocketed. He kept patting the comforting bulge inside his coat, thinking about seeing Toppy again. She hadn't returned his texts or phone calls after she disappeared that night. A few days later he had lamely gone to the secretarial college where she was studying and asked reception how he could find her. After some consultation, the receptionist was allowed to tell him that she had dropped out of her course and gone back to London. And now, fifteen years later, here she was in his life again. Toppy Mrazek.

When he got to the restaurant, he was disappointed that he was the first to arrive. What if she had changed her mind? The restaurant was an Italian place near South Kensington Tube that he sometimes took guests to. It was sufficiently out of the way from the hospital not to be seen by prying eyes.

Why are you so afraid of being seen? he asked himself. This is a perfectly justifiable meeting between a hospital chief executive and a patient who is suing the hospital, trying to reach an out-of-court settlement, he reasoned.

Stop kidding yourself. You're here because the moment you are alone together, you plan to betray your wife and the mother of your child with a woman you have dreamed about ever since she rejected you.

And truth be told, he still dreamed about her – even after nine years of marriage. The dreams came infrequently, as if there was something unresolved he had to work out. Why is it we always want the ones who don't want us? He compared the two women: Snow White and Rose Red. Jemma was an intrinsically good person, a rare thing to find; and yet, if he was being honest, she was just a little boring. Having been married for so long, they knew each other's views on everything from the prime minister to wallpaper. Everything in Jemma's life revolved around either their son or her work at the hospital. There was never any time for him. He was having trouble remembering why they got married in the first place. Don't be a bloody fool, his other voice remonstrated, you're about to throw everything away for a dream...

"I expect you thought I wasn't coming," Toppy said.

He had been thinking so hard he hadn't even noticed her coming in. She was standing over the table, still on crutches. A waiter fussed about, pulling out a chair for her, and Tony stood up. He realised his mouth was quite dry. She was wearing a fetching brown velvet jacket over a grey V-neck jumper.

"I hope you like this restaurant. They know me here," he said once they were both seated. "Would you like something to drink? I thought we could get a bottle of wine."

"Not for me. Water will be fine. It's funny seeing you again. When my lawyer mentioned your name, I wondered if it was you. How long has it been?"

"Fifteen years," Tony laughed nervously. "Not that I'm counting."

"So, you're married now with a child. Marriage suits you. You've put on weight."

"Marriage does that to you. Creeping contentment."

"Your wife, the surgeon, what's she like? When I realised it was you, I wanted to stop, but the legal wheels were already in motion. My solicitor is convinced we can win."

"Toppy, what happened in the hospital, I'm sorry. You must know that Jemma's a good doctor, a bloody good doctor in fact. If there had been any other way to prevent what happened, she would have done it. Your lawyer is badly advising you. There are no grounds to sue."

"That's not what my lawyer says."

"Is there anything I can say or do to stop you going ahead

with this? It's all so unnecessary. And you will lose."

"Ah yes, I'd forgotten how you medical people stick together," Toppy said, closing her menu. She gave her order to the hovering waiter. Tony did the same.

They paused until the waiter had moved away. "Actually, there is one thing you can do that would make me go away," Toppy continued.

"And what's that?" Tony said eagerly.

"What do you think? You never were the sharpest knife in the drawer, Tony. I think that's one of the things I love about you."

Of course, money. Tony unconsciously touched the wad of cash in his jacket pocket. "And if we came to an arrangement between ourselves, keeping the lawyers out of it, would you drop it? This suspension is hurting my wife."

"I might consider it."

If he paid her off from the money Nibley was giving him, nobody would ever know about it. They talked about nothing much while they waited for their food to arrive. Toppy told him that she worked as an office manager for an investment bank in the City. No, she had never married. Tony talked about his own life, careful not to mention Jemma or his son, partly because he did not want to hurt her feelings and partly because he wanted to make himself appear more available. Even as he was talking, he wondered what it would be like to slip his hand under her jumper and learn the feel of her breast.

"Your wife, does she know about us? That we already know each other?"

Tony shook his head. Putting his knife and fork together, he said: "When I left you that night and you disappeared, I was surprised, to say the least. You never returned my calls or my texts. The secretarial college said you'd gone back to London."

"I was barely more than a schoolgirl. I could see the look in your eyes. I wasn't ready for a relationship."

"And now, I mean, the father of your child, does he know what's going on?"

Now it was Toppy's turn to shake her head. "Another ship passing in the night, I'm afraid. You must think I'm a terrible person."

"I would never think that," he said clumsily.

Her face waxed in front of him until it occupied the whole of his vision. The hubbub around them submerged as if the other tables were underwater. All he felt was his heartbeat and how difficult it was to speak. He felt high. Tony reached out and touched her hand. She did not resist.

"I hope you don't mind, but I've booked a room at a nearby hotel" – Christ, why was he sounding so bloody English? – "and I need to let them know if we don't want it."

She smiled, and he noticed her tiny vulpine teeth; a thousand questions being asked and answered. "Why should I mind?" she said.

The sound of the room came back.

CHAPTER NINE

MEMORIES. MOTES OF DUST DANCING in the sunlight of her childhood home, a mansion flat in Knightsbridge. Her anguish at being separated from her doll as a room divider was pulled across their sitting room. Seeing her mother standing naked in a bath cooling the water with her feet, and holding her baby brother's tiny hand in hers as she lifted him out of his cot showing him the London plane trees. Then the sick-making moment as he slipped out of his blanket, going faster and faster; a woman screaming in the street below and her seven-year-old self knowing she had done something terribly wrong. She stood on tiptoes and peered over the balcony to glimpse his small white body lying at a funny angle in the street below. A crowd had gathered. Her mother brushing past while she shrank into a corner of the bedroom. Then Mummy opening her mouth and making this awful keening sound.

Her parents sent her to see a psychiatrist when she began cutting herself. Anything to feel something. She cut herself on her inner thigh to try and hide what she was doing. The psychiatrist had said it was because she felt so guilty about what she had done. In her heart she knew she had wanted him to die. All the attention had been hers before he arrived.

Now she was being punished again. A second child had been taken away from her. Except this time she was not going to take a knife to herself. No. She was going to hunt down the woman who had done this to her and make her pay.

Toppy Mrazek ran her hand over the thick caesarean scar across her belly and looked at herself critically in the mirror. Shifting her weight to one hip, she pirouetted a little in her underwear. Not bad. The bruises on her face had faded to yellow marks, and the cuts had disappeared almost completely. You would not have known that six months ago she had been in intensive care.

"Can't wait to see you, darling, and feel your strong arms around me," was what she had said in her text message. She picked up the silk dressing gown lying across the foot of the bed and put it on, trying its belt before helping herself to a glass of chilled white wine. He would be here any moment. The bottle was beaded with cold as she lifted it out, rattling ice cubes in the stainless steel ice bucket. Taking a sip, she stared meditatively at the net curtains. Not that there was much to see. The hotel bedroom looked onto a bleak courtyard, and if you opened the double glazing all you heard was air conditioning. Neither were the bedroom's chintz bedcover and reproduction furniture to her taste, but the room was anonymous and it suited her purposes.

Thinking about her baby brother, her thoughts turned to those first awful days in hospital.

Lying there in intensive care, feeling as if the only thing that made any sense had been ripped out of her, she thought about the woman doctor who had done this. How she hated the surgeon's brisk cheerfulness and practical aura; you could tell everything she did was efficient and well-managed. Toppy had wondered whether she had children, and, if she did, she pictured them going to church on Sunday morning dressed up in smart little overcoats and polished buckled shoes. It made her want to vomit. What future did she have? The father of her child didn't even know she was having his baby. They had met in a nightclub and gone back to her flat that night. They had been to bed together only that once, and the sex had been so awkward she was surprised to find herself pregnant. Not that she would ever have a baby now. Doctor Sands had seen to that. She realised that her hatred of Doctor Jemma Sands was slowly poisoning everything she thought about.

It was the young Indian doctor who told her that, in his opinion, his superior had acted hastily. If Doctor Sands had not panicked, she would not have needed to perform an emergency hysterectomy, he said earnestly. How puffed up and officious he was as he sat by her bedside. The doctor explained how the complaints procedure worked. She felt so angry she could only take in half of what he was saying.

Blood roared in her ears while he opened and closed his mouth.

Her company private health insurance kicked in, and she was transferred to a big private hospital near the mansion block where she had grown up.

Her biggest stroke of luck was when she realised she already knew Tony Sands. She dimly remembered him from a one-night stand years ago. Those had been the bad years, when she was doing anything to blunt the pain: booze, drugs, even a spell in a psychiatric hospital.

It was only when she met the hospital chief executive and his solicitor in her lawyer's office that she started thinking about revenge. She realised that the hospital boss was married to her, this woman who had snatched the one thing she wanted more than anything else in life. When he slid his business card across to her, she knew full well what he wanted. She went to see him at his office in the hospital and there, on his desk, was a photograph of the three of them together – him and his accursed wife, this woman who had taken her future away, sitting with a plump baby on her lap.

Tony Sands could not have been more solicitous, as well he might have been, considering she was about to sue his hospital for hundreds of thousands of pounds. Saying goodbye, the hospital chief executive had held her gaze for slightly longer than he should have, and that was when she knew. It was during their second meeting that he rested his finger on the top of her hand, suggesting they discuss things over lunch. It would be less costly for everybody, he said, if lawyers were kept out of this until the last possible moment. This transparent lie suited them both.

After that, they began meeting in this hotel room once a week. She reached into her holdall and brought out the Diana Krall CD he enjoyed listening to. He liked to sway with her, dancing, smelling her hair and telling her how much he loved her before they made love. It made her skin crawl. Lying there in bed, she would encourage him to tell her about his home life while she played with his chest hair. Like every other married man she had been with, he was only too happy to whine about his wife: how she spent all her time complaining about how tired she was and squandered all her attention on their five-year-old son. Oh grow up, she felt like saying, stop being such a whiny baby. Instead, she just lay there listening, and remembering. The type of car his wife drove. The layout of their home. Where she took Matthew to school each morning. She made sure she remembered it all.

A knock at the door interrupted her thoughts. Checking herself in the mirror one last time, she went to answer it. Tony stood in the corridor wearing a big overcoat and a romantic-looking hat. She posed a little in the doorway, and smiling, he pushed her gently back into the room. Tony took off his silly fedora and threw it onto the dressing table before pulling her towards him, running his finger down the plunge of her chest. He was practically licking his lips in anticipation. Good. It was so easy to lead men around by their cocks.

"I ordered some white wine," she said. "The one you like so much."

"I like it, but it doesn't like me. In fact, I shouldn't really drink. That diabetes I was telling you about."

"Surely one little drink wouldn't hurt? It will help you relax."

"All right. I'll join you."

Toppy poured him a glass of wine and they clinked glasses. He started pulling at her dressing cord, and her silk robe whispered to the carpet.

"I wore my nicest underwear for you. I hope you appreciate it."

"Very nice," he said running his eyes over her appreciatively. "Oh, there's something I want to show you."

He reached into his overcoat pocket and pulled out a wad of fifty-pound notes. "Here you go, baby. From now on there's going to be plenty more where this came from."

He threw the notes into the air and, like confetti, they helicoptered onto the bedspread.

"My God, I've never seen so much money. Where did it come from?" she said, gazing in amazement at the money-strewn bed.

"Don't worry, darling. From now on we are never going to have to worry about money again."

"How much money are we talking about?"

"More cheddar than you could possibly imagine."

"I don't know," she said doubtfully. "I can imagine a lot."

She pulled him towards her and they kissed, sinking down onto the coverlet. She felt the crunch of paper behind her as he gently started undressing her.

Later, lying in bed next to her, Tony asked what the time was. "The time is now," she replied touching his face. He rolled away from her and got out of bed, saying he was late for getting back to the hospital. She watched him dress and then sank back on her pillow. Where had Tony been getting this money from, and what did he mean when he said there was plenty more of it to come? She gazed up at the hairline crack in the ceiling and began thinking of another way she was going to pull his little family apart.

CHAPTER TEN

THINGS CHANGED AFTER JEMMA'S SUSPENSION.
St John David gave her silly things to do around the
hospital while her list of post-natal patients dried up.
Jemma found out that Toppy Mrazek's car had narrowly
missed another vehicle speeding on the motorway, rolled
upside down and burst into flames. The paramedics had to
drag her from the burning wreckage. She was lucky to be
alive. Negotiations with Mrazek's solicitor dragged on, with
her lawsuit claiming hundreds of thousands of pounds'
worth of compensation. It was apparently all Jemma's fault
that Toppy would never be able to have children. Oddly,
there was never any mention of who the father of her lost
child was. Perhaps Toppy was one of those career women
who'd grown tired of waiting.

Doing her patient visits, Jemma had the sense she was
being pushed out by the rest of the pack. For most people
she had become an embarrassment. They didn't want her
hanging around.

Tony had become increasingly distant as well. Far from
being supportive, he appeared to side with David and his
deputy on the ethics committee. Something had changed

between them, but Tony grew evasive whenever she brought the matter up, reassuring her everything was fine.

The lawsuit was always there hanging over them. Even when they took Matthew for a walk, trying to get away from it, it was all they ever talked about. But there was something else bothering Tony, something deeper – like that darker patch out at sea where the strong current is. He became distant and snappy, and he started criticising things Jemma did. She began to feel chilled without knowing why.

There was one bad night with Matthew where he kept waking up with a tummy ache. Rather than disturb Tony, Jemma flopped into the spare bed. After that she carried on sleeping in the guest room. There was an unspoken agreement that it was better that way.

The argument blew up one night after she had put Matthew to bed. By now she had been suspended for a couple of months. Matthew eventually drifted off after hearing the same story over and over, but he woke every time Jemma crept towards the door. She resigned herself to sitting there in the dark, even though there was a stew cooking in the oven. She would just have to wait until she heard Matthew shudder and sigh, which meant he was finally asleep. In her head she counted her dwindling list of patients. She must have lost track of how long she was sitting there, because supper was black and congealed when she finally came back downstairs and took it out of the oven.

"You think about that boy more than you ever think about me," Tony said behind her.

Here it comes at last, she thought, squatting in front of the oven. Whatever it was, let it come down.

"Matthew has trouble going to sleep at night. You know that."

"But it's nearly ten o'clock. You were in there for two hours. I've got to be up at six. We never ever spend time together."

"It wouldn't hurt if you went in and put him to bed for once, you know."

"Here we go. Same old stuck record."

She took a deep breath. She felt herself wanting to say wilder and wilder things – anything to get whatever what was really coming between them out in the open.

"You're never here anyway. You're always in your office at the hospital. Single-handedly saving the NHS."

"I've got a heavy-duty budget presentation this week to all the line managers."

"Is that where you really are? Your mobile was switched off when I called the hospital last night. Reception said you'd left hours ago."

For a moment Jemma thought Tony was going to hit her. This was the pressure cooker that had been building up for weeks. She stood rooted to the spot, shocked that he had even contemplated violence.

Matthew began wailing upstairs. They both looked at each other accusingly. "I'll go," she said, relieved to be breaking the tension.

Their son was standing at the top of the landing in tears. Jemma scooped him up, feeling his heavy solid warmth on her hip. He needed changing. Lately Matthew had started wetting the bed at night, and she had put him back into disposable pants. Through the wall she heard Emily and her husband moving around next door. Were they as angry with each other as she and Tony were? A malicious thought popped into her head – what if she and Matthew were left on their own? No Tony. She wished she could un-think it, but it was too late. The feeling wouldn't budge.

The floorboard creaked as Tony came upstairs. He stood in the dim bedroom watching her wrestle Matthew into dry underpants. She sensed he wanted to apologise. They had never gone so near the precipice – she felt dizzy. Tony came farther into the room and put his arm around her. She could feel the pain in her heart dissolving. Matthew looked up at his parents standing together and smiled. She had almost forgotten what it was like having Tony's arms around her. She resolved to hang on to their marriage, no matter what it took.

They left Matthew finally asleep.

Blinking under the landing light, Tony said: "I'm sorry.

Sometimes I feel as if I've got this tsunami of work hanging over me. You leave it for a few hours, and the emails and voicemails and text messages start piling up. Let's go downstairs and have a drink, yeah? It was my fault I didn't check the oven. I think there are some eggs left in the fridge."

"We knew this was going to be difficult, what with us both working. Do you remember what your mother said? 'Make the most of Matthew growing up, because it all goes so quickly.' I remember thinking, what do you mean? I've been awake for the past five years."

Tony laughed.

They had omelettes at the kitchen table and, for once, didn't talk about her suspension. Instead, they gossiped about friends. Tony kept refilling her glass, and she began to feel pleasingly squiffy. Tony was being his most urbane and charming, and she remembered why she loved him.

Tony cleared the plates, stacked the dishwasher and said he was going upstairs to have a shower. Halfway up the stairs, he said: "My jacket needs dry cleaning. I managed to get Bolognese on my sleeve at lunchtime."

She heard him turn the shower on. He had left his jacket hanging up in the porch. For some reason she felt apprehensive the moment his mobile started ringing. It was unusual for somebody to be calling this late. This could only mean bad news. She fished the phone out of his pocket and saw that it was a London number. Jemma was about to call up the stairs but answered it instead.

"Please may I speak to Mr Tony Sands? This is the Kensington Hotel."

"I'm afraid he's busy right now. He can't come to the phone. Can I pass on a message?"

"Please could you tell him the Kensington Hotel called? One of our chambermaids found the earring his wife reported lost yesterday. It's waiting at reception if he wants to come and collect it."

His wife? For a moment she felt physically sick and hung on to the wall for support.

"Are you sure you have the right number? I haven't been to the Kensington Hotel."

"This is the number he gave us. Are you Mrs Sands?"

"Yes."

"Then we'll keep your earring in reception until you next come in. Oh, and please would you tell your husband that we've reserved your usual room."

"Yes. I'll be sure to tell him," she said numbly.

Her mind began scrabbling wildly. Something clicked in her head. The way that he found fault with everything she did; how nothing was ever good enough for him anymore. Now she understood.

Her husband was having an affair.

Jemma ended the call and felt herself going into shock. For

a moment she stood there not feeling or seeing anything. Then she heard the shower upstairs snapping off and Tony emerging onto the landing. He came downstairs wearing a towelling dressing gown and drying his hair. "Everything all right?" he asked. The picture of innocence.

CHAPTER ELEVEN

JEMMA HARDLY SLEPT THAT NIGHT. Lurid images of Tony and this woman, whoever she was, revolved in her head. She wanted to storm into their bedroom and tear him into a thousand pieces for what he had done. How could he? How could he do this to their little family?

Flashback. Her dad's funeral service in a ghastly crematorium. Jemma had noticed a brassy blonde with a hard little face sitting on her own towards the back of the pews. Dad's mistress. She reeked of sex. All these years, and her mother had never suspected. Yet all around them people knew what was going on. Jemma was not going to let that happen to her. She felt her mother's humiliation. She was going to make Tony pay for what he had done. And she had to protect herself and her son. Nothing else mattered. Most of all, she must remain calm and not give anything away. First, she had to collect evidence – this was a war, and you didn't tell the enemy what your strategy was.

Eventually she must have drifted into fitful sleep, because the next thing she heard was Matthew treading downstairs. The first planes had started going overhead. She looked at her watch: 5:30am. She was gritty-eyed from lack of sleep. Willing herself out of bed, she felt the rough carpet beneath her feet. Then the bleak realisation of what had happened last night hit her again. It was true. Tony was having an affair.

Matthew was already sitting on the sofa downstairs watching TV. She kissed the top of his head fiercely. Then she went into the kitchen and switched on the radio, waiting for the kettle to boil, and listened to the well-fed voices on Radio 4. A typical day, except of course it wasn't typical, not at all. She wanted to march upstairs to where Tony was sleeping and scream and shout. But what would this do to her beloved son? If Tony showed remorse, then they could try again; yes, that's what they would do. After all, a bone that has been broken often mends stronger. Her thoughts see-sawed back and forth. It was bewildering. Exhausting.

She went upstairs with a cup of tea for Tony: he must not realise that she knew about his betrayal. She rustled into their dark bedroom, placing the mug on his bedside table. He raised his face to kiss her, but she couldn't do it – the idea of touching him revolted her. Instead, she opened the curtains; it was light outside, and a man was already on his way to work.

The three of them had breakfast together, pretending that nothing was wrong. Jemma had never been a very good actress. She was due to take Matthew to school – she could not wait to get out of the house. Tony asked her if she would take his laptop in to Renfield, the hospital's head of IT, to be mended. He was giving a presentation to other local NHS chief executives, and the battery lasted only half an hour before it died. Jemma nodded dully.

She bundled her protesting son outside; for once they were not going to be late. Crossing the road towards the bus stop, she was surprised by how cold it was. The pigeon-grey sky meant winter was coming.

Numbly she dropped Matthew off at the school gates and caught the bus to the hospital.

Renfield lived in the basement surrounded by computer innards. She always pictured him as a wizard in a cave. His desk was littered with bits of motherboard, while hard drives were piled up behind him. There was a huge magnifying glass on an extending arm and a trail of smoke from the soldering iron he was tinkering with. Jemma knocked lightly. The most surprising thing about Renfield was his voice. A West Indian, his kinky black hair was scrunched into tiny dreadlocks and his gold tooth added to his pirate air, but his voice was pure ee-by-gum Yorkshire. His parents had immigrated to Barnsley from Kingston, Jamaica.

"I've brought Tony's computer in to be mended. He says the battery needs replacing."

"Bloody 'eck, I've told him again and again. But will he listen? Will he ever."

"He's asked if there's any chance you can fix it this morning. He needs it for a presentation."

"I've told him not to leave it on standby. It drains the fookin' battery."

"Can you do it?"

"Aye, I think I've got one in stores. That's why everybody has the same bloody computer. I'm clever, me."

He tapped his head. While the laptop was powering up on his desk, he scrolled through the list of management user passwords he kept on his desktop PC. He fired up Tony's computer before leaving the laptop open and running while he went to find the spare part.

"Right. I'm just going to get another battery from t'stores. Don't touch nowt."

Renfield winked at Jemma as he walked past. His Aladdin's cave was farther down the corridor.

Keeping an eye on the door, she swiftly launched the internet browser. If Renfield asked, she would say that she was just surfing the Web. Instead, she scrolled through the list of Tony's favourite websites. There was The Guardian, the BBC and a couple of scuba diving sites. Then she noticed the log-in page for a French bank. Why had Tony bookmarked Crédit Mercantile? They had been to France a couple of times on holiday but it wasn't as if–

"Summat the matter?" Renfield asked.

She hadn't heard him come in. She smiled blankly, but she must have looked awfully guilty. "No, I was just checking my appointments."

"I haven't got the battery. I'll have to order one in. It should be here tomorrow. You can still run it off mains, you know."

"Fine, I'll tell Tony to do that," she said, snapping the lid shut.

Coming upstairs after the quiet of Renfield's office, you could hear the hubbub of the ground floor. The hospital atrium was full of visitors. Jemma was about to go upstairs for the labour-ward handover meeting when she spotted Tony walking briskly towards the exit. He was obviously in a hurry to be somewhere – probably desperate to be with Her, she thought bitterly. She had to see this through.

"Tony," Jemma called, raising the satchel. Too late. He was already through the revolving door. Damn. She pushed up against the glass. Outside, a porter was wheeling a stunned-looking woman in a wheelchair with a tube up her nose. Tony was hailing a cab. She watched him telling the driver where to go before getting in. The handover meeting would have to start without her. She had to find out where her husband was going.

Another taxi beetled up Fulham Road and she raised her arm. All the while she kept watching Tony's taxi as it did a U-turn and set off towards South Kensington.

"Where to, luv?" asked the cabbie through the window.

"It sounds stupid, but I want you to follow that cab." He grinned at her.

"Hop in."

They were four cars behind Tony all the way down the Fulham Road. The cabbie tried to make conversation, but Jemma ignored him. As she expected, Tony's cab turned left after only a few minutes and pulled up outside an expensive-looking hotel in South Kensington. She told the taxi to pull over. Through the glass she watched Tony pay the driver and then walk up the Kensington Hotel steps. The hotel that had called last night about her missing earring. Her missing earring. What was she going to do now? Burst in and catch them in bed together? How would she even know which room they were in? The driver asked her if she wanted to get out here.

That's when she saw her.

Toppy Mrazek. The woman who was suing the hospital.

There was something serpent-like about her step as she sashayed along the street. Jemma's marriage, her identity, everything she believed in fell apart right at that moment. She wanted to throw herself onto the pavement and claw and scratch and eat the paving stones. The world seemed utterly meaningless. She sat there watching numbly from the back of the cab as Toppy click-clacked up the hotel steps. Pandora's box had been opened, and now she was paying the price, oh yes. She felt as if her husband had just knifed her in the head.

CHAPTER TWELVE

JEMMA FELT PARALYSED AFTER THAT. There was nobody she could talk to, and in any case, she felt ashamed about what had happened to her marriage. Her indecision lingered for weeks. The idea of ending her marriage was like being asked to saw her own arm off. Yet the strain of keeping up this pretence was killing her. Every newspaper article she read, every song she heard on the radio, seemed to be about her failing marriage. Had they been having sex in their bed while she and Matthew were out? Righteous anger filled her; Tony would pay for what he had done. Right now, though, she had to collect evidence before confronting him.

But other times she would wander around the house in a tearful daze. The slightest warmth or soft word from Tony would fill her with optimism. Then something bad would happen, and everything would swing down again. Looking back, she understood that she had been trying to hang on to her marriage, desperately gripping the tether as it slid between her hands. But the balloon was drifting away. Out of reach.

George stopped her one afternoon in the paediatric

department. It had been a month since she found out about the affair.

"Are you all right?" he asked. She told him she was fine. A Disney cartoon played inanely in the background. "Have you seen yourself in a mirror lately?" he said, steering her towards a wall mirror. It was covered in rainbow sparkly stickers. She looked terrible. Her clothes were hanging off her, and she noticed without interest that her blonde hair was turning grey. For Matthew's sake, she knew that she had to start looking after herself, yet inside she felt like she was dead.

"What's going on?" George persisted. "I never see you smile anymore."

There was so much pain in her heart, she longed to tell him, but she couldn't. Pride, she supposed. Her mother, who lived in Cornwall, told her on the phone the other day that her voice sounded strained – was there anything the matter? There was no point in burdening her. Her compass had to be what was best for Matthew, and what was best for Matthew was that Mummy and Daddy stayed together.

"I've got a few issues at home, that's all," Jemma told George, anxious to get away.

Tony had told her he was going to be late home that evening. His brother was coming up to town again, he said, and they were going to see the new Woody Allen film together. Not that she believed him: she didn't believe a word he said anymore. She had cleared what little she had to do in the hospital that afternoon to go and see the film herself. She wasn't quite sure what she was trying to prove.

"Remember those old Snoopy cartoons? The psychiatrist is in, five cents? Well, this psychiatrist is in."

"George, I told you, I'm fine. Really."

"I can't help you if you won't tell me what the matter is."

"Look, I'm late to collect my son from school."

George looked wounded. "Why don't you come with me to collect him one afternoon?" she said. "We can go for a walk in the park and catch up then."

George stood there as she walked away, looking concerned. She raised her hand in farewell, hugging her clipboard to her chest.

Jemma had taken the car into work for once because the film was playing at Westfield, the big west London shopping centre. There was nobody in the hospital basement parking level as she walked towards her car. That was when she heard another car coming down the ramp. The big mustard Mercedes swept past the dented crash barrier. Its headlights were on and its tyres screeched. Then it came to a halt, blocking her Subaru. Oh great.

The driver of the car, a tough looking mixed-race guy, got out and held the back door open. Tony got out, smiling when he saw her.

"Hey, Jemma," he called. "I was just talking about you.

There's somebody I want you to meet. Wade Nibley."

She walked over to the Mercedes. She suspected that Tony might have been drinking at lunch. The driver looked at her flatly with hard piggy eyes. There was something about him that unsettled her.

"Wade, this is my wife, Jemma."

"Hi, howarya?"

Nibley slid over and shook her hand. He had such a silly name that she wanted to laugh.

"Pleased to meet you," she said, peering into the car interior. Leather seats.

"Wade runs the London office of Tri-Med, the American drugs company," Tony continued. "I've been showing him round the hospital."

"Sorry, ma'am, and then I took your husband out for lunch. A very gooooood lunch, I might add," Nibley grinned. It was not an attractive grin. He looked like a guy who smiled too much.

"So you won't be wanting anything to eat, then? What time will you be getting in?" she asked.

"I'll eat with my brother. Don't worry about me."

Give me a call, Nibley mimed to Tony as he climbed into his car. Tony slammed the door with a reassuring thunk, and the car moved off. Jemma and Tony watched the Mercedes circling the car park.

Jemma said, "Look, I'm going to be cooking anyway, so I can save some for you."

"I told you. I'll be getting in too late to eat."

No, but I need to confront you about what you've done, she thought. Watching the Mercedes exit up the ramp, she felt as if she had been buzzed by a dangerous fish, a manta ray perhaps, sinking into the gloom.

That afternoon, Jemma sat in the cinema surrounded by people laughing while tears streamed down her face.

Tony found her smoking in the garden when he got home. He noticed the empty bottle of wine on the draining board.

"How was the film?" she asked, exhaling and blowing the smoke out.

"Really funny. We both enjoyed it."

"What was it about then?"

"Oh, the usual Woody Allen story. An older man and a younger girl. It's a bit like a soufflé. When he gets it right, it's absolutely perfect. You get something wrong, and the whole thing deflates."

Jemma nodded dumbly. She was not going to let him get away with it. Tonight they were going to have it out.

"Anyway," Tony continued, anxious to change the subject, "is there anything to eat in the fridge? I'm starving. We didn't get to eat in the end. Charlie had to get his train home. The tyranny of the train timetable."

"Yeah? What was the ending? How did the film end?"
Jemma asked sharply.

Tony's shoulders slumped as if air was being let out of him.
He had not known until this moment that she knew he was
lying. So the jig was up. "I don't know," he said. "I don't
know how the film ended." Then, in a moment of clarity
like the centre of a storm, he said: "It's over between us,
isn't it?"

She suddenly felt intensely angry. Everything she wanted
to say to him was bottled up and ready to burst. "How
could you?" she hissed. "With my patient?"

His eyes registered surprise that she knew who it was.

"How did you find out?"

"I followed you to that hotel you went to. They rang one
night to tell me that she'd left her earring in your hotel
room. When I saw you going inside, with her, something
died in me. You've killed something. You've murdered my
love."

Tony stepped towards her. "Jemma, I'm sorry. You're too
good a person..."

"Can't you see why she's doing this? She doesn't love you.
She only wants revenge."

"That's not true. I've explained to Toppy that you never had
any option, that you saved her life. Sure, she was angry at
first."

"What have I done to deserve this? Haven't I been a good wife to you?" She could feel the tears starting now.

"It's not that. Jemma, things haven't been good between us for a long time. You know that too. The truth is, even when I was standing at the altar, I knew I was making a terrible mistake."

That really hurt. He was lashing out, trying to say the worst thing he could. Flashback. Tony standing next to her at the altar; his collar stud was so tight it was drawing blood.

"What mistake? You never said anything at the time."

"Jemma, you're a really good person. Too good. I can't live up to your expectations of me. Let's face it, our marriage died after Matthew was born. We never sleep together any more. We've just become two co-workers who share the same house."

"But why her? Of all people?"

"Jemma, there's something you should know. I knew Toppy years ago. Before I ever met you. I'm sorry I never told you, but it didn't seem important. We were together only once, but I never managed to get her out of my head. And then, when I saw her again in her lawyer's office, I'd never experienced anything like it before. A coup de foudre. I had to have her. It's madness, I know but..."

"Everything that we built together, all our plans and dreams..."

Tony shook his head. What had she expected? That he

was going to fall on his knees and beg forgiveness? With a sinking feeling, she realised it was already too late for that.

"Have you thought how this is going to affect our son?"

She was playing the guilt card, wanting to keep his focus on what was important.

"It's better that it happens now rather than later. He won't feel the pain now. What's the usual line, 'Mummy and Daddy don't live together any more, but they love you very much'?"

There was something so glib about the way he said this, and Jemma could have killed him there and then. He had broken the trust between them, and now he was almost joking about it.

"I'm sorry that you're still in love. I'm not."

There was a knife block on the kitchen counter. She imagined grabbing a knife and plunging it into his heart. Her fingers itched.

"Where are you going to go? Are you moving in with her?"

"I'll rent a flat near the hospital. We can work out the financial arrangements later."

They were getting a divorce?

"Tony, please. We could start again. Move somewhere else." She felt herself becoming desperate and tearful.

Tony shook his head. "I'm sorry," he said. "We both know this is unmendable."

He left her alone in the kitchen, and she heard him moving around upstairs. She realised he was packing his things. She sat down at the dining table and felt herself going into shock. What would become of them and, worse, how would this affect their little boy? Somehow, she had always pictured them growing old together. It was a hard dream to say goodbye to. There was so much pain in her heart it was seeping into her bloodstream.

CHAPTER THIRTEEN

THOSE FIRST COUPLE OF WEEKS without Tony were the worst. Jemma buried herself in work, spending as much time as she could at the hospital. Then that anaesthetic wore off and the pain of Tony's desertion really hit. It was as sharp as a scalpel. Every night after putting Matthew to bed she would sit at the kitchen table working her way through most of a bottle of wine. She would stare at the phone on the kitchen wall, willing it to ring – anything to break this loneliness. She wanted to go to Tony for comfort, to feel his warmth protecting her, but of course, he was the one causing her all this pain. All she had now was her son. And one day he, too, would grow up and leave her; it was as if childhood was one long wave goodbye.

One weekend, Jemma arranged to take Matthew to see his grandmother, who had been badgering to see the boy for weeks. Mum was still living in the same house in Falmouth that Jemma had grown up in. Matthew ran on ahead while Jemma crunched down the passage to the back door. The trees were bending in the wind – gales had been forecast for the weekend. Jemma knew that Mum had been lonely since Dad died. Only now did she understand her loneliness.

The back door shuddered as Jemma struggled in with their bags, and the kitchen windows were cloudy with steam. Mum came out to greet them with her arms outstretched. "Hello, luv," she said, hugging her tightly. They walked into the kitchen, where Mum was cooking lunch, and memories came flooding in. It seemed like only five minutes ago that Jemma had been having breakfast at this same kitchen table, her hair in braids while Dad read bits of the Daily Mail aloud. His death after a series of strokes was partly the reason she had become a doctor.

"Mum and I are fine, Dad, we're all fine," she had told him as he lay there stricken on the hospital bed. The strokes had robbed him of speech, and he had gazed up at her with wild, frightened eyes. The phone was already ringing by the time they had arrived home. The nurse said Dad had died minutes after they had left. It was almost as if he had been waiting for permission to go.

So it was a shock to discover after his death that Dad had a mistress. Mum never mentioned her except to say that she was common. Her mouth would tighten whenever the woman's name came up.

Matthew was standing against the door frame while Mum measured him. "You've grown so much," she said, marking the line of the top of his head with a pencil while he wriggled to get away. He wanted to play with the collection of Dad's old things Mum kept in a drawer: a pipe-cleaning tool, a military compass and a pen that revealed a lady in a bathing suit when you tipped it upside down.

Mum was mashing potatoes on the stove when Jemma told her about Tony's affair.

"Oh, Mum, why does life have to be so fucking awful?"

Jemma felt herself welling up; the emotion that she had dammed up for the past few months was bursting through. Suddenly her shoulders heaved, and she was racked with sobs.

Mum stopped what she was doing and put her arms around her daughter.

"Darling, I'm so sorry. How long has this been going on? Why didn't you tell me?"

"Three months, I suppose," Jemma managed to say between sobs. "Pretty much since I saved this woman's life. At first I thought it was all some plot of hers to get back at me. Now I think he really is in love with her."

"You've been keeping this all inside for three months? No wonder you sounded so strained on the phone. Is Tony still living with you?"

Mum stepped back, still grasping her shoulders. Jemma shook her head, unable to speak through her tears.

"Jemma, stop crying, love. I know you're upset, but feeling sorry for yourself is not going to help."

Mum handed her a tissue and she blew her nose. She felt a tremendous weight had been lifted off her shoulders now that she had told somebody. Calming down, she said, "He moved out when I told him I knew about the affair. He's renting a house in Pimlico."

"Where's he getting all this money from, renting a house I mean?"

"I don't know. We've always kept separate bank accounts. He took care of the bills."

"He's probably keeping this woman out of your money." A thought struck Mum. "He's not going to go for custody of Matthew, is he?"

"No, I don't think so. It's embarrassing how quickly he's lost interest in his son. He's completely wrapped up in this woman, intoxicated by her."

Lately she had realised that although she'd told herself she had the perfect marriage, the flaw had always been there, and now the glass had shattered. She thought about the uneven distribution of childcare, the hours she had spent taking Matthew out in his buggy so that Tony could rest at the weekends.

"Have you spoken to a solicitor yet? You need to have somebody on your side."

"Sometimes I feel like tearing him into a thousand pieces. Then I think, what makes you so special? He's just met another woman, that's all. It happens every day."

"Jemma, this is not the time to be soft. Matthew is the important one now. Tony has stabbed you in the back, just as your father betrayed me. Even now, I still feel the knife between my shoulder blades. The hurt never goes away."

The weather was so bad that weekend that they stayed inside while rain lashed the windows. Mum was good about keeping Matthew entertained, building playing-card houses with him on the sitting-room floor while Jemma fretted and paced. Toppy had already moved in with Tony. Despite what Mum said, Jemma did not want to get divorced. She felt stuck, unable to move one way or another.

Mum was on the telephone when Jemma came down with their bags packed, ready to say goodbye. Their direct flight to London had been cancelled because of bad weather. Instead, they would take an old-fashioned propeller plane to Plymouth and change to the regular flight to Gatwick. Newquay Airport was one of the few places that still operated prop-driven planes. Mum scribbled something on a piece of paper and rang off. "Here is Dennis's email address," she said, handing her daughter the paper slip. Dennis had been their family solicitor for years. "He wants you to write down everything that has happened, keeping emotion out of it. Just dates and places. And he wants you to keep a diary from now on. He'll call you once you've written to him."

Jemma first noticed the young mother while they sat in the departure lounge. She was a few seats away holding a baby. Jemma thought it odd that she was wearing dark glasses even inside the gate. She realised the woman was crying and wondered what she was so upset about; there was so much unhappiness in the world, she reflected. The woman stood up with her baby and wandered off to the toilet at the back of the departure lounge. Feeling the need to go too, Jemma told Matthew to stay where he was reading his comic. He nodded and continued swinging his legs against the plastic chair.

Pushing open the door to the women's WC, Jemma could hear the woman crying. Her sobs were amplified by the white-tiled walls. The woman was bent over the pull-down plastic mat, changing her baby. Jemma felt awkward standing there and thought she ought to say something.

"Excuse me, I'm a doctor," Jemma said. "Are you feeling all right? Is there anything I can do to help?"

"That's great, that's all I need, another doctor in my life."

The woman turned around. She had taken off her glasses, and her eyes were raw with tears.

"If it wasn't for you doctors, my head wouldn't be like this. Why don't you just leave me alone?"

Affronted, Jemma apologised again and locked herself in one of the stalls. She heard the woman crooning to her baby, occasionally gulping her sobs. Jemma listened to the words of the song, which seemed to be about how much the woman loved her baby despite everything that had happened to her. She was making up the words to the lullaby. The pull-down table banged upright, and Jemma heard the clack of the woman's heels and the suck of the toilet door closing. She sat there on the toilet seat ruminating on what had just occurred; what had happened to this woman to make her so dreadfully unhappy?

Sitting back down next to Matthew, Jemma deliberately ignored the woman now back sitting opposite her. Her train of thought was interrupted by the boarding announcement for their flight. Jemma briefly registered the woman pushing her baby in a stroller ahead of them. There were only a few of them flying back to Plymouth. Matthew was so excited about going on a propeller-driven plane she thought he might explode. How wonderful to be so full of life, she thought, remembering how she had been at his age.

There was a short flight of steps down to the tarmac and then a walk across to the twin-propeller plane. Their steps rang out on the metal staircase. The noise was terrific as the plane revved its engines. A makeshift fence of plastic tape strung between bollards flapped in the wind, stopping anybody from straying too near the whirling blades. The queue shuffled towards the aircraft steps. Jemma noticed the mother breaking away from the line. The woman's baby stroller was parked right in front of her, and Jemma could see the outline of her baby's back. The woman was walking towards the propeller. Somebody shouted. That was when Jemma realised what was happening.

The mother was trying to kill herself.

Everybody in the queue shrank back, willing somebody else to do something. Without thinking, Jemma ran up to the mother and grabbed her shoulder, but the woman pulled away. "Leave me alone," she shouted. She said something else that was lost in the noise. Any moment now she would touch the spinning blade. A man ran up once he saw what was going on, and he shot Jemma a scared look. Together they manhandled the woman away from the propeller.

"Help. Could somebody help us please?" Jemma called. The woman was twisting and trying to yank herself away, dragging her feet on the runway. She was determined to throw herself into the propeller. Jemma didn't know how long they could hold on. By now airport staff were involved. Two burly men wearing ear protectors and hi-vis jackets were running towards them while the girl from the check-in desk was shouting into a walkie-talkie. An emergency vehicle with its lights going was tearing across the tarmac.

Two police officers got out, and together they wrestled the woman to the ground. You could see the policeman was surprised by how strong she was. Eventually they managed to get the woman into the back of their car. She was still screaming and shouting and putting up one hell of a fight.

Matthew looked shocked.

"It's all right, darling. Everything's okay now," Jemma soothed.

"Mum, why was that lady so cross? Will the police take her to hospital?"

"That's right. They'll take her to hospital and make her better."

The girl from the check-in desk was doing her best to calm the screaming baby. "Excuse me," Jemma interrupted, "I'm a doctor." All the baby needed was unbuckling from its straps and being picked up. Human touch was so important. Matthew watched as his mother calmed the baby, hugging him to her chest. It was something she did every day of her life. Together mother and son walked back towards the terminal while Jemma rubbed the baby's back.

Trying to kill yourself by walking into a whirling propeller. It was the damnedest thing she had ever seen.

CHAPTER FOURTEEN

WHEN THEY GOT BACK TO London, there was a letter from Patient Advice and Liaison Services on the doormat along with the bills. "Dear Doctor Sands," the letter began, "We are writing to inform you that Ms Toppy Mrazek has dropped her threat of legal action over supposed negligence. Her solicitor has written to advise us that she will not be taking Ms Mrazek's case any further. Therefore, St Luke's own investigation into the events of Saturday, September 18, has now ended."

Tony must have persuaded Toppy to drop the case; this was probably something she could thank Tony for. Jemma's suspension from duty had gone on for four months now. There was also a personal letter addressed to Jemma, and she recognised St John David's handwriting on the envelope as she pulled out the stiff, almost card-like cream notepaper. His spidery writing was difficult to read.

"Dear Jemma," David had written in fountain pen. "In light of the malpractice suit being dropped, I am delighted to reinstate you to full surgical duty. I regret all the distress you have been through waiting for this investigation to be completed, and I am relieved to invite you back full-time onto the obstetric staff. This hospital can ill afford to lose you."

Satisfied, Jemma went back into the kitchen. At least that particular nightmare was over. Matthew was drawing a picture on the floor, and she started getting his plastic lunch box ready. It was his nursery school nativity play tomorrow afternoon, and his costume still wasn't finished. She noticed Matthew drawing snakes slithering inside the windows of a house.

"Why isn't Daddy living with us anymore?" he said, colouring in a snake.

That brought her up short. They had agreed to say that Tony was working away from home, so desperate was she not to hurt their little boy. Perhaps it was best to tell him the truth though. Gently and simply. She knelt down beside him.

"Daddy and Mummy had a big fight. Daddy doesn't want to live with us anymore. It doesn't mean that he doesn't love you, though. It's me he's cross with."

It was becoming difficult to swallow, and Jemma felt her eyes pricking. Matthew did not look up, but she could tell he was listening intently, as if a big cartoon ear had grown out of the side of his head.

"Why did you and Daddy have a fight?"

"Because Daddy met another lady that he likes more than Mummy. That made Mummy sad."

Christ, she was sounding like something off children's television. Why not just tell him the truth? Because your daddy is a selfish bastard who put his own pleasure before that of his family. Because he's hooked up with a bitch who tried to ruin my career after I saved her life. And once she's done that, she'll dump him. Jemma reined herself in: the one thing she had promised to herself never to do was to disparage his father.

"Do you like Daddy's new friend? I think she's nice."

He's met her already? She and Tony had never agreed on this. They said that Toppy would have to be introduced carefully – if at all.

"When did you see Daddy's new friend?"

"Oh, we went to the park and then we went to the ice-cream shop where we went with Daddy. I had a banana split."

Going for a walk on Hampstead Heath and then going to the ice-cream bar on Chalk Farm Road had been their thing. Obviously Tony couldn't care less about his old life now.

Jemma was grateful to be back on duty the next morning. Guaram sat down with her and ran though the list of patients she had inherited from other consultants. Doing her rounds that afternoon, she talked to a girl in neo-natal who'd been brought in for an emergency caesarean. Christmas was coming, and a few Oriental-looking baubles hung desultorily from the ceiling. Guaram told her that it had been very messy after this girl's sixteen-hour labour.

She looked as if she had been through the ringer, pale and washed out with her newborn lying beside her. The baby was fast asleep, and his tiny hand was balled into a fist. Jemma leant down and breathed in that heavenly new-baby smell. This was what she did the job for.

"He's a fighter, that one," Jemma said. "See that determined look on his face."

"Yes. I was really frightened. I didn't know if he was going to make it."

"And how are you feeling now?"

"Terrible. I woke up this morning, opened my eyes and burst into tears. Doctor, I don't know what's wrong with me. I've never felt so bad before. It isn't how I expected to feel. People talk about the joy of motherhood. Can I ask you something in private?

"Of course. That's what I'm here for."

She looked over at her sleeping baby. "I have these terrible thoughts about him. God knows it's a bad thing to say, but I keep thinking he'd be better off without me. I know it's crazy."

"Listen to me," said Jemma. "It sounds as if you might be suffering from the baby blues. One in ten women suffer from them."

The girl glanced at the clear plastic tub in which her baby lay. "But I don't feel normal. I don't feel anything towards him."

"It's nothing to be ashamed of. It's a chemical imbalance caused by giving birth. We have an excellent psychiatrist here who runs a group for new mothers like you. His name's Doctor Malvern. I can ask him to get in touch if you like."

The girl gulped and nodded, and Jemma scribbled on her notes that she was recommending that George monitor her.

She found her friend leaning over the nurse's station on the second-floor geriatric ward. George straightened up when he saw her.

"Doctor Malvern. Can I talk to you for a minute? I'd like to you to keep an eye on one of my patients, Renee Pieterse. She's anxious about not bonding with her baby. Standard post-partum depression. I suggested she sign up for your new-mothers group."

"Of course. I can introduce myself when I do my rounds if you like. We've got four mothers in the group at the moment. I'm sure they find it helpful."

"Thank you." She paused. "There's something else that I'd like to talk to you about. In private."

Jemma nodded towards the ward double doors. She did not want the nurses to overhear her; the nurse's station was always the gossip hub in a hospital. George gathered his papers and followed her out into the corridor. The two of them started walking down the hallway, Jemma staring straight ahead. She was not sure where to begin, and she always did her best thinking while pacing.

"Tony and I have separated. He told me he's been having an affair with the woman whose life I saved, the one I was suspended over. I thought you ought to know."

George stopped and touched her shoulder. "Oh, Jemma, I am so sorry. How long have you known? I knew that something was wrong. You haven't been yourself for weeks now."

Jemma nodded, feeling her throat tighten again. She was relieved it was finally out in the open. "You're the first person I've told apart from my mother. I just– I wasn't ready to talk to anybody about it."

"What about your son? Does he know what's going on?"

"He's five years old. He knows that Daddy doesn't live with us anymore. I'm trying to keep his routine exactly the same. I just don't want anything to affect him."

George muttered something about "stupid" and shook his head before looking deep into Jemma's eyes. She felt warmth in her chest, but she wasn't ready to go there just yet. In time, perhaps. Instead, she met George's concerned gaze while their faces moved imperceptibly closer. "Listen to me," George said. "You're my friend. I don't want anything bad to happen to you. If you need anything, and I mean anything, you come and talk to me."

"George, I can't tell you what it means–"

A beeper cut through what she was about to say next, and they both looked down at their pagers. "Yours or mine?" asked George ruefully.

CHAPTER FIFTEEN

THEY GOT THROUGH CHRISTMAS AND those first weeks of January when everything seemed frozen and dead. Jemma buried herself in work. Then, one day, the sun reappeared, and she detected the faintest whiff of spring in the air. It was now March. Mum had told her on the phone that she might not be able to see it now, but the kaleidoscope would shift: things would get better. At the time, Jemma hadn't believed her. Slowly, though, things were starting to change. She felt the wound healing.

Her mother brought her up short one night. She had been on the phone complaining about how badly Tony had behaved when Mum said, "You can either be a victim or do something about it. It's all your emotions. You can either feel sorry for yourself or you can fight." She remembered what George had said about her looking so terrible. Emily, her next-door neighbour, was giving a birthday party for her daughter, Matilda, tomorrow afternoon at the local leisure centre. Rather than stand around with the other mothers watching the children play in the ball pond, Jemma decided to do something for herself.

The leisure centre had a rock-climbing wall. Before

Matthew was born, Tony used to take her mountain walking on rainy weekends in north Wales. At first she had loathed the hard scrabble up mountains under the glowering Welsh sky. Then she grew to love it. One evening they had fallen onto the bed of the pub they were staying in after a nasty climb, and she felt a sense of perfect peace. Something achieved. Now, wearing her pinching climbing shoes, she strained for the next handhold as she climbed the indoor wall. The wall arced overhead so she found herself almost hanging from the ceiling. There. If she could just stretch her leg a little farther along... She felt herself going and resigned herself to the drop. She landed with a bang on the vinyl crash mat. Opening her eyes, Jemma realised she felt glad to be alive for the first time in weeks.

One afternoon, George joined her in collecting Matthew after nursery. Matthew ran out and flung his arms around her. She was so pleased to see him that she felt her chest welling. These days she had little interest in anything else apart from Matthew. Whether or not this was a good thing she wasn't sure.

"Matthew, do you remember my friend George?" she said as they set off towards the park.

Matthew ignored her and went on jabbering about his day. It was that cosy time revolving around beans on toast and children's telly.

Sitting on a park bench watching Matthew clamber over

a climbing frame, Jemma noticed a young couple playing with their toddler in the train Matthew liked to hide in. She tried to remember Tony playing with Matthew but she couldn't. He had always been at work. All she could remember was standing by herself in the playground watching Matthew. Or pushing him around the streets in his buggy. Jemma's mother told her that her marriage had exploded without warning, like the Challenger space shuttle. That was the line Jemma repeated to other people, but in her heart she knew it was not true – the problems had been there right from the beginning; it was just that she had chosen to ignore them.

Matthew was running alongside the roundabout, trying to make it go faster, while another little boy was sitting in the middle contentedly whirling round. Jemma was still gazing at the young family when George asked her how she was bearing up.

"Better. Sometimes I can get through a whole morning without thinking about it. This is the kind of thing that happens to other people, not to me."

"How are things between the two of you?"

"Not good. I had hoped we'd be grown up enough to do what's best for Matthew. Somehow the words get tangled in the air between us. We just end up shouting at each other."

The couple had scooped up their son and were nuzzling him. The wife had her arm around her husband and she looked so happy. Jemma felt as if she had her face pressed against a glass window of other people's happiness, peering inside.

"How come you haven't found anybody, George?"

"I don't know. Never met the right person, I guess. I was so busy with my career that I didn't make time to get out there."

George turned to her and that secret understanding flashed between them. She knew that George had always been a little in love with her and that if circumstances had been different... But circumstances were different now, so what was stopping them? She imagined what George would look like sitting at their kitchen table.

She said, "It's funny, but looking at that couple over there, sometimes I resent other people's happiness. It's like one moment I was happily dancing with my husband, then I was tapped on the shoulder and asked to leave the dance floor. I was good at being married. It wasn't my fault my marriage ended. Tony took a hammer to it."

"Jemma, do you think you're the only person who's ever been betrayed? In a relationship, somebody always puts the boot in. Everybody betrays each other in the end."

Suddenly she heard Matthew scream.

Jemma stood up. She could not see him. George started running towards the roundabout. He had seen something she couldn't. Catching up with him, Jemma saw Matthew lying face down with his head trapped beneath the oundabout. The little boy was still sitting going round and round. Matthew was really screaming. George was hanging on to a metal bar, trying to slow the roundabout down; Jemma tried grabbing another one, but it was going too fast. Her fingers flew off. Next time she held on and pulled back as hard as she could. The pull was terrific. Between them they slowed the roundabout to walking pace, but if anything Matthew's screams got louder. He had got his head jammed between the roundabout skirt and the Astroturf. Instinctively, George tried pulling him out, but Jemma told him to stop. She felt underneath the roundabout as wood slid over her fingers. Sure enough, she felt an exposed nail, which must be digging into her son's head every time it went round. George slowed the roundabout to a stop. The toddler's dad had come over asking if he could help. Jemma reached in beside Matthew's head and cradled her fingers around his skull. He was really yelling, and part of her wanted him to stop.

"Matthew, we are going to get you out of this, okay?" she said.

Slowly, the two of them started easing him out. Please, God, don't let him be hurt. Inside she was screaming like any young mother whose child had been hurt – she almost felt his pain herself – yet another part of her was detached and assessing the situation, as if she was watching herself bent over her son. Always the professional. Finally, Matthew's head worked itself free, and Jemma saw the gash. She was

SLOW BLEED

split between shouting at him for having been so stupid and wanting to hug him. Instead, she said, "I'll need to take him to A&E and get this stitched up. He'll need a tetanus jab."

Jemma cleaned up Matthew's wound herself when they got to St Luke's. Wiped free of blood, it was not as bad as it looked. Jemma picked out bits of grit with tweezers, dropping them into a kidney dish. She told Matthew that the tetanus jab would be just like a cat's scratch. Putting in the stitches, she tried to be as gentle as she could, but she could see George wince every time the needle went in. Her darling son was being very brave. Jemma looked up and saw Tony arriving through the children's Outpatients gate.

"I only just got your message," he said, coming in to their cubicle. "Is he all right? What happened?"

He looked down at Matthew, who was lying on the bed looking pale.

"He got his head trapped beneath the roundabout in the park. I've put some stitches in. It looks worse than it is. I've given him a tetanus shot."

Tony acknowledged George before he leant down and stroked his son's face. "You all right, little fella? You gave us all a big scare. Promise me you'll never do anything like that again, okay?"

Matthew nodded wanly, and Tony asked his son if he wanted to see where he worked. Turning to Jemma, he said, "Is that all right?"

"We've got to get home," Jemma said. "Early bath and bed. He's exhausted."

Jemma had no idea why she said that; it was her automatic blocking response whenever they negotiated over Matthew. Tony and Matthew both looked up at her beseechingly, and she felt her resolve crumbling.

The three of them said goodbye to George, and they took the lift up to Tony's office.

Her solicitor had written that morning setting out what Tony wanted from the divorce. He had employed an expensive divorce lawyer, and again she wondered where he was getting the money from. Dennis, her divorce lawyer, had written that Tony's solicitor had come in with a ridiculously low maintenance offer that just wasn't acceptable. At least there wasn't any question of him having custody. What Tony wanted was pretty standard: every other weekend, a fortnight during the summer and every other Christmas.

"I got a letter from my solicitor this morning. About access arrangements," Jemma said tightly, watching the floor numbers change.

"I wanted to talk to you about that. I'm renting a villa in the South of France for three weeks. I'd like to have Matthew for the whole time. You can have Christmas."

"Will she be there?"

"Jemma, you are going to have to accept the fact that we don't live together anymore. I love this woman."

She chose to ignore him. "When exactly? Do you have dates yet?"

"The last two weeks of August and the first week of September."

Jemma shook her head. "That will cut into the start of his new school."

"Then you'll have to come out and collect him, won't you?"

Tony's office was on the top floor of the hospital. It was still light outside, and the office had a fantastic view over the rooftops. Great flocks of starlings wheeled around in the dusk. Tony pointed out the various London landmarks to Matthew: Battersea Power Station, the London Eye and, farther west, the Empress State Building. Jemma joined them looking out over the grey sprawl and noticed darker rain trails on the horizon. Tony asked if he could take Matthew downstairs and buy him an ice cream as a reward for being so brave. He hadn't cried once during his stitches. Jemma nodded. A little blood had seeped through the gauze above Matthew's eye, and his dressing would need changing when they got home.

Jemma stood by the window and listened to the lift being summoned to their floor. The abstract gold painting she had given Tony for his birthday hung on the wall. She had always imagined that there would be more birthdays, that they would do everything together. And now the dream was gone.

She walked over to his desk and trailed her fingers along his papers. There, among the pharma company brochures and NHS Best Practice pamphlets, she noticed a printed-off email peeking out from the other papers. Idly, she worked it free and scanned it quickly. It seemed to be a patient's testimony of one sort or another. The lift machinery started up again: Tony and Matthew were coming back upstairs. Keeping one eye on the glass wall running along the side of the office, Jemma read: "I have this recurring nightmare where I wake up screaming, and I hear myself screaming too."

Tony and Matthew were getting closer behind the frosted glass.

"When I woke up, I turned to the man lying next to me and asked him, 'Who are you?' He told me he was my husband. And I asked him if I was married, and then I asked, 'Who am I?'"

Tony and Matthew were at the office door.

She heard the doorknob turning.

They found her still standing by the window overlooking the rooftops. Except that it was almost dark outside.

"Everything all right?" Tony asked.

"Sure. Just thinking."

He was no fool. He knew that she had been up to something.

"Come on, Matthew, it's time to go home," she said, taking her little boy's hand. "Tony, I've been thinking some more about what you said, about the summer, I mean. I was being unfair. I wasn't thinking about what would be best for Matthew. Of course he can come. If you can meet him at the airport as an unaccompanied minor, then I'll come and collect him. He'll still need to start school that first week of September."

Tony smiled. "We'll have a fantastic time. I'm renting a boat."

CHAPTER SIXTEEN

SUMMER ROLLED AROUND, AND TONY took Matthew on holiday. It was the first time Jemma had been separated from her son, and she felt a keening loss at his absence. Once again, work became the anaesthetic. Matthew would be away for only three weeks, she told herself. The question of where Tony was getting all this money from still rankled, though. The letterhead of his divorce lawyers looked expensive.

One lunchtime, she left the hospital and crossed the road to the local Tesco. She was daydreaming by a selection of ready meals when she realised she was standing beside the South African estate agent whose baby she had delivered, what, seven months ago? The woman looked terrible. Her face was sallow, and she had put on a lot of weight. Anti-depressants did that to you.

"Renee, isn't it?" Jemma said.

"Doctor Sands, I was just going to the hospital. For my weekly group session."

"How are you feeling now? Better, I hope."

"Oh, yes. I feel like a totally new person." She hesitated. "I do have trouble remembering things, though. Yes, I have to make lists for everything I have to do."

Renee looked furtively up at the convex mirror above their heads reflecting shoppers. She jerked her head over to a blind spot where they could not be seen. Intrigued, Jemma followed. They stood beside the freezer cabinet, and Renee checked to make sure nobody could overhear them.

She lowered her voice, "These drugs that Doctor Malvern gives me. They're not good. They make me feel terrible. I keep thinking that something awful is about to happen, just out of sight where I can't see it."

"Have you told Doctor Malvern about this? You're obviously having some kind of reaction. Something's not right."

"I have the feeling that I've gone off somewhere and I can't come back."

"Sounds like you're having an allergic reaction. What has Doctor Malvern been prescribing you?"

"He says that some people have this bad reaction, and that I have to stick with the medication."

"Look, let me have a word with him. Would that help?"

Renee nodded gratefully. "He says that I'm not ready to come off the meds yet, and that I need to see the course through."

As soon as Jemma finished doing her rounds, she went to see George.

His office was at one end of the first-floor psychiatric department. Intrigued, she looked through the window of one of the meeting rooms. Four women, one of them Renee, were stretched out on reclining chairs. The lighting had been dimmed, and they looked as if they were asleep. There was also muffled talking going on. Jemma put her ear to the glass and listened. She heard some kind of recording. The voice was neutral, even a little fey: "You mean to get well. To do this, you must let your feelings come out. It is all right to express your anger. You want to stop your husband bossing you around. Begin to assert yourself first in little things, and soon you will be able to meet him on an equal basis. You will then be free to be a wife and mother just like other women."

Jemma reached for the door handle.

A hand touched her shoulder.

"Hey, what's up?" said George.

"Christ, you gave me a shock. I nearly jumped out of my skin. Can I have a word with you for a minute? Somewhere private?"

"Of course. Come into my office."

George's office was farther down the corridor.

"Those women in there," Jemma continued. "One of them was a patient of mine I referred to you. Is that your postpartum depression group? What's going on? Were they asleep?"

"Meditating. It's a new technique called 'depatterning'. It's been very popular in the States, so we're trying it over here. The results have been fantastic. You combine neuro-linguistic programming with group therapy and anti-depressants."

"Not according to the patient I sent to you. She says she feels even worse since you started giving her whatever you're prescribing."

"I guess you're talking about Renee Pieterse, that South African woman. You saw her just now. She didn't look upset to me. I warned her that this latest generation of SSRIs has side effects. Some people do have adverse reactions, so I've reduced her dosage. If she continues feeling bad, we'll go back to something else. But she has to stick with it. She was suicidal when you first sent her to me. The meds do work."

Jemma thought back to that other mother she had seen walking into the propeller blade. How terrible for a mother not to bond with her child. When she had Matthew, she felt as if all her questions had been answered; from now on everything she did would be for the betterment of her child. There was a Bob Dylan song that she and Tony used to listen to, something about having to serve somebody – it did not matter whether it was Jesus or Mohammed or, in this case, a child, but we all had to work for something bigger than ourselves.

"She was mildly depressed, George. This afternoon she scared me with what she was saying."

"Look, I'm not telling her to take anti-depressants because I'm a bad person. I don't enjoy seeing her so unhappy. But she's the outlier in this group. The rest of them have seen a dramatic improvement."

George's office was scruffy with overloaded bookshelves, a paper-covered desk and his mountain bike propped against one wall. He cleared some papers off the chair, making room for her to sit.

"There's something else I need to talk to you about, something personal."

"I told you before. The psychiatrist is in."

"Tony has taken Matthew on holiday in the South of France, where he's rented this amazing villa."

"Sounds great. Can I come? I'd love to be going to the Riviera."

"He's also hired one of the most expensive divorce lawyers in London. And he's rented a flat in Pimlico so he can be near the hospital. The question is, where's he getting all this money from? Even with our two salaries, it used to be a struggle to reach the end of the month sometimes."

George began making instant coffee for both of them.

"Savings? Help from his girlfriend you were telling me about? What if she's wealthy? It's not really any of your concern, is it?"

"There's something else going on. I know him. He's not

telling me everything."

She felt her BlackBerry buzzing in her doctor's coat. Probably Guaram giving her an update on the woman with the ectopic pregnancy. She reached down and pulled it from her pocket. Glancing at the screen, she saw it was a text message from Tony:

"Urgent. Am under arrest. Please come and get Matthew. Will explain everything."

CHAPTER SEVENTEEN

LIKE MOST ARGUMENTS, THIS ONE had started with something trivial. Toppy had snooped on his iPhone and seen a text message from another woman who signed off with a kiss. The fact that it was from Christine Matlock, Tony's deputy chief executive and somebody who was a good twenty years older than him, didn't seem to register. Anything seemed to set Toppy off these days. It was nearly a year into their relationship, and now that the sex was fading, he realised what he had on his hands was a mentally unstable woman.

When they first reconnected, nothing else seemed important, not his work or the woman he had married. Everything in Jemma's life revolved around either their son or her work at the hospital. There was never any time for him. It had reached the stage that he was having trouble remembering why they'd got married in the first place. Somehow the most important thing had been lying in bed with this woman and simply talking to her. He pictured Toppy lying in bed with that look of wanton abandonment. It had been a lovely thing to behold.

Tony was surprised at how quickly their relationship

had soured. Any adulterous relationship was built on quicksand; how could you trust the other person if they were so quick to betray others? Now, Toppy went into incoherent rages, screaming and thumping the table, before a sudden lurch into self-pity. There were moments when Tony honestly thought she was nuts. This was one of those moments. After a screaming match where she accused him of having an affair with another woman, she had locked herself in the bathroom.

The worst of it was that Matthew had to hear it. The walls were thin. Yesterday morning, when Toppy was shouting at Tony in the kitchen, his six-year-old son stepped in and physically separated them. First him and Jemma, now him and Toppy. How would this affect Matthew's view of men and women?

After waiting a few minutes for Toppy to calm down, Tony knocked gently on the bathroom door. "Toppy, it's me," he said. "Can you let me in?" No reply. He put his ear to the wood and heard her moving about in the bath. He tried again. "Toppy. Open the door. Then we can talk about it." He could hear her crying. Tony uselessly agitated the lock. "Toppy, please," he pleaded. "We need to talk. This is all in your head." No response.

He remembered that awful evening when she had first accused him of seeing other women – she had locked herself in the bathroom and refused to come out, then swallowed most of a bottle of ibuprofen. He had cradled her head over the toilet bowl while she vomited it up. Rowing with Toppy made him feel sick to his stomach.

Suddenly he felt righteous anger. Who was she to treat him like this when he had done nothing wrong? He took a step back and kicked the door as hard as he could. The flimsy lock gave way, and the door crashed open with a bang. Toppy was crouched in the bath with her arms across her chest. The water was misty with blood.

"Jesus Christ," Tony said.

He knelt down beside the bath and put his arm around Toppy's wet back. She was trembling.

"Toppy, it's all right," he said. "You can show me."

Slowly, like a flower opening, Toppy relaxed her arms. She had slashed one of her wrists. Thankfully, he could see it was superficial – she had cut herself across her artery and not along it. This was a plea for help, not a suicide attempt.

To his horror, Matthew was standing right behind him, seeing everything. Tony slammed the door shut.

"Toppy," he said. "I want you to stay in the bath and keep your wrist under the water."

At least the water would keep it feeling numb. What he needed now was something to wrap her arm in and then to take her to the doctor in the village where they were staying. It was at least a half-hour walk down to the port, and there were no cars on the island. In any case, he didn't know whom to call.

Matthew was standing outside looking frightened as Tony pushed past him, closing the bathroom door behind him. Banging a kitchen drawer open, he rattled around until he found a tea towel. It would have to do until he got Toppy to the doctor.

Back in the bathroom, Toppy was shivering.

"Are you ready to get out now?" he asked. Toppy nodded. She stood up and stepped out of the cloudy water. A spider's web of blood spread across her wet skin. Tony wrapped her in a bath towel and sat her on the toilet.

"Why did you do that, you silly girl? Don't you know that I love you? This jealousy of yours, you've got to stop it. I left my wife for you. What more do you want?"

"I don't know what I would do if you ever left me. All through my life people have walked away. I want them to stay, but they don't."

"This is madness. You're just being insecure. You've got to learn to trust people a little, okay?" he said, stroking her hair. He felt pity for her – the death of any relationship. Toppy sniffed and nodded while he wrapped her wrist in the tea towel. It would be a good forty-minute walk into town and it was nearly noon.

Outside, the gnarled, desiccated trees looked as if every drop of moisture had been sucked out of them. Their sandals scraped along the dusty track while Matthew skipped on ahead, occasionally kicking stones. The sun was pitiless – soon Tony's T-shirt was soaked with sweat. Cicadas grated. Cyclists whizzed past them, peaceful holiday-makers ambled alongside them. Matthew ran his stick along the school railings as they started downhill. In the square, men played boules and waiters dashed between tables yelling "Attends, attends".

Sitting there in the doctor's surgery, Tony felt shame when asked what had happened. The doctor didn't believe for a minute that it was an accident. Tony wanted to confide in this young Arabic woman about what he was dealing with, that he was living with somebody who was mentally unstable, but his French wasn't good enough. Instead, he resolved to break with Toppy when they got back to London. There was no use trying to be gentle about it.

Watching the doctor stitch the wound together, Tony's thoughts turned to the boat he had rented for that afternoon. To his surprise, Toppy had never learnt to swim. They had previously agreed that she would stay on the cabin cruiser looking after Matthew while he did a short twenty-minute dive in the morning. There was a nineteenth-century wreck he wanted to explore. He and Jemma had learnt to scuba dive on their honeymoon. He wouldn't be able to do that now, Tony thought bitterly. And it was too late to cancel, otherwise he would lose his deposit. Instead, he would have to watch Toppy closely. The idea of leaving his precious son alone with her on the boat didn't sit right, not after this. Yes, he would break with her the moment they got back to London. He had begun to wonder if Jemma would have him back; this had all been a dreadful mistake. Tony wished he had never walked out on his marriage in the first place.

The doctor made four anchors, pulling the skin together. As he suspected, it wouldn't be pretty, and Toppy would be left with a nasty jagged scar for the rest of her life. The doctor also prescribed some tranquilisers, temazepam, "to 'help you sleep'", she said, handing Toppy the bottle.

After she had calmed down, Toppy kept apologising for what she had done. She said she was fine about sticking to their plan to take the boat out. Tony had misgivings but agreed to go along with what Toppy wanted. Anything to avoid another row.

They went down to the port again later that afternoon, carrying overnight bags for their trip. The wind was picking up.

The boat Tony had chartered was a real gin palace. Smoked-glass doors led to a sitting room that could have been designed for an African dictator in the seventies. Day-glo orange carpet covered the walls and ceiling. Tony watched Toppy unpacking a carrier bag of supplies from the island shop. Apart from the bandage on her wrist, you wouldn't have known anything was wrong. She seemed a bit distant, that's all, probably the result of the temazepam. Matthew, meanwhile, was running around the boat exploring everything. Tony was going to watch his son like a hawk. He didn't feel comfortable with Matthew being around a woman who only hours before had tried to kill herself.

Seagulls barked overhead as Tony revved the Marie-Christine's engine and the craft glided out of the harbour, occasionally lurching down as it hit a wave. The water was choppier than he had expected. One of the other yachtsmen had warned that a storm was coming, one of those sudden downpours you get in August, but you wouldn't have known it that afternoon. The weather was glorious, if windy.

It clouded over quickly that night, though, the air heavy with approaching thunder. You could feel the tension, but still the storm would not break. Humidity pressed down like a hot towel on Tony's face. "It's close tonight," he remarked to Toppy, who was preparing their picnic supper in the galley kitchen. Matthew had already eaten and was downstairs asleep in his bunk. Now that Toppy was her normal self again, he could not resist broaching the subject of going diving tomorrow. The diving shop had already left a fully pressurised scuba tank and breathing apparatus on board. He hadn't had time to cancel his order for the equipment. The wetsuit was hanging up in a cupboard waiting for him.

"Toppy, how would you feel if I went for a short dive tomorrow morning? After all, it's what I came here to do. It's such a shame you can't come, too. I think you'd love it. There's this wonderful sense of peace down there. Nobody can contact you, so you might as well enjoy the experience."

"If you want to go, then go. I'll be fine with Matthew. I'm sorry about this morning. Sometimes I don't know what comes over me."

Thank God it's going to be a good night, Tony thought as they sat together eating cheese and ham. But Toppy kept refilling her glass, and Tony became alarmed at how quickly she was drinking. Two or three gulps and her glass would be empty. Making conversation, Tony talked about how he and Jemma had learned to dive on their honeymoon. The man they had rented their honeymoon villa from had taken them out in his small boat, and they had spent the afternoons diving in a quiet cove. It had been glorious.

"Why do you talk about your ex-wife so much?" Toppy asked. "Don't you realise how hurtful it is?"

"I was just talking about scuba diving, that's all. I would love to do it with you, darling," Tony said, reaching across the table for her hand. Toppy withdrew.

"Jemma this, Jemma that," she said in a sarcastic sing-song voice. "I am so sick of hearing that name. If you love her so much, why don't you go back to her?"

Here it comes, he thought. "Whoa, whoa, who said anything about going back to her? We experienced a lot together.

I'm bound to mention her name sometimes. You're the one I love, not her. Listen, rather than arguing about my ex-wife, let's think about how we're going to spend the money. In a few weeks' time, you and I are going to be richer than we could possibly imagine."

He was doing his best to divert her from another row, trying to be his most reasonable and placatory. It wasn't working. Toppy was draining another glass of wine, her rationality dimming with each sip.

"You left her only because she wasn't paying you enough attention. You men are such babies. Looking at you, I'm beginning to see why she found you boring."

"Toppy, please stop it before you say something you regret."

"Oh, I should have known. I should have listened to what my friends said. They told me not to get involved with a married man. It's my fault; I should have never let you sleep with me." She rose from the table and was pacing the cabin, twisting the ring on her finger. He might as well not have been there. "I only slept with you out of pity. I felt sorry for you, this little man whose wife ignored him. I see why now."

Tony got up from the table and grabbed her arm. He was so tired of listening to this nonsense. He wanted it to end, right now. Toppy was on the upswing of one of her moods, and he didn't want her to go there. This rollercoaster of emotions was happening more and more frequently. At first they were every other month or so, then weekly; now there would be only a few hours' respite before she would start laying into him again.

"How dare you touch me?" she snapped, pulling away. "You're always siding with her, not me. Don't forget, she's the one who fixed it so that I could never have children."

"Toppy. That's not true. She saved your life after the accident; you at least owe her that much. I've explained to you again and again that it was either you or the baby."

"Oh, how easy it is for all you medical people to band together. The moment there's any trouble, you close ranks. It's clear to me now that you and she conspired against me. I should have known that the two of you were in this together. Anything to stop your precious wife from losing her job. That's probably why you started fucking me, to stop me from suing your precious hospital. Oh yes, you made sure that didn't happen."

Part of him wanted to clamp his hands over his ears; he was so fed up listening to these wild accusations. He knew what she was doing. She was pushing him, jabbing him in the chest until he reacted and lost his temper. He wasn't going to take any more of this and, without thinking, he slapped her face. Hard.

For a moment they both stood there in shocked silence. He had never done anything like this before.

Instantly, he regretted what he had done: "Toppy, I am so

sorry. I didn't mean to–"

"Get the fuck away from me," she snarled.

He remembered something that George the hospital psychiatrist had said when he had broached the subject of Toppy's erratic behaviour. Not that Tony had used her name. When you are dealing with somebody who is mentally unstable, George counselled, the only thing you can do is back away. It's as if she is holding out a stick, George explained, wanting you to grasp it so you can both be shaken around. Well, he wasn't going to play that game. Besides, he realised that he'd had too much to drink himself; all he wanted to do was go downstairs and sleep it off. "I'm going to bed," he said, lifting his hands in surrender. "You can stay up if you want. I don't want to fight with you anymore."

Lying in the small double bed, he could hear Toppy moving about upstairs. He thought about her black implacable anger and shivered; what had he done getting involved with this crazy woman? Eventually she would calm down and realise how unreasonable she was being. They would kiss and make up and have I'm-sorry sex; there would be a few good days and then the cycle would begin again. Toppy seemed constantly dissatisfied; nothing he did seemed good enough. Tony was determined to break with her when they got back to London. He had really fucked up his life. Perhaps if Jemma would have him back...

Something woke him in the middle of the night. Toppy was

not in bed next to him. He felt he had closed his eyes only a few moments ago, but it must have been longer. His watch said it was half past three in the morning. Tony sat up in bed, and the awful lurching sensation told him they were in the midst of a storm.

He lurched into the tiny corridor as the bow pitched down and the floor dropped away, throwing him off balance. He felt sick as the floor smacked up again, and he hung on to the wall to steady himself.

Everything was rolling around in the cabin. Matthew was downstairs asleep in his bunk bed, and Tony was torn between checking on him and searching for Toppy. The room was yawing from side to side, making it difficult to stand upright. He fought a rising panic as he scanned the room. The boat wasn't that big – perhaps she had been swept overboard? He couldn't see her. She had been so drunk last night that she could have lost her footing. That was when he spotted the empty temazepam bottle rolling across the carpet. Picking it up, he could see she must have swallowed the whole lot. Jesus wept.

On deck, the scything rain was like nothing he had ever experienced. His T-shirt and boxer shorts were soaked instantly as he leant over the rail shouting Toppy's name. The storm swallowed up his shouts. There was no way Toppy could hear him. He thought of her somewhere out there, watching the boat as the sleeping pills took hold and water closed over her head.

Tony climbed the ladder up to the flying bridge. At least it was dry in here. He reached down for the boat radio, flipping the safety toggle off the emergency button. Pressing the red button would instantly transmit his position via GPS to the coastguard, right down to within a few yards. Channel sixteen would also cut into every other ship's radio. Anybody within range would have to divert and come to his rescue.

The coastguard immediately came on the line.

"Ici le garde-côte de Port Croix. Quelle est votre position? Terminé."

"This is the..." Tony looked around, trying to remember the boat's name. "We have a man overboard. Repeat. Man overboard."

There was some static and radio atmospherics.

"Parlez-voo anglais? Nous sommes anglais."

"Ne bougez pas. Nous arrivons. Nous serons là dans peu de temps. Terminé."

The windscreen wipers were ineffectually trying to sweep the wall of rain away. Every trough the boat hit was like somebody smacking the flat of their hand on something hard.

He heard Matthew's voice calling from downstairs. The poor boy must be terrified.

Matthew was still in his bunk. "What's happening, Daddy? I'm frightened. Don't leave me alone." Down here, the hull

SLOW BLEED

amplified the sound of pounding waves. No wonder his darling son was scared.

"There's been an accident. I think Auntie Toppy might have fallen into the sea. We have to wait for the coastguard to get here. Then they can help me find her."

"Auntie Toppy told me she couldn't swim," he said.

The boat lurched violently.

He helped Matthew into his yellow lifejacket and took him upstairs to the flying bridge. Tony scanned the darkness for a boat, any boat.

The coastguard took about half an hour to reach them, but it felt much longer. The storm had spent itself by now. The man on deck threw a rope across to tether the two boats together before jumping across, leaving another man on the coastguard-cutter bridge. Beneath the hood of his wet gear, the coastguard who had jumped across looked a tough customer. Tony told him the whole story, and the man regarded him with contempt. You could imagine him thinking, just another silly tourist out of his depth.

They spent another hour searching for Toppy. In the lunar dawn the rain turned to a light drifting mist, but all three men knew it was hopeless.

Father and son transferred to the simple white motor boat. My God, Matthew, what have I got you into? Tony thought. He felt out of his mind with worry. The other coastguard would follow back to port in the Marie-Christine.

Tony felt utterly defeated and physically sick. He still could not quite get his head around what had just happened. This woman he had once been obsessed about, who he had left his wife for, was somewhere out there. Was she still struggling to keep her head above water, too exhausted to shout, watching with disbelief as the two boats set off back to harbour? No, she must have drowned already. She couldn't swim, and he pictured her sinking in the gloom, her body twisting and her hair cloudily spread out before coming to rest on the seabed. Ophelia.

If he was honest, though, there was also a tiny spark deep inside him that was secretly relieved. He thought of all that money sitting in the French bank account. One million euros that he wouldn't have to share with anyone. And then he felt ashamed of his thoughts.

"Dad, are we going to find Auntie Toppy?" Matthew said, snapping him back to reality.

"I don't know. Another boat might have picked her up and brought her back home. She's probably waiting for us back at the villa." He tried giving Matthew a brave little smile.

Matthew looked doubtful. "She told me she didn't like the sea."

The coastguard dropped down into the cabin and jerked his chin at Tony. "When we get to the harbour, you will come with me to the police," he said. "They want to interview you."

"Interview me about what? I've told you everything that happened. We had an argument, and my girlfriend jumped overboard."

The coastguard shrugged as if to say, that might be your story, but we don't believe you.

CHAPTER EIGHTEEN

THE AIR WAS SO CLEAR it was almost crystalline.
A couple of jet skiers followed the ferry, jumping across
its wake like mechanical porpoises while tourists took
photographs. It was too windy for Jemma at the stern of
the boat, so she went back inside. Passengers lolled on
benches filling the ferry interior. A guide was pointing
out landmarks over the loudspeaker system, but Jemma's
French wasn't good enough to follow what she was saying.
She rejoined the French family with whom she had left
her holdall. London had been rain-sodden when she had
got her flight from Stansted, but here the weather was
beautiful.

The moment she had got Tony's text she had tried phoning
him back, but the call went through to voicemail. Tony
had returned her call an hour later. He had told her the
whole story: about how Toppy had made a pathetic suicide
attempt yesterday morning, the day he had chartered his
boat; how they had taken the boat out anyway seeing he
had already paid for it; and how Toppy and he had started
arguing again. Then the storm and the fruitless search for
her at sea.

Even as Tony was speaking, part of Jemma was satisfied that everything had ended so tragically: she knew Toppy Mrazek was trouble the moment she set eyes on her. Here was another of those self-absorbed, damaged women Tony had been attracted to until he met her.

Tony continued: "Once, I found her sitting on the edge of the bed. You remember that scene in The Shining, the one where Jack Nicholson has completely lost it? It was like that. There was this sunken look in her eyes. I remember how cold the room was. It was weird. I just thought, I'm out of my depth here. There's nothing I can do to help you anymore."

You're the one who got into bed with her, Jemma thought uncharitably. You made your bed, and now you're lying in it.

"Sometimes I would wake up in the middle of the night and hear her crying. She was convinced I was having an affair. Which I'm not, by the way. You begin something like this and it's dark and dangerous and exciting, and then you realise, no, she's just a crazy woman. It's been like living with a suicide bomber who's about to press the detonator."

"How is Matthew doing? Can I speak to him?"

"Sure" – she heard French conversation going on in the background – "he's doing okay. I don't think he really understands what's going on."

Matthew came on the line. "Hello, darling, it's Mummy. Are

you all right? I just wanted to make sure you were okay."

"Mum, are you coming to get me? The policewoman here is very nice. I've been drawing pictures with her."

Jemma was relieved to hear how normal Matthew sounded. Perhaps Tony was right and he didn't really comprehend what had happened. My God, she thought, what a situation. Part of her was glad that Toppy had gone missing. After all, what had Toppy Mrazek brought to their lives apart from chaos and unhappiness? The thought crossed Jemma's mind that Tony might think they were getting back together. Well, he could forget about that. She could still feel the imaginary knife caked in gore that he had plunged between her shoulder blades.

The ferry was heading to an island that was just a line of rock on the horizon. It was four o'clock in the afternoon, and they had been on the boat for more than an hour now. Jemma glanced at the front page of the local newspaper over someone's shoulder: forest fires had razed all the hills round a village; the search continued for a woman tourist gone missing; a Hollywood star posed next to one of those big yachts in St Tropez harbour. The news about a British woman who had fallen overboard hadn't made it into the paper yet.

Jemma's thoughts turned back to what Tony had told her about the tiny island. There was one little harbour town – the rest of Port Croix consisted of holiday villas and isolated beaches. The stony, stark island loomed closer through the salt-flecked window, olive trees clinging to copper-red rocks. Jemma guessed they were about to arrive. The faded ice-cream colours of the port were drawing closer. There was a bump as they docked.

She saw the policeman waiting for her on the quay as she came down the gangway. The glare outside was dazzling, and she shielded her eyes with one hand as she came down the gangway.

"Doctor Sands?" he asked, offering to take her overnight bag. "Your 'usband and son are waiting for us at the gendarmerie. My colleagues will be arriving from Toulon to take your husband to the mainland."

"Is he under arrest? What are you arresting him for?"

"No, he is not under arrest. My superiors want to ask him more questions."

"Have you found the woman's body yet? She might have washed up somewhere."

"We have alerted all the local fishermen and the harbour master. The coastguard continued its search at first light."

"I want to see my husband. Please will you take me to him?"

They walked past bike-rental shops and ice-cream stands. Families on holiday wheeled bicycles through the main street, laughing and joking. How happy they seemed. They approached the gendarmerie – it looked more like a Wendy house than a police station.

The policeman ushered her into a small waiting room facing a counter. Matthew was sitting next to a pretty blonde policewoman banging his legs against the wooden bench. He was bored. The policewoman was reading a French storybook to him in faltering English. Matthew jumped up and flung himself at his mother the moment he saw her. Jemma hugged Matthew as hard as she could, unable to believe how much she loved him. Something about him didn't smell right, though. It was uncomfortably hot in the police station, and there wasn't any air conditioning. Somewhere a mosquito was buzzing, just out of sight. Over Matthew's little shoulder she spied Tony through a window, sitting in an office. There was a counter and beyond that an office like in a hotel reception. Tony stood up when he saw her and tried to smile. The policeman lifted up the hinged counter and walked through.

Tony emerged and he and Jemma hugged awkwardly, their bodies not quite touching. Always that conflicting tug of intimacy and repulsion.

"My colleagues are waiting down at the harbour," the policeman said. "Mr Sands, if you would follow me?"

Jemma said, "When will my husband be coming back? My son and I are taking the night flight back to London this evening."

"Désolé, mais... that will not be possible. I need you both to stay on the island until your husband is released."

"When will that be? You don't understand. I have to get

SLOW BLEED

161

back to London. I have a job, responsibilities..."

"Doctor Sands, I am sure this will just be a formality. Your husband will be released tomorrow, bien sûr. Then you will be free to leave."

"Jemma, I swear on Matthew's life that I had nothing to do with Toppy jumping overboard," Tony said. "You must know that."

"We both know the truth. The police have to take you in for more questioning. It's just routine. Like the policeman said, you'll be back tomorrow."

Already she was thinking that they would have to cancel that night's flight and rebook for tomorrow.

"Thank you for believing me, Jemma. It means a lot. We both need to be strong for Matthew."

The policeman put his hand on Tony's shoulder and began leading him out. Her husband looked so shaken that Jemma was afraid he was going to cry. She wanted to say something, to reassure him that everything was going to be all right.

"Tony, you have nothing to be ashamed of. She was hysterical..."

Tony paused in the doorway. He gave a tired smile. "You know, I've been thinking. Do you know where the word hysterical comes from? It comes from the Greek word for hysterectomy. It means somebody who's had their womb removed."

And with that he stepped into the afternoon glare.

They waited for the gendarme to come back from the dock. As Matthew played with his Game Boy, Jemma reflected that she had never seen Tony shaken like this; he had always been so confident, so in control. She reassured herself that if he told the truth, they had nothing to worry about.

The gendarme walked back into the office wiping the sweat from his forehead with his wrist. "Mon Dieu, qu'il fait chaud," he muttered. There were dark patches beneath his armpits. He led Jemma into his office, and she quickly realised he wanted to question her, too. An electric insect-killer hung in one corner, its blue bars gleaming. The French president smiled self-consciously in an official photograph behind the gendarme's head. The gendarme waved for Jemma to sit down.

The young officer sat back in his chair and played with his pen. There was a pop as an insect incinerated itself on the bars.

"Your husband told me that this woman who has gone missing... she was his mistress?"

"She was his girlfriend, yes. They met after she was a patient at the hospital where we both work."

"So you knew this woman? You say that she was a patient of yours. What were you treating her for?"

"I am an obstetric surgeon. Toppy Mrazek was brought

into hospital after she had been in a car accident. There were complications."

"Mr Sands said that you operated on this woman and she lost her baby. She was angry with you. Did you know about his affair?"

Jemma sensed she was digging a hole for herself, and she wanted to stop. "My husband and I are getting divorced, that's true. I never had any sense until now that the woman was mentally ill."

"But your husband says she had mood swings, that she was, uh, volatile, is that the word?"

"Look, all of this is my husband's private life. I just want to take my son and go back to London. We have nothing to do with this. Tony said that she tried to slash her wrists yesterday morning. Surely that's evidence enough that she wasn't in her right frame of mind. Can't you check with the village doctor? She will corroborate what my husband is saying."

The gendarme ran his hand over the iron filings of his hair. "Suppose your husband realised he had made a mistake leaving you for this other woman. After all, here is this woman who has tried to kill herself. And then there's you – sensible, attractive," he said. "Divorce is expensive, he loses his son... Suppose he takes advantage? She is drunk and he pushes her off?"

He let his words hang in the air.

"My husband is no murderer," Jemma said coldly.

The policeman reiterated that she and Matthew would have to remain on the island until Tony was released from questioning. That was just a formality, he assured her. In the meantime, she should buy some groceries, and he would take them up to their accommodation for the night.

The policeman drove them up to the villa. The number of cyclists petered out, and soon they were on their own. The rocky track got steeper, and Jemma could see where they were heading: a modest-looking house perched on the side of the hill. It was funny, but she had expected something grander. There was also a castle on the hill crest above it.

The track finished beside an olive grove leading up to the house. The policeman parked the van and switched off the engine. "From here we walk," he said.

It was scorpion hot. They jumped across a ditch and began walking uphill towards the villa, twigs crunching beneath their feet. Cicadas chirped all around them, and Jemma had to stop for a moment to catch her breath. She was not used to this heat, and her eyes were stinging with sweat. The air became dangerously still, almost liquid. Finally, they reached the house. The policeman fiddled with keys and unlocked the French windows leading inside. The villa interior looked cool and dark and inviting. So this was what Tony had rented. Together Jemma and the gendarme stepped in to a Provençal-pink sitting room where Matthew's half-assembled Lego helicopter lay on the tiled floor.

The policeman said, "Can you make sure you have your portable, um, mobile phone, with you?"

She fingered the business card he had given her as she watched him leave. René Duverger, the name said.

That evening she forced herself to eat, waiting for her mobile to ring. Guaram Chandra had not sounded too bothered when she told him her flight had been postponed. She was meant to be on duty tomorrow, so he would have to find somebody to cover for her. There had been a problem, she told him vaguely; and she would be home as soon as she could.

It was only the next morning, after a sleepless night filled with anxiety, that Jemma could see how truly beautiful the island was. Out at sea, there were white lines that the early-morning water-skiers had carved in the water. And there was a softness in the air that you got only in the South of France. Matthew and Jemma spent the rest of the morning in a sandy cove at the bottom of the hill. The sand was pebbly, and it hurt to wade into the sea without shoes on. The water was shallow a long way out, so Matthew was not in any danger. Jemma sat on her towel, occasionally brushing a fly away from her face. She felt her mind oozing in the heat. Tony still hadn't called. Wanting to kill time, she decided they would explore the castle she had spotted on the drive up to the villa.

The castle was perched on the hill like a vulture. It was a stiff climb up between the olive trees, and the smell of pine and lavender was almost overpowering.

She wandered over and joined a group of tourists, listening intently to a tour guide. "The castle was built by British prisoners of war during the Napoleonic War with England," the guide said. "Napoleon was convinced that the English would attack by sea, and he built a series of defences along the coast. This is one of them. The islanders were certain that the British were about to invade, so they dug tunnels underneath where we're standing. These tunnels were used to store food and ammunition. The islanders planned to live in the tunnels and defend the castle until Napoleon's troops broke the siege."

The sunlight bleached the colour out of everything. Matthew was standing beneath a brass plaque on the wall. He looked terribly hot. Jemma worried about him in this heat because he wasn't wearing a hat. Glancing at the wall, she read: "Le 23 août 1942, 26 juifs, dont 12 enfants habitant Port Croix, furent livrés aux Nazis par le gouvernement de Vichy et déportés vers Auschwitz. Que ceux qui ont tenté de leur venir en aide soient remerciés." Her French was just about good enough to understand that the plaque commemorated Jewish families who had been deported during the war.

"This plaque," Jemma asked. "What does it mean?"

The guide looked down and stirred dirt with the tip of his

shoe. "During the war, the Nazis rounded up all the Jews on the island and deported them. There were a lot of Germans stationed here. They renovated the tunnels beneath us. The idea was that the Vichy government would hide in them if they lost the war."

"What happened to the Jewish families?"

"The parents were sent to Auschwitz, while the children stayed here. What was shameful is that it was the islanders themselves who gave the Jews away. It's not something people will talk about, even today. It's their secret shame."

"So the children stayed here?"

"Yes and no. The Germans had a hospital here on the island. The story is that Doctor Mengele, the Auschwitz doctor, came out and experimented on the children. None of them were seen again."

People turned to each other and began muttering.

"Personally, I think it's a myth. The children were shot and they were then thrown into the sea. It's believed that was why their bodies were never found. That's what the historians think anyway."

The guide's story crystallised her sense of unease about the island. There was something not quite right about this place.

Back at the villa, Tony finally rang when they were eating dinner. Her mobile reception was so bad he sounded like a robot being drowned in the bath.

"Tony, what's happening? Have you found a lawyer yet? You need to have somebody with you."

"They haven't charged me with anything. They keep pushing me to confess. But I just keep telling them what happened. I think even they are beginning to realise that I had absolutely nothing to do with it."

She could hear the stress in his voice and pictured him running his hand through his thinning hair. "You must phone me if they charge you. I'll try and get you a lawyer from this end. You can't just let them bully you like this. What's a number I can call you on? Have you got your mobile on you?"

"The detective told me I would probably be free to go home tomorrow. I'll come back to the villa and pack. There's no need for you to stay. Why don't you and Matthew get a flight home this evening?"

"The police said we had to stay until you were released."

She wanted to reassure him, but the words stuck in her throat. Tony rang off. Almost instantly the phone rang again, startling her.

She recognised Duverger's voice. "Hello? This is Port Croix police. Your friend's body, it has been found. You must come to the hospital in Hyères to identify her. I am sorry. There is nobody else we can ask."

"Of course," she said. She felt as if somebody had jump-started her heart with the paddles. "Where did you find her?"

"Some fishermen caught her in their nets. Once you have identified the body, then you will be free to fly back to England. We will take you to the airport. Your husband is still being questioned."

She pictured a sagging, dripping fish haul, one grey arm dangling through the netting.

"Yes, I know. He just called."

Hurriedly, Jemma swept the villa of belongings and stuffed them into their bags. At this rate, they might be able to get the evening flight home. Twenty minutes later she heard the police van making its way up the road.

Edging along the track in his van, listening to the nasty scraping of stones, the gendarme said: "The pathologist says your friend probably hit her head before falling into the sea. He still has to do a full post-mortem. We won't know the results for days."

"My husband was telling the truth. You've found the body. She drowned at sea."

"My superiors want to detain your husband until the laboratory report comes back."

Matthew spent the crossing excitedly running around the boat while Jemma gazed out of the window. She looked at the indifferent sea and wondered whether she had the guts to go through with this. Of course she had seen dead bodies before, but somehow this felt different. This was somebody she had actually known.

The hospital was a terracotta building on the outskirts of town.

The mortuary attendant was younger than she expected, tall, with café-au-lait skin and startling blue eyes, bluer than his hospital gown. "Venez par ici, s'il vous plaît," he said quietly with a faint lisp. He gestured for her to accompany him. She had assumed she would be asked to identify Toppy through a window – that was how they did it back at St. Luke's – but no, she was being taken to inspect the body up close. She rose with a queer feeling that this was all happening to somebody else. She had to get through this, she must. "Matthew, you stay here, sweetie," she said. "Mummy's got to go and do something."

The attendant held the door open, and they walked through into the mortuary.

It was colder on this side. There was the hum of powerful air conditioning, and the white walls were glaringly antiseptic. One wall was taken up with drawers where they kept the corpses. A sign read: "Veuillez s'il vous plaît vous assurer que les corps soient mis tête en avant dans les unités de rangement." The morgue looked like an operating theatre, except more basic: a stainless steel counter ran along a back wall used for eviscerating organs, blue hoses neatly coiled on top. Toppy's body was laid out beyond the attendant, and it struck Jemma that it was as if the morgue worker was standing between life and death itself. Her husband's lover was lying on a hospital gurney wrapped in a plastic shroud, her head-end towards the metal sink.

The two of them stood over the body, and the attendant waited a moment before unzipping the plastic bag. The bag split open with the most nauseating fishy smell. Jemma stepped back. The woman's lolling breasts were exposed inside the milky plastic, and red welts and jellyfish stings covered her arms and torso. Her slack flesh was turning the colour of potter's clay, grey and bloated. Her jaw sagged, giving her a double chin. Even though the attendant had turned her good side towards Jemma, trying to hide the worst of the damage, she could see part of the head had been eaten away. Fish, eels perhaps, had taken great chunks out of it. Even in death she looked surprised at what had happened to her.

Jemma said, "That's not Toppy Mrazek."

CHAPTER NINETEEN

AUTUMN SEEMED TO HAVE DESCENDED since they had been away. Name-tape weather, her mum called it, that time of year when you were meant to be getting children ready for school. Matthew was starting at his new primary school in a few days' time. "Home, home and happy to be here," her mind trilled as she let them both into the house. African tribesmen talked about sitting down and waiting for their souls to catch up with them once they had arrived somewhere, which was just how she felt.

Jemma was unpacking their holdalls, marvelling at how sand always managed to get into them, when the telephone rang.

It was Tony. "They released me without charge. I think they realised I was telling the truth. My story never changed no matter how much they leant on me."

She could hear the relief in her husband's voice, which sounded choked with emotion.

"Tony, where are you now? Are you going back to the villa?"

"I'm going to stay overnight in Hyères and go back

tomorrow morning. I'll close up the villa and hand the keys in to the agents. I don't care if I never set foot on that island again."

"Tony, they took me to see what they thought was Toppy's body in the hospital morgue this afternoon, did they tell you?"

"They think she's a German tourist who went missing a few days ago. They're checking her dental records to see if they can identify her."

"What will happen if they don't recover Toppy? Will she be certified dead or missing, or what?"

"I don't know. I keep thinking there's somebody I ought to be speaking to, somebody in Toppy's family. She never talked about her relatives. You would have thought she was an orphan. I don't know if her parents are alive or not. Or even if she had any brothers or sisters. She was very private about things."

"What about that lawyer you went to see? Surely she must know somebody."

"I suppose so," Tony said doubtfully. "Jemma... I keep replaying everything in my mind, wondering if there was something I could have done. I feel so responsible."

"Tony. It was an accident. You have got to stop crucifying yourself. She was drunk and she fell overboard. Tony, from everything you've told me, it was almost as if she had a death wish. There was nothing you could have done."

Nevertheless, Tony and Jemma avoided each other when he got back. It was as if they had both been involved in something shameful, not that either of them had anything to be ashamed of. She imagined Toppy underwater, reaching out to her, hair waving around her white face, imploring Jemma to do something. Toppy was sinking deeper and deeper, arms outstretched, swallowed up by the misty wall.

Jemma returned from the hospital after her first day back on duty dog-tired, and Matthew took forever to get to bed. There had been a mention in one of the newspapers' in-brief column that morning about Toppy's disappearance. "British Woman Presumed Drowned," said the headline. So the police must have decided that Toppy was dead, her body never to be recovered. The news-in-brief item mentioned that about eighty British tourists drown on holiday abroad each year.

Now all Jemma wanted to do was watch something dopey on television. She had just taken her first sip of white wine when her BlackBerry rang. Thinking it was either Tony or her mother calling, she picked it up without glancing at who the caller was.

"Is that Doctor Sands? I am sorry to be disturbing you at home. My name is Eva Mrazek. I am Toppy's mother."

At this Jemma sat upright on the sofa. "Oh, Mrs Mrazek, I'm so glad you called. My husband was trying to find you. We both feel terrible about what's happened. We had no way to reach you. Even Toppy's solicitor had no way of contacting any of her family."

"Yes, I was hoping to speak to your husband. Is he there?"

"Er, no... the thing is that we don't live together any more. Mrs Mrazek, I wanted to say how sorry I am about what has happened. It was a tragic accident."

"Yes. I don't have to tell you how I felt when the police came to see me." A parent losing a child was the worst thing Jemma could imagine.

Eva Mrazek continued, "In a strange way, I always knew something like this would happen, even from when Toppy was a little girl. It's something I've been dreading for years. There was always something different about her. You were friends with Toppy, yes?"

"Not exactly." Jemma was unsure how to proceed. "Toppy was my husband's girlfriend. It's complicated. My husband took our son on holiday with Toppy to the South of France. That's where the accident happened."

"Yes, Port Croix. We used to have a holiday home there. The police at Toulon gave me the number of your hospital. They said your husband rented a boat and that Toppy fell overboard. Please, I need to talk to you. What they said in the newspaper was so... bald. It would help me understand things better if I knew a little more."

"Of course. Do you know how to get to St Luke's hospital in west London? I could see you tomorrow if you like. Just tell me when would work best for you."

They arranged to meet in the ground-floor café tomorrow morning at eleven o'clock.

Jemma thought about what Eva Mrazek had said as she got ready for bed. What did she mean when she said that Toppy's death was something she'd been dreading for years? Did Toppy's mental problems, her manic behaviour, stretch further back than when Tony first met her, further back even than from when Jemma performed the hysterectomy? If Toppy had a history of mental illness, that would have coloured the lawsuit she had threatened the hospital with. Perhaps that was why there was never any mention of the family. A relative could have testified about her mental state if Toppy had gone through with her legal action.

Time dragged in the obstetric consultants' meeting next morning. Jemma wanted to see George before her meeting with Eva Mrazek. Finally the meeting broke up, and Jemma hurried down the hall to George's office. His door was unlocked. Jemma stood there for a moment wondering what to do before deciding to wait. George's desk was such a mess, and she wondered how he got anything done. Papers and files spilled over the desktop, threatening to topple onto the carpet. Wanting to help, she went over to the desk and started straightening things up when her coat must have caught on something and a pile of folders slid onto the floor. She cursed and crouched down, picking the files up. Jemma realised how this would look, rummaging through somebody's desk, if somebody did walk in. She picked up the last batch of hanging files when she noticed the typed name beneath the plastic tab: Pieterse, Renee. Unable to resist, she began reading his patient notes: " ...an exceedingly complicated 26-year-old woman, who from a very early age has shown serious neurotic tendencies with strong feelings of hostility towards her mother, expressing themselves ultimately in frank statements of hatred. She also had profoundly disturbing incestuous preoccupations with and fear of her father and hatred of her own body... the patient's references to her unconscious homosexual feelings concerning the mother are much more frequent..." – Jemma dropped her eyes to the bottom of the page – "... about her mother being hot, moist and sticky and the feeling that her mother was smothering her."

Jemma skipped to the next page and read on: "The mother means work, perfection and discipline, and burdening. This always ended up in abandonment, injury and death through childbirth. The father means charm, pleasure, a mess and unsatisfied needfulness. The patient shuffles between these two extremes and tries to remain something of a mess, but not quite father, something of a perfectionist, but not quite mother... Childbirth itself was experienced as both a mutilation and an annihilation."

George had prescribed 100mgms of MC4703 to be taken orally every day. Jemma did not recognise the name of the drug – it must have been that American wonder drug

George had mentioned to her, one of the new-generation SSRIs. She turned to the keyboard and googled MC4703, but nothing came up even vaguely like what she was looking for. How odd. There wasn't a single mention of MC4703 as an anti-depressant in the search results.

She glanced at her watch and wrote the words "George. Call me. Jemma" on a Post-It note before leaving it on his desk. It was five minutes to eleven.

When she met Mrs Mrazek in the café, Jemma ordered two white coffees and carried them over to the table, careful not to spill any. Eva Mrazek must have been beautiful when she was younger. Even now she was chicly dressed and startlingly thin. The first thing you noticed was how blue her eyes were. She smelled of face powder and perfume, her hair an expensively coiffured cloud.

"Thank you. How much do I owe you?" she said, reaching into her handbag.

"Please, don't even think about it."

"So, this place. How long have you been a doctor?"

"I'm an obstetric consultant, actually. I get called in to deliver difficult babies and oversee the obstetric staff generally." Again, she didn't know what to say next. "Mrs Mrazek, I don't know quite how to tell you this, but Toppy was pregnant when I first met her. She had been in a car accident and the baby was stillborn. I'm so sorry."

Toppy's mother pursed her lips, absorbing the information.

"Do you know who the father was?" she said finally.

"We never knew. Toppy was angry and upset about what had happened, and she tried suing the hospital. That was how my husband met her. Or should I say, met her again. Apparently they knew each other when they were younger."

Mrs Mrazek stared numbly at the table. "So I would have been a grandmother. Jack would have loved that. Jack was Toppy's father, but he died many years ago."

"Tony was worried that there was somebody we ought to contact. We had no idea of how to get in touch with you."

"No, she had a brother once… That was when her problems began…"

Mrs Mrazek's hands knotted as she searched for the right words. Her voice sounded absurdly familiar; Jemma realised it was the same as Toppy's except a little more papery.

"I was a stewardess on Czech Airlines. That was how I met Toppy's father. He was a businessman in London who had a factory in Prague. We married and had Toppy a couple of years later. Toppy's father was a wealthy man. I remember him standing over her cot saying that he was going to take our baby daughter to Hamleys every weekend. She could have whatever she wanted. Please God, no, I thought. And I was right. He spoiled Toppy completely. Anything she wanted, she could have."

"You said that Toppy had a brother?"

"When Toppy was six years old, we had another baby, a boy this time. We were living in a mansion flat then. I had put the baby in his pram out on the balcony in the sun. I remember I was in the kitchen on the telephone when the baby started crying. I was too selfish to end the call. Toppy must have heard the baby crying and tried to soothe it. She picked her baby brother up and rocked him. I think she wanted to show him the trees and the street below…"

Mrs Mrazek faltered. Even after all these years the memory was too painful. "The baby must have slipped. At least, that is what I tell myself. Our flat was on the seventh floor. Toppy was never the same after that. Something changed inside her."

She gripped Jemma's hand tightly, and the doctor noticed the liver spots on her wrist. "It's something I blame myself for every day, do you understand?" Mrs Mrazek continued. "Toppy felt responsible for her brother's death. First, she wouldn't eat at all. Then she would gorge herself and make herself sick. She started cutting herself. Her father and I didn't know what to do. We sent her to the best psychiatric hospital, but the doctors only told us what we already knew, that Toppy's mind had turned with guilt over what had happened. She became lying and manipulative. My husband eventually died of a heart attack. I don't think he ever got over the grief of having lost our little boy. He left Toppy a lot of money and things became worse. Drugs. Bad people. She squandered her inheritance. In the end, I moved abroad because I could not cope with her any longer. She was like a sinking ship that was pulling everybody down with her. I had to get away. Otherwise I would have been sucked down too."

Mrs Mrazek still had a sorrowful beauty about her, as if her capacity for thinking the world was a good place had died on the drive leading to that psychiatric hospital.

Jemma remembered what Tony had said about Toppy's black, implacable anger. "Perhaps Toppy was just lashing out, trying to hurt anybody because she felt so guilty, and you were the nearest person to hand."

"Well, that is kind of you to say," Mrs Mrazek said, recovering. She dabbed her eyes with a tissue. "So now you tell me about how she drowned, yes?"

"Well, as I said, Toppy was my husband's girlfriend and..." Mrs Mrazek was about to console Jemma, who shook her head. "No, it's all right. Tony rented a villa in France last month and took our son on holiday with them. What I didn't know was that Toppy and my husband weren't getting on very well. Tony said your daughter was jealous. She kept imagining that my husband was having an affair, and they had a row about it on the morning she died. She tried slashing her wrists in the bath... let me know if this is too much for you" – now it was Eva Mrazek's turn to shake her head – "and Tony took her to the doctor. That's when the accident happened. Tony had rented a boat because he wanted to go scuba diving. So Toppy said she would stay on the boat with Matthew, seeing that she couldn't swim…"

At this, Mrs Mrazek widened her intense blue eyes. "Couldn't swim? Why, Toppy was an excellent swimmer. She loved swimming. She was a schoolgirl swimming champion. Here, let me show you…"

Mrs Mrazek rummaged in her handbag and pulled out her purse. Facing the credit cards was a plastic-covered holiday snapshot. It showed a younger Eva Mrazek sitting beside a handsome man who Jemma supposed was Toppy's father. They were sitting on the stone bench of a holiday villa with their teenage daughter sitting between them.

Toppy was wearing a wetsuit.

CHAPTER TWENTY

THE SLOVAKIAN GIRL WHO SOMETIMES looked after Matthew until Jemma got home had told her that night she was going home for Christmas. Her mother in Bratislava was ill. And Jemma's next-door neighbour, Emily, had taken her kids to Dorset for the weekend to see her parents. Jemma was stuck for childcare. There was nobody she could turn to for help with looking after Matthew at such short notice. She would have to take Matthew into work with her. Going through today's appointments, she realised she could cancel them all apart from one first thing this morning. One hour of being bored would not kill her six-year-old; the nurses in the children's Outpatients would make a fuss of him, and there were toys to play with. Then she would have to take the rest of the day off to look after him, which meant more time away from work and handing her patients over to one of the other consultants. Sometimes single parenthood felt like being one of Matthew's toys, a rubber man whose arms you stretched to breaking point. When she was at work, she felt guilty about leaving early, and when she had to fetch Matthew late from school, she felt bad about leaving him there. She wasn't doing her job well, and she wasn't being a good mother either.

They stopped at the newsagent's on the way to the hospital to buy Matthew a comic. The newsagent was an old Indian woman whose face lit up whenever Matthew came in. They had a ritual where Matthew would tell her a joke. "A man and a woman fell down a well. Which one got out first?" Matthew asked shyly. Mrs Sharma said she didn't know. Jemma listened as she put some coins down on the newspaper pile. "The woman, because she had a ladder in her stocking," Matthew replied. Jemma could tell Matthew did not really understand the punchline. The Indian woman offered Matthew one of the cheap sweets she kept on the counter for schoolchildren spending their pocket money. Jemma nodded and said, "Say thank you, Matthew" while glancing at her watch. Matthew unwrapped the penny sweet and put it in his mouth. They were already late.

Outside it felt cold enough to snow. Walking up Fulham Road towards the hospital, Jemma could see that a crowd had gathered outside the main entrance. Perhaps somebody famous had arrived: politicians were always holding up St Luke's as a beacon of the NHS. Or maybe a reality television star. She lifted up her eyes and followed what the crowd was looking at: a woman was standing on the edge of the roof dressed in a hospital nightgown. Her heart lurched when she realised it was Renee, the South African estate agent who had once been her patient. She looked poised to jump. Oh my God, why wasn't there anybody up there with her?

Cars hooted as Jemma dragged Matthew across Fulham Road. How had Renee managed to get on the roof? Was there anybody up there trying to talk her down? She hadn't seen anybody. Renee was George's patient. Perhaps he was on the roof with her.

The receptionist slowly looked up as Jemma slammed both hands down on the desk. Would anything ever shake this woman out of her complacency?

"How can I help you?"

"I need you to page Doctor Malvern. Urgently. A patient of his is on the roof. I think she's going to jump. Alert security."

The woman nodded as if this happened every day and reached for the internal telephone. Jemma stood there, impatiently holding Matthew's hand. There was no reply after seven or eight rings. The receptionist shook her head and replaced the handset.

Jemma realised that she would have to go and find George. She was conflicted between searching for the hospital psychiatrist and going up onto the roof herself. Somebody had to talk Renee down. She grabbed Matthew's hand, and together they hurried along the ground-floor atrium to the cafe.

Sitting Matthew down at a table, she looked into his face

and told him she would be back in a few minutes. She had to go and find Doctor George, remember, the man they went to the park with? Matthew nodded.

Then she started running.

One of the security guards who worked on reception was already ahead of her. They were both heading for the lift. She remembered him telling her that his name was Bart and that his family had fled Uganda in the seventies.

"Wait," Jemma called. "I'm coming with you."

People on the ground floor dropped away as the lift ascended.

"What I don't understand," Jemma said, "is how she got up on the roof on the first place."

"I do not understand either. That door is alarmed."

A stairwell she hadn't noticed before led from the top floor to the rooftop. Jemma and Bart clattered up the stairs, pushing the door open onto a roof cluttered with pipes and ceiling vents. There was nobody up there apart from Renee, who was standing on the parapet dressed only in a hospital nightgown. Large feathery snowflakes began drifting from the sky. She must have been freezing.

"Renee, come down. You don't want to do this," Jemma called.

Renee turned around when she heard Jemma's voice. Now the balls of her feet were over the drop. One false move and she would plunge over the edge.

"Doctor Sands, I kept trying to tell you, but nobody listens to me."

Wind whipped her nightgown, which she hugged to herself.

"I'm listening to you now."

"Don't you understand? I'm all wrong inside. I'm so tired of it, and it makes me feel sick. I don't think I even like you anymore."

Her feet shuffled a little closer to the edge. The soles of her feet looked raw, and the parapet was icy. Jemma felt sick just looking at her. The pavement was six stories beneath them.

"This is all in your head, Renee," Jemma said. "Here, take my hand. You have my word no harm will come to you."

The surgeon held out her hand towards the young mother.

"Do you know what it feels like? You're going to fall off the step, and yes, you're going to hell because it's so far, and you're so little. You see, there's a pill that makes you big like Alice, and then you're a mouse, and you can't get out of the running wheel because somebody's coming after you."

Jemma remembered the name of the drug George had prescribed for her, the antidepressant she had never even heard of, the one Renee was being weaned off. Usually the hospital doled out citalopram, the cheapest anti-depressant on the market. Whatever it was, Renee was clearly having a terrible reaction to it. George had promised he was cutting down on the dosage, and now this had happened.

"Renee, please. Take my hand."

Renee pushed some hair away from her face. "I just want it to stop."

Jemma said, "I promise. You won't have to take those pills anymore." She stretched out her fingers even farther.

Renee finally stepped on to the gravel, and Jemma put both arms round the frightened young woman, hugging her tight. She could feel how cold she was beneath the hospital nightgown. A snowflake landed on Jemma's shoulder like a benediction. Renee started crying. "You won't have to take those filthy pills again, okay?" Jemma said, leading her back across the roof. Inside, she was seething at George for letting one of his patients get into this state. First, she was going to give George a piece of her mind and then she was going to tell Tony what had happened – until she remembered that he was away at some medical conference that morning.

Nurse Agyemang and another colleague were waiting in the stairwell ready to take Renee downstairs. At the same time George was coming up round the corner. He looked as if he had seen a ghost.

"I'm so sorry," he said. "I was across the road when my pager bleeped–"

"How could you let one of your patients get up onto the roof like this? I've never seen somebody in such a state. The poor girl was terrified." She was about to question him about the prescription when she remembered that Matthew was still downstairs where she had left him. "George, I haven't got time to get into this right now. You haven't heard the last of this, believe me." She felt so angry with him she could hardly speak.

She strained to see her little boy beneath her as the lift descended. It seemed to take forever going back down. She felt a little grain of personal terror growing inside her.

When she got to the café, Matthew was not where she had left him. The gnawing feeling got stronger.

Matthew had disappeared.

There was a hollow, painful feeling in her stomach as she walked up to the café counter. The teenage girl behind the till was chatting to her friend. "Excuse me," Jemma interrupted. "Have you seen my son? He was sitting right over there." The surgeon gestured to the empty table. The girl looked at Jemma strangely. "But you came to collect him," she said. "I remember seeing you."

Panic caught the back of Jemma's throat.

Not wanting to waste any more time talking, Jemma set off along the ground floor, scanning left and right. What did the girl mean, I remember seeing you? Matthew must have just wandered off to look at something, she reasoned – children do it all the time. All that stuff you read in papers about paedophiles preying on toddlers was just scaremongering. Please God, don't let anything have happened to him, she thought, I love my little boy so much. He had gone missing once in a department store, and there had been an awful five minutes where she had not known where he was. She was almost in tears when he came round the corner, holding the hand of a woman from the perfume counter and looking pleased as punch. She hadn't known whether to shake the living daylights out of him or hug him close and never let him go.

She broke into a controlled run, not wanting people to know that inside she was panicking. Then, not caring what anybody thought, she started calling out Matthew's name. Still nothing. She stood there with visitors streaming past her, not knowing which way to turn.

Bart, the security guard who had been with her on the roof, ambled up asking if anything was wrong. "It's my son. He's gone missing. I left him in the café, and now he's gone." Bart looked at her with his soft, cow-like eyes and said he would telephone his boss. He spoke into his walkie-talkie and together they waited. The radio squawked back and Bart shook his head. Matthew had not been handed in to his colleagues in security.

"He has probably just wandered off. He will be back soon."

"Look, I know you're just trying to keep me calm, but the problem is that my son is missing. People do things to little children. Sick things. Do you understand?"

Glancing up, she noticed the black bulb of the closed-circuit television camera above them. Of course, CCTV cameras would have been watching the café. Every corner of the hospital was monitored.

They found Renfield, the hospital's head of IT, in his junkyard of broken computer equipment. He smiled when he saw Jemma, flashing his gold tooth.

"My son has gone missing. I left him in the café, and now he's gone. Can you find out where he's wandered off to?"

"Nowt can 'appen in this place without it being on bloody CCTV. Surveillance bloody Britain this is. Don't worry, luv, we'll find your kid."

Jemma felt so relieved she could have kissed him.

Three minutes later, Bart was standing beside her in the cramped CCTV surveillance room. Renfield was facing a bank of monitors showing the hospital from every angle. Views blinked between busy corridors and empty stairwells. "He was sitting on his own in the café," Jemma said, resting her hand on Renfield's shoulder. Please, please find my little boy. Renfield flicked to an overhead view of the café showing customers blurrily walking up to the counter. Matthew's table was clearly visible. Another couple was sitting at it now. "That's it," she said excitedly. "That's the one where he was sitting. Now go back five minutes." Parallel white lines zigzagged on screen as the feed rewound. People walked crazily backwards in and out of frame. Now the table was empty and then, right there, was her little boy. The machine clunked to a stop. Renfield twisted the dial, edging the CCTV footage forward. Matthew was sitting reading his comic when a woman in a white doctor's coat walked up to her son, keeping her back to the camera. Jemma noticed that, like her, she wore her blonde hair short. They spoke for a bit before Matthew hopped down and the woman led him away by the hand.

The reality of who had kidnapped her son knifed in.

The woman on television was Jemma Sands.

Somehow, Jemma herself was the woman on the CCTV footage.

CHAPTER TWENTY-ONE

THERE WERE SIX OF THEM in the back of the Bedford. Nobody spoke as the van swayed from side to side. Every day SO19, the armed division of the Metropolitan Police, raided at least three homes in London. It was always like this on the way to a dig-out. Apprehension. Just wanting to get the job over with. They were on their way to arrest a couple of Jamaicans suspected of murdering another gang member. Detective Chief Inspector Niall Walker's job was to find the murder weapon.

The van stopped. The back door opened and DCI Walker stepped out gingerly, feeling every one of his forty-eight years. They were parked beneath a White City tower block, one of those seventies' council monstrosities that the lads sniggeringly referred to as self-cleaning ovens. There were so many shootings here, they joked, why not just let them get on with it?

All four SO19 officers jogged to the tower block entrance. Walker and his detective inspector, Reggie Balogun, hung back. Balogun, who was in his early thirties, had been brought up single-handedly by his mother on a west London housing estate just like this one. Like many of the kids on his estate, Balogun had never known his father. He had fallen in with a gang and was arrested at the age of thirteen for carrying a knife. That had been enough for his mother, who got them out of the estate and moved to a suburb in east London. She wasn't going to see her son become another knife-crime statistic. The way Balogun told it, he had been raised by the local evangelical church. The complaint that there wasn't much difference between police and criminals rang true in his case. Balogun admitted that if it hadn't been for the Met, he would have been a gang leader or in jail, or even dead by now. Still, there was a simmering anger about his DI that Walker was mindful of. Which was why, he guessed, his detective superintendent had thrown them together. Good cop, bad cop.

The sergeant signalled for two of his men to take the stairs up to the ninth floor. The method-of-entry officer holding the battering ram would take the lift with Walker and Balogun.

The lift slid up the building: one, two, three, four... Grey metal walls covered with obscene graffiti greeted them. The sergeant mimed to his colleague with the battering ram to go first.

The flat under surveillance was diagonally across the hall. The MOE man stood poised with the battering ram on one side of the front door. Nicknamed The Enforcer, the red battering ram weighed nearly sixty pounds. The sergeant put his head around the stairwell and nodded to the other two waiting on the stairs before taking up position himself. Raising his hand in the air, he counted down with his fingers. Three. Two. One.

The battering ram slammed into the front door, nearly taking it off its hinges on first impact. The MOE officer swung the post back for a second attempt. This time the sergeant helped by kicking in what was left of the panel, and the door gave way completely. Both officers charged over it, crunching glass underfoot. The two Murder Squad detectives followed close behind. The armed police swept the hall with their guns, practised moves falling into place. Eyes everywhere. All communication done through hand signals. Cover here. Move there. Identify, locate, contain. One of the Jamaicans might spring out from behind a door, blasting them with a sawn-off shotgun.

Walker heard shouting behind him. Balogun had burst into a bedroom and must have found a suspect in bed. Balogun enjoyed violence. Now he was yelling, "Show me your hands. Show me your hands. Now."

Walker finished checking whether anybody was hiding in the sitting room. Clear. He turned back to the bedroom, where the suspect was sitting up in bed. "Get down on the floor. On your face," Balogun said. The Jamaican raised his arms as he clambered out of bed, too slowly for the DI's liking. "Get down on the floor," he repeated, pulling him to the ground. "I have rights," the yardie shouted. He squatted on his hands and knees wearing only his underpants. The copper pushed him down farther, putting his boot between the shoulder blades.

"Just hold there and shut up."

"I got rights, you know."

"Switch on, shut up and do what you're told."

The DI pulled out a pair of plasticuffs, quickly handcuffing him behind his back.

"Bedroom one, clear."

"Sitting room, clear. Kitchen, clear."

The back-up constables hustled both suspects out of the flat. Methodically, the two other policemen overturned the rest of the flat, pulling books out of bookshelves, upending drawers and ripping sofa cushions.

An hour later, the two detectives had found no trace of a murder weapon. The place was ransacked: clothes strewn over bedroom floors, the sitting room a mess of feathers and upended furniture, the kitchen linoleum slicked with oily foodstuffs. Nothing.

Balogun walked into the kitchen, carefully avoiding the mess.

"Complete waste of time," he said.

"We know he didn't get rid of the sword in the pub. He was seen carrying it into the building."

"He must have chucked it in the river by now."

Walker took one last look at the filthy cooker congealed with fat and the sagging kitchen units. As they walked back down the hall, a floorboard creaked beneath his shoe. He stopped.

"Go round the other flats and see if any of them have hammer and chisels. I want these floorboards taken up."

They rolled up the hall carpet and set to work banging and hammering as they levered up each floorboard. By mid-morning most of the floor was exposed, showing brass central heating pipes running along the length of the hall. They had been pulling up floorboards for a couple of hours now, and Walker felt tired. He strained with the effort of levering up one plank but finally it came, throwing him off balance. He landed on his bottom, which made Balogun laugh.

There, lying in dust and dirt between ceiling joists, was something hidden in a bin liner. Walker reached in and pulled it out. Wrapped inside was a nasty looking machete smeared with dried blood.

"Would you look at that?" Walker said.

"Bingo. His prints must be all over it."

"Send it to forensics to see if there's a blood match. Even if it's not the victim's, it'll be some other poor bastard's."

Walker's mobile trilled in his jacket hanging on the back of the door. Getting up off his knees to answer it, he wished he had time to wash his hands.

"DCI Walker."

It was his detective superintendent on the phone. "Niall, a kid's gone missing at St Luke's Hospital. It's been a couple of hours now and he hasn't turned up. We've got uniformed officers combing the building. I want you to get down there and talk to the mother. She's a doctor at the hospital."

Walker understood why the DS was calling in homicide: The murder squad was automatically brought in to handle any misper case involving a child. Any child who had been missing for more than three hours was always treated as a murder victim.

CHAPTER TWENTY-TWO

TOPPY'S HEART THUMPED AS SHE came out of the hospital revolving door holding the little boy's hand. Her mouth felt dry as she gripped his trusting fingers. Surely everybody must be able to hear her heart pounding. Any moment now she expected to feel a hand on her shoulder as they walked quickly to where her car was parked. It had all been so ridiculously easy.

Toppy had been watching Jemma and her son for days. How she envied this woman doctor with her beautiful son. Toppy would never know what it was like to take her child to school. She felt faint imagining the smell of her unborn son's sweet-smelling hair, the feel of his body and the touch of his skin.

This woman had taken all that away from her. Her hatred of Doctor Jemma Sands knew no bounds. First, Toppy had taken her husband, and now she would steal the person she loved even more. Jemma Sands was going to be made to suffer. Only then would she understand the hurt she had inflicted.

Toppy had been watching their entire routine, from when they woke up in the morning to when Jemma took

Matthew shopping at Sainsbury's. She had thought about taking him from the supermarket; Doctor Sands had a habit of leaving her son on his own reading comics by the entrance while she went round the aisles. This morning she had followed them into the hospital and saw Jemma leave her little boy in the café. It was now or never. And now, here he was, walking along the wintry pavement with his hand in hers, apparently completely trusting that she had come back from the dead.

When Tony Sands told her that he planned to fund their new life together out of the proceeds of the fast-tracked drugs trial, she knew what she had to do. She had to have that money. Tony knew nothing about what she had in mind for his little family. He thought that she loved him, but there was an oiliness about Tony Sands that made her skin crawl. She despised him.

For a moment she couldn't feel the safety deposit box key in her hip pocket, and her heart lurched until she patted it again to make sure. Passers-by jostled past, barely giving them a second glance. A Salvation Army band was playing Silent Night on the street corner. Just another mother and son out shopping on a wintry December morning. Her mouth felt dry with apprehension. Any moment now somebody would raise the alarm, and the whole thing would be over.

They walked to the side street where she had left her rented car, and Toppy blipped it open and got into it quickly.

"Where are we going?" Matthew asked as she pushed him into the passenger seat, buckling his safety belt.

"I told you. Mummy wants me to look after you until she comes home from work. First, you're going to have your photograph taken. Would you like that?"

"Mum told me to wait for her."

"I'm going to take you to where I live. There are toys for you to play with."

Toppy fought her instinct to get away from there as fast as possible. She didn't want to draw attention to herself. Instead, she drove carefully up through Earls Court and out towards Shepherd's Bush and Acton, constantly checking her rear-view mirror.

The first thing they would need if they were going to get out of the country was passports. She had already thought about that. They were on their way to the west London council estate where she had been told she could buy everything she needed.

The wail of the siren cut through her like a knife.

Panicking, she almost didn't dare check her rear-view mirror. The noise was so loud it almost hurt as the ambulance worked its way through the crawling traffic. The car in front pulled over and she did the same, keeping her head down.

That half-hour drive out to Acton felt like hours. Eventually they parked beneath one of the bleak tower blocks and she led Matthew by the hand up the concrete steps, afraid of being spotted. The stairwell smelt of piss and vomit. Kids shouted below as they walked along the windswept gantry, and a football rattled a chain-link fence. Toppy stopped and looked over the balcony, where a group of teenagers, their faces covered and some of them on bicycles, was gathering round her hire car. In their hoodies and tracksuits they looked like dead people.

The council flat where she'd been told she could get passports was right at the end of the walkway. A CCTV camera overlooked the approach to the flat, so they were obviously being watched. Toppy knocked on the metal door behind the barred gate. A young boy, who could have been only a few years older than Matthew, peered out from inside with a sullen, starved look.

"We're here to see Goldie."

"Dad," the boy called. "We got visitors."

The council flat looked more like a warehouse than a home. Boxes stacked everywhere. Blu-ray players. Laptops. PlayStations. Most of the stuff was stolen by junkies needing quick cash. It would all end up on eBay within a few days.

Toppy caught a glimpse of a teenage girl hiding behind a bead curtain.

Goldie came out. From his nickname, she had expected a Jamaican gangsta, all tattoos and gold teeth. Instead,

Goldie was an overweight, middle-aged white man swaddled in black pyjamas. His feet were bare, which unsettled her. He padded up to Toppy and Matthew, extending a hand. There was a softness about him that was repellent.

"We need passports. I called earlier."

"Did you bring photos with you?"

Goldie spoke with a touch of a lisp, and he sounded a bit asthmatic.

Toppy shook her head. "We need to get them taken here."

"Not a problem."

"How much will they cost?"

"A grand each. Half now and half on delivery."

"That's a lot of money."

"Things cost if you want good work. You won't get any hassle."

"How long will they take?"

"My lad will bring them to you. I don't want you coming here again. The two of you can arrange to meet."

"That'll take too long. I need them quicker than that. Can you do them in three days?"

"That will cost you more."

"How much are we talking about?"

"Three grand."

"I've got only a thousand on me. I'll give your son the rest."

Matthew sat on a stool in front of the wall while Goldie tried taking his photograph. Although the six-year-old didn't know what was going on, he was already beginning to look upset. "I want my mummy," he said. His eyes brimmed as Goldie tried taking his photo with a camera on a tripod. "I can't do anything with him if he's crying. Can't you get him to stop?" Goldie complained. Toppy promised Matthew an ice cream if he gave them a smile. Matthew nodded and did his best to look happy. He still looked like a frightened little boy and, for the first time, she felt a pang of misgiving.

Not for long, however. It was all Jemma's fault for doing this to her, she reasoned. Jemma Sands had been in a hurry to get rid of her baby, so she was taking hers. Tit for tat. She imagined the two of them together on a beach somewhere in the Far East, Matthew happily playing in the sand while she watched him. He would not remember what had happened. Like with a circumcision, he would still be too young to register the pain.

Watching him have his photograph taken, Toppy's mind shifted to the night she had faked her own death. Bubbles had exploded around her as she righted herself and floated back up to the surface, her head breaking the water as she sucked in stale rubbery air. How odd the scuba-tank mouthpiece had felt between her teeth. She needed to get away from the lights of the pleasure cruiser, which was rocking from side to side in the storm. Rain was sheeting down. It had taken her an hour to swim back to the island, and the only sound had been the suck of oxygen. She had hauled herself out of the shallows and collapsed on the beach breaded in sand.

"That's better," Goldie cooed from behind the camera.

It was time to go. Goldie's boy told Toppy he would meet her at the bandstand on Wormwood Scrubs common on Wednesday. They would complete the handover then. Toppy wanted to get out of here as quickly as she could.

Waiting to be let out, Toppy looked up and saw two schoolchildren standing outside on the CCTV monitor. "I'll see you on Wednesday, then?" she said to Goldie's son, who nodded and opened up the barred gate and then the metal door. Both boys waiting were dressed in school uniform. Goldie padded up and glanced to see if anybody was looking, fluttering his fingers. "Hey, mister, have you got any trips?" one of the kids asked. He could not have been more than eleven. Goldie smiled and beckoned them inside.

An old woman was scrubbing her doorstep as Toppy and Matthew hurried along the walkway. She lifted her head and scowled. Toppy hugged Matthew, glad his face was hidden in a hoodie. Would he cry out and give them away? "I know what goes on in there," the old woman said. She stared after them with watery blue eyes, muttered something and went back to scrubbing her front step.

The house Toppy had rented was only a ten-minute drive away.

A couple of kids playing in the street stared as she parked the car. This northwest London street looked ready for demolition. Some of the other mock Tudor houses were burnt out and had metal sheets over their windows. Even the bricked-up windows had graffiti on them.

"I don't think my mum wants me to be here," Matthew said.

"I told you. Mummy is going to come here later. She wants me to look after you until she picks you up."

"Please could I phone her? I want to speak to my mum."

"Are you stupid or something? I told you. Your mother's really busy."

There was a moment when he looked stung by what she'd just said. His face screwed up and he started bawling. It only made her want to hit him even more: anything to shut him up.

Matthew was still snivelling as Toppy let them into the house. An overpowering smell of cat piss greeted them as the front door shuddered open. The previous occupant had been a widower who had let the house rot when his wife died. The landlord had accepted cash and hadn't asked for any references or paperwork, only too pleased to find somebody to rent the house before it was knocked down. The walls were painted a sickly green, and the kitchen had an indefinable, rancid smell. Muddy newspapers were strewn on the kitchen linoleum. You felt dirty just standing there.

"There are some toys in the bedroom upstairs. Would you like something to drink?"

Matthew didn't say anything.

"You run upstairs and I'll bring it up to you."

Toppy watched the milk rise and skin over in the pan. Matthew would be fast asleep soon after he had this, she thought, stirring sleeping pills into his drink.

Matthew was upstairs in the bedroom playing with the toy cars on the filthy carpet. They were going to be there only a few days. What did a bit of dirt matter?

"Here. Take this mug. I've put some cold milk in it to cool it down."

"It's too hot."

"I'll sit here and watch you drink it. Do you like the toys I bought you?"

"When is my mummy coming? I want to go home."

"Mummy phoned to say that she's only going to be a bit longer."

Downstairs she waited by the kitchen window, looking out over an ugly rubbish-strewn patio until she could be sure he was asleep.

When she went back upstairs, Matthew had fallen over on the carpet where she had left him. She lifted him onto the bed with its filthy sheets. Unbuckling his trousers, she noticed a sour smell from where he had wet himself.

Closing his bedroom door softly, Toppy swung the hasp shut and padlocked it.

He was hers now.

CHAPTER TWENTY-THREE

MATTHEW HAD BEEN MISSING FOR an hour. Tony had gone off to a conference of NHS executives in Birmingham that morning. How do you tell a father that his son has gone missing, and that it is all your fault? Voicemail. Tony's rich voice told Jemma to leave a message. Relieved she did not have to speak to him, she asked Tony to phone her back.

She resumed her seat in the corner office of Christine Matlock, Tony's deputy chief executive. They had been told to wait for the detective chief inspector. The police had arrived quickly once they knew a child had disappeared. They were combing the hospital for her little boy right now. She dared to hope it would be only a couple of hours before they found him.

There was a soft knock behind her, and a middle-aged man put his head round the door. "Christine Matlock?" he asked. "DCI Walker. Notting Hill CID. Your reception told me to come straight up." Both women got to their feet.

The policeman had the oddest face: his oversized features and large blue eyes made him look like a garden gnome come to life. Vain, too. Jemma noticed that he was so worried about losing his hair that he'd had a hair transplant; tuft extensions were planted across the top of his head.

The DCI stepped in to the room accompanied by a younger black man dressed in a sharp-looking Prince of Wales-check suit.

"This is my colleague, DI Balogun. You must be the mother," the detective said, turning to Jemma. There was an Ulster bark to his voice.

"Yes, this is Doctor Sands," said Matlock. "It's her little boy who's gone missing."

Matlock came round from behind her desk, and all four of them sat down at the circular conference table.

Walker said, "Doctor Sands, please would you tell me what's happened?"

Jemma went through the whole story again: from bringing Matthew to the hospital, to Renee threatening to jump from the roof and to discovering Matthew was not where she had left him.

"The important thing is that you've acted quickly," Walker said. "The more we do now, the quicker we'll find your son. Doctor Sands, the truth is that children going missing are as rare as wooden horse droppings. If we wait a few hours, I am sure he will turn up, just you see. After all, this hospital is about the size of the QE2."

"Yes," Jemma said, "but what about the woman on the

CCTV footage? This isn't about Matthew wandering off. Somebody has taken my son."

Walker looked puzzled and glanced at the other policeman.

"Didn't they tell you?" Matlock said. "We already know that a woman has taken Doctor Sands' son."

They stood over the deputy chief executive's desk watching the CCTV footage that Renfield had burned onto a disc. Jemma felt anxiety pooling in her stomach as they reached the moment when this woman, her doppelganger, walked up to the café table. There was something about her she recognised, something in the way she moved: more like a glide than an ordinary walk. Jemma racked her brains trying to think where she had seen her before. It wasn't just because they looked so much alike, there was something else about her, something... "Look how she's keeping her back to the camera the entire time. She knows where the CCTV camera is," Walker commented. Matthew looked up and there, right there, Jemma knew in her heart who this woman was.

Toppy Mrazek.

Of course. This woman who had taken her husband. It was so obvious. Except that Toppy Mrazek was missing, presumed dead, wasn't she? Jemma felt the jigsaw pieces clicking into place. "Do you have any idea who this woman is?" Walker said. "Do you have any enemies? Why would somebody want to kidnap your son?" Jemma's mind was screaming, yes, I know exactly who this woman is. It's

Toppy Mrazek, the person who has tried to destroy my life, before she realised how mad this sounded.

"You can steal a doctor's coat from anywhere," said Matlock.

"I understand from the statement you gave to the PC that you and the boy's father are separated. Most missing person cases involving children usually turn out to be one parent taking the child away to hurt the other."

Matlock interrupted. "I am sorry, but I cannot allow that statement to go unchallenged. Tony Sands is chief executive of this hospital," she said. "In any case, he couldn't have anything to do with this. He's away at a conference in Birmingham."

Jemma shook her head, "Christine's right. No, it's not like that. Tony has nothing to do with this. We might be separated, but we get on for Matthew's sake."

"Is there anybody else you can think of who has a grudge against you? Who would want to hurt you like this?"

"Yes," Jemma said. "I know exactly who has stolen my son."

Both policemen leaned forward and Jemma's mobile started vibrating in her lap. Looking down, the caller ID said it was Tony. Putting the phone to her ear, she mouthed "Tony" to Matlock and mimed an apology to the policemen. Stepping out of the office, she closed the door behind her.

This was the moment she had dreaded.

"I got a missed call from you," Tony said. Everything all right?"

"Tony, it's Matthew. He's gone missing."

"What do you mean, 'gone missing'? Where are you? I thought he was at home today with the au pair."

"She had to go back home to see her mother. I had to bring Matthew in to work. Tony, I…"

"So you're at the hospital now? How long's he been missing?"

"An hour. The police say he'll turn up any minute."

"Christ, Jemma, how could you…"

"I had to leave him in the café while I dealt with an emergency. One of George's patients had climbed onto the roof and…"

"You left our six-year-old son on his own? What were you thinking?"

"There wasn't anybody else who could look after him."

She realised how defensive she sounded. "The police are certain he'll turn up if we just wait."

"How could you leave him on his own like that?"

"What do you want me to say, Tony? I would crawl over broken glass if I thought it would make things better. That's not going to help bring Matthew back, is it? We need to be calm."

She pictured Tony staring at the hideously swirly carpet of his Midlands hotel. She thought about telling him that she already knew who had stolen their son and how crazy it sounded. No, not yet. There was silence on the other end.

"Tony... hello?"

"I was thinking," he paused. "I'll come straight down. I should be back at the hospital in three or four hours."

"Tony, there's no point. It's not as if either of us can do anything. Matthew will probably have turned up by then, I hope to God."

"So you're saying there's nothing either of us can do? That we just have to wait?"

"Think about it. We just have to sit tight. Remember that time he wandered off on holiday?" she said, trying to sound confident. Inside, she felt as if she was going to sick. Then it had been five minutes that felt like an hour. Now it was much, much worse.

She rang off, promising to call the moment she had news. Why couldn't she tell him that their son hadn't just wandered off, that this was kidnap? And that she knew exactly who was doing this to them? Well, he would find out soon enough. Right now, though, this was a conversation she did not want to get into.

Back with the two detectives, Walker resumed his questioning.

"So, you were saying," Walker said. "You know the woman

who has taken your son."

"Her name is Toppy Mrazek. She's my husband's girlfriend." She spoke with the exaggerated calm of somebody in shock.

Walker sat with his pen poised over his notebook. "What's her address? Where can we find her? Do you have a phone number?"

"She went missing at sea this summer. Presumed drowned."

Both men exchanged a look and Walker leaned forward. "You're in shock, everybody understands that. So what are you saying? That your husband's girlfriend who drowned has come back from the dead?"

Jemma slapped her hand down on the table. "Don't patronise me. I know what I'm saying. She must have faked her death so that people like you think this way. If everybody thinks that she's dead, why go looking for her?"

Matlock looked concerned but did her best to support her staff member. "Toppy Mrazek was a patient of Doctor Sands. There were complications after she lost her baby. Doctor Sands saved her life."

"Sounds like a funny way of repaying you," said Balogun.

"There was nothing I could do to save the child," Jemma said. "She's hated me ever since. That's why she started having an affair with my husband. This is revenge."

Walker said, "Doctor Sands. Take a step back. Ninety-nine

per cent of the time the child turns up within a few hours."

DCI Walker was wrong.

Matthew did not turn up either at the hospital or a police station.

The police drove Jemma home. Walker had told Jemma that if Matthew hadn't turned up by morning he wanted to hold a press conference as soon as possible. He called it feeding the dogs. Walker told her frankly that a middle-class woman like Jemma and an attractive child like Matthew would get a big response. It was the Afro-Caribbean and Eastern European children that they really had to fight to get media coverage for, he said bluntly. Somebody out there must know something; you don't just steal a child and vanish into thin air, Walker reassured her. All it needed was for one person to come forward and say they knew who the woman on CCTV was. But what if the suspect you were looking for was dead already, Jemma wondered.

As they drove past Holland Park, she remembered happy afternoons she and Matthew had spent there: watching Matthew crouched over the sandpit, or pushing him on a swing as he said laughing, "Higher, Mummy, higher." Memories that made her chest hurt. Now she imagined him sitting withdrawn in a corner, his knees drawn up against his chest, with a dark patch on his jeans.

The first thing she did when she got home was climb the stairs to Matthew's bedroom. She had to do this. Opening the door, Jemma stood there, letting her eyes rest on his single bed with the patchwork quilt she had made for him. Nothing had changed. Everything was still waiting for him. His Thomas the Tank Engine books were propped up in a row on the bookshelf, and his teddy bear lay on his pillow. She reached down and picked up the cuddly toy. It smelled of him.

The doorbell rang and Jemma hurried downstairs. Tony had taken the first train down from Birmingham that he could. They hugged and for once she was grateful for the touch of his body. She led him into the sitting room.

Tony said, "First Toppy goes missing at sea, and now this. You read about this stuff in the papers and think, how unlucky can one family be. It's like we've been hit by lightning."

"Tony, there's something I need to tell you," she said, not quite knowing where to begin. The hell with it. She would just plunge in and tell him the truth. "Tony... I know who has stolen our son."

"Yes, the police said that they've got it all on CCTV. The officer I spoke to told me they were checking all the cameras outside the hospital."

"No, it's not that. What I mean is that I know who she is. Tony, it's Toppy."

Tony frowned and said, "That's ridiculous. Toppy's dead. Even the French police now accept that."

"No, Tony, that's not true. Her body was never recovered. Don't you see, the woman on CCTV is your girlfriend. She's torturing me for taking Matthew. This has been her plan all along. First, she steals you from me, and then she takes my son."

"Jemma, this is crazy talk. Toppy drowned at sea on holiday. I know that you're obsessed with her and, look, I'm sorry about everything that happened, but you have to let it go."

"I'm telling you that she's still alive and that she's taken our son. Why won't you believe me?"

"Jemma, listen," Tony said, taking a step towards her. "You're in shock. We both are."

"For God's sake, don't you patronise me as well. First the police, now you. I'm telling you that Toppy is alive and that she has our son."

"What evidence do you have?"

"You saw the CCTV footage. She's dyed her hair to look like me. Can't you see that it's her?"

"I saw a woman who looks vaguely like you, yes. But do you realise how crazy you sound?"

Jemma sat down on the sofa and covered her face with her hands. "I'm going out of my mind. I don't know what to do."

Tony sat down beside her and gently placed his hand on her knee. "All right. Supposing Toppy has taken our son, now what? What are you proposing?"

"I told the police what I think. They're keeping an open mind. All we can do is wait. The police will want us both at the press conference tomorrow. Let's hope to God that Matthew has turned up by then."

Tony took one of Jemma's hands away from her face. "Jemma, listen to me. I'm truly sorry for what I did, for bringing Toppy into our lives, I mean. I wish it had never happened. We have to be strong for each other. For Matthew."

Jemma nodded, recovering. Despite everything, he was still the father of her child. Together they would get through this. Somehow.

Once Tony had left, Jemma spent the rest of the night willing the telephone to ring. Any moment now the police would tell her they had found her darling. She was sure of it. Her sense of guilt was overpowering, though. Lurid images filled her head of those two boys leading Jamie Bulger away by the hand, or Myra Hindley staring at the camera with her brassy peroxide bouffant. Her last memory of Matthew was of watching him sitting at the café table, poring over his comic. Now she realised that Toppy Mrazek had been watching him, too. She imagined herself running up to them and grabbing Toppy by the shoulder, saving Matthew before it was too late.

The next morning it was hard putting one foot in front of the other. Jemma had to try and get on with normal life, she knew that. It felt like being on a tightrope. All she could do was keep looking straight ahead and never down. Parting the bedroom curtains, she spotted three men in bulky down jackets standing outside, their breath steaming in the cold. One of them looked up. So somebody had tipped off the press already.

Jemma kept the curtains drawn for the rest of the morning. The telephone kept ringing, but she never answered. She was too afraid of who it might be. Instead, she sat rooted in the darkened room compulsively checking her BlackBerry for the text Walker said he would send. She felt numb, unable to move. Her anxiety made it painful to breathe, and the compass dial in her mind swung wildly from one scenario to another.

So it was a relief when there was a knock at the door. Jemma had lost track of how long she had been sitting there. Walker had told her that a family liaison officer would be coming to see her. She got up from the sofa and parted the curtain cautiously. Her neighbour Emily turned when she saw the movement.

"My God, Jemma, are you all right?" she said as Jemma let her in. Jemma shut the door quickly. "I only just heard on the news," Emily said. "You must be going out of your mind. When did you realise Matthew had gone missing?"

"Yesterday. At the hospital. I had to take him in to work with me because Eliska has gone home for Christmas. I left him alone in the café for five minutes. There was an emergency. He had gone by the time I came back."

"What do the police say?"

"Most missing children turn up within twenty-four hours. But it's been that already. They're holding a press conference this afternoon. They want me to be there," said Jemma, leading them both into the kitchen. She went through the whole story again, leaving out her suspicion that she already knew who had taken Matthew.

"What else are you doing apart from the press conference? We need to print posters, start a Twitter campaign. Somebody must know who has taken Matthew," said Emily, putting the kettle on.

"I'm just doing what the police tell me to do," replied Jemma dully.

"You can't just sit here waiting for something to happen. You've got to get the word out. The more people who know that Matthew has gone missing, the greater the chances are of finding him."

"I just want to curl up in a ball and wait for this to go away. I've never felt this much pain. It's indescribable."

Emily handed her a cup of tea, which Jemma sipped gratefully. Everything that had happened was so overwhelming; she needed to be looked after. Her neighbour looked at her carefully.

"Jemma, I know you just want to wait until this has all gone away, but you can't. And you can't just rely on the police.

We need to get posters up in everybody's window, like for that Madeleine McCann girl."

Jemma shook her head. "The police have told me not to say anything. They want a news blackout until the press conference."

Emily gestured towards the front door. "It's too late for that. They're already out there. The story's already out there, Jemma. What are you going to do about it?"

"I don't know," she said. "I really don't know."

CHAPTER TWENTY-FOUR

TONY WAS ALREADY IN THE police car that came to collect her that afternoon.

They drove through the blue folding gates of Notting Hill police station, parking alongside a police van.

Walker was waiting for them in a canary-yellow corridor. There were less than twenty minutes to go before the start of the press conference, and Jemma felt faintly ridiculous standing there holding Matthew's singed teddy. The detective had asked if Matthew had a favourite cuddly toy – sentimental objects were very effective, Walker told her.

Tony asked Walker what he wanted him to say during the press conference, and Walker looked down at the blue floor. "I'm sorry," he said. "It would be better if it was just your wife alone. The press doesn't like it when a husband and wife are separated. It confuses the story, and they'll start digging into your private life. We'll just tell them that you're too upset to take part. They'll start digging, and all that business about your girlfriend drowning this summer will come out."

The woman who stole Matthew, Jemma thought. She needed to convince this policeman that Toppy was still alive. Only then would she get her son back. She knew it.

Walker led them to the Murder Squad room, which, with its whiteboard and cheap pine desks, could have been any sales office. Tony sat down to wait on one of the hard blue chairs.

The press conference was surreal, something she had seen so often on TV but never thought she would experience at first hand. Walker sat next to her facing the press, who were mostly younger than she had expected. Their faces were difficult to see beyond the television lights. There was the hubbub of conversation. The reporters gossiped or checked their Dictaphones. Walker tapped his microphone and called for everybody's attention.

"Thank you, ladies and gentlemen of the press, for coming here at such short notice," he began. "We are holding this press conference to bring you up to speed with our investigation into the kidnapping of Matthew Sands. We hope that whoever is holding six-year-old Matthew – or if anybody knows the boy's whereabouts – will step forward. Our first concern is for Matthew's safety." The DCI glanced towards Jemma before continuing. "At approximately nine-fifteen yesterday morning, Matthew was sitting alone in the ground-floor café of St Luke's Hospital in west London when a woman wearing a doctor's coat approached him and led him away by the hand. Closed-circuit television footage shows the two of them leaving the building. We have no further information as to their whereabouts after that. Matthew's mother, Jemma, will now read out a statement on behalf of Matthew's family."

The focus of the room shifted to Jemma, whose hands trembled as she read out what she had been told to say. "Matthew is a sweet, shy and rather nervous boy," she began. "I would like to say a few words to the person who is with Matthew, or has been with Matthew. Please do not scare him. Please let us know where to find Matthew or put him in a place of safety. I beg you to let Matthew come home. I need my Matthew. He's my reason for getting up in the morning. Anybody who knows where he is – and somebody does – please get in touch and bring my Matthew home." Her voice cracked with emotion, and it was hard to swallow. She was determined not to cry, but she rubbed her eye with her finger. Flashbulbs shredded the room.

"Now, we have a few minutes available to answer questions," said Walker. "Yes, over there?"

Beyond the TV lights, she could just make out a youth with his hand in the air.

"Surely whoever took Matthew was tracked outside by CCTV cameras?"

"They would have been, but we have no further images outside the hospital."

Another voice said, "Why do you think the woman who has taken Matthew looks so much like his mother? Do you think it's a coincidence?"

"We're not here to speculate," Walker replied, shielding his eyes.

"I understand the boy's parents are separated. Do you think that has something to do with the case?"

"We will be interviewing all family members as part of our enquiry."

After that, they seemed to compete as to who could ask the rudest question. One suggested Jemma had been negligent leaving Matthew alone in the café. Eventually, an attractive but tough-looking blonde raised her hand. Walker pointed with his finger, as he obviously knew her. "I need some more colour for my readers," she said, glancing at her notes. "Doctor Sands – Jemma – how does it feel to be a mother whose son has gone missing? Can you describe to my readers how you're feeling?"

I need some more colour for my readers? Did she think Jemma was there just to provide copy for her tabloid rubbish? "Right now I feel as if I'm walking through a solid wall of pain," Jemma said hesitantly. "I can't believe it's possible to experience this much agony." There was a murmur of approval as reporters scribbled down her words. They had found tomorrow morning's headline.

Another reporter, emboldened by his colleague, stuck his hand in the air and asked what sort of things Matthew liked. As she was describing his favourite wooden train set, an image of Matthew cuddled next to her on the sofa watching television flashed before her eyes. The thought of never being able to do that again was too awful. Out of the corner of her eye, she noticed a policeman lean down and whisper into Walker's ear. The DCI nodded and wrote something on a piece of notepaper, which he slid across to her. The note said, "He's been found."

CHAPTER TWENTY-FIVE

BLUE-AND-WHITE INCIDENT TAPE CRACKLED IN the wind beyond the police car window. Police officers, some of them wearing crash helmets, stood around talking at the housing estate entrance. Atlee Road was full of parked up cars and vans, their blue lights strobing silently. All the exits had been sealed. Somebody had tipped off the police that Matthew was being held in one of the council houses. They had torn down there, siren wailing, as soon as the press conference had broken up. A lone policewoman was going to knock on the front door of the suspect's house. He was a middle-aged man who was known to the police and on the sex offenders' register. Other people living on the estate had made his life hell once they discovered who he was, regularly smashing his windows and smearing shit on his front door. A couple of lads, one of them on a bicycle, watched Jemma's parked car from the street corner. Her stomach hurt with anxiety until she spotted Walker coming back towards the car. She started to sit up before she realised he was shaking his head.

"I'm sorry, it was a false alarm," he said, getting in beside her. "Prank call. They torment this poor bastard day and night." In her heart she had known Matthew was not there.

No, Toppy Mrazek was out there somewhere, waiting for her. She kept seeing Matthew lying glassy-eyed on a mortuary slab, his skin grey like putty. Her pain, dread and sense of helplessness were as suffocating as a doctor's mask.

"What are you doing about finding the woman I told you about?" Jemma said. "I tell you, she's the one who kidnapped Matthew."

Walker frowned. "Doctor Sands, we've spoken to the French authorities. They are convinced your husband's girlfriend drowned at sea. Apparently it's not unusual for bodies not to be recovered. Your husband's boat was beyond coastal waters."

"So that's it, is it? You're not going to do anything. You know that it's not me on the CCTV footage. I'm telling you, she has my son."

"With respect, the only evidence we have so far is video footage of a woman who looks very much like you taking Matthew. In my experience, once we have eliminated family and friends, we can broaden the search."

Jemma folded her arms and looked out the window. Every minute they wasted, Matthew was getting farther away.

Walker continued, "Look, Doctor Sands, our incident room is getting hundreds of calls. We have to follow up every call, every lead. Believe me, we're going to get your son back. It's just that what you're saying is so... outlandish."

Jemma didn't say another word as they drove her home. Inside she felt stuck, unable to move one way or another.

It was surreal seeing Matthew's face on Sky News that night. The police had asked for a photograph, and she had given them one snapped on the boat during the summer, the most recent one she could find. Matthew was looking off to one side, as if he had just heard something. It was the first photo she had seen of him that showed what he might look like as a young man and now here it was on the evening news.

Guilt pressed down on her like water crushing a diver. She had to convince somebody, just one person, that Toppy was still alive. George had left a message on her voicemail saying he would be at home this evening if she wanted to talk. She telephoned him and said, yes, she couldn't face another night on her own. George offered her supper if she wanted, and she had gratefully accepted; she had hardly eaten anything since Matthew disappeared. Changing for dinner and looking at herself in the full-length mirror she thought, damn you, Toppy Mrazek.

She was walking up to her Subaru, preoccupied with everything that had happened, when a man stepped in front of her. "Doctor Sands?" he asked. He was short and round and wore a Barbour jacket. For some reason, he reminded her of a dumpy comedian she had seen on television, except there was nothing funny about him. "Are you the woman on the TV footage? What have you done with your son?" He kept badgering her as she fiddled with her car keys. "Do you know where your son is, Doctor Sands? The police think that you have something to do with him going missing." Jemma said, "Leave me alone. I've got nothing to say to you." She finally got into the car and locked the doors. "Are you the woman on CCTV, Doctor Sands?" the man called out as she started reversing out of the parking space.

Rattled, she drove over to George's with her mind churning. What did the reporter mean when he said the police believed she had something to do with Matthew's disappearance? Did they honestly think she had kidnapped her own son? What possible reason would she have?

George lived on the second floor of a Victorian mansion block about ten minutes away. A single wrought-iron streetlamp weakly lit up the courtyard as she searched for George's name on the entryphone system. Christ, after everything she had been through today she needed a drink.

The apartment-block landing smelled of fried food, and the walls badly needed repainting. George was standing in his second floor doorway waiting for her.

"They showed a bit of the press conference on the news this evening," he said. "Somebody must know where Matthew is."

Jemma stepped into his hall.

"They've been getting a lot of calls. There are a lot of leads to follow up. The police keep telling me to be patient. They say the more they do now, the faster Matthew will turn up." She suddenly felt terribly tired, and her bones ached.

"Do you want a drink? I've opened a bottle of red wine. I was about to pour myself one."

George led her into his kitchen by the front door. The paintwork looked grubby here, too, and the cupboards were hanging off their hinges. Standing there in George's kitchen, she felt the familiar tension between them. As if reading her mind, George said: "It's rented, so I've never done anything with it. You wouldn't believe how expensive it is."

He handed her a glass of red wine. It tasted velvety and delicious.

"So, how are you feeling?" he asked.

"As if I'm going out of my mind. I don't sleep. I don't eat. Everything I see, everything I touch, reminds me of Matthew."

"Considering everything you're going through, that's hardly surprising. One of my consultants could see you. If you need to talk, the talking cure is often best."

"George, there's something else." She paused. "I know who has taken Matthew. You remember Tony's girlfriend who drowned? Well, I'm convinced it's her. She's come back from the dead to steal my son. I know it sounds absurd."

George looked thoughtful as he sat down at the kitchen

table. "Why would she want to steal your son?" he asked.

"I don't know. Because she's angry and she wants revenge, I suppose. It wasn't enough to steal my husband. Now she has my son as well."

"Have you told anybody else about this? Tony, for instance?"

"Yes. I told him when he came to see me last night. He doesn't believe me. Neither do the police. But I'm telling you, it's her."

"To be honest, Jemma, this all makes you sound a bit unhinged. The wronged woman. I mean, it's not as if you have any proof that – what was her name? Toppy? – had anything to do with this. And didn't you identify her body anyway?"

"It wasn't her. Another tourist had drowned at sea. Don't you see? She planned it this way. First she goes missing, and now she has the perfect alibi."

George rubbed his temples before he spoke. "Jemma, people don't come back from the dead. Look, I've offered you counselling. You're grieving, I understand that. Grief is a funny thing. People I've spoken to say it's like visiting another country. All the illusions you had are stripped away, and you see things as they really are." He paused. "Sometimes that kind of reality can be overwhelming. We need illusions. At the very least we could prescribe you something to help you sleep."

"What, more drugs? Do you want to find me up on the roof like that poor girl yesterday?"

George widened his eyes when Jemma said this. She had never attacked him in this way before. He looked affronted by what she had just said.

Jemma pressed on, "And what is MC4703 anyway? Why did you prescribe it to her? Nothing comes up when you Google it. You said it was a new drug that's been imported from America. Has it even got its FDA licence yet?"

George ran his hands through his hair before replying. "Jemma, before I tell you this, remember I signed a non-disclosure agreement. I could get into a lot of trouble."

"Who cares about the non-disclosure agreement? One of your patients tried to kill herself yesterday."

"Don't you think I know that? All my life, I've tried to help people. I keep replaying in my mind what could have happened if she'd jumped."

"Why don't you tell me what's been going on? This drug you prescribed, where does it come from? Who gave you permission to start prescribing it?"

George suddenly got up from the table, as if he could not bear to sit down any longer. He started pacing the galley kitchen. "It was all Tony's idea. He was contacted by Tri-Med, one of the American pharma companies. It's not up there with Glaxo or Astra-Zeneca, but it's ambitious. Until now they've mostly repackaged other people's drugs whose patents have expired. Anyway, they wanted the hospital to test this new anti-depressant they'd been working on. Replicating their lab tests. The Americans call it 'microwave testing'. They try and do as many drug trials as they can simultaneously around the world before they get a new discovery licensed. They're paranoid about piracy. The results were off the scale, un-fucking-believable – no side effects, no weight gain. All the upside of Prozac and none of the short-term problems. Tony said they were offering the hospital a lot of money to do this, enough to stop him having to make redundancies. You have no idea of the pressure he's put me under to cut the budget."

"So let me get this straight. You agreed to do a trial on an experimental anti-depressant for an American drugs company? A trial without ethics committee approval? Does the MHRA know about this? " she said, referring to the pharmaceuticals regulatory agency. "Do you have any idea of the trouble you're in?"

She had heard of Big Pharma conducting illegal drug trials in Africa and India, but never in Europe or America.

George continued, his voice faltering slightly. "The data they sent over from America was fantastic. Really fast turnarounds. Usually people have to be on SSRIs for weeks before there's any change. With this stuff, we were talking hours. Remember how much money Eli Lilly made with Prozac? This is going to be even bigger. Tri-Med is convinced it has a wonder drug on its hands. They wanted to rush things through and see its share price rocket. So I started the trial with a small group of patients. Just four, in fact. Renee was one of them. I halved her dosage when she started having side effects. You can't just come off SSRIs like that."

"Do you know what's going to happen when the authorities find out? You'll lose your licence, and for what, money?"

So this was how Tony could afford his new life – by taking kickbacks from an American pharma giant. Jemma wondered how much had lined his own pocket, and how much had gone to the hospital. Not much, she bet. Tony spent money faster than butter melting in a frying pan.

"I've told Tri-Med I won't have anything more to do with it," George said. "Tony as well. Jemma, I'm begging you not to say anything. No lasting harm has been done. St Luke's has made a lot of money out of this, enough money to keep people's jobs, people you and I work with."

She felt so ashamed of him she did not know how to respond. His career would end over this. Possibly he would even go to jail. And now he was asking her to put her own reputation on the line to help cover up a drugs scandal that could sink the hospital.

"George, you've put me in an impossible situation. I don't know what I'm going to do. If I don't report this, I could lose my licence."

"Please, Jemma. It's all over now. I've never asked anything of you before." He looked earnestly into her face. "As a friend, I'm begging you."

CHAPTER TWENTY-SIX

Sex, Tony reflected, needed a touch of cruelty in it, like angostura bitters clouding a glass of gin. There were no thanks for being too loving. Once he had met Toppy, nothing else seemed as important, not his work or the woman he had married. Somehow the most important thing had been lying in bed with this woman and simply talking to her. And now she was dead. Despite all the rows before the end, he still felt as if somebody had plunged their hands into his heart and was twisting it in opposite directions.

He was in so much pain. Unbidden memories kept coming back to him: watching Toppy hungrily while she sat with her back to him on the beach, and putting his arms round her while she cooked in the mews kitchen, smelling her hair as they danced in the hotel room, and the moment he saw her again and the moment they chinked glasses in the Cambridge pub. He felt a terrible sense of loss, as if he was searching from room to room, unable to find her. Come back to me, Toppy, his mind wailed.

By now he was walking past the strip of shops and restaurants where he had first met her for lunch. He stopped outside the Italian restaurant and peered through the window. Couples having dinner. He pictured how nervous he had been waiting for Toppy to arrive that lunchtime, and the moment he placed his hand over hers and everything had been settled. She had less than one year to live.

A mobile phone was ringing, and Tony glanced around before realising it was his. He fished the mobile out of his pocket while glancing in a shop window. "George" said the caller ID. What did he want now? He had already had one slightly hysterical conversation with his chief psychiatrist in his office that morning. George said he didn't want anything more to do with the Tri-Med tests. Tony told him to calm down and agreed to end MC4703 testing immediately. He would tell Nibley that they were pulling out of the trial. Tony had then spent the rest of the morning interviewing everybody who had been on the roof, telling them not to speak to anybody. Any reporters who got wind of the attempted suicide were to be referred to the press office.

"Yes, George, how can I help you?"

"Jemma has just been to see me. She knows about the drugs trial. She's threatening to go to the MHRA."

"Wait a minute. You could have been prescribing any anti-depressant. How did she find out about Tri-Med? You must have told her."

"She already knew everything. I had to fill in the blanks.

Tony, she's still your wife. You've got to stop her. I could lose my job. This could end both our careers. And believe me, if I'm going down, I'm taking you with me."

"Whoa, are you threatening me?" said Tony, shocked at how quickly the conversation had turned. He glanced around to see if anybody was listening. "I told you, George," he said quietly. "You need to hold your nerve. I will talk to her and explain the damage she would cause if she went public. I told you, we're winding down the trial. Nobody was hurt."

"You do that, Tony, and phone me back. I wish I had never got into this."

Yes, but you were only too happy to take the money, Tony thought. "I'll call you later," he said.

He buried his mobile in his coat pocket and walked past late-night Christmas shoppers. People streamed by chatting and laughing. Inside he felt as if he was being torn apart. His son was missing, taken by the woman he had seen on CCTV. What if what Jemma was saying was true, and that Toppy had come back from the dead? No, that was impossible. The boat had been in the middle of the sea. Nobody could have swum that far back to shore. In any case, she couldn't even swim. His thoughts turned to Matthew. I have failed you, my darling, he thought. My one job had been to protect you, and I couldn't even do that.

That lunchtime he had wandered into a church, sat down in a pew and pressed his head against the sticky polished wood. He had pushed against the pew until his head hurt, in what, an act of contrition? What was he going to do, give the money back? He had spent a chunk of it on his new life with Toppy, and the rest was sitting in cash in the bank. And who was he going to give the money back to anyway? Nibley had gone into an otherworldly rant down the phone when Tony said the trial was over. Judas must have wanted to give the thirty pieces of silver back, too.

By now Tony was walking past furniture shops and interior designers on his way back home. He remembered the day he had spent with Toppy just wandering around. They had not done anything in particular, and yet it was one of the happiest days of his life. Now she was dead. His son was missing. There was no doubt in his mind he was being punished. His thoughts turned again to suicide. That would be the easy way out, doubly failing your son. No, there had to be a way to make amends. Everything in his life had fallen apart because of his lust and greed, he knew that. He resolved to put things right, even if it took the rest of his life.

A supermarket was coming up on the left, and Tony needed some bits to take home. He wandered into the vegetable aisle and noticed the television suspended from the ceiling. A woman reporter was standing outside St Luke's and a picture flashed up of Matthew. Then Jemma looking tearful at the press conference. That stopped him in his tracks. He paused for a moment standing beside one of the other shoppers in the aisle and then hurried on, anxious to get out of there as quickly as possible. Dumping his few groceries at the till, he began to have the feeling that everybody was watching him, that they knew who he was. The Asian girl behind the till began scanning his purchases. Was there the faint glimpse of recognition in her eyes?

Turning the key in his front door lock, he recapped everything he had thought about on his walk back home. Stooping down, he collected today's bills and estate agent circulars and then walked upstairs to the kitchen, dumping his groceries on the table. Despite having little appetite, he would force himself to eat.

The flat was cold and dark, and he moved to switch some lights on. That way he might stop feeling morbid. It wasn't going to help Matthew if his father was shuffling like a dead person. But I am dead inside and you killed me, he thought, reaching for the table-lamp flex. That was when he realised there was somebody else in the room. A woman sitting in darkness. "Hello, Tony," said her familiar voice.

CHAPTER TWENTY-SEVEN

Jemma was in two minds as to whether to drive straight over to Tony's home and confront him about what she knew, or wait until she had decided on her own course of action. Her best friend faced being struck off, while Tony could go to jail for accepting bribes. What a dilemma. In the end she took the plunge and phoned Tony.

"Tony, it's Jemma. I need to come and see you. There's something we need to talk about. Face to face." She could be at his rented mews house within twenty minutes. "Sure, but could you come round in around half an hour? I've got somebody with me," he said. His voice sounded odd, and she wondered if George had already been on the phone, warning him she was about to turn whistleblower.

Pulling into his street, Jemma noticed how quiet it was. That's what you pay for, she thought, locking the car and putting the keys in her shoulder bag. It would be safe in a residents' parking bay this time of night. The imposing white stucco houses were part of a Victorian housing boom that had gone bust by the time they had finished building. Most had been turned into flats. Tony's mews was where they used to stable the horses. Her heels clacked on the cobbles as she counted off house numbers. Tony's house had a green-painted door next to a garage. She pressed the door bell unthinkingly, stepped back and waited. It was only then that she noticed the front door was ajar. The catch was not quite locked.

Pushing the door with her fingers, it slowly opened onto a tight hallway leading upstairs. She called out Tony's name and began climbing the stairs, noticing the squeak of a floorboard. Her senses told her that something was very wrong. "Tony?" she called again stepping out onto the landing. The sitting room was directly in front of her, and beyond that were what she assumed were bedrooms. To her right was the doorway to a largish kitchen.

That was when she heard him.

He was lying on the floor beyond the kitchen table, his head beneath the sink. Running over to him, her first thought was that her husband was dead. She squatted beside him, convinced she was already too late. Then Tony blinked. She recoiled with surprise, her back pressed up against a kitchen cupboard. His diabetic syringe was lying beneath the kitchen table, and his insulin bottle had rolled a little farther away. He must have dropped the syringe when he injected himself. Her husband had taken an overdose and was now sinking into a diabetic coma.

Her mind scrabbled as she banged the fridge door open, searching for a soft drink. Nothing. He had never taken very good care of himself. She pulled open kitchen cupboards hunting for sugar. Glasses. Biscuits. Coffee. Where was the effing sugar? She started going through pots on the counter and finally found a packet. Crouching over him, she tried stuffing the granules into his mouth, but they spilled everywhere. Tony was drifting in and out of consciousness.

She dug her BlackBerry out of her shoulder bag and dialled 999. Ironically, St Luke's was probably the closest accident-and-emergency unit. She waited for the operator, keeping her eyes on Tony sprawled on the floor. The operator came on, and Jemma told her she needed an ambulance immediately. "My husband is going into a diabetic coma," Jemma said. "He could die. Please hurry." The woman asked for the address, and Jemma realised she didn't know exactly where she was. She began searching wildly for a bill or something else with the house number on.

Jemma sat beside Tony, holding his hand and willing the ambulance to arrive.

"Jemma," Tony said. His voice was so faint she had to bring her face down to his. "Toppy," he whispered. "You were right. She came to see me. She's still alive and she has Matthew." His voice sounded very far away. "There's money for you. Remember, Matthew's birthday. For you and Matthew."

That was when the banging on the front door started.

Getting up, she looked down from the window and saw the ambulance parked in the mews, its blue lights churning.

Her husband was dying in front of her, and there was nothing she could do. She felt her legs turning to water.

CHAPTER TWENTY-EIGHT

"Thank God you've come," Jemma gasped to the ambulance crew. "My husband is dying. Please hurry." The two men clumped upstairs behind her. Their footfalls were heavy, and they seemed to be going unnecessarily slowly. She willed them to hurry up.

Tony lay sprawled on the linoleum where she had left him. Something had changed, though. His skin looked grey, and there was a sweetish smell in the air. Jemma realised with a thud that he was dead. The green-uniformed paramedic crouched over her husband's body, raised his eyes and shook his head. "We have to wait for the police," he said. "We can't do anything until they get here."

The colour seemed to drain out of the room. Jemma slumped into one of the kitchen chairs. She felt as if her hands and feet had been cut off with an electric bone saw. Her husband, the man she had once planned to share the rest of her life with, was lying dead on the floor in front of her. It was as if she was looking at herself through the wrong end of a telescope.

The rest was a blur. She couldn't hear anything, couldn't see anything, couldn't feel anything. She just sat numbly in the chair. Toppy missing, presumed dead. Matthew disappeared. And now her husband lying dead on the floor. Two uniformed police constables arrived quickly afterwards. One of the ambulance men let them in, and Jemma roused herself enough to tell them the whole story, from arriving at the mews to finding Tony unconscious on the floor. She was showing them the insulin bottle and the hypodermic she had found when a third voice behind her said, "Put the vial down, Jemma, and the syringe."

To her surprise, DCI Walker stepped into the room. He was wearing a mackintosh and he looked dishevelled. Jemma placed both items on the kitchen table. "I came to see Tony and found him already on the floor like this..." she began. Walker raised his hand, cutting her off. "That syringe. I want it fingerprinted," he said.

Jemma said, "We had things to talk about."

"What, about Matthew?"

"Is there any news? Have you found him yet?"

Walker shook his head. "The appeal went out only this afternoon. You have to be patient. We've got hundreds of leads to follow up, and now this. I'm going to have to take you down to the station."

"You can't think I had anything to do with this. I tried to save his life."

"I'm not saying that."

"So what are you saying?"

"Doctor Sands, like it or not, you are a person of interest in the kidnapping of your son. It's standard procedure. We always have to rule out the immediate family first. And now the boy's father is dead of a drugs overdose. What do you expect me to say?"

Walker drove her back to Notting Hill police station in his Audi. Shop windows were still lit up as the car tore through Knightsbridge. Normal life carrying on as before. Jemma suspected Walker thought she knew more than she was telling. First Toppy, then Matthew and now Tony – all three were either dead or had gone missing. And Jemma was the one person who connected them all.

The custody suite looked brand new. A blonde policewoman stood behind a curved Plexiglas shield and wrote down Jemma's name and address. She stared down at the powder-blue floor, not quite able to comprehend what was happening. Her husband was dead and her child was missing. Another policewoman, this one with a pony tail, touched her arm and escorted her to the interview room.

The walls of the windowless room were painted municipal grey. A steel strip, some kind of panic button, ran along one wall, and two video cameras surveyed them from above.

The blonde policewoman set down a plastic cup of coffee on the table and gave her a compassionate smile. Normally Jemma did not take sugar, but she was so overwhelmed she could have folded her arms and gone to sleep right then and there. Laced with sugar, the coffee tasted silky and delicious.

Walker strode in accompanied by Balogun. The DCI reached across to the chunky Neal recorder, like a hi-fi amplifier, sitting on the table. The red light came on.

"Thursday. December the seventeenth. The time is eleven thirteen pm. Present in the room are Doctor Jemma Sands, mother of missing toddler Matthew Sands, myself, Detective Chief Inspector Niall Walker, and my colleague, Detective Inspector Reggie Balogun of Kensington and Chelsea CID. Could you identify yourself, please?"

Jemma did so.

"At eight thirty-four this evening police were called to 17 Eccleston Mews, Pimlico. On arrival, PC Wynn found your husband dead, we suspect at this stage, from an overdose of insulin. Would you say that's a fair summary, Doctor Sands?"

Jemma nodded. "Yes, that's right. Inspector, there's something I haven't told you," she said. "Before he died, Tony told me that Toppy Mrazek, the woman I was telling you about, was alive and had taken our son."

Silence. The striplight overhead was strobing ever so slightly, just enough to bring on a headache.

"The woman who went missing in France?" he said.

"My husband's girlfriend. Tony told me that she has

Matthew. Those were his dying words."

"Doctor Sands, I think you ought to read this. Your husband left a suicide note."

Walker slid a piece of paper across to her. A chill prickled down her back. It was a photocopy of Tony's handwriting.

"To whomever finds this note. I have decided to take my own life because I cannot live with the guilt that I murdered Toppy Mrazek any longer. On August 31st this year, I rented a boat with my girlfriend. We got into a fight after dinner. We had both had too much to drink. I lost my temper and pushed her overboard, knowing she could not swim. When I told my wife about it, she told me not to tell anybody but pretend it was an accident. But I can't live with this any longer. It's tearing me apart. I am sorry about what happened. And I am sorry about my son. Perhaps his going missing is God's punishment for what I have done. Tony Sands."

Jemma stared at the note, dumbfounded. The only thing she could think of us was that Toppy must have forced Tony to write this.

"The thing is, Doctor Sands," said Walker. "I can't decide whether you're a witness or a suspect."

"This doesn't make sense. What father kills himself while his son is missing? She made him write this to implicate me. Can't you see that?"

"You knew he'd pushed this poor girl overboard, but you

didn't do anything about it. You then perverted the course of justice by telling him to keep quiet. Then you sent us on a wild goose chase to find this dead woman. I reckon that alone is worth ten years in prison."

"Wait a minute" – she felt her indignation rising – "I'm the one who's in the wrong here? It's my son who's gone missing. My husband is dead. Tony might have been many things, but he was no murderer. She planned all this. She faked her own death, and now she's taken our son. She wants revenge. I couldn't save her baby, so now she wants mine."

Her voice cracked with emotion, and she swallowed hard to stop the tears coming. She was not going to give Walker the satisfaction of seeing her cry.

"Why don't we look at it another way? Your husband and his girlfriend get into a fight. Perhaps he regrets walking out on you. He pushes her overboard. You tell him to keep quiet, pretend it was an accident. How does that sound? You know she's dead, and you know your husband did it."

The atmosphere in the room thickened. You bastard, she thought, stop trying to push me into a corner. But all she said was, "I've told you. That's not what happened."

"Why don't you tell us where your son is? Wouldn't it be a relief to tell the truth? Isn't it a strain, holding it all in? Then we can get this whole mess sorted out. Toppy Mrazek is dead. Your son must be very frightened, wherever you've hidden him. It's over, Jemma, you can let go now."

The ground was opening up beneath her, swallowing her whole. She felt as if she was being buried alive, and it was useless struggling against it.

Walker continued, "I think your husband wanted to confess, but you didn't want him to."

"I had nothing to do with Tony's death," she repeated. "He was murdered, and she killed him. Don't you understand? I haven't just lost my son, I've lost my entire future."

Walker placed both hands on the interview table. "Doctor Jemma Sands, I am arresting you on suspicion of the murder of your husband."

CHAPTER TWENTY-NINE

Her cell consisted of a grey slab to lie on and a blue vinyl mat. She sat down in the corner and drew her knees up to her chest. The duty solicitor told Jemma they could hold her for twenty-four hours without charging her. Under arrest and being charged were two different things, he explained. Jemma tried closing her eyes, but she couldn't because the electric light was never switched off. If she told the truth, she thought, nothing bad could happen to her. Only good things happen to good people. Discuss. Sitting there, listening to doors bang and shouts from other cells, she felt as if she was trapped in some outer rim of hell.

They let her go early next morning. Walker told her he had no option but to release her because there was not enough evidence to charge her at this stage. He was keeping an open mind as to whether she had murdered her husband. It would take a week for Tony's blood and urine tests to come through. Walker himself had driven her back home to Fulham.

She felt so ghostly with tiredness that all she could do was crawl into bed. She tried to sleep, but the events of the past few days had been ghastly: Toppy's waving hair as she disappeared into a misty seawater wall; Matthew slipping off his chair and putting his hand into Toppy's; and Tony's sugar-crusted lips brushing her ear. Images kept revolving in her head. There had to be a reason all this was happening to her. She wondered if she was being punished for past error. Eventually she pulled herself out of bed and blearily pulled on her dressing gown.

Parting the curtains, Jemma looked down into the street. Cars were parked on both sides all the way up to the Fulham Road. One man was sitting behind the wheel watching her house. So the police had her under surveillance. They must be keeping tabs on her to see if she would lead them to Matthew. Jemma let the curtain drop.

The sudden ringing of the phone was startling.

"Jemma, it's George. I just wanted to know what you'd decided."

For a moment she wondered what he was talking about. "George, I... I haven't decided about anything. After I left you I went to see Tony and..."

"What did he say? He must have told you I washed my hands of the whole thing. I told him I didn't want anything more to do with it. Please, Jemma, don't rush into making a decision. I was trying to do the right thing. I told you, I'm truly sorry for what I did."

"George, there's something else you need to know. Tony

died last night. He took an overdose of insulin."

There was silence on the other end of the phone as George absorbed her words.

"Hello? Are you still there? George, I'm really frightened. First Matthew disappears, and now this. I don't know why this is happening to me. It's all too much."

"What do you mean, Tony's dead? I spoke to him only yesterday."

"I went round to his flat and found him dying. It gets worse. He left a suicide note. Tony confessed to killing his girlfriend that night on holiday. He pushed her overboard."

"Jemma, you need to tell me everything."

She sat down on the bed and went through the events of the past twenty-four hours, from leaving George's flat to the police taking her home.

"Do you think that Tri-Med could have had anything to do with Tony's death?" George asked. "When I spoke to him, he said he'd just had an extremely unpleasant conversation with Wade Nibley, the man who runs the London division. Nibley was not happy about us terminating the MC4073 trial. Tony said the American was ranting so much he put the phone down on him."

"No, that doesn't make sense. Toppy made him write that suicide note. Now everybody believes she's dead."

"For goodness' sake, Jemma, let it go. Toppy Mrazek died

four months ago. The only person who thinks she's still alive is you."

Jemma paused. "Perhaps you're right. I don't know what to think any more. Matthew going missing, and now Tony dying. The police think I had something to do with Matthew's disappearance. The detective accused me of sending them on a wild goose chase to protect Tony. They think I knew Toppy was dead all along."

"Do you want me to come over? You shouldn't be on your own. I could be with you in half an hour."

Jemma gave a mirthless little laugh. "Oh, I'm not on my own. The police are watching right now. They've got me under surveillance."

She stood up and parted the curtains once again. The man was still in the car. There was no doubt about it. She was being watched.

Eventually she had enough of being inside the house. She felt like a caged animal. Pulling her coat on, she picked up her keys from the hall radiator and stepped outside into the street. Locking the front door, she turned right towards the park, mindful of the man watching her. Out of the corner of her eye she saw him getting out of his car and start to follow her, trying to be inconspicuous. As a tail it was pretty blatant. Fine, let him follow her. All she was doing was trying to get her head straight.

Irresistibly she was drawn to the park with the roundabout

and swings where she had taken Matthew most days after nursery. Sitting down on a park bench, she stared into the middle distance past the train that Matthew liked to hide in. The empty playground only reminded her of Matthew even more. Thinking about her little boy clutched at her heart. Where was he now, and what was he doing? The idea of never seeing him again was too terrible to contemplate.

An American voice behind her said, "Why Doctor Sands, how nice to see you again."

Jemma turned and found herself face to face with Nibley. The way he greeted her sounded like a threat. She felt a chill of premonition.

"It's Wade Nibley, isn't it? What on earth are you doing here?"

"Do you mind if I sit down? We need to have a little talk, Doctor Sands."

Nibley ran his fingers along the back of the park bench with a kind of exaggerated ease, as if to underline that he was the one in charge.

"I'm sorry, I was just about to leave," said Jemma, standing up. "You caught me at a bad moment."

Nibley's driver, the tough-looking mixed-race man, oozed imperceptibly closer and folded his arms. His eyes were as expressionless as mackerel.

"Please sit down, Doctor Sands," Nibley said, waving the driver away. "You and I have something to discuss."

Jemma didn't say anything but hoped to God her police tail was watching all this.

"I hear you're none too happy with our drugs trial," Nibley continued. "That you're thinking of going to the authorities."

George must have spilled the beans. "That's right. Doctor Malvern told me about you rushing clinical tests. You're very lucky you didn't have a dead patient on your hands. One of Doctor Malvern's patients tried throwing herself off the roof two days ago."

Was it really only on Tuesday that she had talked Renee Pieterse down from that roof? It felt like a lifetime ago.

"Do you have any idea how competitive the global drugs market is, Doctor Sands? Each year, my company spends millions in Britain developing new patents. This drug, MC4703, came out of our lab in Ashford. We employ hundreds of research chemists here in England. We've spent years developing what could be the cure for depression. Yet with one click of a mouse, our intellectual property could be pirated and made free to rest of the world. We might as well have ripped up our dollars in the street. That's why we're so keen to get this drug tested quickly."

"You can't hurry research like this. Side effects become apparent only years afterwards."

"That's old-fashioned thinking. If you throw enough people

at the problem in enough countries, you get the same result. Your husband agreed, too. That's why he took our money."

"My husband died yesterday, haven't you heard? I want you to leave me alone."

Where on earth was that policeman? Why wasn't he doing anything?

"I am truly sorry for your loss. Here's the thing, Doctor Sands. Your husband took a lot of money from us. Now that he's dead, we want our money back."

"My husband and I were getting divorced. Our financial affairs were quite separate."

Nibley sighed and pulled his camel coat tighter around him. "That's unfortunate. I was afraid you were going to say that. Let me ask you a question. How much do you love your son?"

Jemma was so astonished by what he'd just said she didn't know how to react. "My son has gone missing. Surely you must know that. It's been all over the news."

"Exactly. The way you love your son is just how I feel about this company. I will do anything to protect it. Anything that threatens its future, anything that stands in its way." He mimed shooing a fly. "I am not saying that Tri-Med is bigger than Buddha, but when we go to war, we go to war to win."

Jemma turned to face him. "Are you threatening me, Mister

Nibley? Please, I'm begging you, if you know anything about the whereabouts of my son, you must tell me."

Nibley grinned. "I don't threaten, Doctor Sands. But if you mess with people, you have got to be prepared to be messed with. Listen, I am a consequence man" – that smile again – "and if you mess with me, there will be consequences."

CHAPTER THIRTY

The Tube carriage reeked of fried food and perfume. Two teenage boys sitting opposite were playing music loudly on a mobile phone, sharing a set of mini headphones. One of them started rapping with words indecipherable to Walker, while the other just made noises that sounded like mud being sucked through a pump.

Walker stood up, glad to be getting out of the crush and smell as the train decelerated into St James's Park.

Clouds sagged with rain. There was a roll of thunder, and Walker felt the first fat drops of rain striking his forehead. Suddenly the clouds burst open, and raindrops were exploding on the pavement. He ran along the street to New Scotland Yard, desperate to get out of the wet and shielding the papers he was holding in his raincoat. His appointment with the Commander was for five thirty. Umar Okumu was one of the brightest officers he knew. It was as if he could see farther than Walker, make connections faster. They had started at Hendon Police College together in the mid-eighties during the long hot summer of the Brixton riots. Okumu once told Walker he assumed he would be welcomed into the Met with open arms. There was so much talk of how the police needed to mend relations with the black community. Instead, it was one of the few times he had experienced racism. Okumu remembered the shock when another recruit told him, "I know all about you. You're that nigger from north London." Institutional racism was a bland term for what Okumu had put up with, Walker reflected. When the rest of them sloped off to the pub on Friday nights, Okumu would be doing laps on the running track. He had polished his image as hard as he buffed his shoes, so it was no surprise when he won the Baton of Honour. Now, while Walker's career seemed to have stalled, he watched bemused as Okumu rose swiftly thought the ranks. There was even talk of him being the next Metropolitan Police Commissioner. Some carped that his rapid promotion was due to positive discrimination. Yet Walker knew different. Whenever Walker had to debrief the Commander, he felt as if he was guiding a metal wand along an electric switchback, one of those games you see at summer fetes. Okumu would spot some flaw in his thinking, the buzzer would sound, and Walker would have to start all over again.

When Walker knocked, he found the Commander gazing out over St James's Park as if he was scanning nearby roofs for snipers. Trafalgar Square lay in the distance. Okumu's office was bright and modern. Sky News was playing quietly, showing riots in the Middle East. In one corner was a prayer mat, a compass sewn into it so that Okumu would always know where Mecca was.

The Commander turned from the window. "From up here those people look like ants, don't they?" he said.

Okumu walked over to his desk and sat down. He did not invite Walker to take one of the two chairs opposite him, and Walker remembered that the last time he was in this office he had been on the receiving end of a bollocking. Sloppy evidence-gathering had led to the collapse of a trial at the Old Bailey.

"Tell me about this Sands woman," Okumu said. "The Commissioner is afraid that this might come back and bite us. We don't need another public embarrassment from you."

"She reported her son missing. You've seen the CCTV footage. A woman who looks just like her leading the boy away. Then we get an emergency-crew call about her husband. When we get there, he's dead on the floor and she's standing over him. He'd written a suicide note saying that he'd pushed his girlfriend overboard on holiday in France. They'd had an argument on a boat. When he told his wife about it, she told him to keep quiet. He couldn't handle the guilt, apparently."

"So you've got her for perverting the course of justice."

"She denies everything. In fact, she says it was the girlfriend who kidnapped her son."

"I don't understand. I thought you said the girlfriend drowned in France?"

"Sands says it's all an elaborate plot to steal her son. Apparently the husband was taking cash out of the hospital to pay for his new life with his girlfriend. Sands says they met after an operation went wrong trying to save the woman's baby. The baby died, and now the girlfriend has kidnapped the little boy out of revenge."

"Does she have anything to back up what she's saying? What about the CCTV footage? That shows her leading her son away, for God's sake."

"She says it's not her. She's adamant it's the woman who drowned."

"Dead people don't kidnap children."

"We've been doing some digging into the girlfriend's background. She had a spell as a patient in a mental hospital in south London. Then there's this…"

Walker passed Okumu the photocopy he was holding of an eighties' newspaper clipping. The print was reversed on the microfiche clipping so that it was white on black. X-rays of people's faces stared out from the page. "Tragic Baby Falls To Death," read the headline.

"The girlfriend, Toppy Mrazek, accidentally dropped her baby brother from a seventh-floor balcony when she was a kid. After that, she was in and out of mental hospitals," Walker explained.

Okumu looked at him witheringly. It was difficult to remember sometimes that they had once been friends. "Do you really believe in this Pied Piper nonsense? A woman comes back from the dead to lead this boy away, and they're never heard from again? I want you to lean on this Sands woman hard. She knows more than she's telling. You follow her, and she'll take us to the boy. She's just spreading some shit to get us chasing our own tails."

Okumu was obviously being leaned on by the Assistant Commissioner, who was probably getting it in the neck from the Commissioner. He imagined a scaffold of them, all pressing down on each other's necks.

He thought for a moment. If Okumu wanted this airtight, there could be only one next step. "Everything we have so far is circumstantial. I want a search warrant for Doctor Sands' home."

Okumu nodded and turned to his phone. "Give me an hour, and I'll get you what you need."

CHAPTER THIRTY-ONE

It was a nightmare she wanted to wake up from but couldn't. Looking down from Matthew's window, Jemma saw a police constable searching their garden with ground-penetrating radar. It looked like a lawnmower being trundled over the flagstones. The police were also digging up the flower bed she had put so much work into, heaping soil onto the patio.

Walker had come back with a search warrant, and his POLSA team was tearing her house apart. The press were standing around in their cordoned-off corner of the street. Bulky men in thick down jackets with cameras slung round their necks were sipping tea. Reporters chatted with one another or on mobile phones, their mouths steaming as they talked. Already the whispering campaign had started. The police had released spare details about Tony's suicide without mentioning that Jemma was the one who had discovered him. Now the press were speculating that husband and wife both had something to do with Matthew's disappearance, and that Tony had killed himself out of remorse. That morning's Daily Express had splashed with the headline, "What Isn't She Telling Us?" Jemma had become the story, not Matthew. Looking down at Matthew's empty bed now, she yearned to hug his body smelling of bed warmth and milk.

Her thoughts were interrupted by another PC coming into the bedroom. "The DCI would like to see you downstairs," he said.

Her living room was in chaos. All the books had been pulled from the shelves and were lying in an untidy heap on the floor. Matthew's toy basket had been upended, covers stripped from the sofa. A power drill whined as two policemen crouched over the floorboards. They were even taking up the wooden floor. The police had unrolled plastic matting stretching from the front to the back garden door, but still their muddy footprints were all over the hall.

The kitchen was in even more of a state. Cans and bottles had been pulled down from the cupboards, and there was an oily slick where one had smashed. Would things ever be normal again?

Walker was standing with his back to the kitchen counter. "One of the nurses we interviewed at the hospital told us somebody has been stealing Rohypnol," he said.

"What does that have to do with me?"

"Apparently, you have access to the drug store." He brought out an empty foil pill strip from behind his back. "We found this in the bottom of your car glove compartment."

His latex-covered fingers offered her a busted-open foil package.

"I have never seen those before in my life."

"Are you saying these pills don't belong to you? That you have no idea how they got there?"

"Why can't you see what's in front of you? I keep telling you, Toppy Mrazek is framing me for my husband's murder."

"There's no evidence that she's alive, Doctor Sands. What I do have is CCTV footage showing a woman who looks like you taking your son away. And your husband confessing that you helped cover up his girlfriend's murder. Now I find this date-rape drug in your car. Did you use it on your boy to keep him quiet, eh?"

The world shifted on its axis before righting itself. Jemma was not going to be railroaded like this, despite invisible hands squeezing her neck.

She said, with as much calm as she could muster, "Are you going to charge me with Matthew's murder, too?"

"Get this pill strip to forensics," Walker told another officer. "I want a full report as quick as you can." Then, turning to Jemma, "As for you, I would suggest you get yourself a lawyer."

Jemma thought of Dennis, their family lawyer who had been handling her divorce. He should have retired by now and had taken her case as a favour to her mother. She thought of him struggling to put on his suit of armour, once again trying to protect her. No, she would have to find somebody else, somebody better equipped to deal with what she was going through.

The police spent the rest of the day combing her house for evidence. The phone kept going, too – journalists pestering her for interviews. When the police left, she sat down on the floor with her back to the sink cupboard and wept. Her yearning for her little boy had come on her like madness. She had vowed to devote herself to her son, and she had failed. She had failed in her solemn duty to protect him. This was all her fault. She kept seeing Matthew sitting alone in that café as that woman approached him, extending her hand, and Matthew, so trusting, jumping down from his seat. She felt as if her heart was being pulled out through her mouth.

She was still berating herself when her mobile pinged with a text message. She got up off the floor to see who it was from. "Worried about you. Saw news on TV tonight. Need to talk? Emily x" the message read. It was from her next-door neighbour. Jemma crossed the sitting room and parted the curtains. A police constable was guarding her front door, watching the reporters standing around in the cold. There was even a satellite truck parked farther up the street. She dropped the curtain back. Picking up her mobile from the kitchen counter, Jemma texted back, "Trapped inside house. Reporters outside. Can u come to me?" Moments after she pressed send, she heard Emily calling her over the garden wall.

"Jemma, can you climb over?" she asked.

"There's a step-ladder under the stairs."

"See if you can use that."

Resting the step-ladder against the fence, Jemma thought there was something vaguely comical about climbing over into her next-door neighbour's garden. If she had not felt so sick with anxiety, she would have even laughed.

Jumping down into Emily's garden, she met her next-door neighbour's concerned eyes. "Do you want a drink?" she asked. Jemma nodded dumbly, this unexpected display of kindness robbing her of speech for a moment. Emily led her into her back kitchen, where her husband was putting ice cubes into glasses. "Pour gin on your troubles?" he said, handing her a full tumbler. The three of them touched glasses. Jemma took a grateful sip and felt the alcohol slowly and blissfully take hold.

Emily led her through to their sitting room where, for once, the plastic toys had been packed away. Emily's drawing board was set up in the corner – Jemma realised she had never seen her work before. A saccharine pastel drawing of a Yorkshire terrier with thyroid eyes stared up at her. "Hideous, isn't it?" said Emily cheerfully. "I went to art school thinking I was going to be the next Tracey Emin, and I end up drawing cats and dogs for birthday cards." She moved across to the sofa and patted a cushion for Jemma to sit down beside her.

"I saw the television news this evening. I can't imagine how you're coping, the kind of pressure you're under. First Matthew going missing, and now this. What Tony did to himself, it's beyond belief. Did he leave a note? Do you have any idea why he did it?"

Jemma took a deep breath. "Tony didn't kill himself. He was murdered."

Emily looked shocked. "What do you mean, murdered? The news said it was suicide."

It was a relief to tell her story to someone who actually seemed to want to listen. Not wishing to complicate things, she left out the part about the illegal drugs trial. Adam, Emily's husband, came and stood in the doorway. At one point Emily leaned forward and hugged her. The human contact was almost unbearably comforting.

"And you've told the police everything you know?" said Emily.

"Of course. They believe Tony's suicide note was genuine. They think I've invented this story about his girlfriend stealing Matthew because I knew about him pushing Toppy overboard, that I told him to pretend it was an accident."

"What mother kidnaps her own child? It doesn't make any sense."

"The police think I have Matthew hidden somewhere. They think I've done it to make them think Toppy is still alive.

And then they found this Rohypnol bottle in my car this afternoon."

"Which was nothing to do with you?" Adam said carefully.

"Of course not," said Jemma, shocked he would even think such a thing. "She planted it there, I know it."

"So what are you going to do now?"

"I don't know," she said shaking her head. "I simply don't know. The noose is tightening, I can feel it."

"Why don't you stay here tonight in our spare room? You shouldn't be on your own."

"The police might call. I need to be at home. They might have found Matthew. What if they bring him home and his mummy isn't there?"

She felt herself on the verge of tears. She knew it was time to leave and she stood up. "God only sends us what we can just about cope with, right?" she said bravely.

Adam, who had been watching both women, stepped farther into the room. "It's important to be clear about this. If what Jemma's saying is correct, this woman could be anywhere by now. You can't just stay at home," he said, turning to Jemma. "You've got to get out there and find her. It sounds like the police have already made up their minds. You're not going to be any good to Matthew just sitting here."

Tony had always found Adam pompous in his investmentbanker way, but for once Jemma was grateful to be lectured. She would tell Tony how helpful Adam had been until she remembered, a microsecond later, that she would never be able to tell Tony anything again.

"The police are watching my house," Jemma said. "There are policemen outside my front door and at the back. They're coming to arrest me, I can feel it."

"What are you saying?" said Emily to her husband. "That we ought to find this woman? I wouldn't even know where to start."

"No, not that," said Adam, "but Jemma can't just sit here waiting to be arrested. I'm sorry Jemma. I know it's hard, but you've got to get out of here. Before it's too late."

Emily turned to her. "Adam is right. We'll do anything we can. But every moment is a fresh start. You have to believe that."

CHAPTER THIRTY-TWO

Half past three in the morning. Walker took a final sip from his cup of coffee and set it down next to the hand brake. "Right, let's get on with it," he said to his detective inspector, who was behind the steering wheel. He wanted this done as quietly and with as little fuss as possible. The press had drifted away and here they were, sitting in an unmarked police car, doing an Obo in a west London street. The lab results from the Rohypnol had not come back yet, and he had wanted to be doubly sure, but Okumu was insistent. "Stop prevaricating" were his final words.

Balogun picked up his walkie-talkie. "Red to Control, Red to Control. Is Yellow still at Green, over?" He waited a moment before nodding to Walker.

Both men got out of the car and walked over to the PC standing guard outside the house.

"Anything?" asked Walker.

The constable shook his head. "No, sir. She went to bed early and switched the upstairs light off at around ten. Nobody's been in or out since."

"What about the alley down the back? Anything going on?"

The PC cocked his head and spoke into the walkie-talkie on his shoulder. Static squawked during his brief exchange with the constable posted round the back. The PC shook his head.

Pushing their way past the gate, Balogun stepped up to press the doorbell. Both men stood back and waited. Nothing. It was cold tonight, and Walker wanted to get back to the warmth and fug of the canteen. "Try again," he told Balogun, stepping farther back to get a good look at the bedroom window. Light switched on behind the curtains. Balogun shifted his weight from one foot to the other. "I wish she'd hurry up. I'm freezing my bollocks off out here," he said.

Walker looked farther up the street. Something didn't feel right.

"Try her again," he ordered. "I don't care about the noise."

Balogun stepped back into the porch and this time thumped the door. Hard. Both men waited. "This is the police. Open up," Balogun said loudly. Walker glanced around to see curtains over the road opening a little, just enough for somebody to peek down. A dog barked over the road.

The PC's walkie-talkie burst into life. "She's making a run for it," exclaimed the constable. "She's climbed over the garden wall."

"Reggie, get that bloody door open."

Balogun stepped back and took a hefty kick at the door. The woodwork rattled. Balogun started kicking at it frenziedly before the wood splintered and the door burst open.

The alarm went off at ear-piercing volume.

Walker winced as they pitched into the hall. The noise was so loud it fibrillated his eardrums. Despite the pain, he could see that the double doors into the back garden were wide open. "She's gone out the back," he shouted, already running through the kitchen. He crashed past the French windows and took a running jump at the brick wall, barking his shins as he hauled himself up. To his left he saw the PC who had been guarding the alley chasing after Doctor Sands.

The drop was about ten feet and he landed awkwardly, hobbling a little as he gave chase. The suspect was about thirty feet ahead, and the PC was gaining. "Suspect. Parsons Green Lane," he was shouting. Sands slowed to a stop beneath the street lamp, almost waiting for the constable to catch up with her. What the hell was she playing at? Walker was catching up, too, feeling the weight of every one of his forty-eight years. Thank God she had seen sense – did she really think she was going to outrun the entire Metropolitan Police? The track-suited figure turned around to face them, taking down her hood. "Yes, officer, is there anything I can help you with?" she asked.

"Who the hell are you?" Walker couldn't help but ask.

Whoever this woman was, she wasn't Doctor Jemma Sands.

SLOW BLEED

CHAPTER THIRTY-THREE

Jemma stood waiting by the back door of Emily's garden. All she felt was the thump of her heart. She heard Emily burst through her French doors, clambering over her rear wall, which was her cue. She felt the trellis shake as Emily jumped to the ground. Jemma slid the bolt free and opened the door a crack. She glimpsed Emily sprinting away up the alley chased by the policeman. His boots rang on the pavement. "Hey, stop," he shouted. That was when her house alarm went off, which meant the police were already inside. Move. Now.

She slipped out the back entrance and began walking purposefully away from Emily's house, hugging the wall. Behind her another man clattered over her bamboo trellis. She heard him land and shout, "Stop. Police." It sounded like Walker's Ulster accent. Please don't see me, she thought, keeping her head down. Her plan was to drive to a multi-storey car park in south London and dump the car near a station. Then she would take a suburban train back into the City and begin her search. She would find Toppy Mrazek on her own, so help her God.

Turning into the street where her car was parked, she

stopped dead. The word "Murderer" was aerosoled along the side of her car. There was no time to take it in. She had no idea where or which way to go now. All she knew was that she had to get out of there. Digging her hands deeper in her pockets, she walked briskly to Fulham Road, which was empty at this time of night. A taxi gleamed orange in the gloom. She raised her arm, and the driver pulled over sharply. Out of the corner of her eye, Jemma sensed the policeman gaining ground. A police car hammered towards them from the other direction, lights flashing, nearly colliding with the waiting cab as it tore through the street. "Late for his breakfast," the cabbie muttered as Jemma slammed the door behind her.

It was difficult to resist a peek through the rear window. Her heart was pounding as the taxi bumped along Fulham Road. She felt completely helpless. Any policeman would have already noted down the taxi number plate, and speed cameras would now be tracking their every move. It was probably only a matter of seconds before the game was up. She had only sixty pounds left in her wallet – hardly enough to go on the run with. Leaning forward, she told the taxi driver to pull over at the nearest cashpoint.

Keying in her PIN with shaking hands, she flinched at the sound of the approaching police siren. Every policeman in London would be looking for her. What was she thinking, chasing after a ghost? This was madness. Did she really think she could evade the entire Metropolitan Police force?

Her mind hardened. Toppy Mrazek had murdered her husband and she had stolen her son. Like a Fury, Jemma would pursue her to the ends of the earth.

A message flashed up on the cashpoint screen: "Insufficient funds. Please contact your card issuer." With a sinking stomach, she keyed in her PIN one more time. Same thing. She cursed herself for not transferring her money to a separate account as she had been planning to.

What was she going to do without any money? One thing she knew was that she had to get off the street.

Dingy-looking hotels lined the Earls Court crescent. She had enough money for just one night.

The hotel reception smelled of hot dust and cooking, and the radiators must have been on full blast. An obese Indian man perched on a bar stool smiled sadly as she walked in. He didn't look surprised to see a lone woman wanting a room at four o'clock in the morning. She handed over forty pounds, praying she wouldn't be asked for her passport. Turning on his stool, he unhooked her bedroom key.

It was the ugliest hotel room she had ever seen. A blown-up snapshot of the Austrian Tyrol in summer, sunlight streaming through pixelated trees, covered one wall. There was just one power socket, so you could switch on the bedside lamp or the electric heater or the television, but not more than one at the same time. She could either watch TV in darkness or try and read in the cold. All she wanted to do was lie down and go to sleep, but she had to keep going. I'll sleep when I've got my son back, she thought. Diligently, she set to work.

She bought a half-bottle of vodka from a 24-hour shop down the road, along with hair dye and a pair of scissors. She was tempted to have a sip now to steel her nerves, but she needed a clear head.

Staring at herself in the bathroom mirror, she wondered how she was going to find Toppy. She must have been the person Tony told her was with him on the night he died. That was why he had sounded so odd on the phone. There had to be some clue as to where Toppy was. The first place to start would be the mews house Tony was renting. People don't just disappear without a trace.

She pulled off the polythene gloves stained with dye and grabbed the scissors. Cutting all her now-dark hair took longer than expected. Hanks of dark hair fell into the washbasin.

The final touch was a pair of cheap see-through glasses she had found at the back of the shop. Putting them on, she turned her head in the mirror. She certainly wouldn't be lacking for free drinks in a lesbian bar, she thought with a grim smile.

An hour later she was done. It was time to venture outside again.

Earls Court Tube was busy even at this hour of the morning. Jemma pushed her way through the automatic gates along with the commuters. Her heart thumped violently – what if somebody recognised her? At least she hadn't made it onto the front page of that morning's free newspaper. Jemma swayed in the fug of the Tube carriage, counting down the stops to Victoria.

Tony's mews house was a ten-minute walk from Victoria around the back of Eccleston Square, and she took a seat in the café opposite where a few builders were having breakfast. Steam hissed and the radio chattered in the background. From her stool she had a good view of the mews entrance. A policeman was standing on duty outside Tony's house, the front door criss-crossed with incident tape. There was no way of getting in, she thought.

Then she spotted the postman trundling his red-plastic delivery box along the pavement. She slipped out of the café and crossed the road. The postman was just about to turn into the mews when she stopped him. "Anything for number seventeen?" she said brightly. "I'm just on my way there." The postman, who was holding a pile of letters, gave her the once-over and decided she looked respectable enough. He riffled through the pile and gave her an assortment held together with a red elastic band. "Here you go," he said. "Mostly bills, luv." Jemma thanked him and turned into the mews, waving goodbye. Quickly, she walked in front of the on-duty policeman, who nodded to her as she strode briskly past, keeping her head down. It took all her self-restraint not to break into a run. Any moment now a hand would clasp her on the shoulder.

Sitting on the top deck of the bus, Jemma avoided eye contact. She did not want to be caught on CCTV. She tore the envelopes open. They were mostly estate agents' circulars, but one of them was Tony's mobile phone bill. She ran her finger down his itemised calls and kept seeing the same mobile number. It had to be hers, it just had to be. Tony had kept calling this one number in the weeks following his return from France. Had he known all along she was still alive? Somehow she did not believe that. No, he really had believed she was dead; perhaps he was calling this number as a way of making sure.

Back in her lonely hotel room, she felt sick about even keying in the number. This was her only clue. She prevaricated. Her mother would be sick with worry when she heard the news that Jemma had gone on the run. She needed to reassure her, tell her that everything was going to be okay. Instead, she telephoned Falmouth; would the police be able to trace even a brief phone call? In the movies they always needed time to trace mobile phones. She pictured her mother's telephone ringing on the sideboard.

"Hello, Mum? It's Jemma."

"Jemma, thank God. The police have been here. They're searching for you. You need to come home."

"Mum. I'm all right. I'm trying to do the right thing. I know who's taken Matthew. The police don't believe me. Nobody believes me."

"Listen to me. You can't do this on your own. I love you. Everybody loves you."

Jemma felt herself becoming tearful. Every second that elapsed brought the police closer. She was so desperate to come in from the cold.

"Mum, I'm going to be fine. I'm not coming back without my son."

"Jemma, please..."

She snapped the phone off, breathing heavily. Her thoughts turned back to Toppy. It was now or never. She keyed in the number from the mobile phone bill. Putting her BlackBerry to her ear, she listened to the dialling tone. Even if it was the right number, why should she have any better luck than Tony?

"Hello, who is this?"

The unmistakable voice of Toppy Mrazek answered.

CHAPTER THIRTY-FOUR

Cutting the phone off immediately, all Jemma felt was the roar of blood in her head. So she had been right. Toppy was still alive. She thought about the card DCI Walker had given her. Why not just call him, tell him she had proof Toppy Mrazek was still alive? The police would finally arrest the right woman. But her heart burned for her little boy; every cell in her body yearned to be reunited with him. She tapped out a text message: "Toppy. I know you're alive. Please give me my son back. I won't tell anybody about you. I just need my son back. Jemma." Oh God, I know that I have been a terrible person all my life, she thought, but please don't let anything happen to my little boy. I love him so much. She pressed send and stared at the BlackBerry, willing her nemesis to respond. Moments later, the BlackBerry pinged: "Mt me cafe opp Cptl Sfe Dpsits, Bell Lne. 1 hr."

Fifteen minutes later, Jemma was back on the Tube, taking an eastbound District Line train.

Dirty newspapers were trod underfoot as people hurried out of Liverpool Street station. Bell Lane was somewhere on the other side of the main road. After crossing Bishopsgate, the streets became narrower. Bank headquarters loomed over tiny side streets where shops catered to wealthy office workers. This was Jack the Ripper territory, although nearly every trace of old Spitalfields, where he had plied his evil trade, had been demolished.

From the look of it, the café on Bell Lane catered to builders. Inside, the atmosphere was thick with steam and grease. A woman stood behind the counter slopping tea from an oversized teapot. Jemma spotted Toppy sitting at the back watching the entrance, and she slid into the booth facing her, their knees almost touching.

"Where's my son?" she hissed quietly.

To her surprise, Toppy looked frightened. "Christ, I could use a cigarette," she said.

"I want my son back. I'll kill you right now if you don't tell me."

"Cigarette?"

"Tell me where Matthew is." Jemma grabbed the lapels of Toppy's coat.

"I didn't kidnap your son. They did."

That brought Jemma up short. She stared at Toppy incredulously.

"What do you mean? Who are 'They'?"

"Do you think this is about you or Matthew? Don't you see, it's bigger than that."

Toppy's hand shook as she picked up her coffee cup. One rheumy-eyed old man sitting across from them wrapped up in an overcoat was reading a copy of The Sun. To Jemma's horror, her photo was on the front page beneath the headline "Cops Hunt Toddler Mum."

Toppy went on, "You want the whole story? You want to stop threatening me?"

Jemma released her grip and sat a little farther back in her chair. "Go on."

"You must have figured out that the Americans were paying Tony to let them run the drugs test. But there was more to it than that. He promised them the hospital's entire drugs supply. A contract worth millions. Tony said he would swing it for them. He wanted a lot of money up front. Half now and half when the deal was done. Tony came up with the idea of me faking my own death. He wanted me to take the money and then he would join me. But they got suspicious and wanted their money back. That's why they took your son. As ransom. They wanted to make sure Tony repaid what he'd taken." She leaned forward. "Look, I want to get out of this just as much as you do. Both of us are trapped. They get their money back, and your son goes free. Everybody gets what they want."

So why hadn't the American said anything about this when he came to see her in the park? She'd looked into his eyes when she asked if he knew anything about Matthew but had seen nothing.

Toppy continued to ramble. "If Nibley hadn't changed his mind, the whole thing would've worked."

"But now they want their money back, right?" Even as she was saying it, she realised how unlikely it all sounded. Nothing she was hearing made any sense. "How much cash are you talking about?"

"There's a safety deposit box across the road with about half a million pounds left."

"So give them their money back."

"I can't."

"What do you mean, you can't?"

"Tony gave me the key to the safety deposit box, but he never told me what the code was. You need both the key and the code to get into the vault downstairs."

So her husband had not quite trusted this woman. This way, both of them would need to be in the same room at the same time to open the safety deposit box.

Toppy's voice was pleading. "They've promised to release Matthew unharmed. They said on the news that you discovered Tony's body. They must have got the code out of him and then forced Tony to kill himself."

She imagined Nibley confidently walking round Tony's kitchen while her husband lay dying on the floor. They didn't have the key. Only Toppy had that. She remembered what Nibley said about wanting his money back.

Toppy continued, "When you found him, was he still alive? Did he say anything to you? Getting into that safety deposit box is the only way to save Matthew."

She remembered Tony's warm breath on her ear as he whispered. What had he said? 'Matthew's birthday'. "Finish your coffee," Jemma said. "We're going to get that money. Then you are going to get my son back."

CHAPTER THIRTY-FIVE

Walker ran his hand across the map of London pinned to the notice board. Doctor Sands had been missing for eight hours now, and every available officer in the Met was looking for her. She had to turn up somewhere. There were eleven thousand CCTV cameras covering the Tube network alone. You couldn't just disappear into like that. Not in the metropolis.

"What I don't understand is where she could have gone to," said Walker, turning to face DI Balogun. "We're watching her mother's house, but she hasn't tried contacting her. She has no other family."

Balogun stopped eating and held his yoghurt-covered spoon in mid-air.

"If you ask me, she's gone rogue. That woman she keeps talking about. She's gone after her, see?"

Walker pulled a face. "I've been through HOLMES," he said, referring to the Home Office crime database. "Toppy Mrazek didn't have a criminal record. I've got an officer at the last psychiatric hospital she was admitted to when she was younger. Maybe they have something."

"So what's your thinking, boss? Coming round to her side?"

"Like I told the Commander, I'm not interested in sides. I just want the truth."

"Okumu put the boot in, did he?"

"You could say that. Let me put it this way. He wasn't too pleased that our only suspect has gone missing."

"What if she's telling the truth and this other woman has taken her son?"

"I don't care. Right now she's a suspect in a murder investigation. She's running away from something. She hasn't just popped out for a pint of milk."

"What if she tries leaving the country?"

"I've already logged an All Ports Warning with the Police National Computer. They've got her description and a photograph."

"Yeah, fat lot of good that will do. They just look at your passport and wave you through, don't they."

"Look. You know and I know that the Border Agency couldn't find Osama bloody Bin Laden in an all-girls' choir. But it's important that we're seen to be doing the right thing."

"Sounds like you've got everything as tight as a mother superior's bum," Balogun said with a grin. He returned to his yoghurt.

Was that really true? Walker wondered. Had he really thought of everything? Was there one thing, one tiny detail he had overlooked? He still felt shaken from Okumu's phone call. Walker rubbed the corner of his eye with the heel of his palm. It was only eleven o'clock, and already he was bone-tired. He had slipped into bed next to his wife in the early hours of the morning and apologised for being so late. "Doesn't matter, love," she had murmured before turning away. And he had been up and out of the house before she was awake.

"What mother kidnaps her own son?" Walker thought aloud.

Balogun licked his spoon clean. "Maybe it's like that case up north, that mum who kept her daughter in a bedroom. She was only two streets away. What if the Commander is right? It's a wild goose chase. She was covering for her husband, and now she's been rumbled."

There was a knock at the door, and a woman constable came in holding a manila envelope.

"This has just arrived from forensics, sir. They're sorry it's so late. They know you put a rush on it. It's just that they're backed up."

The DCI pulled out the forensics report on the Rohypnol bottle they had found in the well of the doctor's car. The bottle had been examined using specialist lighting and put in a glue chamber. The serrated edge of a plastic cap was not good for fingerprints, so that had been swabbed for DNA. Forensics had found a recent partial smudge on the bottle itself. However, nothing matched on the national fingerprint database – including the doctor's own fingerprints. Walker quickly scanned past the jargon to the conclusion at the foot of the page.

Whoever had left that print on the bottle was not Doctor Jemma Sands.

CHAPTER THIRTY-SIX

Capital Safe Deposits was covered in scaffolding and plastic sheeting. A sandwich board pointed the way inside. Toppy swiped a plastic card and a buzzer sounded. Inside was a shabby room with a bureau de change window. Toppy swiped her card again, and both women pushed through into a second room. From the CCTV cameras, Jemma guessed this was the mantrap: you wouldn't get any farther if they didn't like the look of you. This reception room had a dainty, rather frigid atmosphere, like a funeral parlour. There was even a small vase of plastic flowers on a scratched reproduction table. Toppy slid her card into an old-fashioned beige card reader and keypad on the wall and turned to Jemma expectantly. Now it was her turn: Please, God, let this be the right number. Jemma tapped in the date of Matthew's birthday.

They waited.

Nothing.

Her heart lurched. Without the code, they could not get into the vault. The safety deposit box with the money to set Matthew free would stay alarmed.

"Try again," Toppy said tensely.

Panicked, Jemma rekeyed the date of Matthew's birthday. Still nothing. She wanted to bang the keypad with her fist in frustration.

"You must have got the number wrong."

"I told you. The last words Tony said to me were 'Matthew's birthday'. It has to be right, it just has to be."

A memory. Matthew's last birthday party. Tony had come home early from the hospital to help Jemma tidy up. Some of the nursery school mothers were in the kitchen drinking wine. Tony was charming them, and she listened to their laughter as she prowled the sitting room playing Sleeping Tigers with the children. Matthew's kindergarten friends lay on the floor pretending to be asleep. Later, Tony had helped her clear up, scraping chocolate cake off Toy Story plastic plates. "I've done something a bit extravagant," he said with a tired smile. "I've bought our son a twenty-first birthday present. A case of wine." She remembered saying that the year 2028 sounded very far away; they would all be whizzing around in flying cars with pills for food and wearing spacesuits by then, she told him.

She keyed in the year of Matthew's twenty-first birthday. The green liquid crystal display changed to "Approved". Her knees almost buckled in relief.

The vault door was already ajar as they stepped down into the basement. Beyond the bars, the vault was lined with thousands of burgundy-leather boxes, each with its own brass lock. Toppy explained that the vault was encased by a two-foot-thick cement-and-steel wall. All that stuff you saw on TV about people clipping an alarm cable with a pair of bolt cutters was nonsense. There were at least five different alarms, each of them independently run. Five separate alarm companies held keys. There was also a motion sensor at night. Anybody caught walking in the vault would set off the alarm.

Toppy walked down the corridor of boxes looking for the right one. Jemma wondered what was in the other boxes lining the room. Gold and paperwork mostly, she guessed. Jemma heard somebody else coming downstairs. If she was spotted, it would all be over. She wiped her hands down the side of her jeans in fear. Toppy was waiting for her at the far end, and she went up to join her. She had already put the key in the lock.

"Ready?" she asked.

Somebody touched Jemma on the shoulder.

A dumpy woman was standing right behind her. She was shorter than Jemma, with hard flinty eyes and thin determined lips.

"You're her, aren't you?" she said. "The doctor whose son has gone missing."

This was it. It was all over. Jemma nodded, finding it difficult to swallow.

"I am sorry about what you're going through. You must be in hell. If anything happened to my two…"

"Thank you. That's very kind." Jemma nodded dumbly.

To her surprise, the woman came forward and hugged her. For a moment, the two of them stood there, locked in an awkward embrace.

"I put a candle in my window for Matthew," she said, stepping back. "There were candles all down our street last night."

Obviously her well-wisher was unaware that a warrant had been issued for her arrest. Jemma almost felt like laughing. The woman wandered off in search of her own safety-deposit box.

"Breathe," said Toppy.

Jemma exhaled deeply. Toppy turned the key, and the burgundy-leather box swung open. Inside was a grey metal drawer, which Toppy slid out and carried to a privacy booth, whisking the blue curtain shut behind them. She placed the drawer down on a desk. Jemma's heart pounded so hard it hurt. As Toppy levered the lid open, she imagined plastic-wrapped bundles of fifty-pound notes jammed together.

Instead, the shoebox was empty.

CHAPTER THIRTY-SEVEN

Jemma did not pretend to hide her disappointment. It was so unfair – Matthew seemed just as far away as ever. Toppy reached in and pulled out an origami bird that Jemma had not spotted. "You didn't think it was going to be full of money, did you?" Toppy asked. Jemma didn't like her patronising tone of voice. Toppy unfolded the swan. "It's a message telling us where the money is," she said. "We give them this, and then we can get your son back. We all walk away and never see each other again." With a sinking stomach, Jemma realised just what she had done. She felt sick. By wheedling the code out of her, Toppy had made her reveal where Tony had really hidden the money – something that even he had not trusted her with. Lured by the prospect of being reunited with her son, Jemma had dumbly gone along with the plan. Now Toppy could get her hands on everything she wanted; Jemma had thrown away the only card she held.

Out in the street, a police siren was getting louder. Both women looked at each other. "Somebody must have recognised you," Toppy said. "Quick. Follow me."

They exited the building as fast as they could and started

running down the street, pushing their way through startled pedestrians.

"How are we going to get out of this?" Jemma panted.

"My car's parked round the corner," Toppy said over her shoulder.

They barged their way through a pavement full of people. A man shouted as she jostled his cup of coffee. Toppy turned down a side street towards a multi-storey car park. Jemma was not far behind, but she was struggling to keep up. She must have shut her eyes for only a couple of minutes last night, and her exhaustion was catching up with her. Her calves felt stiff and her chest hurt like hell. Come on, you lazy cow, come on. She felt as if she was running through a long, dark tunnel.

They clattered up a piss-stinking car park stairwell. Pulling the door open at the top, they emerged onto the second-floor parking level. Tyres screeched as a saloon swung round looking for a space. Toppy was making for a black hatchback parked up ahead. Its lights flashed as she unlocked it.

They slammed both doors shut, and Toppy fumbled with the key in the ignition. Just in time, too: a police car charged up the ramp, swinging round towards them. Toppy started the engine and reversed out sharply. Jemma was thrown forward as Toppy slammed on the brakes and put the car in first as they hammered towards the exit. The police would have to zigzag through the entire car park system if they wanted to catch up.

Now their car was plunging down the corkscrew tunnel, tyres screeching as Toppy turned the wheel hard left. Jemma hung on to the passenger-seat strap, her heart in her mouth. They plunged round tight bends at dizzying speed. Any moment now they were going to hit the wall, she knew it.

The road flattened out as they approached the crash barrier.

"We didn't pay for our ticket," Toppy remembered.

Pulling up outside the ticket booth, Jemma leapt from the car. She heard the police car's tyres screeching as it came down the ramp.

"Please," she said, rapping on the glass. An overweight man ambled towards the counter. "Two pounds fifty," he said, pointing to his till display. Jemma dug into her jeans and pushed her last crumpled five pound note through the tray. "Wait a minute. I'll go and get you change," he said. The car park manager wandered off towards the back of his office. "It doesn't matter," Jemma almost shouted. "Just give me the ticket." She glanced back and saw the police car screeching round the corner. The cashier shrugged.

After what seemed like an age, the crash barrier lifted. They were out of there. Jemma looked back and, to her satisfaction, the barrier was coming down again, trapping the police car with its headlights flashing and horn blaring.

"Where now?" she gasped, turning back to Toppy.

"We need to make sure we're not being followed."

They were heading east through the City and out towards Bow. It had started raining. Was Matthew being held in some grim East End housing estate? Or was he being kept in a rundown suburb farther out? She pictured her son cowering inside a boarded-up house with an overgrown garden somewhere on the outskirts of the city.

"Is that where they've got him? Somewhere in east London?"

"Pass me my phone. It's in my bag by your feet."

Jemma reached down and fished out Toppy's iPhone. Fat water rivulets chased each other down the windscreen.

Toppy made the call. "I know where the money is now. Yes. I have the account number. You promised you would let him go. Yes. Have you got a pen? Zero-seven-eight-five-five-seven-four-five. The sort code is seventeen-twelve-thirty-nine. I've kept my side of the bargain. Where can we find the boy?"

Pause. Please, God, let them release my little boy unharmed.

"Chalcot Farm. Howarth Road. Near Margate. Is there a post code?"

Toppy's mobile was cradled between her chin and her

neck as she drove, a notepad balanced on her knee as she scribbled down the address. She ended the call, passing the iPhone back to Jemma.

"He's being held in a farm in Kent. They'll send him out when they see the car."

Jemma frowned at what she heard. "I don't understand. You've already told them the account details. They have everything they need. Why can't they just release Matthew now?"

"Release him where? Do you want him picked up by a stranger on the side of a road? It's better that we go and collect him. I told you, this is a dirty business. The deal has gone down twisted."

"What's to stop me going to the police once Matthew is safe? They could all go to jail for years."

"You could do that, but do you really want Tri-Med as your enemy? An American multinational with unlimited resources? They could bury you forever."

Jemma didn't care about Tri-Med, she only wanted to be reunited with her son. "What will you do now?" she couldn't help but ask.

"Dunno. Move away. Live in a different country. Everybody thinks I'm dead anyway." She gave a mirthless laugh, and Jemma saw a flash of the old nastiness, a reminder of why she knew this woman was her enemy the moment she first laid eyes on her. Don't think you're going to get away with this, Jemma thought, you are going to pay for what you have done.

A police siren cut into her thoughts, and she glimpsed the blue lights flashing in her side mirror. "There's a police car following us," Jemma said. They were heading towards the Blackwall Tunnel, and even as they plunged into it, Jemma could see that traffic was slowing down. A traffic jam. The last thing they needed.

Cars crawled along the tunnel bumper to bumper, red lights glancing off the ribbed walls. The police car was still behind them, caught in the same traffic.

They ground to a halt.

"Come on. We've got to get out of here," Toppy said, grabbing her shoulder bag.

Barely knowing what she was doing, Jemma found herself running along the service walkway above the cars with Toppy. The tunnel's walls boomed with engine sounds, and the smell of petrol was nauseating. Green arrows pointed the way ahead. Jemma didn't dare look around to see if police were chasing them on foot. They kept running past the wall-mounted telephones lit up in red with the word "SOS". Save Our Souls indeed. Thankfully, she could see cars edging forward towards the square of daylight up ahead.

Toppy clattered down the steps back onto the road and rapped on a driver's side window.

The man inside warily wound his window down.

"Please. You must help me," said Toppy. "My car's back there. I think my husband has had a heart attack." The driver reacted immediately.

"Do you want me to call an ambulance? I've got a mobile phone."

"Please. I need your help."

The driver started getting out of his car. Jemma glanced behind her. Two police officers were running towards them. Before the driver knew what was happening, Toppy was inside his car – it took Jemma a moment to realise she had to get in, too. Toppy locked the car doors with a satisfying thunk. The driver, realising now that he was the victim of car theft, started banging angrily on the window.

Toppy revved the engine and within moments they were moving again, emerging into daylight and into the bleak industrial hinterland of Greenwich: a dreary suburban sprawl of semi-detached houses. Jemma heard the chug of a police helicopter flying overhead. With a stab of relief, she realised the police would have no idea which car they were in now. Toppy was clever, she had to give her that.

Another police car accelerated past them, with its siren ear-piercingly loud.

They drove on in silence, Jemma flinching every time she heard a siren. After about twenty minutes or so, they both relaxed a little. No police car was following them. They had slipped through the net.

Eventually, Toppy pulled over for petrol.

As Toppy stood filling the car, she rapped on the window, and gestured for Jemma to pass her wallet through the window. As Toppy crossed the forecourt to pay, Jemma rummaged in Toppy's bag until she found the origami bird. The pencilled numbers were definitely in Tony's handwriting. Memorising the account number and sort code, she remembered the French bank website that she had noticed bookmarked on Tony's computer. Was this the account that he had set up for his slush fund?

Toppy was heading back towards the car. Jemma froze. Toppy must not see what she was doing. She flung the scrap of paper back down and sat up straight, pretending nothing was wrong. To her relief, Toppy didn't seem to notice anything awry.

The journey continued interminably, rain obscuring the landscape around them. Rain smoked around the back tyres of the cars in front. Jemma asked how long until they got to the farmhouse. "Nearly there," Jemma said peering through the windscreen, which had become a sliding wall of water. They turned left into a main road and then left again down a country lane. Toppy pulled the car over in a lay-by.

"They don't know that you're with me," she said. "Given that you're all over the news, they might panic and call the deal off if they see you."

"You can't just leave me here."

"I'm not saying that. Get in the boot until we've got Matthew. You can get out once the coast is clear."

"You have to be kidding," Jemma said. Toppy just looked away, and they sat there listening to the rain thrumming on the roof. Jemma realised she had no choice. Once again she had to trust this woman, on the basis of what? A thread of a chance that she would see her son again? "Okay," she said finally. After a minute, she got out of the passenger seat, and Toppy pressed the boot-release button. It lifted with a hydraulic suck, and she clambered inside as Toppy slammed it back down. Neither of them spoke.

It was dark inside the boot. Jemma reached with her fingers, exploring the tight space she was in. Part of her was furious for allowing herself to be put in such a vulnerable position, but what other choice did she have? Her knees were tucked up against her chest, and she had to brace herself against the corners. Lying there in the blackness, she tried keeping track of where they were going: first they turned left, then right. Now they seemed to be turning in on themselves. She gave up. Instead, she pictured the isolated farmhouse, a vicious dog barking, and a man with a shotgun stepping outside gripping the arm of her frightened son; Matthew would see his mummy and they would run, run towards each other...

Jemma's daydream was interrupted as the car stopped. She heard Toppy getting out. The sound of a metal fence clanging open. Then they were on the move once more, water sloshing beneath the car as it lurched through potholes. The car pulled up again, the engine was switched off and, again, it sounded as if Toppy was getting out. They must be at the farm, Jemma thought, adrenaline coursing through her. Any moment now she would be reunited with Matthew. She braced herself but, no, they were on the move again. This wasn't normal driving, this was just rolling forward; the engine hadn't actually been switched on this time. The car was picking up speed.

Jemma suddenly understood what was happening: Toppy was pushing the back of the car. She heard her grunt with the effort. Jemma was too petrified to scream. Instead, she just lay there, rigid with fear. The car began moving faster and faster, and suddenly it tipped forward violently. A horrible weightless moment, and Jemma felt her world falling through the air. "Not like this," she thought. "Please God, not like this."

CHAPTER THIRTY-EIGHT

She felt like she was in a grand piano being dropped on cement. Her head banged on the roof so hard, she almost bit her tongue off. Blood filled her mouth, and the pain from her skull was excruciating. But worst of all, her feet were soaking.

The car boot was taking in water.

Her mind scrabbled. There must be some kind of button she could press to open the boot from inside. Water was really streaming in now – it felt so cold sloshing around her in the pitch darkness. She felt for a catch or a lever. Nothing. The car lurched unexpectedly forward. The front end must already be under water. Strangely, she felt no panic, no need to scream. She was going to get out of this. She had to.

Reaching behind her, she felt for the back seats. Good. They were the type you folded down. Now, if she could just manoeuvre around. She tried getting into a position where she could start kicking at one of the back seats, but she was so cramped it was almost impossible. The boot must have been one third full now, with the water rising fast. She realised her teeth were chattering with the cold.

There was an ominous metallic groaning sound. By now, the car was almost standing straight up. She kicked with all her might. At any moment the car would be underwater. She felt the right-hand seat give way a little, and she started kicking at it frantically with everything she had. The seat moved a little more before suddenly breaking completely. Water rushed in as she slid down, but there was still air to breathe. She still had a few more seconds. Now, if she could just edge her way down into the driver's seat...

The car was sinking fast. Jemma was thrown backwards. Regaining her balance, she clambered between the front seats onto the driver's side.

Dark water pressed against the windows. If she could just open the door, she could swim to the surface. But when she tried to open the driver's door, it would not budge. There was too much pressure keeping the door closed. What about the window? If she could just open it, then more water would gush in and the pressure would equalize. Her fingers searched for the electronic switch. Jemma prayed the battery was still working. Thank God, the window started to lower. Then it stopped. The battery must have shorted out. She was still trapped.

Gallons of water were pouring in through the gap in the window, pooling around her legs and rising. It was already up to the hand brake. If she could only hang on until the water filled the interior; she remembered enough physics to know that the door would open then. She felt the swift, cold water rising up to her chest. She had five, maybe ten seconds to live. An image of Matthew flashed before her; she could not give up on life, she loved him too much. One last effort, she urged herself. Take one last breath for Matthew. She gasped at the air, pulled herself down towards the door and curled her fingers almost lazily around the catch. The door opened in slow motion. Kicking her way free, she swam to the surface, lungs burning as her head broke the water. Jemma gasped.

Now she wanted to laugh and cry and shout all at the same time. But her joy was short-lived. She was in some kind of quarry. She noticed the rain had stopped, and she could see the hill where the car must have fallen from. Jemma swam to the water's edge, dragged down by her heavy clothes. She was so cold. Feeling her way up the slimy, muddy bank, she fell onto the shingle and rolled over. Jemma had never been so grateful to be alive.

After lying there for a couple of minutes, she was able to take stock. Yes, she was glad to be alive, but she was miles from home, had only a little money left and was still on the run from the police. But for a moment, none of that mattered. That bitch had tried to kill her, and she had escaped. She lay there panting until she was so freezing she had to get up and start moving.

She surveyed the scene and realised the only way to get out of here would be to climb up the side of the quarry. She reached up for her first handhold, bracing herself, using her strongest leg. She launched herself up. It was hard going. A couple of times she just froze with fear, clinging to the side of the rock. She didn't know how to go on. Whatever she did, she knew she must not look down. Once her foot slipped, and she heard pebbles spinning into the dirty water below. Finally, she caught hold of some tough plant roots and hauled herself upwards and onto flat land. Lying face down, she panted with the effort. Her head was thumping, there were cuts and bruises all over her body, and the coldness was almost unbearable, but adrenaline and the thought of revenge kept her mind clear. She had to get into some dry clothes.

Sitting up, Jemma saw padlocked gates and a chain-link fence. Jesus, she said aloud. It was another Everest, but she had no option. Her muscles screamed as she hauled herself upwards. The thought of finding Toppy kept her going. This one's for you, bitch. As she straddled the top of the fence, she heard the swish of cars on the motorway nearby. The normal world was going on without her. Below was a rubbish dump where people fly-tipped things they didn't want: a greasy sofa, bursting dustbin bags, even a child's potty. There was also a nasty-looking spike fused into a concrete lump.

Swinging her other leg over the fence, she jumped down. Even as she was falling, Jemma knew she had miscalculated. Her foot landed on the spike and she felt it puncture her flimsy plimsoll. Sitting down on the grass

verge, she pulled off her shoe and her wet sock. Examining
the nasty hole in her foot, she saw it would need a tetanus
jab. At that, Jemma lay down again and began shaking
uncontrollably. It was all too much for her to comprehend.
So Toppy had planned to kill her all along: all that stuff
about Matthew being held in exchange for a ransom was a
complete lie. Toppy had lured her into the car boot and had
pushed her over the edge.

It was turning into a bright, cold day as the sun came out,
and she felt a little warmth on her face. She must have
closed her eyes for a moment, because the next thing
she knew a dog was excitedly sniffing her and a woman
was crying sharply, "Come away." Jemma raised herself
up on her elbows and saw a car had pulled over with
its hazard lights flashing. Broken glass glittered in the
sunlight. The woman was walking towards her. "Are you all
right?" she asked. "You're wet through." She was vaguely
horsey-looking, one of those mums you see taking their
kids to school in tank-like four-wheel drives. Jemma said
something about rambling and getting lost. "I can give
you a lift into town if you like," the woman said. She was
taking her daughter swimming at a nearby leisure centre
and could drop Jemma at the train station. Jemma hobbled
after her. The daughter had her face pressed against
the rear window. The car radio was playing: "Police are
still searching for Doctor Jemma Sands, the 34-year-old
mother whose son Matthew, five, has been missing since
Wednesday. Police arrested Doctor Sands..." Jemma's heart

was thumping. Would this woman make the connection? Thankfully, she started the engine, interrupting the news bulletin, and the newsreader had already moved on when the radio cut back in.

Five minutes later they were driving into one of the Medway towns, the highlight of which seemed to be a discount supermarket.

The woman asked Jemma only a few questions on the way to the railway station, while the daughter just stared. The warm blast of the car heater was a blessing, but Jemma knew she had to steel herself for yet another massive effort. She was not safe yet.

Jemma sat on the platform letting the sun dry her wet jeans and sodden fleece. She reckoned she had just enough pound coins to get herself back to London. Once on the train, she locked herself in the toilet. Catching sight of herself in the mirror, she saw a face grey with pain. She tried to clean herself using the trickle of cold water from the tap. As she did so, her mind whirred. Toppy was the one calling the shots now. She had everything while Jemma had nothing. After all, the bitch had the bank account details where Tony had deposited the cash: all she had to do now was go and get it. Then she would disappear forever with Matthew and half a million pounds of Tri-Med's money. Jemma imagined Matthew, older and with his hair cut differently, standing in a street market in Vietnam or Cambodia, somewhere in the Far East. There was a hurt look on his face, as if he could not understand why his mummy had not tried to find him.

Back at Victoria station, Jemma spotted a couple of policeman chatting to one another in the ticket hall, hands in stab vests. Her mouth went dry at the sight of them, and she averted her face as she bought a ticket with the last of her change. The ticket gate banged open. She limped through.

It was just two stops to South Kensington, where she could walk to the hospital.

Limping into the main entrance, she knew she was taking one hell of a risk. Every step would be monitored on closed-circuit television. Her foot was throbbing like a pump, though, and she must clean and dress it before she did anything else. Stuffing her hands into her anorak pockets, she felt for the plastic shopping bag she had rescued from a rubbish bin. Keeping her head down, she walked confidently past reception and through the atrium until she reached a stairwell. Hanging on to the banister for support, she hobbled downstairs and punched in the key code.

The basement was where they did the patients' laundry, and she sidled past cages full of dirty towels. One of the porters was in the laundry pulling sheets out of a big industrial drier. The air smelt of warmth and fabric conditioner, and for a moment she breathed it in, letting herself be transported to a place where nothing bad could ever happen. Grabbing one of the neatly folded doctors' coats, she limped towards the drugs store.

For a moment her mind went blank, as she strained to think of the right combination on the metal keypad. She keyed in what she thought was the right code and pulled the door.

Nothing.

Then, letting her fingers remember, she tried again. This time the door unlocked as she pulled it open, and she exhaled deeply.

The lights flickered as Jemma went through the shelves pulling out supplies she might need, dropping them into her Tesco bag. She listened out for the door, petrified of being discovered. Hiding in the furthest corner of the room, she took off her sock, which was stiff with blood. She winced as she poured chlorhexidine over the hole in her foot. Once the sole had been cleaned up, she carefully placed a Mepore dressing over it. Her foot felt tender as she gingerly tested it on the ground. She limped over to one of the humming fridges where they kept the tetanus vials. Ripping open a sealed plastic syringe with her teeth, she stuck the needle into the bottle and drew out the liquid, squirting a few drops and flicking the barrel to get rid of any air. Bracing herself against the wall, she squeezed a fleshy ridge on the top of her thigh and jabbed hard.

Taking the stairs back up to the first floor, she opened the door a fraction. Two nurses wearing blue scrubs were standing farther off, chatting to one another. She dug her hands in her doctor's coat and tried to walk normally looking purposeful. One of the nurses looked at her strangely.

George's office was at the far end of the first floor.

He was sitting at his computer as she pushed his door open. She hadn't knocked. As he turned around in surprise, she noticed that he had started wearing glasses. "Good Lord, Jemma," he began, rising from his chair.

Closing the door behind her, she leant against it. This was the first time she had felt safe since the police had come to arrest her. George looked as if he had seen a ghost. "Are you all right? I heard on the news that the police were looking for you. Here, sit down."

Slumping in the chair opposite him, she asked if she could have a cup of tea. She realised she had not eaten anything all day, and her insides gnawed themselves with hunger. George fussed about boiling a kettle and passed her a leftover flapjack and a banana. She wolfed down the food. Now that the adrenaline had worn off, she felt overwhelmingly tired. George handed her a cup of tea laced with sugar, and she slowly told him her story. Halfway through, George walked to his door and locked it. His eyes widened when she told him that Toppy was still alive, and he gaped when she explained how she'd been left to drown in the car boot.

"Nibley came to see me yesterday afternoon," she said.

"He wants his money back. Apparently Tony didn't just take money for your drugs trial. He had promised them the entire hospital drugs supply contract. It's worth millions." Her body shook with a sudden shiver, and she sipped more tea. "Tony got greedy. He wanted a fat upfront payment. It was going to be his running-away money. Toppy conned me into telling her the safety deposit box code. Even Tony hadn't quite trusted her with that. I feel such an idiot. She has everything, George, everything."

"Will you go to the police? You haven't done anything wrong. You've got nothing to hide."

"You have a touching faith in authority, George." She looked up at his caring face. "Do you really think they're going to believe me? They already have a prime suspect. You're looking at her."

"Every single policeman in London will be on the lookout for you. The best thing you can do is turn yourself in, Jemma. You've got no choice."

She could see the sense in what George said, but she had come too far to listen to him. "I'm not going to do that, George. I'm the only one who can get myself out of this. Either you help me, or I leave." She made as if to rise from her chair.

"Jemma, sit down. Drink the tea." He pushed her gently back onto her seat. "You know I will do what I can. But I'm not a detective. I don't know what to do."

"I need proof that Toppy is still alive and that she has Matthew." Jemma's voice had an edge to it. As her body warmed, her mind was whirring back into action.

"What about your mobile phone? That must still have her text on it," George offered.

"I thought of that. It's dead from all the water. It won't switch on."

"Well, what about CCTV footage of the two of you going into that bank vault? That would prove she's still alive."

"That's assuming the police believe me. She and Matthew could be on the other side of the world by the time I convince them. No, there's only one thing I can do." She looked again at George. He was an innocent in all this, a follower not a leader. She couldn't tell him everything. If she worked alone, it would mean she was protected. "Let me think, George. Let me think for a minute."

Her mind went over the early events of today. All the safety deposit box had in it was the account number for another bank, one in France. That was it. Toppy was heading back to the island. Tony had told her that Toppy had a childhood summer house there, and how dead the place was in winter. She could lie low there until she got the money. That was where she had to go then. The island. No matter what it took, Jemma would get her son back.

George looked at her over his half-moon glasses and saw the first smile of the day on his friend's face. "What is it that you want me to do?" he asked.

Jemma thought for a moment. "I need your credit card."

CHAPTER THIRTY-NINE

Walker knew the hospital psychiatrist was lying when he glanced away at the detective's question. Looking to your right rather than your left was a sure-fire way of knowing somebody was not being truthful.

The detective pressed again. "I just want to be clear about this," he said. "You haven't had any contact with Doctor Sands since she absconded? I don't have to tell you how serious the situation is. It's important that we speak to her."

Malvern rubbed his nose. Another tell. "Are you suggesting that I'm not telling the truth? I resent the implication."

"I'm not suggesting anything. All I'm saying is that if you know anything, anything that could help us find her, you must tell us. Not for our sake, but for hers."

"I've already told you. I haven't seen or heard from Jemma since she came to see me in my flat."

Walker looked down at the notepad on his knee. He was convinced Doctor Malvern was lying. But how to persuade him they were on the same side, that increasingly he was coming around to Jemma's version of events?

"All right," said Walker. "Let's go through what you talked

about when she came to see you two days ago. How did she seem?"

"How would you feel? Her six-year-old son had gone missing. She'd just been through a traumatising press conference. She told me that she wasn't sleeping, wasn't eating. And that when she did sleep, she had bad dreams about her son. Classic PTSD. I told her one of my staff could see her. It wouldn't be appropriate for her to see me given that we're friends."

"Did you talk about anything else? Did she mention the name Toppy Mrazek to you?"

Malvern shifted in his seat. "Yes, she told me her theory that her husband's girlfriend had stolen her son. I told her to stop being so ridiculous. I mean, from what I read in the paper, the French police say it was a tragic accident. People don't come back from the dead, do they?"

Balogun, who was leaning against the psychiatrist's desk, interrupted. "You know that we're going through every hour of CCTV footage. We'll soon know if you're telling porkies or not."

Walker raised his hand to shush him. "Detective Inspector, please could you leave me alone with Doctor Malvern for a moment? There's something I'd like to talk to him about." The DI slid off the desk, but not before giving the psychiatrist a hard stare.

Waiting for the door to close, Malvern visibly relaxed once

the other man was outside the room. "I don't think he likes me very much," he said.

"Oh, he doesn't like anybody very much." Walker paused. "Tell me, do you read the Bible?"

Malvern frowned, unsure of where the conversation was going. "Actually I'm an atheist. When it comes to theories, I want to see evidence. I prefer Gradgrindian facts."

"But you know the story of St Paul, the Damascene conversion and all that? He was a Roman whose job was to hunt down early Christians..."

"...until he went over to their side." The psychiatrist smiled. "Are you telling me that you're actually starting to believe Jemma's story?"

Glancing at the door, Walker said, "Listen. I shouldn't be telling you this, but we found a bottle of Rohypnol in the footwell of Doctor Sands' car. Whoever left that bottle there was not Doctor Sands." Malvern's eyes widened. "Somebody is fitting her up. So I'm going to ask you again. If you know anything that might help us find her, you must tell me. She might be in great danger."

Walker sat back. There was nothing more he could do now but wait for Malvern to come to him. He could see the words forming in the psychiatrist's mouth. Come on, tell me where she is, Walker thought. Just then there was a knock on the door. The moment was gone.

Balogun stuck his head round the door. "The incident

room got a call from somebody who's seen the boy. They're convinced it's genuine."

"Thank you, Detective Inspector. I'll be right out," Walker said acidly before rising to leave. One more minute and the doctor would have told him what he needed. Malvern stood up too, clearly relieved the interview was over.

One hour later, and both policemen were standing on the doorstep of an Acton council estate. A community support officer answered the door and led them into a dingy sitting room. Walker took in the drab walls with the butterfly mirror above the fireplace, and large overstuffed chairs draped with antimacassars. The old woman who had contacted the incident room shuffled in with a tea tray.

"So, what are you going to do about it?" she asked.

The CSO coughed and said, "Mrs Freer has made regular complaints about Flat 34 but says the police do nothing."

"That's right," the woman said, nodding. "There's shouting. Doors slamming. Cars. I know what goes on in there."

Walker studied her dried-up face and her startlingly blue eyes. He sipped the tea and said, "You have my word we're going to crack down on this. I can see how aggravating it is. In the meantime, though" – he turned to the plastic document folder he carried everywhere holding the case essentials – "we need to talk to you about this boy."

He handed the woman the blown-up snapshot of Matthew taken on holiday. People had started putting the photo in the windows of their homes above lit candles. The missing boy had caught the public imagination. "Yes," the woman said, "that's him." Feeling his excitement mount, Walker handed the old woman the next photo, a portrait of Doctor Sands. Mrs Freer studied the picture and shook her head. "No, that wasn't her. She's similar, mind, but that's not the woman," she said. Balogun and Walker exchanged a look. The DCI slid the photo back into the plastic file and stood up to leave.

Back outside, Balogun leaned over the balcony. "I was brought up on this estate. My mum could see where this was going. Carrying a knife for one of the older kids. Dead outside the school gates. She wanted to get us out of here sharpish."

Walker joined him, and both men gazed out over the grey sprawl of tower blocks. You could taste the concrete at the back of your throat.

"We don't have a search warrant," Balogun continued. "If he doesn't want to talk to us, that's that."

"I'm not interested in some small-time drugs dealer flogging stuff on eBay. We need to know if she took him to visit this flat, and why. He'll have to face the consequences if he knew this was Matthew and his mother. She wanted something."

"What about a computer? He's a regular Only Fools and Horses, this one."

"There's only one way to find out."

Balogun banged on the metal door behind the iron bars. There was no answer. When he banged again, the sound reverberated along the walkway. A fat middle-aged man carefully opened the door while keeping the gate locked.

"Can I help you, officer?" he said, blinking behind his spectacles. Was there a touch of a lisp?

Balogun said, "We're looking for a missing six-year-old. Matthew Sands. He's been all over the TV and the papers. You must have seen him." He held up the Missing poster, and the drugs dealer pretended to study it.

"I'm sorry, officer, I've never seen the boy before. Now, if you'll excuse me..."

Balogun said, "Do I look as if I've got the word cunt written on my forehead?"

Walker interrupted, putting his hand through the gate to stop the door shutting. "Listen to me. The boy came here with his mother. We know that. You're going to be in a lot of trouble if you don't give us what we want. Why did she come here?"

Goldie hesitated. "Perhaps you'd better come in," he said before unlocking the gate.

Inside was more like a warehouse than a home. Boxes piled everywhere: Samsung, LG, Sony and Apple. Expensive-looking racing bikes stacked against one wall. Probably stolen to order and then shipped to Eastern Europe. A beaded curtain was strung across the hallway, separating what Walker took to be the living area. He sensed what looked like a young girl standing barefoot beyond the curtain. To his Presbyterian mind, this whole place reeked of corruption. Flashback. Holding his mother's hand as they crossed a sheep-filled field to a tiny Armagh church. What would she have made of this place?

Walker said, "We're not here about you selling cannabis to schoolchildren or whatever it is you do. Matthew Sands came to this flat, we know that. Now, we've been very nice to you so far…" Balogun stepped forward meaningfully. "…but that could change."

"She needed passports. For both of them. She wanted them done in a hurry. Money wasn't a problem, she said."

Balogun snarled, "So you knew this was the missing child. Yet you didn't do anything about it."

Goldie appealed to Walker: "I told you. I'd never seen either of them before. I don't ask questions."

Walker was busy digging into his document wallet again. He pulled out the photo of Doctor Sands and showed it to Goldie. "So when this woman said she needed passports, did she say where they were going?"

Goldie shook his head. "No, she didn't say. What I mean is, that's not her. That's not the woman who came to see me."

The two policemen looked at each other. Walker riffled documents again until he found the one he wanted. "Was this her?" he said, passing a photocopied snapshot across. Goldie nodded. "Yes, that was her. Honest, she gave me the creeps. The way she shouted at that little boy, really shook him about. Women like that shouldn't be allowed near children."

And you should? Walker thought, taking the photocopy back. Toppy Mrazek gazed sullenly at him from her passport photograph.

CHAPTER FORTY

She bought a pre-paid mobile from a dodgy-looking phone shop on Earls Court Road. George wanted her to text him her new number. A charity shop next door provided some dry clothes, and she bought something to eat from a convenience store, clocking the CCTV camera as she inspected its sparse shelves. She realised every twist and turn she made would be caught on camera. Every move in this city was date-stamped: you could watch somebody cross from Wembley to Epping just on closed-circuit television, providing the police knew which camera to look at.

The sad hotel manager looked her up and down as she limped back into reception. Her clothes were still damp and muddy. Sliding off his stool, he handed over her room key. "Ah, you have come back," he said. "I am not knowing what to do with your things." She dug into her pocket and paid for another night's stay in cash with money drawn out on George's credit card. God bless George. She didn't know what she would have done without him.

Standing under the shower, she turned the water to as hot as she could bear it, wanting to wash today away. Brown water circled down the plughole. She sat up in bed in a clean T-shirt and knickers eating her sandwich, wiping mustard off her chin with the back of her hand. Very ladylike. She would need all her strength if she was to confront Toppy tomorrow. How would Toppy react when she realised Jemma was still alive? Her heart clutched at the thought of her little boy. Nibley's words came back to her: if you mess with people, prepare to be messed with.

She sent George a text telling him she was getting the Eurostar to Paris, so that he had her new number. One person in the world should know where she was. Then she pulled her duvet around her and fell gratefully asleep. Her alarm was set for 4am.

Bad dreams had come nearly every night since Matthew had gone. In this dream, she was saying goodbye to him at an airport departure gate. She squatted down, grasped his shoulders and looked into his sweet, serious face. His hair needed cutting. "Please don't go," she said, "I don't want you to go." As she put her arms around her little boy, he dissolved into particles of light. Light streamed through her fingers, and her chest felt tight, so tight. "But I'm already dead," he whispered.

She jolted awake and fumbled for her mobile phone, knocking it off the bedside table. Thank God it had been only a dream, but it had felt so real.

St Pancras International was busy even that early in the morning. People lounged around the Victorian pillared hall with their ubiquitous wheeled suitcases or sat around tapping iPhones, while the spot-lit glass ceiling revealed how dark it was outside. Waiting in the ticket queue, Jemma thought longingly of a cup of coffee. There was no time for that. The wall clock was ticking the seconds away. The queue grew restless as an old woman at the front had an involved conversation with the ticket clerk. They all had trains to catch, too. The queue edged forward. Come on, come on. Why was this taking so long? Another minute disappeared off the clock.

It was even worse walking across the concourse.

A big Sky News television screen dominated the station. Passengers stood around looking up at it as she pushed her way through, desperate not to miss her train. She could hear the powerful hum of the waiting Eurostar. It was her face on the television screen, a photo of her standing next to Tony, the pair of them smiling. Then a smash cut to hospital CCTV footage: jerky black-and-white time-lapse imagery of the Jemma lookalike leading Matthew away by the hand. Keeping her head down, she sidled past the gawping people, praying with all her heart that nobody would notice her.

Somebody called out her name. Jemma froze.

"Hey, stop!" a man's voice called. This was it, she was caught.

George was running towards her pulling a wheeled suitcase behind him. He was out of breath by the time he caught up. "I thought about it, what you were saying," he gasped. His voice dropped to a whisper. "You can't just do this on your own," he said. "You've got the police after you. Probably French police, too. It'll be easier if we travel together. They won't be looking for two people." For a moment she felt overwhelmed by his generosity; she had felt so utterly alone. "George, what you're doing... you could get in trouble," Jemma began. "It's better if I'm on my own. Hadn't you heard? I'm bad news." George interrupted her, putting his hand on her shoulder. She felt that familiar warmth spreading across her chest; she so wanted to come in from the cold. "Sometimes you've got to do the right thing," he said.

A soothing automated voice called for any remaining passengers for the 5:40am to Paris to board immediately. There wasn't any time to argue. Automatic gates banged open. They emptied their belongings into plastic trays and went through security. Seconds counting down. Even if police realised she was getting the train to Paris, the trail would go cold there.

The unsmiling French border patrol officer scrutinised her before nodding Jemma through. She grabbed her passport, glimpsing a TV screen full of most-wanted mugshots that the officer had been studying.

It was when they were taking the travelator up to the platform that she heard Matthew crying.

She knew his voice so well. Her son was somewhere up

ahead of her. Jemma started pushing forward, jostling
other passengers out of the way. She had been right all
along; Toppy was taking him to the South of France.
Jemma was not going to let them get away this time.
When she emerged at the top, she spotted the two of them
walking away from her along the platform. The Eurostar's
deep engines were powering up, and the vaulted glass
ceiling juddered as she ran towards her son. It was like one
of those dreams where you are running but you never quite
get anywhere. The platform seemed to last forever. Toppy
was holding Matthew by the hand and she was almost
dragging him onto the train while he struggled to get away.
He was trying to break free, but Toppy had a tight grip on
his wrist. Matthew was crying and screaming. Finally she
caught up with them. Jemma clapped her hand on Toppy's
shoulder.

CHAPTER FORTY-ONE

An astonished-looking stranger turned around to face Jemma. She looked nothing like Toppy, and the boy looked only a little like Matthew, his big eyes wet with tears. The woman, who was chicly dressed and obviously French, regarded Jemma incredulously. "Etes-vous folle?" she hissed. "A quoi pensez-vous?"

"I'm sorry," Jemma mumbled. "I just thought..." Dragging her child with her, the woman boarded the train carriage as the guard blew his whistle. Jemma turned away to see George standing farther off down the platform. She ran back towards him. The guard blew his whistle again. The train would be leaving any second.

The train began moving out, and the platform slid past. They both stood there panting in the corridor, not quite believing they had made it, then burst out laughing. They sidled into the carriage to find their seats while the train picked up speed.

"I'm sorry. I thought I heard Matthew. That mother with her son." Jemma was still breathing heavily. "I thought it was them. They looked just like them."

George took her hand and squeezed it. "It's okay. I just

didn't... it doesn't matter. Just don't run off like that. Let me help. We're doing this together now."

Jemma felt warm in George's presence. She felt a sense of peace whenever she was around him, so unlike Tony. The two men were completely different. Having him to lean on right now was exactly what she needed.

They found two spare seats together without any trouble in a half-full carriage near the back of the train. They were ignored by the other passengers, many of whom were already trying to get to sleep, draping jackets over their heads.

They sat in silence as the Eurostar hurtled through the Kent countryside. Jemma was sure she recognised the quarry where Toppy had left her to die, and then it was gone.

There was a burst of light through the train window; they were through the tunnel. A fat snowflake landed on the window and melted.

"What will you do when you find her?" George asked quietly. Checking to see if anybody was listening, Jemma whispered, "I just want my son back. I'm not interested in revenge. Anyway, the Americans still want their money. They will pursue her to the ends of the Earth. Whatever they do to her will be punishment enough."

In the Gare du Nord, George and Jemma walked briskly past men holding boards with passengers' names at the ticket barrier. The station had that peculiarly French smell, a mixture of piss and freshly baked bread. Christmas decorations were hanging in the cafés – Jemma had forgotten it was nearly Christmas.

They both fell into their seats on the Nice-bound train, which began moving almost imperceptibly out of the Gare de Lyon. Gaudy Christmas presents peeked out of carrier bags. Jemma guessed they were people who had come up to Paris for some Christmas shopping.

They sat there in silence for the first part of the journey, deep in their own thoughts. It was snowing harder now, and great fat flakes drove past the window as she watched the bleak French countryside slide past. The light was failing outside even though it was only mid-afternoon, and pretty rose lights lit up the carriage. "Why don't you try and sleep?" said George after they had eaten some sandwiches. Jemma smiled, grateful he was there to watch over her, and said she would close her eyes for a bit.

She dozed fitfully for a couple of hours but woke again when the train braked sharply. She sensed something was wrong when she saw the station signs; they were not meant to be stopping in Avignon.

Tough-looking French police dressed in black lined the station platform. They were not regular police – they had dogs. The train guard made an announcement over the intercom and a groan went up from the other passengers, but Jemma's French was too poor to follow what the guard was saying. "He says we're making an unscheduled stop in Avignon," George interpreted. "The police have asked to empty the train. Everybody has to get off." Anxiety pressed down on Jemma, squeezing her lungs. Somebody must have recognised her in the Gare de Lyon. "But they'll ask to see my passport, and then it's all over," she whispered, gripping George's wrist tightly. "Not necessarily," he replied. "Remember, they're looking for a woman travelling alone. Not a husband and wife. Here, put these on," he said, passing Jemma his new glasses. "They're not going to ask for your passport. Why should they? Most of the people on this train are local. Listen, I'm a white-goods salesman, and you're my wife. We've just been up to Paris to see relatives. How good is your French?" Not very good, she admitted. George looked out of the window at his reflection and ran his hand over his chin. By now the train had stopped and passengers were getting out onto the platform, some of them trudging past their window. The police had started emptying carriages from the back – soon it would be their turn. "You're my wife and you're deaf, okay?" he said. George pointed his two index fingers at Jemma and flicked them over his shoulders. "That means 'I don't understand' in sign language. Got it?" he asked. She nodded and repeated what he had just shown her. "Good. If the conversation gets any more complicated, we're in trouble," he whispered, rising from his seat. Passengers standing outside were stamping their feet in the cold. You could see their breath beneath the harsh platform lights. People grumbled in their carriage as they stood up to queue. Slowly, everybody began filing forward towards the exit.

A couple of police in black riot gear were waiting outside their train door. One of them was checking people's faces against a piece of paper. One by one people stepped down onto the platform. Now it was their turn. George squeezed her hand as he helped her down. They were just about to walk off when the policeman barred her way, putting his arm across her chest. Panic rose in Jemma's throat. The game was up.

CHAPTER FORTY-TWO

Set your watch back to 1963, Walker thought as he tripped up the stone steps of the Travellers Club. Gentlemen's clubs ran along most of Pall Mall. Okumu had telephoned him that morning saying the Commissioner wanted to see him personally. Whatever it was about, Walker doubted that the head of the Met wanted to congratulate him. He was still reeling from the dressing-down Okumu had given him after being told that Doctor Sands had fled the country. Any moment now the press would get hold of the information, making a laughing stock of the entire Metropolitan Police.

The porter at reception told him that the Commissioner and Commander Okumu were waiting for him downstairs in the bar. "Straight on through," he said, taking Walker's sodden raincoat from him. Walker decided to ignore the sign telling members to switch off their mobile phones. Interpol had promised to phone him the moment Doctor Sands was under arrest. He thought about the dozens of officers hunched over their work stations coordinating the manhunt from Lyon; vast interlocking databases grinding their way through millions of emails, text messages and Twitter posts, anything that might lead them to Doctor Jemma Sands.

The downstairs bar was cosily furnished with button-back velvet sofas and Spy cartoons on the walls. The room felt like a maiden aunt clutching you to her well-upholstered bosom. Okumu and the Commissioner were standing at the bar talking to a couple of men. The Commander raised his hand when he saw Walker, who ran his hand over his wet hair as he prepared for this uncomfortable meeting.

"Commissioner, this is Detective Chief Inspector Walker, the investigating officer on the case."

"Ah, Walker. Glad you could join us."

"How do you do, ma'am."

They shook hands and Walker felt the Commissioner's scrutiny. Ann Oldfield was one of a handful of women who had risen to the top of the security services. She was dressed in uniform, with her expensively coloured hair swept back from her face. On first impression, she seemed like a disapproving headmistress of a girls' school. Like Okumu, she had risen through the ranks. Her star moment had been coordinating the Met's response to the 7/7 terror attacks. People who worked with her found her slightly supercilious manner off-putting. On the other hand, she had a reputation for being an adroit political operator who plotted the endgame while others were still figuring out where to move their first pawn. Such was her power that she was the sole exception to the Travellers Club's no-women rule at the bar.

The Commissioner turned to the men standing beside her, one of whom she introduced as the MP for Corby North, and the other as an official who worked for HM Revenue and Customs. Walker didn't quite catch their names.

The DCI ordered a Diet Coke and listened to the conversation about how the Prime Minister should handle a rebel minister challenging his authority. Politics made Walker feel uncomfortable. As far as he was concerned, all politicians did was feather their own nests while spending other people's money. Eventually, the woman behind the bar told them their table was ready. To his surprise, Walker was being invited for lunch. He had expected what Okumu had referred coldly to as "a chat without coffee".

"Gentlemen, if you will excuse us, we have shop talk to discuss," said Oldfield. Both men drifted away.

Walking up the main staircase, Walker felt a little overawed by his surroundings. Oil paintings hung all the way up the stairs, and the carpet was so thick it absorbed the sound of their footfalls.

The head waiter took their names at the dining room entrance. Walker looked around the room. Mostly elderly men and women having lunch beneath the chandeliers. A row of windows overlooked Pall Mall. Waiters hurried about uncorking bottles, or pushing a trolley groaning with puddings. It was not hard to imagine the fates of nations being decided in this room. At the same time, you had the sense that nothing bad could ever really happen here.

The Commissioner put on a pair of half-moon glasses and began studying the menu. Whatever they wanted to talk about, they were keen to get the niceties over with first.

"Today on the trolley we have saddle of lamb," the waiter said. He was from somewhere in Eastern Europe.

Oldfield pulled a face. "I'll have the Dover sole and spinach. My doctor tells me I have to eat what he calls flat food. But you have what's on the trolley. The food's very good here," she said, closing the menu.

"I'll have the lamb," said Okumu.

Walker nodded that he would have the same, and the waiter snapped his menu shut.

"We'll have water to drink. Tap water is fine."

The waiter gave a little bow and moved away.

The Commissioner fixed Walker with what he could only describe as her laser stare, and he felt his kneecaps dissolving. "The Home Secretary was on the phone to me this morning asking what the hell was going on. I don't understand how this woman got out of the country. Do you?"

Walker said, "With respect ma'am, the Border Agency is at best a string bag. Especially for people leaving the country."

"Oh, please. Don't start blaming other people for your mistakes. Do you have any idea how bad this makes us look? You've damaged the reputation of the entire Metropolitan Police force."

"Yes, ma'am, I understand that." Walker pictured himself prostrated before the Commissioner like some jungle deity; his best option would be to throw himself on her mercy.

"What about tracking her mobile phone or her credit cards?"

"We traced her mobile phone to a bedsit in Earls Court where she stayed last night. It was thrown in the bin. Her bank has been helpful, though. We got a magistrate's order to freeze her bank account, seeing that she's a fugitive from justice."

"Once she's got to Paris, she could be anywhere," Okumu observed. "The borders are so porous. She's probably not even in France anymore. More likely Spain or Italy."

"I don't think so. I think I know exactly where she's going."

Oldfield paused. "What makes you say that?"

"She's not on the run. She's hunting somebody down. All along she's been convinced that her husband's girlfriend, the one who supposedly drowned in France, has kidnapped her son."

"But we know this is just a wild-goose chase," Okumu grunted. "She's hidden the boy somewhere, and now the game is up. She's saving her own skin."

"A small-time drug dealer know to Acton CID identified Toppy Mrazek. She came to see him to get passports. She's obviously taken the boy out of the country. Sands thinks the same thing."

"What about the Rohypnol you found in her car?"

"That doesn't prove anything one way or another. There were no prints on the bottle. It could have been planted."

"Could have, would have, should have. There's a lot of supposition here, Walker," Okumu said coldly.

"Yes, sir, but what if she is innocent?"

Oldfield said, "Right now, I don't care if she's innocent. She's a fugitive from justice, and I want her back here under lock and key."

"Well, sir, I do have some news. We've already issued a European Arrest Warrant. The Gendarmerie identified her boarding a train to Marseilles twenty minutes ago. French police are pulling the train over in Avignon and getting the passengers off. I'm expecting the call any moment."

"Well perhaps we can snatch triumph from the jaws of adversity," Oldfield said. "I want you to go out there and bring her back. Chief Inspector, I want you in on the kill." She turned to the Commander. "Oh, and Umar, I want the full press works on this, the Met always gets its man, all that nonsense." She shook her head. "What a morning."

The waiter arrived with their main courses. The Commissioner's sole and spinach looked, well, flat. Walker cut into his lamb oozing a redcurrant-tinged jus. It was just as delicious as the Commissioner had promised.

CHAPTER FORTY-THREE

Each moment gathered weight like a drop of water about to fall. The policeman's face was emotionless. He stared at her and said a phrase in French that Jemma could not make out. This was her cue. She flicked her fingers over her shoulders just as George had taught her, showing that she was deaf and didn't understand. George began speaking quickly to the policeman. Whatever they were saying was too fast for Jemma to make sense of. George turned to her and made a complicated series of hand gestures, dragging his fingers across his wrist and then making a stirring motion before stroking his face with his finger. "Police. Looking. Woman," he said as he signed. He then made what looked like the devil's sign that rock fans use, corkscrewing his raised index finger into his neck. "Suspected. Murder." She nodded that she understood as he spoke to the gendarme again. The policeman looked at her dubiously for a moment before waving them both through. She was too rigid with fear to speak until they were safe inside the space-age ticket hall.

"Wow, that was close. You did well," George said as they sat down together. "They're looking for you, though. I told him we wanted to get off here as it was closer to home."

"Thank you, George." Jemma gave him a peck on the cheek. "I didn't think he was going to let me go."

George forced a smile and took her hand. Jemma looked to him like she was ready to collapse: she had very dark rings under her eyes, and her face was horribly pale. He looked her straight in the eyes. "Right now we need to find somewhere safe. They'll be watching all the train stations. Let's find a hotel and stay overnight. We can hire a car in the morning."

"But that will be too late. She could have moved on, and..."

"Look, Jemma, listen to me. It's not as if she's going anywhere, is it? She's probably just as frightened as we are," George said with an edge in his voice. "Let me do this. Let me take care of you."

A taxi dropped them off at an unpretentious hotel in an Avignon side street. Jemma was worried that the big blonde behind reception might ask to see her passport, but apparently George's was good enough. He pretended they were husband and wife again.

Once in the room, Jemma fell onto the bed fully clothed and was asleep within a couple of minutes. George covered her with a duvet. It was a comfort knowing he was there.

That night they had dinner in the hotel restaurant at a cosy table tucked against the wall. "I think we could both use a real drink," George said. They had a gin and tonic each, and she felt the anaesthetic of the alcohol working through her body. They spoke little at first and enjoyed the fine French cuisine.

They eventually talked about the police search for her in England – she wondered how Walker knew she had fled the country. Walker was a good name for him, she remarked; she pictured him striding across the country, stalking her until he ran her to ground. George had ordered a carafe of the house red wine and, after one large glass on top of the gin, Jemma felt pleasantly tipsy – it was a relief, a brief respite from the tension that gripped her like steel. "Where did you learn to use sign language like that?" she asked.

"My older sister's deaf, so I learned when we were kids. Her sight's going now, too. Such a beautiful girl. Sometimes life can be really awful."

Jemma took another sip from her wine glass. "I can relate to that."

George nodded in sympathy and raised his own glass. "Here's to life when it's not awful."

Jemma looked into the middle distance. "Sometimes, what I'm going through, it feels like a crucifixion. I can't understand what it means. Normally I'm quite good at finding out the meaning of things, but this I just don't understand. I can't figure out what lesson it is I'm meant to be learning."

George refilled his own wine glass from the carafe. "Perhaps it's a test. You are being tested as to how much you love your son. Crucifixion wasn't the end of it. Jesus was reborn, wasn't he? Yes, perhaps this is what it's about, a test and rebirth. The hero has to go through trials and is then reborn once he has the prize."

Madame had replenished the bread basket, and their fingers touched as they reached for it. Jemma felt a frisson that surprised her. She fumbled with the bread, dropping it into the middle of her plate by mistake.

"Sounds like hippie shit to me," she said, trying to ignore what had just happened.

George was busy ripping his bread in two. He had noticed nothing. "What I'm saying is, perhaps this is all about the love between you and Matthew. It's shown you how much you love your son." He chewed on another piece of the baguette and then, as if waking from a dream, he said, "We can hire a car when the rental agency opens tomorrow morning. It'll take only a few hours to get to the coast. Didn't you say that there's a ferry from Hyères?"

"There's only a couple a week in winter. They leave at two in the afternoon."

"That gives us plenty of time. Tell me again what makes you so sure that Toppy is on the island?"

"She used to go there with her parents. She knows it really well. It's deserted in winter. Tony was keeping Tri-Med's money in a French bank account. I think she's gone back to France to get the money out."

Madame reappeared holding two dinner plates. She set George's steak down and then Jemma's chicken, waiting for the couple's approval. They both smiled and thanked her. George cut a piece of bloody meat and put it in his mouth.

"I know I'm tired, but I think this is the best steak I've ever eaten," he said.

Jemma was staring at the plate. "I feel guilty every time I touch food. It's time wasted when I could be searching for Matthew."

George set down his knife and fork. "You've got to stop beating yourself up. Listen to yourself: nobody could have done more than you have."

He devoured everything on his plate, and even tried a few pieces of the chicken. Jemma pecked at the food, her hunger dampened by the wine, her mind going into tailspin yet again.

Cleaning her teeth in their tiny sloping bathroom, she wondered whether the pretence of her marriage extended to the bedroom. Her marriage had collapsed more than a year ago, and she had not been with anybody since then. She yearned for human touch. And now, because of the train wreck of events that had started with somebody losing control of her car on the motorway and led to this, she was alone with a man she had often thought about. Would he try it on with her? She wasn't sure how she felt about that. Perhaps it was too soon. But who knew what would happen once Matthew was safe and this nightmare was over, she thought, spitting into the basin.

George was already sitting in the wicker chair with a blanket over him reading Nice-Matin when she emerged. Jemma limped over to the bed and peeled off the dressing on her foot; it was throbbing again. Inspecting the wound, she saw that it was suppurating but healing quite nicely. "Looks nasty," said George from the other side of the room. He appeared so uncomfortable sitting in his rattan chair that she was tempted to ask him to share the bed with her. She sat upright on the edge of the bed applying another gauze pad, which she then taped up before swallowing a couple of oxycodone for the pain. She began making a list of supplies they would need for tomorrow. Exhausted, she finally crawled in between the clean white sheets. George, meanwhile, had been torn between watching her and reading his paper.

"George, why don't you come and lie next to me on the bed." She moved towards the edge of her side of the mattress and patted the white space.

"Are you sure?" He looked at her, trying to gauge the moment.

"But no funny business, okay?" She tried to sound playful, and George raised both his hands in surrender.

"Jemma, the only thing that's on my mind is a race to see who can fall asleep first." He rose from the chair with his blanket and stretched out beside her.

He lay as rigid as the statue on a tomb and seemed to crash straight into sleep. Jemma switched off the bedside lamp. Lying there in the dark, she wondered what it would be like to touch George, to learn the feel of his skin and feel his hands on her body. She brushed his thigh as if getting more comfortable. Already she could feel his hardness. He rolled over and she felt his breath on her neck. "Are you sure this is a good idea?" he whispered. Without speaking, she searched for his face and pressed herself against his lips. Their mouths parted and their tongues explored each other hungrily. For a moment the air solidified and stood still before warmth spread across her chest and dropped to her crotch. All the while she kept feeling him through his trousers. Please, George, I want this, her mind begged. She so desperately needed to feel the touch of another human being. "Wait," he said. As if reading her thoughts, she felt him get off the bed and tear at his clothes. Sitting up, she lifted off her vest and slipped out of her panties. Then he was back, devouring her. Oh, it felt so good. She ran her hand down his back while he buried himself in her neck. She had forgotten what it was like to be with a man. "I've wanted to do this for such a long time," he said thickly. He worked his way down to her breasts, kissing her stiff nipples. Oh yes, kiss them harder, darling. Jemma shifted her position, wanting to make things easier for him. She was sopping. Reaching for his cock, she guided him into her. There was no time for foreplay, she just wanted him inside her. Now. Her inner lips parted, and she felt how big he was. "Yes," she moaned, grabbing his buttocks and pulling him deeper. She felt incredibly full, and yet everything was right, all was as it should be: finally they were one. Then it began. He was thrusting against her, buried up to the hilt. She licked her upper lip and hung on to the bedstead for support. "Oh, George," she sighed. It was growing inside her, wave after wave, building up, gaining momentum. There was nothing either of them could do to stop it. George, slow down, not so fast. She wanted to savour this moment, remember it perhaps for a very long time. She sensed it would not be long now, and she gripped him urgently. That's it, darling, yes, yes! Even as she thought this, George made a noise somewhere between a snarl and growl. Too late. She felt him flooding her, and she wrapped him tighter, milking his cock.

George flopped down and sought her mouth. She felt the crush of him on top of her. His cock was still spasming. They kissed again, and she ran her fingers through his hair. Don't go, I want you to stay there. She held him lightly, trying to think of words, the right words to say, but they wouldn't come. "Hold me tight," she said. They lay for a moment before George rolled onto his back. Her best friend laughed, although it sounded more like a sob. "I'm sorry," he said. "It's been a long time." "For me, too," she said, wanting to make him feel better. He crawled up the bed and they embraced again, wrapped around each other, not speaking. Idly she stroked his forearm.

"If we find her, will you call the police?"

"I told you. Matthew is the only thing I'm interested in. Once I've got him back, then we'll see."

"She's not going to give him up without a fight. You know that."

"She'll be more interested in saving her own skin. She's not mad. I'll give her a head start with the money. I just want to get my boy home."

"You're sure she's taken all the cash to the island?"

"I'm certain of it. The money was in the French bank in Cavalaire. That's why she wanted to go back. To get the money out."

Somewhere was the distant two-tone siren of a French police car. George rested his head on her chest. Here they were, lovers at last, tangled in the sheets and protected from the dangers of this night. The thing she had dreamed of for so long had happened. She hugged George tighter, relishing the feel of his skin. Why was it that you truly find happiness only with another person? Jemma felt herself drifting off, falling backwards like a diver from the highest platform. Oblivion.

Next thing she knew, she couldn't breathe.

Something was clamped over her face. A pillow.

She kicked out, but somebody was pressing down with all his weight. Where was George? Jemma struggled until the roaring inside her head became unbearable: everything was turning red, then purple, then black. Her hand banged against the bedside table as she scrabbled for a weapon, anything to fight with. Grabbing the pencil, she started wildly stabbing her attacker. She heard a scream, and she was free. Rolling off the bed, she crouched on the floor gathering her senses while George hopped around the room clutching his thigh. "You fucking bitch," he shouted.

Yanking her rucksack, she pulled the bedroom door open and ran down the corridor. She could hear George coming after her. An owlish-looking man came out of his bedroom in his dressing gown, no doubt wondering what all the noise was about. "Monsieur," he remonstrated, blocking George's way.

Jemma jumped down each stairwell, one flight at a time. There was nobody in reception as she ran out into the street. She ran down the deserted Avignon road, careful not to slip on the ice. Here she was, a naked woman running down the middle of the street; surely somebody must rescue her. "Help, help. Police," she shrieked over and over again. Her scream was as piercing as a whistle. Then she remembered that she was the one the police were hunting.

The air was so sharp that it was painful to breathe, and the snow had settled into dirty frozen slush. There were no cars about for her to flag down. She had no idea where she was going or what to do next. Her mind reeled as her bare feet slapped down the icy road. Her best friend had just tried to kill her. To be betrayed by the one person she trusted more than anybody else. How could George have done this to her? Were he and Toppy in this together? There was nobody she could turn to. She had never felt more frightened, or more alone.

CHAPTER FORTY-FOUR

Her legs were shaking uncontrollably as she pulled her jeans and fleece on in an alleyway. She could not get dressed fast enough. It was still dark as she crunched towards what she hoped was the city centre. The streets were rigid with cold, and her clothes felt like tissue paper. Eventually a car slushed past, heading in the same direction. Up ahead she saw lights from what looked like a café, and an old-fashioned train station hove into view on her left.

Standing up at the zinc, Jemma ordered a coffee. A fruit machine blipped behind her. At this hour of the morning there was just one drunk slumped on a bar stool. The warmth of the café felt so good after the cold outside.

She could not even begin to comprehend what had just happened. It was impossible to make any sense of. She remembered telling Guaram that George was "the best person" she had ever met. What bullshit. She was talking about somebody who had just tried suffocating her with a pillow. How could she have been so naive?

As she paid, she asked the barman where the nearest car rental office was. After some miming on her part, he gestured farther down the street.

Standing in a shop doorway, she waited for the car rental office to open up. After what felt like hours, an immaculately dressed woman appeared, her hair put up in a complicated coiffure, struggling with the metal shutters. It was eight o'clock in the morning. Jemma waited until all the lights were on before crossing the road. The surgeon's palms felt damp with sweat as she filled out the car rental form, crossing her fingers as she promised she would return the car the next day. The car rental manager checked her passport, and Jemma prayed she would not spot that her credit card was in somebody else's name. Thankfully, she slid the chip-and-pin machine across and averted her eyes while Jemma keyed in George's PIN. She was finished if George had thought ahead and cancelled his credit card. They both stared at the machine while it made a connection, Jemma willing the payment to go through. Finally, the machine came to life, and the receipt scrolled off the top.

Her little car was one of a line parked around the back. Gingerly, she edged backwards out of the parking space and pulled out into the Avignon traffic, following the directions for the motorway.

The snow got heavier on the autoroute. Snowflakes were falling so thickly that she could barely see through the windscreen. Even on full speed, the wipers were ineffectual; it was like driving into a tunnel of stars. She pulled over at a service station and bought some chocolate and a map. By now the autoroute had become three parallel black lines in the snow as cars trailed each other. Just past Aix-en-Provence, overhead signs began warning of road closures. Sure enough, traffic ground to a standstill. A policeman bundled against the weather was directing traffic off the road to the right. How long would they be here? She hadn't brought any food or blankets with her, and the prospect of sleeping in the car as ice formed over the inside of the windows was not appealing. A few drivers got out of their parked vehicles and stretched. Eventually cars began edging forward again. That was when she saw the queue on the slip road.

She had got lost somewhere after a town called Rians.

A gentle hill on a normal day felt insurmountable with this snow. People had abandoned cars on the side of the road. Jemma was angry with herself for having taken a wrong turn, but all she could do was push on. Glancing at the map, she guessed she was entering something called the Gorges du Verdon. She was out of her depth, and she wanted to stop. The road had become a narrow mountain pass with a sheer drop to her left. Gripping the steering wheel tightly, she hugged the mountainside. She must have been crawling uphill for another fifteen minutes or so when she realised she had driven into a thick mist. She was so high up that the car must have driven into cloud cover, and the yellow headlights reflected the fog blankly like a damp, clinging shroud. Jemma had no idea where she was going. At any moment she could plunge over the mountainside and into the valley below.

Things got easier once she came down the other side. Fiddling with the car radio, she found a choice of French rap, an impassioned and incomprehensible discussion, or carols. She opted for carols. Listening to the mawkish songs, her mind strayed to what she and Matthew would do when they were reunited. She was so busy daydreaming that she hadn't noticed the police car following her. How had they found her in the middle of nowhere? This was madness. Her first thought was to outrun them, but a little rental car could never escape the French police, surely. She steeled herself anyway and put her foot on the accelerator. She had to get away.

All she felt was nauseating, gripping fear.

The road was nasty and twisty, and she prayed nothing was coming round the other way. The small engine whined in protest as she took another blind corner. What she was doing was crazy. There was a right turn up ahead, and she pulled the wheel sharply, sending the car out of sight of the road. Checking her mirror again, she saw the police car shoot past with driving snow hammering against its headlights. Turning her attention back to the road, she drove hard towards some kind of turning circle. In summer this must be an observation point or dropping-off place for the valley below. What must have been a steep S-bend in summer had become a sheet of ice.

She felt herself losing control of the car. It swayed beneath her as the wheels locked. The frame juddered. Too late, she realised this was a dead-end, and she was sliding out of control towards a brick wall. As if anticipating the crash, Jemma tasted metal in her mouth, and she threw her arm across her face to block the impact. This is it, she thought, the moment of my death.

CHAPTER FORTY-FIVE

There was a terrific bang, and Jemma was thrown forward. Her airbag exploded and she was yanked back, pinned to her seat. When Jemma opened her eyes, she was gripping the steering wheel as hard as she could, afraid to let go, smelling smoke and battery acid in the sudden stillness. There was nothing quite like the smell of a car accident. One thing, though, was that she couldn't hear. For a moment she felt hollow with panic – had she gone deaf for good? – until she became aware of the hiss of steam from the broken engine as her hearing returned. She couldn't believe she was still alive.

She guessed that she had crashed into something very solid, a brick wall probably. Her tears tasted salty as they trickled down her face and into her mouth. But this was no time for tears. The police would double back and find her. The only thing she knew was that she had to keep moving.

Levering herself out of the car, she remembered that her rucksack was still on the back seat. Her body had taken quite a battering, and it hurt when she breathed. The front end of the hire car had concertinaed, and the bonnet was sticking up at a right angle. The shattered windscreen had spidered into a glittering web, and the car's black innards were spewed on the snow.

Looking down over the parapet, she saw a frozen river hundreds of feet beneath her. Its edges looked as if they were solid ice, although water was still running clear in the middle. A waterfall had frozen in mid-air, its icicles suspended over the cliff. If it was this cold so far south, what must it be like back home? There was some kind of gantry staircase running down to the river and she hobbled down it, her foot throbbing again and her body aching. The handrail was so frosty, her flesh resisted before coming away again. It took everything she had just to put one foot in front of another.

A tunnel ran beside the river. Jemma staggered through the dark, her trainers splashing through icy puddles. All she could hear in the stillness was the sound of her ragged breathing. Half-running, half-limping through the tunnel, she saw the end up ahead.

She stopped and listened, trembling as she reached the tunnel mouth. Everything was frozen and quiet. Nobody was following her. Yet.

There was a trail running alongside the canyon that she guessed eventually also led down to the river. She had no choice but to follow it. Sometimes the trail disappeared completely and she had to clamber over rocks. Snow lay in deep pockets in between boulders, and her hands were stiff with cold. Working her way down, she fell and fell again.

As she had hoped, the trail ended at the river's edge. A dog barked in the distance. Her skin prickled with fear. If it was a police dog, she would have to throw them off the scent. Stop prevaricating, she told herself. She slung her pack off her back and braced herself to enter the water. If she made it to the other side, she would lose them. Her first steps on the ice felt solid enough. She took another step and felt herself lose balance. One moment she was standing upright, and the next she was flat on her back. Bracing herself on her elbows, she got back up and took another tentative step. There was a cracking sound and she felt the ice sinking, water seeping over the sides. Before she fully realised what was happening, she was up to her waist. The cold was unbelievable, yet somehow she swallowed a scream. Every fibre of her being was willing her to get out of the freezing river. Instead, she raised her rucksack over her head and waded deeper, trying to balance on the slippery rocks. The swift current was unbearable. Eventually she could fight it no longer and allowed it to take her. The water was so cold that, for a moment, she felt almost warm. She let the river carry her on her back towards the other side. Snowflakes drifted down onto her hair and face as she floated through shards of icy water. Hugging her rucksack, she gazed up at the overcast sky, frog-kicking her way downstream. The dog's bark echoed somewhere along the canyon. Jemma crossed her arms and let the current do the work. Too late she realised that she was picking up speed and losing control. Panicking, she thrashed round and saw the water disappearing between rocks and over the edge.

She was on a collision course with a waterfall.

There was nothing she could do about it. She screwed her eyes shut and mentally braced herself for whatever was coming. This was going to hurt.

Suddenly she was tumbling inside the spuming, exploding waterfall. The cold took her breath away. Righting herself, she gasped as her head broke the surface. The next thing she heard was the dog's bark getting louder. If anything, she had swum towards what she feared was the police dog and its handler. The canyon walls must have messed up the acoustics.

Jemma hauled herself up the other side and clambered over more rocks. Her sodden clothes clung to her body. When would this stop? She thought longingly of her mother; she yearned for someone to look after her, to tell her it was all going to be okay. This was almost too much for her to bear. What she had to do now, though, was climb: get above the police search party and the dog handler. And the only way to do that was to scramble as high as she could.

It was a hard scrabble up the canyon side. All those sessions at the climbing centre had certainly paid off, Jemma thought grimly. Searching for handholds, she was edging along a canyon wall around twenty feet above the water when she saw him. The police handler turned the corner, restraining the animal. It was a nasty-looking brute. Jemma froze. She was spread-eagled against the wall, her cheek pressed against the rock, petrified with fear. The policeman and his dog were right below. All he had to do was look up. She moaned with fright and pressed herself against the stone. She could feel her right foot slipping, and she was about to lose her footing entirely. Her plimsoll slipped again. She couldn't hold on any longer. The dog started barking even more hysterically and the policeman swore, reining him in. Then they moved off again along the path. Jemma's hand convulsed for a plant root – anything to hold on to – and she stifled a sob. That was close. She waited until she was sure the dog team was farther along the valley before she let herself down, slipping over rocks.

She trudged along the path for as long as she could, but soon she had to rest. If police dogs were after her, surely they must have lost the scent by now. She couldn't hear any more barking. Jemma zippered open her rucksack and pulled out the half-eaten bar of chocolate she had saved from the car. Brushing some snow from a boulder, she sat watching the dark river. Matthew, I am so sorry, she thought, I just can't do this anymore. Even as she was thinking this, she knew her only option was to keep going. She felt the goodness of the chocolate suffuse her body. It would have to last – she had no idea when she would eat again.

Night was starting to fall. The moon sailed higher and

higher as the cold bit deeper. She was trudging through another icy cove when she first heard the throb of the helicopter. A beam of light fell alongside her. They were using a searchlight. The helicopter throbbed closer, the long finger of light probing anything that might be hiding in the rocks. Jemma shrank into the cliff wall, willing herself into the rock. She was too afraid to even breathe. The noise was incredible. Fear deafened her. The helicopter hung there, directing the full blast of its searchlight onto her hiding place. It was blinding. She threw up her hands, trying to block the light. But it was too late.

CHAPTER FORTY-SIX

The light was so blinding that she could not see anything.
Then, to her astonishment, the helicopter started moving
away, its light sweeping farther along the canyon wall.
How could they not have spotted her? It was incredible.
The outcropping must have been hiding her better than
she thought. She watched the helicopter move farther off
down the valley as she caught her breath, its searchlight
scanning the opposite cliff now. You could just make out its
ugly torpedo shape in the blackness.

Morning came so slowly as to be almost imperceptible.
Jemma was clambering over some rocks when she saw
a bridge spanning the canyon. She must have reached
the end. What had likely been a strip of beach during
the summer resembled Arctic tundra in late December.
Through the pollarded trees she could see a petrol station
on the other side of the road; thankfully, it was open. She
had one more change of dry clothes left in her rucksack: a
pair of tracksuit bottoms and an oily jumper that Mum had
given her for Christmas. Jemma got changed in the filthy
toilet, doing her best to wash with hot water from the hand
basin. The heat on her body was painful, but she knew she
had to raise her body temperature. Drying herself with

the tepid hand drier also helped, but when she looked at her face in the mirror, it was gaunt. She barely recognised herself.

There was a coffee vending machine inside the petrol station shop, and she gratefully sipped the bitter espresso while the girl behind the counter glanced up at her. Jemma could not tell whether she looked at her suspiciously or not. Given the police at Avignon train station and now calling in a helicopter for the manhunt, Jemma was probably front-page news. The sugary coffee gave her a glimmer of hope, a tiny glow of warmth. Eating a sandwich, she scanned the station forecourt outside. Her first proper food in more than a day. The sandwich tasted so good, and she ran her tongue around her teeth. Her stomach gnawed for more, but she had to save what money was left. A Mini with its fog lights on pulled up out of the gloom. A tall, stork-like man levered himself out of the car and waded to the petrol pump.

"Excuse me," she said to the man, crossing the forecourt. "Do you speak English?"

"What can I do for you?" To her surprise, the motorist was not French but American.

The man put his hands on his hips and surveyed her. She made up some silly story about having had a row with her boyfriend and he had driven off, leaving her stranded. We were on our way to Hyères to meet friends, she gabbled, could he give her a lift to the next town? She must have looked quite a sight, but the man seemed intrigued by her. "He'll probably feel bad about ten minutes down the road," she continued. "But if you're heading that way, I could really use a lift. I know where we're all meeting. You can just drop me off anywhere there."

"Couldn't you phone him?"

"The battery's dead on my phone." She was now stretching her acting talents with a winsome look to extract maximum sympathy.

The man considered for a moment, cocking his head to one side.

"All right," he sighed. "You'd better get in."

The Mini was a filthy mess inside. She had to move empty drinks cans, sandwich wrappers and papers off the passenger seat.

Once they were back on the road, the man told her his name was Brian and that he worked for a wealthy New York couple. He was driving to their summer house to collect some things, taking them back to the Paris apartment. He was from Los Angeles. "The husband puts up with me, but it's the wife who's my meal ticket. She's what the Chinese would call my iron rice bowl. With her around, I always get to eat," he said. He turned to her and pulled a silly face, pursing his lips before yukking with laughter, revealing his yellow horse's teeth. Despite herself, Jemma started laughing, too. It felt like years since she had even smiled.

It began snowing again, and she felt her eyelids growing heavy. "Driving is so boring. I wish we had some pot," Brian remarked. He switched on the car radio, and they listened to a boys' choir singing carols, their tender voices spiralling up towards the infinite. She thought of Matthew with a pang, his warm body next to hers as she watched him opening his Christmas presents. He had been just old enough to understand Christmas that year, and her thoughts flicked back to an earlier Christmas soon after he was born: sitting beside Tony, both of them exhausted but happy listening at the kitchen table to this very same carol on the radio.

"What was your fight with your boyfriend about?" Brian asked, finding another station, abrasive French hip-hop this time.

Her mind blanked. She would have to make something up. "I discovered he'd been texting another woman. Sexting, they call it."

"That sucks, darlin'. If I found out my boyfriend was cheating on me, I would beat him up real bad."

"You can't make somebody love you. A friend once said to me that in every relationship, somebody always puts the boot in. One of you is always going to end it."

"That's not true. You don't have to suck it up" – Brian started chuckling again – "You can still fuck them up on your way out."

The American dropped her at a strip of closed-up shops on the beach road to Hyères. Jemma did not want him to know where she was really heading. Snow dusted the road even this far south. In summer, this drag had been full of shops selling postcards and inflatables, but in winter, everything was closed down and drab.

The marina was emptier than she remembered, with a few dinghies covered up for winter. She walked along the quayside checking her watch. Five minutes to two. She would have to hurry if she was going to catch the ferry. Jemma jogged along the road towards where the ferry would be waiting. Sure enough, she saw it in the distance. It sounded its horn as it prepared to cast off. Thank God the ticket booth was still open. She dug into her rucksack for her sodden purse and, stepping up to the window, bought a return ticket to Port Croix, willing the girl behind the glass to hurry up. Could she be any slower? Two minutes.

That was when she saw him.

The island gendarme who had questioned her after Toppy's disappearance was standing guard by the gangplank.

She was never going to get to the island.

CHAPTER FORTY-SEVEN

She ducked behind the ticket office again to weigh up her options. After everything that had happened at Avignon train station and the police helicopter in the Gorges du Verdon, she knew that the manhunt had been extended to France. The island policeman who had interviewed her that day she went to collect Matthew would be watching for her. How many others would be waiting on the island? She racked her brains trying to think of who else but George knew her destination.

George. Even now she could not believe the extent of his betrayal, the one person she had placed her trust in. We are all on our own, she thought. In winter, just two ferries sailed to the island each week, so she would have to find some other means of getting across. She heard the whine of machinery as the gangway lifted. Sounding its horn again, the ferry started to move. There had to be a way to get across to the island, there just had to be. Putting her head round the corner, she saw that the ferry was already clearing the harbour. Seagulls screamed overhead. The gendarme must have got on board already. Perhaps there was still a chance.

Jemma walked back along the quay, eyes scouring for ideas. Oily water lapped against the dock. To have come all this way and not make it across was so unfair. Her need to be reunited with her son was now another physical pain in her already throbbing body.

A sailor stood watching her from the stern of his boat, a cabin cruiser that had seen better days. He was good-looking in a gypsy-ish way, with hair like black ice cream. He watched her coolly as she walked past, just another woman going about her business. Then an idea formed in her mind. Jemma turned back and, almost as if she sensed another woman occupying her husband's attention, a woman emerged on deck. She was older than the sailor, stout with peroxide blonde hair: a pear-shaped bumble bee. Jemma waved hello and explained in pidgin French that she needed to get to Port Croix today. "You've just missed the ferry," the man said, jerking his chin. Would he take her across? How much would it cost? The boatman shook his head, but his wife, who had been watching them with a cunning look on her face, interrupted. "Deux cents euros," she said shrewdly. Two hundred euros? That was double what she had on her, and that was the last of her money. On top of everything else, she would have to find money on the island. "Fine," Jemma replied. "Half now and half when we get back." "Tant mieux," the wife said with a shrug.

The boatman took her hand as he helped her on board and, for the second time today, she made up a story, this time about how she was collecting some things from one of the island's holiday homes, and that she to get across or she would miss her flight.

They cast off and followed the ferry. Jemma could see its stern up ahead; it was already well clear of the harbour area. It was bitter and raw up on deck. It would take a couple of hours to reach the island. The boat ploughed on through the silt-thick slushy water, everything so grey and cold it was hard to tell where the horizon began and the sea ended. Beyond you could just about make out the Iles d'Hyères lying flat and ominous in the distance.

"The sea looks as if it's about to freeze over," Jemma said.

"Global warming," the sailor replied with a hard little laugh. There was a coffee pot downstairs, he said; would she go and make some coffee for them both? Jemma still felt dirty from her trek through the canyon. She asked if there was a shower she could use. The sailor said that was fine, and that there were towels in a drawer under one of the beds down below.

She decided to make the coffee first, and balanced the old-fashioned pot unsteadily on a gas ring. There was a table in the cabin surrounded by a banquette that converted into beds. She soon found a white, fluffy towel.

With the coffee made, she half-climbed the stairs to the main deck and handed the boat captain his mug.

"Merci," he said with an admiring glance. "My name is

Franck, by the way."

"De rien. I'm going to shower," said Jemma, who automatically pushed her hair behind her right ear when she noticed his appraising gaze.

The shower cubicle was tiny. Like everything else on the boat, the cubicle had been scaled down, and she felt a little like Gulliver when she stepped into the shower tray. She gratefully began washing her hair. It felt so good to be warm again.

Towelling off, she got dressed and wished she had something else she could change into. That was when she heard the diesel shutting down. Franck must have killed the engine. The water slapped against the hull as the boat sat drifting on the choppy tide. The sailor came halfway down the steps, holding his coffee cup and hanging on to the roof for support.

"Are you hungry?" he asked. "I have something to eat if you want."

Jemma realised that all she'd eaten in the previous twenty-four hours was a sandwich and a bar of chocolate. Franck lifted a plastic bag of groceries on the counter and began slicing a tomato.

"It is not much, but you are welcome," he said, putting the tomato to one side and producing some fresh bread rolls. Jemma could have pushed him out of the way and devoured them then and there.

"Your English is very good," she said, watching him make the sandwiches. "Have you spent time in England?"

"I used to live in Basingstoke with my wife and daughter." The way he said "Basingstoke" made it sound like the most exotic place on Earth.

"The woman I met coming off the boat?" Jemma asked.

Franck shook his head. "No, the woman you met, we are not married. My wife is English. We met in Plymouth when I was on shore leave. I like England very much. Where are you from?"

"Oh, London," she said vaguely. "I've been living in Paris with my employer. It's their house on the island."

"What is so important that you have to go Port Croix and back in a day? Your employer should be grateful to you."

"Some papers, that kind of thing." Jemma said, anxious to change the subject. "When will you return to England? There can't be much work for you this time of year."

"I live here now. My wife and I are, uh, how would you say, separated?"

"Ah, I'm sorry. I had no idea."

"Why should you? We had a daughter soon after we married and lived with her parents. I know it was hard for her when I was away at sea for so long."

"So you were a sailor even then? Were you in the French navy?"

"Merchant marine. I lost my job," the sailor said with a shrug. "I started drinking. It's not something I'm proud of. My drinking got worse. My wife's parents were really scared, you know? They tried doing all the usual things, hiding bottles. Looking back, I cannot understand why I did it. I was mad. One night I punched Susan in the face in front of our daughter. Susan's parents called the police, and they threw me out. I don't blame them. After that, things got worse. I broke into cars and slept in them. I went back to France and drifted down south. There isn't any farther south you can go than down here. It's where everybody washes up."

Jemma was warming to this man who was sharing his troubles. She longed to tell him her own: who she really was and everything she had been through, but of course she couldn't.

Franck carried the sandwiches over to the cabin table. "Is there any coffee left?"

"So, what did you do then?" Jemma asked, refilling his mug.

"The woman you met runs a café in Hyères during the winter and had this boat doing tours of the islands in the summer. She was looking for somebody to look after it. That's how we met." Franck took a bite. "After a while I tried to get in touch with my daughter. Susan was very angry. I wrote every week, with no reply. Then one day, a packet arrived. All my letters to my daughter torn up like..."

He made a sprinkling motion with his hand.

"Like confetti?"

"That's right. Like confetti. I found out that she had met another man and moved away. Susan didn't tell me her new address. I don't know where my daughter is now."

"That must have been very painful."

"One day my daughter will try and find me. She will come and visit for a summer holiday. She will be old enough to make her own decisions."

"Do you think you will see your daughter again?" What Jemma really wanted to ask was whether she would be reunited with Matthew. She felt like somebody blindly searching a horoscope for a clue to the future. She so wanted to tell her new friend everything, this man who had been the first person since George to show her some compassion. Even now she could feel his hands around her neck, pressing down inexorably. She shook her head, trying to get rid of the memory.

Franck gave a little smile. "Bien sûr. Sometimes you just need to have a little faith, you know."

They finished their picnic lunch, and Franck climbed back up to the bridge while Jemma collected plates. She quickly looked round the cabin to see if there was anything she could use. Part of her hated herself for doing this, knowing how kind the sailor had been to her, but she was going to war to get her son back. And in war, she concluded, right and wrong was forgotten. Her search of the cupboards yielded slim pickings: a few snorkels and a sun-faded swimsuit that was too big for her. All she found was a sour-smelling T-shirt and some wet gear, a pair of waterproof trousers and a matching jacket. She rolled them into a Carrefour plastic bag, hoping that would keep them dry in her rucksack. She wrapped her medical kit in another plastic bag along with a towel. Scanning the cabin for anything else she might need, she spotted a pair of binoculars on a shelf.

Jemma tried closing her eyes and lying down on the banquette for the rest of the journey, but she was too eaten up with anxiety to sleep.

Up on deck, a fog had descended, obscuring the island. The fog wall drew closer, enveloping the boat. "Mon Dieu," muttered Franck, who slowed right down as the boat entered the cloud. Fog clung to them with impenetrable blankness. Steering the boat through the fog bank was like feeling the way with your eyes shut; any moment Jemma expected to hear a horrible wrenching sound as they ran aground. Slowly, though, parts of the fog lifted, and she caught glimpses of Port Croix. They were much closer than she thought. The cold grey beach lay ahead of them. A few boats remained in the harbour, some of them covered in tarpaulin. Jemma hoped the policeman would not come down to the jetty to investigate this new arrival.

"I can come with you if you like," said Franck after they

docked. He was tying the boat up. "If you have anything heavy that needs carrying."

"It's all right. As I said, it's just papers and some jewellery."

"How long do you need? I want to set off by five if that is possible. Otherwise it gets too dark."

"That still gives me an hour. It's more than enough."

Jemma was walking along the jetty before Franck called her name. "Hey, Madame," he shouted. Jemma turned. Franck rubbed his thumb and fingers together significantly.

Jemma walked through the village past the cafés and restaurants with their shutters down. Everything was closed for winter. She turned left past a school and along the track that led to the beaches and the villa. Snow had settled on the island, too, and everything looked different as she trudged through sparkling diamond snow. She had no idea what was going to happen when she got to the villa, but that didn't stop her.

Fog obscured most of the hillside that led up to the house. It was utterly quiet apart from the slap of her rucksack and the crunch of her trainers. She stood for a moment trying to remember the way through the olive grove.

The villa materialised out of the fog, as if somebody had breathed on glass.

Jemma leant against a tree and unslung her rucksack, rummaging for the binoculars. There was a terrace at the back of the villa. The wooden shutters were open, even if the French windows were closed. That could mean only one thing. Somebody was definitely inside.

CHAPTER FORTY-EIGHT

She put the binoculars away and started up the steep part of the hill, trying to be as quiet as possible. Her breath steamed in front of her. Icy steps led up to the terrace at the back of the villa. Grasping the frozen handrail, Jemma tiptoed upwards, watching for any movement through the French windows.

Toppy was standing at the far end of the sitting room with her back to the windows, just as Jemma had known she would be.

Jemma sidled stealthily round the side of the terrace. She wanted to surprise the bitch. As Jemma moved, Toppy walked briskly across the room holding the pile of clothes she had been ironing. Now was her chance.

Jemma sprang catlike across the patio.

The French windows shuddered a little on opening. Thank God Toppy had not bothered to lock them. Stepping on to the tiled floor, Jemma crept inside the villa, slipped off her rucksack and lowered it gently to the ground. The silence was so intense it felt as if a tuning fork had been tapped against her ear. The hum held for a moment and then faded. All she was conscious of was immense danger all around her. Her mouth was completely dry.

She crept towards the bedroom and heard the scrape of a bedside table drawer being opened.

Jemma gently pushed the bedroom door and saw Toppy standing over the bed packing a holdall. She had her back to her. Bricks of polythene-wrapped euros peeked out from the bag.

"Going somewhere?" Jemma asked.

Toppy paused, then turned around slowly. Her once dark hair was now cut short and dyed blonde like Jemma's used to be. Toppy was pointing a revolver. "You're persistent, I'll give you that," she said. "I think it's what I like most about you."

Jemma raised her hands in the air. "I just want my son. Give him back and you can keep the money. The police don't even believe you're still alive."

"What's to stop you telling them everything once you have Matthew again?"

Jemma was so close to being reunited with her child she could taste it. "Please, Toppy, you have my word. You have no idea what I've gone through to get here." She started to drop her hands to her sides. The two women were only a few feet apart. "How far do you think you're going to get anyway? The police are searching for Matthew. You can get much farther by yourself, you know."

"You can't un-ring a bell."

"Please, Toppy. Just take me to my son. I'm begging you." Jemma stared at Toppy and searched for some kind of human compassion. But there was nothing.

Toppy was unmoved. "How did you get here? Took the ferry, I suppose."

Jemma tried to stop her voice from cracking. "I hired a boat; the captain is still waiting for me at the port. If you give me my son back, you'll never hear from me again. I swear."

Toppy thought for a moment and gestured for Jemma to start walking while she grabbed the holdall from the bed. "I'll take you to Matthew, and then you are going to get me onto that boat. We were going to leave on tomorrow's ferry, but this is better."

"What do you need my son for? You have the money."

By now they were walking across the sitting room towards the French windows. It was already dark outside.

"Here, take this," said Toppy giving her the holdall. "I never expected to see you again. You're certainly resourceful."

"Toppy, where is Matthew? I need to see him. You have no idea…"

"No idea?" Toppy stopped and stared. "You still don't get it do you? You ripped something out of me. You killed my little boy. My bones ache for him every day. There won't be any photographs of me and my son. No watching him learn to ride a bike or blow out candles at his birthday party.

You robbed me of that. Nothing I have means anything. You have everything and I have nothing. That was why I decided to punish you, to make you understand what it felt like."

"There are other things in life. Friends. Work."

Toppy shook her head. "I will never heal. Being a mother was what I was supposed to do, what I was born to do. I will never be loved in the way that you are loved."

"Toppy, I'm sorry. I understand now. I've learned my lesson."

Toppy considered what Jemma had just said. Then she gestured Jemma forward with the gun. "Believe me, Jemma, you don't know you're born," she said.

Jemma went first down the patio steps, with Toppy following. They stepped down into the olive grove, Toppy holding the gun in one hand and a torch in the other, pointing the way ahead. The moon had risen, giving the bay below a ghostly sheen.

"Where are you taking me?" Jemma asked.

"I'm taking you to your son. Isn't that what you want? First we get Matthew, and then we get off this island. You will tell whoever brought you here that we're old friends and you're giving us a lift to the mainland. After that, we go our separate ways."

"You're just going to let me have him? Just like that?"

"You keep your little boy, and I keep the money."

"After all this, what's changed?"

"I thought that taking what you had would make me feel better. I was wrong. The pain never stops. Matthew will never love me the way he loves you."

Jemma had to stop to digest what Toppy had told her. "So, let me get this straight. All this has been about punishing me. Don't you see I had no choice? I couldn't save your baby."

"That's not what the Indian doctor said. He said you panicked, that you could have saved us both."

"That's not true, Toppy. I swear on Matthew's life. If I could have saved you both, I would have done."

Toppy prodded her in the small of her back, and they kept on marching. Jemma wanted to get the sequence of events clear in her head.

"So, first you decided to punish me, and then Tony told you about the Tri-Med money?"

"He thought we were going to run away together and set up a new life somewhere in the South Seas. Tony said that Bora Bora was the most beautiful place on Earth. All the time I was thinking, this wasn't enough, that you had to be punished..."

"So you faked your own death. That way nobody would come looking."

"It was easy to return to England and lie low watching you. I got to find out a lot about you, Jemma. You're a very neglectful mother. You leave Matthew alone a lot of times. Supermarkets. Parks. If he was my son, I would never leave him alone like that, never."

"What about Tony? He was dying of an insulin overdose when I found him. At first I believed he killed himself out of shame over what he had done. Defrauding Tri-Med, I mean. Then I realised, no, you forced him to kill himself."

"He'd already given me the key to the safety deposit box. It was only when I got there I realised that he'd double-crossed me, that you needed a code as well. I guessed he must have told you what the code was..."

"...and once you had the PIN code to the French account, you didn't need me anymore. So you left me to die in that reservoir."

"As I said, you're very resourceful. The Rohypnol in the car should have been enough to convict you. But no, you escape from the police and here you are again."

"What about George? Was he in on the plan? He tried to kill me. Or did you put him up to that too?"

Toppy shook her head. "Once he figured out what was going on, he wanted to be cut in on the deal. He was a useful way of keeping tabs on you. When you escaped from the reservoir and said you were coming after me, I needed a way to slow you down. I never told him to go that far. I needed more time."

They trudged on through the snow, and Jemma lost the feeling in her fingers. Her clothes felt paper-thin. "How much farther?" she asked.

Suddenly Toppy stopped. A steel trapdoor lay at their feet. You wouldn't have known it was there unless you were looking for it. "He's down here," Toppy said, handing Jemma a bunch of keys. Jemma dropped to her knees and began sweeping the snow away. Her hands shook with the knowledge that her son was so close.

Jemma slid the key into the lock and turned the stiff tumblers. She lifted up one side of the trapdoor and then the other. The steel blast doors were heavy, and it was a strain lifting them. "There's a step ladder that leads down to a tunnel," said Toppy behind her. She gesticulated with the gun and told Jemma to go down first. Jemma clambered down until her head and shoulders disappeared from view.

Descending into the dark, she resisted calling out Matthew's name. Lights flickered on, showing her where she was going. Rubber cables and electricity wires ran down the walls of the tight service hatch. "Achtung, Hochspannung!" read one sign. She remembered the guide telling her that during the Second World War the Germans had renovated the Napoleonic tunnels leading up to the castle. This must be one of them. The Vichy collaborators had planned to hide here if they lost the war. The ladder stopped a couple of feet short of the ground, and Jemma jumped down onto packed dirt. The place had a damp, cobwebby feel, and the brickwork crumbled as she brushed it with her fingers. The walls were close to collapse.

There was a door in front of her that glowed with a weird green light behind its frosted-glass panel.

Jemma was looking at a tiled corridor strung with low-hanging government-issue lamps. Some of the lights had fused, and there were puddles and rubbish underfoot. Dripping water ran down the walls. It smelt of staleness and decay. Once this must have been some kind of hospital, she thought. Slowly it dawned on her that she knew exactly where they were – the place the Nazis had experimented on Jewish children. The sense of horror was so overpowering it made her shudder.

Toppy's boots clanged down the step ladder behind her. "He's down there on the right," she said, slightly out of breath. They started walking down the corridor past filing cabinets covered in German writing. The whole place was like a time capsule from the Second World War.

They stopped in front of some heavy double doors. "He's in here," Toppy said. Jemma clumsily fiddled with the keys, desperate to find the right one. Finally the moment she had dreamt about: she was about to be reunited with her son.

Matthew was sitting on a trolley in a filthy operating theatre. She did not recognise the clothes he was wearing. He looked up when he saw her, not quite believing his eyes.

"Mummy?" he asked. She rushed over, crushing him to her chest. To hold him again, to feel his thin body against hers – the relief was overwhelming. She felt the pain dissolve for the first time since he had gone missing. They were both crying. Slowly she released him and looked carefully into his dirty face. "Are you okay? Did she hurt you?" Over his shoulder, she could see the squalor he had lived in. Everything was smashed and filthy, rags and old bottles and junk piled up in one corner.

"Where have you been?" Matthew managed to say through his sobs.

"My darling, I'm sorry," Jemma said. "Nothing will separate us again, I promise."

"She said you didn't love me," Matthew said. "She said she was going to be my mummy now."

"I don't know what she told you, but I would never let you go. I love you more than life itself. You and I are never going to be parted again, do you understand?"

"Mummy, I'm frightened."

"Everything's going to be all right." How many times had she said that since this whole nightmare started? Nothing ever seemed to get better.

"I want to go home."

"I know, my love. Come on, we're going home now."

"We have to hurry," Toppy said. "How long did the

boatman say he would wait for you?"

Jemma hissed: "For God's sake, we're coming. All right?" She glanced at her watch. Franck had said he would wait for her for an hour, and the time was almost up.

She scooped Matthew up, and he clung to her hip as they sloshed through the puddles back down the corridor. He was trembling. Jemma wanted to get out of this infernal place as quickly as she could.

Jemma began to climb up the step ladder, carrying Matthew as she did so. It was a long way to the top. Matthew was getting heavy and she wished she could move him to her other hip, but she was terrified of letting him go. Toppy clanged up behind them. Jemma hauled the two of them up rung by rung until they reached the surface.

She gratefully slid Matthew to the ground, but the boy still clung to his mother's leg. Toppy emerged from the hatch. "Start walking," she said.

What had been a happy track in summer, leading tourists to beaches, now felt dark and forbidding. Thick overhanging branches made a black canopy. Jemma's trainers crunched through snow. The sound of snow on their boots was like frogs croaking.

Nobody said a word. Now they were walking downhill to the village. There was not a single light on apart from a solitary streetlamp. The ice-cream-coloured houses had been locked up for winter, and the restaurants in the square were boarded up. Where was the policeman she had seen boarding the ferry? Surely he had to be here. In her heart she had hoped he would be their saviour. That all-too-familiar feeling of panic fluttered in her stomach. She strained, listening to the silence. The village was deserted. Nobody was coming to save them.

Some of the bigger boats were covered up for winter, and the tocking of rigging against their aluminium masts sounded like wind chimes. They turned the corner of the jetty and there – where Franck had said he would be waiting – was an empty space. Franck had already turned back for the mainland without her.

The boat that was meant to be taking them to freedom had gone.

CHAPTER FORTY-NINE

Walker looked down into the spuming, cascading waterfall and wondered how anybody could have survived the forty-foot drop into the next stretch of river. You've got guts, girlie, I'll give you that, he thought. Farther downstream, dog handlers were working the next section of the canyon.

"I'm not getting my shoes wet," said Balogun, standing beside him.

Walker looked up at the failing afternoon light. Soon it would be dark. "Come on, we're wasting our time here. She's long gone. Let's go back to the car."

Both men turned and began walking back up through the trees to the road. Walker was amused to see his DI picking up the hems of his suit trousers to stop the frozen mud dirtying them. It was a hard uphill walk through the trees, and bitingly cold. Walker pulled his thin overcoat tighter around him. Neither of them spoke until they were back on the road. Their hire car was parked in a lay-by, while the Gendarmerie dog-handling van and Criminal Investigation Technicians were parked farther off. Walker walked up to a gendarme and made a circular motion with his index finger. "Helicopter?" the DCI asked. The gendarme shrugged as if to say this was nothing to do with him.

"Not being very helpful, are they boss?" Balogun said when they were back inside the car.

"Remember, they're leading this investigation. How would you like some French coppers nosing around one of ours?"

"Fair play. So what do we do now?"

Walker rubbed his chin with his fingers. "I bet my eye teeth she's going back to the island, the one where that woman drowned. I'm sure of it."

Balogun was studying the road atlas. "Port Croix." He pronounced it Port Croy-Ix.

"Yes, that's the one."

"I reckon it's a four-hour drive to the coast. Are you sure there's a ferry that can take us across? What if she's right and this woman does have her son? What do we do then?"

Walker sighed. "Then it's squeaky-bum time for you and me," he said. "We return in triumph with the fugitive and her son." He felt his mobile vibrating in his pocket. Fishing it out, he saw it was Okumu on the caller ID phoning for an update. He decided to ignore it. Sorry, sir, no signal.

They stopped once for petrol and sandwiches on their way down south, Balogun bellyaching that all he'd had to eat since leaving London was either pasta or sandwiches. "Bread, bread, bread. That's all the French seem to eat," he grumbled. Walker flicked back to a memorable meal he'd had somewhere around here on his honeymoon, what, twenty-five years ago. Confit de canard served on a trestle table beside a petrol station. His Presbyterian nose wrinkled at what had happened to this part of France: it was all P. Diddy and superyachts and bling now.

It was dark by the time they arrived in Hyères, which in summer must have been an old-fashioned family seaside town. In winter it seemed a half-dead sort of place, with all the shutters down and nobody around. They found their way to the port, and Walker told his DI to pull over. "Come on, let's see if we can find some way to get across," he said.

They walked along the quay past shrouded dinghies wrapped up for winter and listened to the slap of water against the dock. It was deathly quiet. "Would you look at that?" said Balogun admiringly. He pointed to an enormous covered-up yacht moored in the distance. Walker saw what looked like a closed ticket office at the end of the jetty. No ferry. Then, in the distance, he saw what looked like a pleasure cruiser coming in to the harbour with its navigation lights on. "Looks like our luck just changed," he said.

Both men stood watching the boat as it manoeuvred into the harbour and waited for its captain to tie up. The man knew they were there yet he deliberately ignored them. There was something gypsy-ish about him. Walker, who spoke no French, waited until the sailor was securing the last of his lines before he approached. He flashed his warrant card at the man.

"Excuse me, sir, British police. Do you speak English? We need to get across to Port Croix."

The sailor tested the last of his knots before straightening up. "Are you looking for a woman?" he said. He raised his hand in the air. "About this high?"

"Bloody hell," said Balogun. "We've got her."

CHAPTER FIFTY

"So what do we do now?" asked Jemma.

"We go back the way we came," said Toppy. "The next ferry is due in three days."

"What'll we do for food? Have you got enough for the three of us?"

"I'll bring you everything you need. Now get moving."

Jemma realised that Toppy planned to leave them in that infernal hatch. "What do you mean? You can't expect us to go back to that place again. It's inhuman. Let us stay with you, and then we can leave together."

"The police are looking for you. You'll be safer there."

"Out of the way, you mean."

"Shut up and start walking."

They trudged back up through the village and Jemma thought about shouting for help, but who was there to listen? The village had been closed up for winter. All the rich Parisians who lived there in summer had long gone back to the city. She racked her brains trying to think of some way out. Her mind twisted and turned, but they were both trapped.

The moon was bright enough to light their way. Ghostly light bathed the track leading to the beaches, and Jemma could just make out the outline of the castle against the blue-black night sky. Surf boomed from the nearby beach.

They crunched back through snow to a part of the forest she had not seen before. Matthew was gripping her hand tightly. "Carry me," he said, and she lifted him up onto her hip. An owl hooted, and through the trees you could see the moon above a phosphorescent line in the water. The cloud from earlier had disappeared completely, making the clear night very cold.

"I'll never tell anybody about what's happened," Jemma tried again. "Let me and Matthew go, and you'll never hear from us again, I swear."

"What's to stop you going to the police? We wait for the ferry, and then we go our separate ways. You can keep the boy. You have my word."

Your word, thought Jemma bitterly, what use is your word? She began to suspect that perhaps Toppy wasn't leading them back to the hatch after all. Instead, she was taking them deeper into the forest, where she would get rid of her. After all, what did Toppy have to lose? Nobody but Franck knew she was here, and he had given up on her and taken his boat back to the mainland. Toppy still had her son and the money, too. In fact, she had everything. What did she need Jemma for? She pictured Toppy making her kneel in the snow before putting the gun to the back of her head. Dying like a dog. No, she was not going to die today. Not after everything she had been through. She leant into Matthew's face, nuzzling his cold cheek.

"My God, you're heavy," she said, setting him back on the ground and squeezing his hand tightly. "I need to pee, okay?" she said to Toppy, who nodded. Jemma walked over to a clump of trees with Matthew beside her. She hitched up her ski jacket and pretended to unbutton the top of her jeans. Instinctively, Toppy glanced the other way. Jemma grabbed Matthew and started running.

"Jemma, wait..." Toppy shouted.

Running through the moonlit forest was terrifying. Jemma had no idea where she was going – all she knew was that they had to get away from there. She was half-dragging, half-pulling Matthew along with her, and he started to wail. She stumbled through snow that felt like clotted icing sugar. Picking up her son again, she lurched blindly forward, waiting for the flat crack of the gun. But it never came.

Jemma could hear Toppy coming after them as they zigzagged through the trees. She didn't dare look behind her. Anyway, how far did she think she was going to get carrying a six-year-old child? This was insanity. She would never outrun this woman. Her calves felt as if they were going to explode, and even in this cold her T-shirt was soaked with sweat. It was getting painful to breathe. She tripped and fell head over heels into the soft stuff. Picking herself up, she wiped snow from her nose and mouth; it was even inside her clothes. "Are you okay?" she said to Matthew. His face was white with fear. He understood the terrible danger they were now in.

She took Matthew's hand, and they began running again. She scraped her head on one low-hanging branch, which hurt like hell but she ignored the pain. They seemed to be running into a thicker part of the forest now, and she had reached the point where she couldn't run any farther. If only they could stop for a moment; she had to get her breath back. Panting with fatigue, Jemma rested her hands on her knees. Where was Toppy? As she got her breathing under control, the silence reasserted itself. It became so intense that it was almost painful. They crept quietly to the base of one tree and squatted beside it. From here they could hear anybody approaching.

Snow crunched nearby underfoot.

Jemma pressed herself against the tree bark, pulling Matthew in tight against her. She ached with fear. Oh God, please don't discover us, oh God, please don't discover us. The small boy moaned, and Jemma clapped her hand over his mouth. They must not make a sound. Jemma felt a tear forming she was so petrified. She could hear Toppy getting closer. "Jemma, come out," she called.

There was the sound of wood snapping behind her.

Somebody else was in the forest with them.

Whoever it was had a heavier footstep and was approaching from behind. Of course: the policeman she had seen boarding the ferry. He must have seen them walking through the village and come to investigate. She wanted to cry out that Toppy had a gun and he needed to be careful. Instead, she hugged Matthew tight and slowly stood up, preparing to make a run for it. The policeman took another step, and she sensed he was being ultra cautious. He probably did not even realise that she and Matthew were right under his feet. She needed to warn him, to tell him that Toppy was armed.

"She's over there. She's got…" Jemma shouted.

Something white-hot exploded inside her brain.

She found herself face down in the cold, wet snow. After a moment the pain came. "I don't understand…" she mumbled, getting up onto all fours. Blue stars danced in front of her eyes. One part of Jemma was observing the other, gazing down as she lay in the snow. When her vision returned, she glanced up to see George standing beside Toppy. They were both looking down at her. She had her arm around Matthew, who was crying and struggling to get away. If only she could get things in focus; everything seemed to be revolving in figures of eight. Gingerly, she touched the back of her head with her fingers and felt how sticky it was. She had to sniff hard to stop more blood from running into her mouth. The rock that George had struck her with was lying discarded in the snow.

"You should have got rid of her when you had the chance," Toppy said. "Take her deeper into the trees and finish the job." George nodded, and she handed him the revolver. But instead of coming for her, he lifted the gun up and held Toppy by the shoulder.

A loud bang, a flame in the dark.

The sound was so loud, it seemed to detonate inside her head. Toppy flew up into the air, was thrown against the tree, then slithered to the ground. When she came to a stop, her legs were splayed in front of her, as if she were a doll somebody had got bored of playing with and thrown away. For a moment they both looked at her. "My God, what have you done?" Jemma asked.

George hauled Jemma up by her ski jacket, and she felt too dazed to resist. "You should be glad. She wanted you dead."

"You just killed her."

"What do you care?" George walked over to where Toppy had dropped the holdall and picked it up. "Mine, I believe," he said.

"So, what's next?" said Jemma. "Are you going to get rid of me, too?" She tried to stand up but felt as if her legs had turned to jelly. Stand up straight, dammit.

George shook his head. "I'm not interested in you or the boy. I just want what's in the bag."

Despite everything, Jemma's sense of duty nagged at her. Perhaps it was her medical training, but she had to know if

Toppy was still alive. She walked over to where Toppy was lying slumped by the tree. She could see the burn mark in Toppy's jumper beneath her shoulder.

"Please, I can't breathe," Toppy whispered.

"George, she's still alive. You can't just leave her here."

Jemma's fingers trembled with cold as she pulled the collar of Toppy's jumper down and saw where the bullet had entered. It was a nice clean hole about the circumference of her finger. It must have gone straight through. What you didn't want was the bullet shattering the bone or hitting the pleural cavity. Unlike in the movies, there wasn't any blood. Instinctively, Jemma pressed the heel of her palm down onto the wound, applying pressure.

"She needs to be in hospital. There's a place, where she was keeping Matthew..."

"I know. She told me. The old wartime tunnels."

"We need to get her up and take her back to the hatch. There are medical supplies in my bag."

Toppy was wheezing now. "Toppy, it's Jemma. Can you hear me? You've been shot. Don't try and move."

"Leave her. There's nothing we can do. Somebody will find her."

"You can't just leave her here to die."

George hesitated for a moment, and then they both manhandled Toppy into a sitting position. She wheezed and retched.

"Toppy, listen to me. We're going to lift you up, but you're going to have to help, okay?" Her voice must have sounded very distant.

"I don't think I can walk," Toppy said.

Jemma wrapped her arms across Toppy's chest and started hauling her up. My God, she was heavy. This was almost impossible. Halfway up, Toppy's legs started going again, and Jemma felt all her weight sliding down. "Toppy, listen to me. You have got to stand up," she said firmly. This time Toppy seemed to regain a little strength in her legs, and George came round the other side to help. Together they draped Toppy's arms across their shoulders. "We're going to take you back to the tunnel where I can get this bullet out, okay?"

They started half-walking, half-dragging Toppy in the direction of the hatch. The trail they had made before was easy to follow in the moonlight. The temperature was dropping so fast it was difficult to think straight. Toppy started making a ghastly wheezing sound, a bubbling from her throat. The bullet must have nicked the top of her left lung, which, Jemma suspected, was slowly deflating. She was not sure whether she could do anything if the woman's lung was collapsing. She needed to be in a proper hospital.

They walked on in silence, their boots slushing through snow.

"George, I... I thought that I was in love with you," Jemma said.

"I never wanted your kid. That was never part of the plan. She insisted."

"So what was this all about, then?"

George grimaced. "Haven't you got it yet? It doesn't matter what the question is, the answer is always money."

She could see they were coming up to the hatch. Somehow they would have to manoeuvre Toppy back down the ladder and get her into the operating theatre where she had been keeping Matthew. There were supplies there. Matthew clung to Jemma's leg, afraid to let go.

"There's no way we can carry her down," George said. "You take Matthew and go down first. She'll have to climb down herself."

Jemma separated from Toppy, who stood with her hands on her knees nodding dumbly. She picked Matthew up on her hip and started climbing down the ladder again. The only light came from the moon framed by the hatch, and the deeper she got, the darker everything became. Her muscles were crying out for more oxygen as Matthew clung to her. Somehow clambering back down felt even harder than before. One misstep and both their necks would be broken. She reckoned she must be near the bottom by now, and she felt for the ground with her toe. Sure enough, her trainer touched the dirt-packed floor.

Jemma reached for the wall switch, and the row of lamps rippled into life. There was the hum of electricity along with a steady drip of water.

They stood there hand in hand waiting for Toppy to climb down. It was slow going. She must be in incredible pain, and any moment she could lose her footing. Slowly Toppy limped down the step ladder. The way she was pulling at her breath made her sound like a broken steam engine. Above them was the clang of George closing the blast doors, locking them all inside. He started coming down the ladder, too.

Jemma went to help Toppy as she stepped off the last rung onto the mud and broken tiles underfoot. She was barely conscious, and Jemma could see how pale she was. She would have to move fast. That wound had to be staunched before Toppy lost any more blood and her lung collapsed completely.

George jumped down from the ladder, and together they dragged Toppy through the puddles. The room where she had imprisoned Matthew was coming up on the right. Toppy was really gasping now, with a sound like a sucking pump. They paused, and George managed to pull one of the double doors open, leaning against it with the bag in one hand as Jemma opened the other. They carried Toppy towards the hospital trolley.

"Toppy, I need you to get on here, okay?" Jemma said. Toppy nodded and heaved herself up with the last of her energy. Jemma went to her rucksack and got out what few medical supplies she had. Pouring four diazepam into the palm of her hand, she refilled her water bottle from the trickle of water in the sink. "Here, Toppy, drink this," she said, lifting her head up and forcing her mouth open. Jemma placed the pills on her tongue and forced her to swallow. What she really needed was a general anaesthetic. Toppy closed her eyes and her head fell back. She would be asleep soon.

"How long will she be out for?" George asked.

"Until the pain wakes her. George, I need you to find out what supplies are in that cupboard."

"I'm sorry, Jemma. This is where you and I part ways."

"What do you mean?" said Jemma, looking up from the operating table. "I need your help. I can't do this on my own."

"In fact, I'm sorry about everything. Things were never meant to turn out this way."

He shrugged apologetically and picked up the holdall. Jemma felt so tired that it took a moment for her to realise what was going on. George slipped through the wooden door, and there was the sound of a key being turned in the lock. Immediately, Jemma sprang for the doors and tried pulling them open, but she was too late.

"George, wait," she shouted, banging on the door.

"You want to be with your son so much? Well, now you're

going to be together for a very long time," he said from the other side.

"George, please, you can't leave us here. We need to get Toppy to a hospital."

There was no reply. She tried hammering on the doors again, but there was no response. George must already be halfway up the ladder with the money by now. They were prisoners. Jemma tried throwing herself against the doors, but all she did was hurt her shoulder. She tried again. The doors were solid.

George had left all three of them down there to die.

CHAPTER FIFTY-ONE

There was no time for self-pity. Toppy had fallen asleep on the hospital trolley, and Jemma had to decide what to do. She remembered what St John David had once said: "Jemma, the Hippocratic oath isn't something that you swear with your hand on the Bible. Medicine isn't about morality. It's not up to you to decide whom to save." In her heart of hearts she knew what she had to do. She had to get that bullet out and patch Toppy up.

"Matthew, can you go and sit over there?" she asked. Matthew nodded, and she saw a dark circle around his jeans where he had wet himself. Her sense of guilt was overwhelming. She had put her son in even worse danger than Toppy had. She wanted to pick him up and never let him go. But she had work to do.

Most of the glass panes were smashed in the medicine cabinet. There were still medical supplies stacked inside, though; rolls of gauze and dressing packs stamped "Wehrmacht Sanitätskompanie" under a Nazi swastika. Jemma lifted out a cardboard box that had turned brown with age. Inside was a scalpel and even fresh blades wrapped in greaseproof paper. Testing one on her wrist,

SLOW BLEED

411

she was surprised to find it was still sharp. She pulled out some dressings and shook the dust from them. There were also bottles of what she took to be distilled water. Combined with what she had in her bag, she might be able to fix Toppy up enough to get her to hospital. If they ever got out of here, of course.

Jemma scissored through Toppy's T-shirt, exposing the gunshot wound. It was a nice clean hole. She offered up a silent prayer of thanks for this tiny bit of luck. Then she went round the back of Toppy's head and lifted her up, feeling for where the bullet had exited. Even asleep like this, Toppy flinched while she probed. Thank God the bullet hadn't gone through one of the big vessels. Toppy's trachea had not deviated, and her breathing was stable. Plus, she had stopped making that ghastly wheezing sound. Jemma poured water over the hole to try and clean it. What she really needed, though, was alcohol to sterilize the wound. She remembered there was a half bottle of vodka in her rucksack that she had bought from that shop in Earls Court. It was going to hurt, though. Toppy winced and groaned as the alcohol splashed over her wound. The last of the vodka ran down her T-shirt. All Jemma had to do now was pack the wound with gauze and apply a dressing. Toppy would also need a sling to keep the weight off her arm, but all they had here were tiny rolls of bandages.

A quarter of an hour later, Jemma was done. A nursing sister would not have approved her handiwork, but it would do. Jemma reckoned Toppy would be asleep for another half-hour or so before the pain woke her. That shoulder was going to hurt like hell.

Her work over, all Jemma wanted to do was close her eyes for five minutes. She went and sat beside Matthew on the theatre floor. To have gone through all this and be reunited with her son, only to be trapped down here, was too much. George was not coming back. He had all three of them locked underground. Now that he had the money, what was to stop him stealing a boat? Or lying low until the next ferry? Matthew leant across and hugged his mother. To have just one human being believe in her gave her confidence. He had cried himself out, and she kissed his dirty-smelling hair. The joke that Matthew had told Mrs Sharma came back to haunt her: a man and a woman fall down a well, which one gets out first? The woman. Because she had a ladder in her stocking. But there was no ladder in Jemma's stocking.

The operating theatre felt as airless as the moon. It was incredibly stuffy down here. Whoever had worked here during the war must have had ventilation. Jemma got up and began looking for some kind of air vent. She started moving the pile of old clothes and rubbish stacked up against one wall to see what was behind it. Among the rags and bottles she spotted an old photograph. It was a square black-and-white snapshot that must have been left behind when the Germans evacuated. The picture had been taken outdoors and showed soldiers smiling next to each other on what looked like a picnic. A couple in the front row were grinning and holding an old-fashioned two-man saw, its teeth resting on what looked like the top of a man's head. They looked almost proud. Peering closer, Jemma realised they were about to saw a man's head off. Something inside her snapped. She flung the snapshot down in disgust and started pulling at the smelly rags and bottles. She felt rising panic. There had to be a way out of here, there just had to be.

Sure enough, there was a fan in the wall with a big propeller blade. She put her head against the cover and felt fresh air against her face.

Jemma ran to her rucksack and felt for any euro coins. Thank God there were a couple lying in the gritty bottom of a zip-up compartment. The euro edge slotted in neatly with one of the screws holding the cover in place, and she began turning it with as much force as she could. To her dismay, all she was doing was tearing up the slot, making things worse. Soon the coin wouldn't have any grip. Don't give up, it's your only chance, she told herself. She kept going, and sure enough she felt the screw give a little.

It took half an hour or so of patiently working away before all four screws were loose enough that she could finish the job with her fingers. The ventilator cover sagged before she lifted it off and placed it to one side. A crude hole had been knocked into the wall, just big enough for Matthew to crawl through, she thought.

She bent down to her son and grasped him by the shoulders. "Matthew, I want you to climb through and get away as fast as you can, do you understand?" she whispered, frightened of waking Toppy.

Jemma gave him the torch from the rucksack. He looked as if he was about to cry.

"Mummy, I don't want to leave you."

"You won't be. I'll be right behind you," she lied. "I need you to find out what's on the other side of this wall, okay?"

He swallowed and nodded.

Matthew squeezed through the tight space.

"Can you see anything?" she called softly.

"It's very dark, Mummy."

"Try switching on the torch," she whispered. Toppy stirred uneasily on the hospital trolley behind her. Oh God, don't let her wake up. If only the crawl hole was wider, she could crawl through, too. The bricks looked rotten, though, and when she pulled at one, it came away easily. Jemma carefully placed it on the ground. If she kept worrying away at the stones, she could make the hole big enough. The bricks came away with a shower of earth and dusty mortar. What she did not want to do was make any noise.

Toppy coughed and said, "I'm thirsty."

Wiping her hands free of dirt, Jemma walked over to where

she was lying on the gurney. She offered Toppy some distilled water, which ran down the side of her mouth. Toppy nodded and let her head fall back.

Jemma stood frozen to the spot until Toppy had drifted off again.

Making sure that Toppy was asleep, Jemma nagged at the rotten brickwork again. As soon as the hole was wide enough, she got down and began wriggling forward herself. She felt cold air on her face in the impenetrable blackness. She had never experienced dark like this. The air felt colder on this side. She reached with her hands and felt tight-packed dirt beneath her. There was the sound of running water. Jemma made one final heave and slithered onto cold wet ground. Matthew had been watching her efforts and switched the torch back on when his mother was free.

Standing up, Jemma took the torch from her son and shone it along the walls. They were in a dank tunnel just big enough to stand up in; if Jemma stretched out her hands, she could touch both sides. There were weird folds in the rock like grinning skulls, and what looked like teats hung from the calcified ceiling. A rusty metal pipe ran along the tunnel wall; the power cable for the underground hospital, she supposed. She brushed her fingers on the cobwebby limestone. A narrow-gauge railway ran beneath their feet. Jemma could just make out sleepers beneath the mud and wet. This must be the railway prisoners used to transport supplies up to the castle. If there was a railway track, it must lead outside. One way would go up to the fortress, and the other would take them out of here. She swore she had glimpsed an entrance in the rocks leading up to the castle. All they had to do was follow the track downhill. "Matthew, it's going to be all right," she said, trying to sound confident. "There's a way out. Just follow the track, and it will get us out of here."

She had to duck down as they sloshed through water, which came up to her ankles. When the water got too deep, they straddled the rails and edged forward that way. There was a sharp, sour smell in the air. Carbon dioxide, maybe.

They waded through the dirty water, occasionally stopping to listen. It must have just been her imagination, but she swore she could make out the constant murmuring of people talking.

The water got so deep at one point that she had to hang off the rotten pipe and edge along the one rail that was not under water while holding Matthew's hand. Her breath steamed. Jemma could not believe how cold it was.

That was when she saw torchlight glancing behind them. Somebody was coming up the tunnel. Thank God, a rescue party. She was about to shout out when the words died in her mouth.

"Matthew. Jemma," the voice hallooed.

Toppy. How on earth had she come round so quickly? The pain in her shoulder must have woken her.

"Matthew, my darling, we need to start moving quickly. Okay?"

Disconcertingly, the tunnel started rising. They must have gone the wrong way and were now heading back up to the castle. At least it was dry underfoot again. They started jogging along the track until Matthew stopped in front of her.

"Matthew, keep moving. You need to hurry up."

"I'm frightened, Mummy. You go first."

Now she realised what the problem was. What she had thought was rock beneath their feet was really just tight-packed dirt. There must be another shaft beneath this one. She shone the torch along the tracks. The ground had disappeared completely in front of Matthew. The rails were suspended over an even blacker hole. If Matthew lost his balance, he would slip off the rails and fall to his death. Her mouth felt so dry it was difficult to swallow.

Jemma bent to pick up a stone and threw it down the chasm. There was a long wait before it hit something and pinged into nothingness. It was a big drop. And Toppy was coming after them fast.

"Matthew. Get down on your hands and knees and start crawling. You go first. I'll be right behind you."

Her son began edging along the narrow-gauge railway. She

was right behind him, but it was difficult trying to crawl holding the torch in one hand. "Matthew, quickly, hurry up," she urged him. The torchlight was getting nearer, casting longer beams along the rock. Toppy began calling Matthew's name, her voice echoing through the tunnel. Matthew stopped.

"Matthew, there's nothing to be frightened of. But you must keep going."

"I can't."

He was transfixed with fear. She hated herself for doing this to him.

"Matthew. Listen to me. Just move forward one bit at a time."

She felt him shuffle along, rigid with fright. They were right over the abyss. "That's it... keep going." Matthew moved stiffly across the drop. One false move and they would both fall hundreds of feet below. Toppy's siren voice echoed behind them, getting louder. "Matthew... Matthew. It's Auntie Toppy. Don't be frightened." They both ignored Toppy's plea and moved closer to the other side of the chasm. Cautiously, Jemma lifted one hand off the rail and felt for dirt again.

They both stood up and began loping along the tracks.

Her torch was beginning to fail. Oh Christ, not now. The light faded to an orange glow. She rattled the torch, begging for some more juice in the battery, but the bulb had dimmed. Using the little light that was left, she could just make out that the tunnel split in two. Which way to go? Both had railway tracks. Instinctively, she decided to go left. They started crunching along the tunnel, and she realised she had led them into a dead end. The tracks stopped in front of a rock wall with an iron wagon parked up against it. Her torch died completely. The only light came from Toppy's torch, which was getting ever closer. Jemma's mind cycled furiously as her enemy crunched nearer. She turned and raised her arm against the torchlight. Toppy had them just where she wanted.

Jemma could see that Toppy was holding one of the scalpels in her other hand. There was no way out. They were trapped.

"You're not having my son," Jemma called.

Toppy's voice sounded echoey. "Give me the boy. I swear no harm will come to him."

"Leave him with me, and I'll never breathe a word."

"Don't make me hurt you. Just give me what I want."

There was scrunched-up newspaper on the ground and what looked like toilet rolls wrapped in brown paper. Jemma reached down and touched what felt like wax. The waxy lump was sticky with something. Putting her fingers to her nose, she discerned a strong banana smell. No, my God, it was dynamite. She dimly remembered her chemistry teacher telling the class that old dynamite sweated nitroglycerine. Anything could set it off. Digging her hand into her ski jacket, she pulled out her mobile phone. Praying the phone had dried out enough to power up, she switched it on. The bluish light dimly revealed bundles of sweaty dynamite before the phone beeped.

"Matthew, get behind me," she whispered.

Jemma ducked behind the truck where Matthew was already cowering. Gripping the iron edge, she peeked out from behind the wagon. Toppy was almost on top of them, her face red and satanic behind the torchlight.

"Jemma, come out. I don't want to hurt you," she cajoled.

She jabbed the scalpel at Jemma, who felt it just miss her eye.

"Just give me the boy," Toppy said, reaching for Matthew. "Matthew, come to Mummy. Mummy loves you."

Pointing the phone at the ground, Jemma pressed the flash and took a photograph.

The electromagnetic pulse ignited the dynamite.

There was a tremendous bang, and a wall of flame rose over the tunnel roof as if a stoker had pulled open a furnace door. A rushing wind sucked the life out of Jemma, shrivelling her to nothing. Then the blast hit. It was like being struck in the chest with a sledgehammer. Before Jemma knew it, she was lying on her back. Instinctively, she rolled onto her front and covered her head as debris rained down. Yet she felt curiously detached from what was going on. It was not as if she was in any pain. All she felt was warm water all around her until she realised it wasn't water at all; it was her own blood.

CHAPTER FIFTY-TWO

LEDs pulsed softly on the instrument panel, giving the coastguard's face a reddish tinge. Walker stood beside the impassive figure watching the dark sea from behind the wheel. The boat crashed through another wave. The gendarmes were questioning the boatman, who had immediately confessed to taking a lone Englishwoman across to the island. A hurried phone call to the British Consulate in Marseilles had arranged for this coastguard cutter to ferry the two British policemen to Port Croix. Walker looked at his watch, and he suddenly felt terribly tired. Not long now, he thought.

Lights from the harbour hove into view and, as the boat drew closer, Walker saw the island policeman waiting for them on the dock. Balogun and Walker shook hands with the young man once they had disembarked. He introduced himself as René Duverger. They turned and started walking up towards the village, which was so French that Walker could almost hear accordion music.

"The boatman said he dropped the suspect off at around four o'clock," he said. "You didn't see them arrive?"

"No-one comes here in winter," the gendarme said. "This

afternoon I was on the other side of the island. One of the alarms in a villa was ringing. I had to investigate."

"And you haven't seen anybody else on the island? Another young woman with a child, perhaps?"

Duverger shook his head. "So, where do you want to start? The island is not that big. Wherever she is, we will find her quickly."

Balogun said, "What about the villa that the bloke who killed himself rented? Have you tried there?"

"Toulon told me to wait until you got here."

The gendarme led them to where his wagon was parked outside his police station. More like a hut than a police station, Walker thought. Christ, it was cold. The French policeman told them to wait a moment while he got something. Moments later, a black Labrador shot out of the door and padded around, waiting to be let in to the back of the van. "You've got to be having a giraffe," Balogun said when the cop gestured for him to get in after the dog. "Only two seats," Duverger apologised.

The three men set off along the bumpy road, the yellow headlights showing the way ahead. Snow began drifting down again.

"Top of the island, I'm afraid," said the gendarme.

"Have you ever had to deal with anything like this before?" Walker asked. There was a nasty sound as a rock scraped the underside of the van.

"Most of my time is spent dealing with theft. We have a big burglary problem on the island. Especially in winter. Most of these houses are locked up after the summer."

"Are you here all year round?"

"I'm more of a gardien than a policeman. I keep an eye on these houses. I tell the owners when there's a problem. Burst pipes."

"Are you all right in the back?" Walker asked.

"I hate dogs," said Balogun. Walker grinned to himself.

"This woman you are searching for. I met her, you know. During the summer when her husband's girlfriend drowned. And now you say the girlfriend has the boy? Incroyable." The gendarme shook his head.

"We know the girlfriend is alive and that she has the boy. It's what the doctor believes, too. That's why we're here. Whether they're here on the island is another question. Either way, London wants me to take her back. We have a European Arrest Warrant."

The van scraped along the track until it reached the dead end and the headlights faced the start of an olive grove. Duverger said they would have to get out and walk. The gendarme reached into the glove compartment for a torch and opened his door. "Allons-y," he said. His dog was whinnying with excitement to be let out of the vehicle. Balogun glared at his boss as he stepped onto the ground, brushing himself down.

Duverger handed Walker the torch and unbuckled his own from his belt. The three policemen trudged through snow as barren as the moon. It felt as if they were on another world. That and the unearthly cold. "Un instant," Duverger said. They stopped and looked up at the villa. Its lights were clearly on. "I thought you said this place was closed up for winter," Balogun said. The gendarme reached for his sidearm.

Right at that moment, Walker felt the ground shake beneath his feet. It felt like a timpani roll. The sound hit him only a moment later: a tearing, screaming sound, like thousands of tiny hammers raining down along telephone wires.

"What the hell was that?" Walker said.

"Sounds like one of the tunnels," said the gendarme, jogging toward the trees. Panting hard, the two British policemen followed him. "This whole area is a..." Duverger searched for the right word "...web of tunnels. They were built during the Second World War, you know?"

Breathing heavily, Walker said: "Could the suspect have got in to one of the tunnels?"

"Sometimes there are rock falls. We tell tourists to keep out."

It was a stiff ten-minute uphill walk to the tunnel entrance, which was padlocked and blocked off with a metal gate. "Danger. Entrée interdite" warned the sign. The dog was going crazy, though, barking and circling the metal gate. He definitely thought somebody was in there.

"So, what do we do now?" asked Walker.

Duverger rattled the padlock and made a helpless gesture. "The key," he said, "is in my office. I could go back..."

"There's no time for that. We'll have to climb over."

"We need helmets," Duverger said. "It is dangerous in there."

"Effing health and safety," said Balogun, who, to Walker's surprise, began scaling the gate before levering himself awkwardly down the other side. Embarrassed into following, Duverger told Walker to go next. Walker gestured for the torch. The dog squeezed through the bottom bar.

The DCI switched the torch on as they sloshed through wet and dirt. It was so dark down here. Dark and cold. Soon they were ankle deep in icy water. Walker shone the torch into the middle distance. He was sure he could hear something, a murmur of voices – no, just one person; it sounded like a child. "Wait. I think I hear something," he said. All three men stopped and listened. There it was again: the sound of a child crying. There was no doubt about it. Somehow a child must have got in to the tunnel. Walker's heart lurched: what if it was the boy? There was definitely somebody down here.

"Did you hear that?" Walker asked the others. Balogun

nodded, his breath steaming. Then it was unmistakable: a high-pitched, inconsolable wail. Walker swung the torch away from his DI into the impenetrable blackness. There, walking towards them, was the white face of the little boy. Snot and blood were smeared across his face, and he looked as if he was in shock. The boy stumbled towards the light. "M-m-m-Mummy," he said as Walker jogged towards him, torchlight going all over the place. Oh my God, it was Matthew Sands. And if he was here, where was his mother?

Walker embraced the child, lifting him up. "Your ma? Where is your ma?" he repeated. The boy glanced behind him. "Is your mother still in the tunnel?" The boy nodded, too traumatised to speak. What were they doing down here?

Walker handed the boy across to the French policeman. "Get him out of here," he said. "And call for help. We need a rescue team." The gendarme nodded and crunched back through the tunnel at a jog trot. The dog followed them out.

It took about ten minutes of trudging through darkness before they came to the tunnel cave-in. Dust roiled in the air, and it was hard to breathe. Balogun started coughing badly. A woman was lying face down in dirty water, her face masked with blood and dirt. She was lucky to be alive. The tunnel had almost collapsed completely, leaving a gap in the rocks the boy must have squeezed through. Walker passed the torch to Balogun, who kept it trained on the woman's blonde hair. He knelt down and touched the back of the woman's head. "My baby, my baby," the woman murmured. "Come to Mummy. Mummy loves you." So this was Toppy Mrazek. Jemma Sands had been right all along.

"The boy's mother must be behind this wall," Walker said, straightening up.

"Shouldn't we wait? The rescue team is on its way."

"They could still be another hour. She might be dead by then. Come on, give me a hand." Walker looked down at the Mrazek woman. "She's not going anywhere."

Walker reached for a stone beside the gap the boy had crawled through. He grunted with the effort. It was much heavier than he expected, and he threw it to the ground. The DCI started coughing again. By God, he was going to get this woman out alive if it was the last thing he did. He got his hands round the next rock, which wouldn't budge. Straining with everything he had, he still could not move the stone. There must be tons of fallen rock between him and Doctor Sands. Walker felt the claustrophobic weight of earth pressing down on him, ready to collapse at any moment. What if there was another rock fall blocking the way back? Then they would all be trapped. "It's hopeless, sir," said Balogun. "You're never going to get her out."

CHAPTER FIFTY-THREE

Wade Nibley was giving evidence to the committee investigating the drugs scandal on television. That a parliamentary investigation into the workings of the drugs industry was being broadcast live on TV showed how much public interest there was. Newspapers were calling it the biggest medical scandal since Thalidomide. She stared in fascination at the wall-mounted TV inside the prison security gate.

Nibley maintained that the drug trial was the work of a single rogue employee. "But Mr Nibley," interrupted one MP, "we have already heard eyewitness evidence that you did know about MC4073 testing, and that you made threats when Doctor Malvern ended his trial." Nibley stared earnestly back at his interrogator. "Sir, I have no recollection of that."

The police had found George in a Morocco hotel room after he fled the island. He even had the holdall stashed with money under his bed. He had confessed his part in the conspiracy immediately, helping police build their case. Nibley had been arrested and released on bail pending his trial.

"Sands, Jemma," the prison officer said reading names from a clipboard. "Please put your keys, mobile phone or any other metal objects in the tray."

Toppy had been extradited back to England once she was deemed fit for travel and charged with kidnapping and murder. Charges against Jemma were dropped. Jemma spent a week in hospital recuperating while Toppy was kept in intensive care. What had happened shocked Jemma down to the molecular level. Slowly, she felt her cells knitting together and her strength returning. Matthew was flown back to England to be looked after by her mother until she was strong enough to return home.

The photographers and reporters clustered around her front door on their return had been overwhelming. Reporters shouted questions as Jemma and Matthew tried to shove their way in. But this was nothing compared with the emotional scars they were left with. Jemma couldn't sleep without the vision of Toppy's face bearing down on her, while Matthew was withdrawn and went rigid every time he was touched. He had also developed a stammer. Children were resilient, the therapist had told her, he would recover.

Jemma walked through the airport-style metal detector, and a woman guard patted her down. She scanned the list of rules and regulations as the guard ran her hands down her legs. Her fingerprints were taken electronically: the guards wanted to make sure the person leaving prison was the same one going in.

Waiting to be shown into the prison visiting room, Jemma's thoughts turned back to the murder trial. Only somebody who knew Jemma well could have detected the tremor in her voice when she gave evidence. Her right hand was shaking uncontrollably, like a spider injected with adrenaline. She had to grip the rail of the Old Bailey dock to stop it trembling.

The jury cleared Toppy of murdering Tony but convicted her of kidnapping, false imprisonment and attempted murder. The woman who had tried to destroy Jemma would spend the next eight years behind bars. On hearing the sentence, Toppy's mother had covered her face in her hands in the visitors' gallery.

Jemma had written to Toppy several times asking to come and see her. She had so many unanswered questions, but Toppy had never replied. Now, six months after her conviction, Toppy had written to Jemma requesting a prison visit. It had been two years since she had operated on Toppy Mrazek, and once again it was that final huzzah of summer before winter settled in. Often the way something ends is how it begins, she thought.

This would be the first time they had met face to face since the trial.

Toppy was already sitting at a table as they were shown in. She was looking around with a kind of expressionless distaste on her cold, hard face. A couple of warders stood watching from the sides as people sat down at the half-dozen tables. When she saw Jemma, her face softened and she looked almost frightened.

Sitting down, Jemma said, "I wanted to thank you for letting me come and see you. You look well."

'I'm getting fat. There's nothing to do all day apart from sit in your cell watching TV."

Jemma wasn't sure where to begin. "Do you get many visitors?"

"My mother comes and sees me. She's getting frail." Pause. "Matthew, how is he?"

"He's getting better. He's young enough for this all to have seemed like a bad dream."

"There are never any children here. Sometimes I can hear children laughing outside the prison walls. It's one of the things I miss most."

What Jemma wanted to know was whether she felt any remorse for what she had done. She said, "George wrote to me from Wandsworth Prison. He's been helping the police build their case against Tri-Med."

"Yes, he wrote to me, too. He's hoping to get his sentence reduced. He was always weak."

The two women sat for a moment evaluating each other. Jemma knew she had been asked here for a reason. She decided to break the silence. "Toppy, I need to know something. What possessed you? What made you do it? You destroyed Tony's life, and you almost destroyed mine."

"I wasn't in my right mind."

"The jury thought otherwise."

"I understand things better now. There was a wound I was carrying around with me. I thought that if I had a son..."

"But it didn't make you feel better, did it?"

"You read my psychiatric report."

"Yes, it didn't make for pretty reading. Self-harming. Bulimia. Arson."

"The psychiatrist said that I was acting out what happened to my younger brother. That I blamed myself. I told you, I thought that having my own child to look after, to make amends..."

"What happened in the car crash, it was an accident."

"When you told me I was never going to have another baby, something snapped inside my head. I could feel it. My desire for revenge was the only thing that kept me going."

"You could have stopped at any moment. You did have a choice, Toppy."

"I've done bad things, things I'm ashamed of. Ever since I was a little girl I've had this urge to destroy everything I come into contact with. I really don't understand it myself." She shook her head.

Jemma sensed this was a speech Toppy had practised and polished for a long time, the words shaped by months of remorse. At last, the veneer was cracking. Or was this just another layer of deception – a performance played out for her benefit?

Toppy said, "I am truly sorry for what I did. There isn't a day that goes by that I don't bitterly regret everything."

"The Jews say there are only two crimes that can't be forgiven. Adultery and murder. Because neither of them can be undone."

"Do you believe that?"

"I don't know."

"You must forgive me. I'm asking for forgiveness. Please, I'm begging you."

"I don't know, I..."

Abruptly, Toppy reached across and grasped Jemma's wrist tightly before lowering her voice, "I need your help getting out of here."

"No touching," interrupted the warder.

"You have no idea what it's like. Sharing a cell. The lack of privacy. The violence. If I don't get out, I really will go insane."

Of course. It all made sense now. Jemma had come hoping for contrition, and instead she was being offered another deal. She went cold all over.

"Why should I help you?"

"Please, you must. I deserve another chance."

"Despite the jury, we both know you murdered my husband. You kidnapped my son. Whichever way you look at it, it's pretty unequivocal."

"If you wrote to the authorities, I could get out of here. Then I could be in a psychiatric hospital instead of this place."

Jemma stared into Toppy's hard little monkey face. For a moment she was about to say that it wasn't up to her to decide where Toppy was going to spend the rest of her sentence, but all she was seeing was the old malevolence, just another ruse to get what she wanted. She was like one of those Russian dolls – you scratch the surface only to find another layer, then another, then another. Finally you realised there was nothing inside Toppy, just emptiness.

Toppy looked surprised as Jemma stood up from the table.

Jemma said, "The thing is Toppy, I know you have a heart, but I just can't see it."

"You can't leave me here. You're my only hope. I can't stand it anymore."

George's words came back to her. "I'm truly sorry, Toppy. Surely you realise by now. Everybody betrays each other in the end."

Walking out of the prison gate, it took a moment for

Jemma to adjust to the glorious late September sunshine.
Emily, her next-door neighbour, was sitting behind the
steering wheel of her green Subaru in the car park with
Matthew on her lap. He was pretending to drive. She raised
her hand when she saw Jemma and opened the door for
Matthew to get out. Her beloved seven-year-old son ran
across the prison car park and flung himself at his mother.
For a moment she was startled by how much she loved
him. Picking Matthew up, she could not resist nuzzling
that exquisite fat roll beneath his chin, and he chortled
with pleasure. He smelled delicious, as he always did.
What had happened to them was unimaginable, like two
planes appearing out of nowhere and vaporising the Twin
Towers on a clear September morning like this one. There
had been nothing left. Yet at that moment she knew that
nothing bad could ever happen to them again. Her mother
had been wrong. Even Tony's betrayal had faded to a tiny
teardrop-shaped scar deep inside her. The slow bleed of her
heart was finally healing.

| | |

ACKNOWLEDGEMENTS

First, I want to thank my publisher Matthew Smith of Urbane Publications; it has been an honour and a privilege to work with Matthew, and by far the best collaborative experience of my publishing career.

Second, I would like to thank my nonfiction agent Laura Morris and Tom Williams of The Williams Agency, who handles e-book sales of *Slow Bleed* through an exclusive arrangement with Amazon.

One early reader of the manuscript, who did not know my journalistic background, wondered how long I had been a doctor for. My heart sang when she said this, because as a writer, reaching the point where fiction becomes interchangeable with non-fiction, is the apex. Mark Johnson, professor of obstetrics at Chelsea and Westminster Hospital in London advised me on technical aspects of Jemma's working life as an obstetric surgeon, while Dr Owen Bowden-Jones, a consultant psychiatrist and honorary senior lecturer at Imperial College, helped me get facts straight about George Malvern's career as a psychiatrist, as well as the risks he ran organising an unauthorised drugs test. Dr Carmen Welte, an anaesthetist at PKDNMVZ in Frankfurt, Germany also provided much help.

Another career I have never pursued is joining the police. Callum "Cass" Sutherland, a retired detective sergeant on the Murder Squad and Crime Scene Investigator/ Manager for the Serious Crime Directorate, answered my questions about police procedure patiently, and took me for a memorable visit to Lewisham CID, where Detective Inspector Chris Stanley went through what would happen if a seven-year-old boy such as Matthew went missing.

Everybody loves the jacket design by Susanna Hickling, based on my sketchy ideas.

Finally, I want to thank my copy editor Catherine Browne, who went over my manuscript assiduously, brushed my prose until it shone, and corrected my haphazard grammar. Cathy was exceptionally generous with her time, and would not let anything go until she was satisfied that it was accurate.

Tim Adler, London 2016

If you enjoyed *Slow Bleed*, read on for the first chapter of *Surrogate*, the next exciting book from Tim Adler

EXCERPT FROM SURROGATE

CHAPTER ONE

"I LOVE YOU," I SAID thickly, pushing the fifty-pound note down inside the elastic of the girl's panties. "Thank you," the stripper said before straightening up. She began swaying against the pole on stage again, running her hands lubriciously over her stomach. Even in this dimly lit strip club I could see how tired she was; there were dark smudges of exhaustion under her eyes, and for a moment I wondered if she was going to slide to the bottom of the pole, unable to get up again. Meanwhile, the bass of the music was so loud that it churned your insides. Suddenly I wanted to be anywhere but this place. The whole thing was about as erotic as a glass of warm milk.

That was the moment I felt my mobile phone vibrating in my jacket pocket. Fishing it out, I saw that it was a text message from Brian Sibley, the finance director of Berkshire RE, the private reinsurance syndicate I worked for. Hell, I did more than work for it, I was acting chief executive until my father returned to work full time. I glanced at my watch. Jesus, it was past two o'clock in the

SURROGATE

morning. Well, whatever it was, it could wait until tomorrow – or was that later today? I tried not to think about it. I was drunk, and there would be a reckoning in the morning.

The strip club was dark and full of small round tables decorated with rose lampshades. Brushing past one of them, I knocked over an empty glass. "Hey," somebody complained, and I picked it up, apologising with the exaggerated courtesy of the drunk. We were all on a stag night celebrating the marriage next week of an insurer who placed a lot of business with my syndicate. It was half past two in the morning, and I didn't even know him very well.

My best friend Rupert Currie, who worked for a company managing the riches of the super wealthy, waved from across the room. Currie had long been my partner in crime when we were out on the town. He was sitting on a banquette behind the roped-off VIP area, and a hostess in an evening dress was giving him a head massage. Currie leaned back, luxuriating in her massaging fingers. The rest of our group was sprawled behind a table littered with glasses and vodka bottles. Other girls were sitting beside my workmates, playing with their hair and trying to make conversation. I realised there was some kind of rotation system going on with the strippers. Over the noise I could just make out girls' names being called over the tannoy. As soon as a girl came off stage, she would go back to sitting in a customer's lap as if it was completely normal to break off a conversation ("So, where are you going on your holidays?"), upend yourself on a stripping pole and then pick up where you left off. Why did these men come here? Perhaps as a dare or a way of showing off to each other in the office tomorrow morning that they weren't just sad little grey men in cubicles.

Currie interrupted my thoughts. "Oy, oy" he said, breaking free of the girl, who looked as stung as a geisha not giving satisfaction. "You're drunk," he said. I nodded, sitting down heavily. Currie winked and said he had something that would pick me up. I lurched after him to the men's toilet with a pretty good idea of what he had in mind.

Sure enough, Currie pulled out a vial of cocaine as we crammed into the toilet cubicle. He dug the plastic spoon into the bottle and scooped out a hit. "Want some?" he asked, offering me the brown vial. The sharp powder hit the back of my throat and instantly I felt sober. Sibley's text message was still nagging at me, though. Whatever it was must be pretty important for him to text me at two in the morning. Reluctantly I looked at my mobile phone again. Clicking the message open, I read: "Urgent. Please come to office for immediate board meeting."

"Fuck," I said, resting my head against the toilet partition vibrating with the bass from outside. "What's the matter, matey?" said Currie, sniffing hard. Why on earth had I agreed to come out tonight? It wasn't as if I wanted to be here. I didn't even like the guy getting married. At the same time, I could feel the cocaine coursing through my bloodstream, blossoming my senses and promising a good time. My teeth were grinding. How the fuck was I going to deal with a board meeting in a state like this? One good thing was that at least I wouldn't have to face my father.

Perhaps I had better explain.

Although I am acting chief executive of Berkshire RE, I never applied for a job. It was given to me. Indeed, I have never applied for a job in my life. My father, Sir Ronald Cox, created Berkshire RE in the mid-eighties, having joined Lloyd's as a junior underwriter in the early seventies. You might have read about him in the papers. He's always portrayed as a kind of cross between Alan Sugar and Robert Maxwell, a finger-wagging East End market trader turned City financier with, as one newspaper said, a touch of the night about him. Reading the tabloids, you might assume that his effing and blinding was an act for the press. The reality was far worse, let me tell you. ("Your dad is one of those colourful characters in British life designed to cheer us all up," a newspaper reporter once told me.) Back then Lloyd's had been a gentleman's club. Nearly everybody apart from Dad had gone to public school. Dad described the other underwriters as the cream of society – rich and thick. What Ronnie Cox did, though, was clever: he was the first Lloyd's insider to open up the insurance market to the public; it was the era of Freddie Laker and Skytrain, the City of London Big Bang and privatising British Telecom ("Tell Buzby"). Mrs Thatcher knighted him. And Dad always had Mum to deflate him whenever he became too puffed up and rampant.

Dad met Mum when she was working as a flight attendant. We moved from the mansion flat in Knightsbridge where I was born to Sundials, a Georgian country house near Henley with an indoor swimming pool and even its own squash court. Currie used to joke that I wasn't born with a silver spoon in my mouth so much as an entire solid-gold canteen in my gob. I was packed off to boarding school aged thirteen, and that was when I noticed the change happening at home: Mum started drinking because of Dad's affairs – girls at work, the usual kind of thing. He hardly bothered to hide it, which was hurtful. There was one woman in particular, a brassy blonde whose flat he paid for. Mum sent me there once, a lumpy adolescent who surprised them both in their dressing gowns eating boiled eggs.

She was lonely, and retaliated by having her own affair with a builder who was doing work on the house. Dad threw her out. What startled everybody was how vindictive he was when it came to the divorce. Despite being the mother of his only child, Mum got only the minimum owing to her – Dad's lawyers made sure of that. "I'm not paying any cock tax," Dad kept saying. He even kept custody of me.

Mum lives in a bungalow near Hastings now, and the drinking has not got any better. She sits at a window overlooking the street; she says she likes the view. It took me a long time to realise that her real problem is loneliness. Dad, however, lost no time: I remember a succession of girlfriends when I was a teenager, some of them little better than hookers. Eventually Dad married Eliska, a tough little number from the Czech Republic, who, Mum snorted, was more like a nursemaid than a wife.

You see, around this time Dad was diagnosed with kidney failure, and he now has to spend hours each day hooked up to a dialysis machine. Without it his kidneys cannot function. Mum's view is that got his just deserts, instant karma and all that. That he is being poisoned to death because of what he did to her.

Well, that's enough about me. I just thought you needed to know where I was coming from.

"I know what you've been doing in there," the black lavatory attendant said as Currie and I unlocked the cubicle door. That made me feel bad. I probably earned more in a week than the guy did in a year. The attendant had run a basin of water, and I washed my hands and combed my hair in the mirror. My reflection looked funny. I smiled and the reflection grinned back at me, but it was not me grinning. Well, whoever it was didn't matter much right now.

Sibley's text message was still in my jacket pocket, worming away at me. I had to get out of here and try and sober up. Hell, what could be so important as to convene a meeting in the middle of the night? I thought about the toilet attendant again as I lurched after Currie and turned back, dropping a ten-quid note into his tips saucer. If I expected him to show some sort of gratitude, I was wrong. He just nodded and moved off.

The others tried calling me back when I said I was leaving. "The party's just getting started," one of them said. Looking at the table debris, I doubted that.

As I stumbled out of the nightclub, the doorman eyed my expensive coat. It would be dawn soon. I sniffed hard, and cocaine-y mucus slid down the back of my throat. My heart was beating so fast I thought it was going to burst through my chest. What could be so important at half past two in the morning?

A delivery van was parked outside Liverpool Street station, with the driver dumping newspaper bundles onto the pavement. First editions ready for early-morning commuters. A vendor was slitting one of them open, and I glanced down at the headline. That's when I felt my legs turning to water. "Sea Inferno. North Sea Oil Rig Disaster." There was a blurry black-and-white photo of an incandescent ball of light, like one of those night-vision photos showing how accurate American bombing was during the Iraq War. The oil platform was like a stricken skeleton.

I picked up the first edition, throwing down a two-pound coin. "Here mate, your change," the vendor called after me as my eyes drank in the newspaper report: "A biblical pillar of fire rising a thousand feet above sea level, and the only evidence there was even an oil rig at its heart was a vague dark shadow … over fifty million metres of standard cubic feet of gas, enough to power millions of Britain's homes, exploded beneath the Dutch Marquez … eyewitnesses said it was like seeing the birth of a star." I dropped the newspaper in a bin. My teeth were grinding away and my chest was hammering like a fucked clock while I comprehended what had just happened. This was serious.

The Dutch Marquez was one of ours.

I hailed a taxi, and it took me the few streets away to Berkshire RE. The developers had called it 30 St. Mary's Axe, but to everybody else it was known as the Gherkin, a phallic symbol of London's pre-eminence in the financial world. I walked through the airport-style security and submitted to a light frisking. Satisfied, the guard stepped back. Seconds later, I was hurtling upwards at stomach-lurching speed before the lift suddenly decelerated. There was a slight moment of weightlessness as my legs bent and the lift doors opened onto the thirty-ninth floor.

Pressing my plastic access card against the reader, I pushed my way into our space-age reception area. With its red Op Art couches and Apple computers, it looked like the set of a sixties' Czech science-fiction movie. The design brief had been to say that we weren't some boring insurance company like everybody else. The irony was that, out of sight, Berkshire RE was just another office with beige computers and cubicle partitions. Still, the impact was undeniable. Office space like this, right beside the Lloyd's building in the heart of the City of London, did not come cheap.

You could smell the fear as I walked in to the boardroom.

Brian Sibley, our finance director, was standing beside the floor-to-ceiling window that looked down over the panoply of the City at night. Nigel Rosenthal, the company secretary and head of business affairs, was sitting at the board table. "Sorry to drag you out of bed at such short notice," said Sibley, turning from the window. Our accountant was so grey that he had only the faintest elephant's breath of personality. "You'd better sit down. We've had some bad news. Nigel, please could you explain?"

I had always thought of Rosenthal as a cold fish. He had disliked me since his protégé had been passed over for my job, the son also rises and all that. "I don't know if you've heard the news," Rosenthal said. I shook my head, deciding to play dumb. "But late last night a fire broke out on the Dutch Marquez oil platform in the North Sea. The platform was on our books. We don't know yet how many men have been rescued or died, but reports say that the rig has gone. There's nothing left. The entire platform melted down in the inferno."

My brain was fizzing. Would they notice the state I was in? "My God, what a disaster. Do you know what kind of loss we're looking at? Have you come up with a figure yet? Who's insuring it with us?"

I realised I was gabbling, and I told myself to shut up.

In hindsight, I want to look back and laugh. Even then, buoyed by the shit coursing through my system, I was not unduly worried. Reinsurance has also been compared to a tree: by the time the risk has spread down through the roots, there is hardly any exposure left. Sure, we would face a loss, but that loss would be shared with other reinsurers. Sibley cleared his throat. "Here's the thing. Sir Ronald overruled me and insisted we cover the risk ourselves and not bring in any other reinsurers. He said we needed the premium."

Only now was the enormity of what had happened beginning to sink in. I felt myself going into shock, and my arms started shaking uncontrollably. This couldn't be happening, could it? "Jesus," I said finally. "What are we on the hook for?"

"Right now, Berkshire RE is staring at a loss of hundreds of millions of dollars," Rosenthal drawled. "For those of you old enough to remember, Piper Alpha cost the market nearly four billion."

"We don't have enough money in the kitty right now to pay out on the entire loss," Sibley added. "Our current account is a muddy hole in the ground."

"What do you mean there's not enough money?"

The idea that there was not enough cash in the bank had never occurred to me. There was always more money. True, we'd had a run of claims – Hurricane Nora had not helped – and had to go out to our investors cap in hand, asking them to make good the shortfall. You see, unlike bigger reinsurance syndicates, Berkshire RE was funded entirely by private individuals. Back in the early nineties, Lloyd's had nearly collapsed when asbestos claims wiped out many private investors. Since then, Lloyd's had reformed, with insurance companies taking the risk. There was still room, though, for private investors – known as "Names" – although the concept of unlimited liability – basically being on the hook for everything you owned – had almost been phased out completely. We were one of the last to do it: the market allowed colourful Sir Ronnie Cox a bit of leeway. Our investors still had to show they had half a million pounds in the bank in liquid wealth, and they were liable for up to a million pounds each if things went bad. What it meant, though, was that our syndicate had been pushed out by bigger syndicates, the ones that covered the safer bets. Berkshire RE was one of the smallest syndicates in the market. Which was why we had to keep extending into ever riskier areas of coverage. I wonder how many of our investors realised that Berkshire RE had become the dumping ground for risks the big boys didn't want.

"Has anybody spoken to Sir Ronald?" I said. "Is he aware of what's happened?"

"As acting chief executive, it's up to you to make the call," said Rosenthal drily.

"Fine," I said, determined not to be rattled. I reached for the phone in the centre of the table. "I'll wake him up."

I punched in Dad's home number and listened to the dialling tone. After four or five rings, Eliska's sleepy voice answered.

"Eliska, it's Hugo. May I speak to my father, please?"

There was mumbling in the background, and I pictured their bedroom in Berkshire with the dialysis machine next to the bed. My father's voice came out over the speakerphone.

"Do you have any idea what fucking time it is?" he said.

"Dad, you're on speakerphone. I'm in the boardroom with Brian and Nigel. We've had some bad news."

I found myself standing up as I went over our predicament. How many times in the past had I felt my kneecaps dissolve as Dad eviscerated me in this very room over the loudspeaker? There were moments when the boardroom had felt like Hitler's bunker, with the generals glancing nervously at each other while the Führer raged. This time, however, there was silence. What I couldn't understand was why Dad had gone ahead and reinsured Dutch Marquez on our own, ignoring the usual protocols. Then again, you could never underestimate how rapacious Dad was when it came to money. He was like a shark in that he had to keep moving, always searching for the next deal. For him, the deal was the thing; I don't think he had ever had a self-reflective moment in his life.

Finally, Dad said, "Well, there's no choice, is there? We'll have to go out to our investors and get the money from them."

I turned to Rosenthal, who was listening intently with his fingers steepled. "Nigel, you're going to have to be the one who writes to them. How will this go down?"

"We only called on them last year to help us mop up the damage from Hurricane Nora," Rosenthal said. "In my opinion, this is going to wipe out many of them completely. Some are going to lose everything."

The gloom in the room deepened.

Ronnie's voice came over the speakerphone. "If God had not meant them to be sheared, he would not have made them sheep."

| | |

ABOUT THE AUTHOR

TIM ADLER is an author and commissioning editor on *The Telegraph*, who has also written for the *Financial Times* and *The Times*. His debut self-published thriller *Slow Bleed* went to number one in the US Amazon Kindle psychological thriller chart. Its follow-up *Surrogate* stayed in the Top 40 psychological thrillers for more than a year. *The Sunday Times* called Tim's most recent nonfiction book *The House of Redgrave* "compulsively readable" while *The Mail On Sunday* called it "dazzling". Adler's previous book *Hollywood and the Mob* – an exposé of how the Mafia has corrupted the movie industry – was Book of the Week in *The Mail On Sunday* and Critic's Choice in the *Daily Mail*.

Tim is former London Editor of *Deadline Hollywood*, the

US entertainment news website.

Follow Tim on Twitter @timadlerauthor or contact him directly via his author website **www.timadlerauthor.com**

BOOKS BY THE AUTHOR

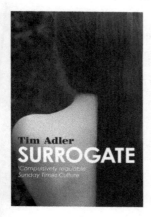

How much is your child worth? That's the question Hugo and Emily Cox must answer when they get a ransom demand for their child – from Alice, the surrogate mother they paid to carry their baby. The police are helpless. No law has been broken – the baby belongs to their surrogate. And Hugo has a secret he's keeping from his wife that makes their search even more desperate.

Now Hugo and Emily must find their missing daughter … even if it costs them everything they own. Fans of Elizabeth Haynes, Sophie Hannah and Mark Edwards will love this gripping and fast-moving thriller.

What the critics say about *Surrogate*:

"*A fantastic read … wonderful plot twists.*" Thriller of the Month – E-thriller.com

'I photographed the moment of my husband's death...'
So begins HOLD STILL, a nerve-twisting thriller from
bestselling author Tim Adler. How much do we really know
about those we love? Kate is visiting Albania with her
husband Paul, a much needed break from Paul's stressful
website business. 'Hold still,' says Kate, taking a picture
as Paul steps onto the hotel room balcony. 'We'll always
be together,' Paul responds. Suddenly there is screaming
below and a blaring car horn. Kate stares down from the
balcony at the broken body of her husband lying lifeless
in the street. Overcome with grief, Kate can't accept the
truth of Paul's tragic death, and replays the incident over
and over again, searching her pictures for a vital clue to
what really happened. When she meets the enigmatic
Priest at a grief support group, they journey together into
a dangerous world of violence and secrets as Kate realises
what Paul really meant when he said he would never leave

her...

What the critics say about *Hold Still*:

'HOLD STILL hooked me from the very beginning and Adler's engaging style and sharp pace kept me glued.' – Peter James, author

'Compulsively readable' – *Sunday Times Culture* magazine

'HOLD STILL is a first rate thriller that deserves to be an essential summer read – and a runaway success.' – Paddy Magrane, author

Urbane Publications is dedicated to developing new author voices, and publishing fiction and non-fiction that challenges, thrills and fascinates.

om page-turning novels to innovative reference books, our goal is to publish what YOU want to read.

Find out more at **urbanepublications.com**